Call of Freedom

Paul C. R. Monk

Bloomtree Press

A BLOOMTREE PRESS book.

First published in 2024 by BLOOMTREE PRESS.

Copyright © Paul C.R. Monk 2024

ISBN 978-1-0686822-5-4

www.paulcrmonk.com

Formatting by Bloomtree Press

Cover design by David Ter-Avanesyan/Ter33Design

CALL OF FREEDOM

Book Four of

The Huguenot Chronicles

by

Paul C. R. Monk

Foreword

In an era when the rise of the nation-state ignited rebellions and shaped destinies, Paul Monk's *Call of Freedom* transports us to the turbulent landscape of the seventeenth-century British Atlantic World. As we journey with the exiled French Huguenot Delpech family from their now familiar shores of Ireland to the unfamiliar world of North America, we are immersed in the struggles and triumphs of their pursuit for religious and personal freedom.

Western Europe in the seventeenth century was in immense upheaval and transformation. Reformation and humanist ideologies threatened order and stability. Theological divisions intensified republican and absolutist struggles for governmental control. French Reformed Protestants, such as the Delpech family, fled French Catholic King Louis XIV's persecution in his realms to seek sanctuary in England and Ireland. Now, like so many other religious refuges, they looked to the British colonies of America for their future. The Leisler Rebellion of 1689, which forms the central backdrop in this novel and a pivotal event in New York's history, was a consequence of the same tensions impacting Europe; tensions between autocratic authority and an awakening spirit of self-determination.

As the founder and director of the Jacob Leisler Institute for the Study of Early New York History, I have devoted most of my career to investigating the nuances of this dynamic period. The author corresponded extensively with me during the writing of his work, discussing the historical contexts and ensuring the authenticity of the events and settings. I was one source among a myriad of contemporary writings and secondary resources being consulted for historical accuracy. As a result, *Call of Freedom* stands out not only for its riveting narrative but also for its meticulous attention to historical detail. The depiction of the Leisler Rebellion and its aftermath captures the complex dynamics and the fervent quest for justice and autonomy that characterized this period. This attention to historical accuracy has resulted in a narrative that is both engaging and historically sound.

Call of Freedom is more than ahistorical fiction; it is a vivid portrayal of the complexities and contradictions of the human experience as fugitives struggle to control their destiny. The Delpechs reflect the broader Huguenot diaspora, highlighting the contributions of these emigres into the fabric of the American story. Their quest for freedom—religious, personal, and communal—resonates deeply with the foundational values of modern America: life, liberty, and the pursuit of happiness.

This novel is a compelling read for anyone interested in the rich tapestry of American history, the dynamics of family sagas, and the timeless themes of love and adventure. Having closely examined the historical contexts and events depicted in *Call of Freedom*, I can confidently assert that the novel presents a carefully researched portrayal of colonial New York at the end of the seventeenth century. It captures the essence of a time when new worlds were discovered, not just in geography but in the human spirit. The accuracy with which it describes the Leisler Rebellion, as well as the daily lives and struggles of the period, provides readers with a reliable lens into this formative chapter of American history.

As you embark on this journey with the Delpech family, may you find inspiration in their resilience and hope in their relentless pursuit of freedom. The historical accuracy, combined with the poignant storytelling, ensures that *Call of Freedom* will remain with you long after you turn the last page.

David William Voorhees, Ph.D.
Director of the Jacob Leisler Institute for the Study of Early New York History
July 14, 2024

Cast of Characters

A selection of key figures

Delpech Family

Jacob Delpech, *merchant*
Jeanne Delpech, *his wife*
Elizabeth Delpech, *their eldest daughter in Montauban*
Paul Delpech, *their adult son*
Isabelle Delpech, *their daughter*
Pierre Delpech, *their young son*

The Darlington Household

Daniel Darlington, *merchant and planter*
Marianne Darlington, *his wife*
Samuel, *their son*
Delphine, *their daughter*
Madame de Fontenay, *Marianne's grandmother*
Claudine, *a maid*
Martha, *the cook*
Ben, a *servant*

The Ducamp Household

Didier Ducamp, *a former French lieutenant*
May Ducamp (formerly Stuart), *his wife*
Francine, *their young daughter*

Lily-Ann, *May's daughter*
Winden, *May's manservant*
Sarah, *the maid*

Aboard the Marie-Ann
Captain Wright, *captain of the Marie-Ann*
Gwyneth Williams, a *Welsh passenger*
Bosun, *a Scotsman*

New York – Leislerians
Jacob Leisler, *de facto governor-lieutenant of New York*
Elsie Thymens Leisler, *his wife*
Jacob Milborne, *Secretary of the Province of New York*
Peter Delanoy, *Mayor of New York*
Domine Daille, *Huguenot pastor*
Ensign Stoll, *supporter of Jacob Leisler*

New York – Anti-Leisler Faction
Nicholas Bayard, *former mayor of New York and leader of the opposition*
Judith Varleth Bayard, *his wife, connected to prominent colonial families*
Stephanus Van Cortlandt, *prominent colonial administrator and former mayor*
Frederick Philipse, *wealthy merchant and landowner*
William Nicholls, *lawyer and political figure*
Davey, *Dutch docker*

John Barbeck, *former shipmaster and agent*

From Montreal

Count Louis de Buade de Frontenac, *Governor of New France*
Jacques Le Moyne de Sainte-Hélène, *leader of the raiding party*
Nicolas de Manthet, *French officer and member of the raiding party*
Kryn, *allied-French Indian Chieftain*
Jean Baptiste Giguieres, *frontiersman and participant in the raid*
René-Robin de Montesson, *French officer involved in the raid*
Pierre Le Moyne d'Iberville, *French officer and explorer*
Jacques Testard de Montigny, *French officer involved in the raid*

Albany

Johannes Wendell, prominent businessman and Alderman of Albany
Captain Jochem Staats, militia officer and military leader in Albany
Reyer Schermerhorn, *brother of Symon, magistrate and representative of Schenectady*
Jan Janse Bleeker, *alderman and representative of Albany*

From England

Governor Sloughter, *Governor of New York appointed by the English Crown*

Major Richard Ingoldsby, *military officer and acting comman-der before Sloughter's arrival*
Chidley Brooke, *councillor and administrative official in New York's colonial government*
William Gething, *gunner*
James, *bombardier*

Schenectady

Aunt Millie, *Daniel Darlington's maternal aunt*
Uncle Alfric, *her husband*
Cornelius, *their eldest son living in Boston*
Gerrit, *their second son*
Senchi, *a Mohawk trader*
Hendrick, *tavern owner*
Old Joe, *Indian tavern attendant*
Chaya, *a young Mohawk woman*
Mrs Philipsen, *a merchant's wife*
Symon Schermerhorn, *a wealthy merchant*
Willempie Schermerhorn, *his wife*
Cornelius Schermerhorn, *Symon's younger brother*
Jannetie Schermerhorn, *Symon's younger sister*
Johannes, Symon's eldest son
Arnout, Symon's youngest son
Joan, *a young slave*
Kanta, *a young slave*
Solomon, *a slave*

Boston

Robert Marley, *general store owner*

Mrs Shrimpton, *guest house owner*
Governor Richard Coote, the Earl of Bellomont, *Governor of New York and Massachusetts*
Town Constable Gibbs, *a local law enforcement officer in Boston*
Captain Thomas Cox, *a pirate chief*

La Rochelle
Monsieur Le Conte, *a Huguenot settler*
Monsieur Bonnefoy, *a Huguenot settler*

CHAPTER 1

June 1699, Dublin

THE DELPECH FAMILY

The 14th of June, 1689

Dear Jacob,

I hope this letter finds you in finer fettle after your long voyage back to England. I can well imagine how burdensome the long separation from your family must have been, especially now that I have a child of my own. Indeed, my dear Marianne has given me the most precious gift a man could ever hold in his two hands. Samuel Darlington was born last April 14th in this year of our Lord 1689.

But alas, he arrives in times of turmoil, and it is especially for this reason that I set quill to paper as I sit here wondering how long we shall hold out. Since your departure, Jacob, much has changed in our beloved New York. Jacob Leisler has taken command of the fort, having been elected by the Committee of Safety composed of two men from each county. With England embroiled in conflict between king and parliament, he and many burghers had feared that the papists in power here would leave our city open to attack from the French and their Indian allies from the north.

Under Leisler's command, we have begun fortifying our city defences and securing provisions and ammunitions in case of attack. We are mercifully better protected now, and the people of our good city, though they hail from different parts of the globe, stand mostly united in the face of the adversary. Therefore, my dear friend, I strongly advise against you bringing your family here at this time. I fervently pray to God that my next correspondence will bring news of how chaos has been ordained and the situation brought under control here.

Your friend and servant,
Daniel Darlington

Standing at the front lattice window of the empty farmhouse in the countryside of Dublin, Jacob Delpech wondered what had become of his friend in New York. He looked again at the date on the letter and counted ten years almost to the day.

It was June 1699. The times of war were hopefully behind them for now, he thought to himself as he heard Jeanne calling to their eight-year-old son from outside. Jacob slipped Darlington's creased and yellowing letter carefully back into his worn leather pouch of correspondence. Then he glanced through the window set with lead cames to see the distorted figure of young Pierre, squatting in the dappled shade of the acorn tree, holding two late-hatched goslings to his cheek. Jacob wondered about Daniel's son, who would be two years older than Pierre.

Standing by the open cart at the end of the garden path, Jeanne watched her daughter, who was dressed for the chilly, damp weather, skipping away from her brother, two years her junior. 'He says he doesn't want to, Mother,' said the girl. 'He says he wants to stay.'

Lifting her skirts, Jeanne said to her daughter, 'Jump into the cart, Isabelle, dear.' Then, taking three strides to the gate, she called out to her son again: 'Pierre! Pierre, put down those chicks and come along. We are leaving!'

Turning to his mother, the boy called back with insistence, 'I want to stay here!'

But it was a young man's voice from the opposite direction that joined the exchange and hollered cheerily, 'Come on, Pierrot!' It belonged to Paul, the boy's elder brother by twelve years, who now closed the front door behind him and turned the large iron key in the lock. Young Pierre put down one of the chicks, which made a dash back to mother goose and its siblings. Moments later, Paul was giving his young brother a comradely pat on the back, as Pierre begrudgingly followed alongside as if he were walking to the gallows.

Knowing the boy's bullishness, in a stern but conciliating tone of voice, Jeanne pressed on, 'I know, Pierre, darling, but if I've told you once, I've told you a thousand times, it is for the best. There will be all sorts of animals where we are going, and you'll find a host of new friends in America too, I'm sure. Besides, everything's ready on the ship. Now come along, the tide won't wait.'

'But...'

The boy tested his mother's patience once more, although deep down he knew there was no point insisting. He was soon sitting tucked in the cart beside her, but nonetheless with a secret smile at the corners of his mouth as he fed the chick in his overcoat pocket some grain to keep it quiet.

Two minutes later, dressed in his great brown cape, woollen breeches, boots, and a flat, broad-brimmed hat, Jacob emerged from the side of the house after securing the back door. He cheerfully called out across the front garden, noticing that the

3

oak tree had at last fully donned its tender green sleeves, 'Everyone aboard and tucked in?'

'Yes, Papa!' replied a chorus of voices in unison.

As Jacob heaved himself onto the cart and took the reins from his eldest son, there came a barking that everyone recognised. 'She's escaped again,' said Paul flatly to his father, then jumped down to greet the setter frantically wagging its tail.

'You ought to be at farmer Raffety's, Jess. Wish we could take you with us, girl, but they won't have dogs aboard the ship.' The dog barked in disagreement.

'You'd better climb up, Paul,' said Jacob. 'We don't want to be late. Mr and Mrs Devanny will be waiting to pick up the cart.' Paul turned back to the dog and told it to stay put.

'She'll follow us,' said Isabelle sharply from the back of the cart.

'Most likely,' said Paul, 'we'll just have to leave her with old Liam on the way.' He then climbed aboard, and Jacob clucked to the horse to giddy up.

A bright spell between the June clouds illuminated the green hills as the family cart turned out of the alley of trees that Jacob had planted eight years earlier. Warmly clad and sharing a woollen cover with her youngest children, Jeanne gave herself a moment to contemplate Les Chênes farmhouse for the last time.

As they rumbled along the stony track, for no particular reason, it occurred to her that some people were home-builders and stay-putters, and others were drifters and make-shifters. She unfalteringly belonged to the former, she thought to herself. She had indeed made a lovely home of their farm in Ireland, she concluded as she viewed the neat little farmhouse with its chimneys still smoking in the chilly June morning. Despite the short summers and the dingy skies compared to those of her homeland of southern France, she did not particularly want to leave these golden green fields. And yet, here she was being bundled away with her children again, not knowing what fortunes would meet them upon their arrival. But did she have a choice? The fact remained that, although they were the rightful owners of their farm, this was not their homeland, and neither was it likely to be that of their children. What could the future here hold in store for them? Would they be considered English, French, or Protestant Irish in a primarily Catholic country? A country where equal rights were being eroded.

So, she had conceded that Jacob was right. They needed a place where newcomers were welcome, a place they could unequivocally call home for generations to come, where the land was fat, the rivers teeming, and preferably, where the sun shone generously in the summer months. Could there be such a promised land on this earth? If so, could it be this New World Jacob had so often harped on about? Would there be room for them in this English colony on the far edge of the ocean? Jacob had reassured her that the charted wilderness alone was many times the size of the counties of France all put together.

As the cart trundled onward, it was all she could do to empty her mind and distance the thought that by leaving Ireland, she was also leaving her eldest daughter to live her life in France with her new husband. There, Protestantism was still banished, the king having "converted" the whole country to the old religion. With the end of the war between England and France, Elisabeth had finally been able to visit her parents the previous year, bringing along Isabelle, her young sister, who had been taken from Jeanne's arms as a baby. Elisabeth had gone back to her life in France, leaving Isabelle with her parents.

But deep down, Jeanne knew that Elizabeth would be fine. Jeanne's sister would see to it. And just as Jeanne herself had poured all her energy into her family after her parents died, when she was quite young, her daughter would lead her life enriched by the memories of her childhood, even though she and Jacob had been removed from Lizzy's world in Montauban.

Leaving the farmstead behind them, the Delpech family headed in the direction of the flat ribbon of stonewalled track that meandered to the port of Dublin, where the ship to New York was waiting for the turn of the tide. 'We managed to get them to load the chests and tools in the hold at the edge, close to the steps where we can see them. Didn't we, Paul?' said Jacob, making an effort to look to the future, having sensed the collective pang of leaving home.

'Good,' said Jeanne, coming back to herself. 'And what about the grain? Did you see to it that it was stored well away from the damp?'

'I did that, every barrel of it,' replied Jacob. 'And even if we did lose one, we'd still have enough grain to see us through our first year.'

'I only hope that land you purchased is as good as you say it is, Jacob.'

'The virgin topsoil of the valley is rich, deep, and is well exposed to the sun. What more can I say?'

Jeanne said nothing more. There was no point in adding doubt to an already risky enterprise. Besides, having been successful once, there was every reason to believe that, with God's grace and the added advantage of experience, they would be successful in an even richer land. Her thoughts were interrupted by Jacob clucking the mare into a steady trot now that the bumpy trail continued into the wider, beaten track. This was the track countryfolk took to cart their produce to market.

Ten minutes later, Jacob turned off and pulled up the reins outside a ramshackle stone cottage where sheep and long-horned goats were penned in and grazing. They looked up in unison and baaed as the horse snorted and nickered on coming to a halt.

Moments later, as Jacob handed Paul the reins and alighted from the cart, a mid-aged man, with a weatherworn face and cheery grey eyes, stepped out from the small wooden door with a welcome chuckle and a wolfhound by his side. He pulled out his pipe from his mouth and doffed his cloth cap in greeting, revealing a thick shock of grey-and-black hair. 'Ah, 'tis truly the day, then,' he said, covering his head again. This was old Liam, a Catholic smallholder who had taken kindly to the French family from their very first spring at the farm. They had helped him save his lambs from the beaks of crows after a snowfall, not long after his wife had died the previous winter.

'It is that. We'll be going,' said Jacob, having joined the old man three steps from the door. 'It's now or never, my old friend.'

'I'll be sorry to see you go, but I do see what you mean, Jacob. You're not getting any younger, are ye? But you'll have the boys. You'll be a'right.'

'Thank you, Liam,' said Jacob as he shook the old man's hand. Then, turning to the subject on every farmer's mind, he said, 'Any more sightings?'

'Two sheep killed at O'Lorregan's. That's why I'm keeping mine around me just in case.' The two men exchanged news of the series of killings from a pack of prowling wolves that had roamed into the district from the forest.

'You take good care, my friend,' said Jacob, who was keen to get on and did not want to let Liam get settled into a long rant. 'Anyway, here's the key.' As Jacob handed over the large wrought iron key, there came a familiar bark, followed by the dog's name being called out by the children tucked in the cart.

Needing no explanation, the old farmer called out to Paul. 'Put her in the barn and bar the door, Paul!'

Jacob thanked the old man and said the dog would return to the farm where Tom Rafferty would find her. Meanwhile, Paul left the reins so that his mother could reach them, then stepped down and led Jess to the barn that adjoined the cottage.

A minute later, crouched in the dusty rays of sunlight that filtered through the barn hatch, Paul said to the dog, 'You can't come, Jess. You have to stay here now, where the smells are familiar to you.' The young man, now alone with the animal, gave it a pat and a boyish hug. 'Stay here now, Jess,' he told her as he closed and barred the wooden door behind him, while the dog yapped its discontent.

Back in front of the cottage, Jacob was saying, 'I have told the solicitor where to find the key.'

'It be safe with me, Jacob, I only wish I could keep me neighbours, but I do understand, given your age, last chance to catch the tide, eh? But you'll be a'right with the boys,' he insisted, as if trying to persuade himself.

Two minutes later, old Liam was bidding farewell to Mrs Delpech and the children. Another two minutes after that, the old man was giving a last wave of his pipe, as the cart bearing the French family disappeared around the bend that took them back onto the beaten track to the city.

Liam joined his sheep and goats with his wolfhound, as he inwardly wished the Delpech family Godspeed. They would need it to cross the expanse of endless ocean, he told himself. The very thought of a lone ship heaving and pitching under the roll of the great waves made him glad to be among his sheep and the undulating hills south of Dublin. At least he knew where he was headed, and it gave him a strange inner comfort to know that one day, he would be lying beside his wife, Lilly, in the land he loved.

An hour later, the cart was trundling toward the gatehouse that gave access to the port, and Jacob suddenly wondered if he still had it in him.

He was a man past fifty. Men past fifty do not head out on an adventure, especially not with wife and children in tow. A man past fifty should be settled. He should have a select number of friends, friends who have stood the test of time. A man past fifty should have his business in good order, and a nest egg in case of times of hardship. A man past fifty should stand in the comforting thought that he and his family had a home for generations to come. Then it occurred to him that he had achieved all this at forty. He had been a jurist, a prominent businessman, a respected planter. Such a fickle friend was life, he thought to himself. But he had the strength back then to start again when he had lost everything. He had found it in God, and in the undying support of his wife, without which he would never have made it out of France.

This time, however, he would be putting his family's lives at the mercy of the vast and indomitable ocean. Yet, the challenges would not end with the sea; they would also have to adapt to a new way of life. True, Paul had done so before, and their daughter Isabelle, who had been raised in France by her older sister and her aunt Susanne, had quickly picked up the language since she came to Ireland the previous spring. But what of little Pierre? He had never left the county, let alone embarked on a voyage to another world.

As they approached the tithe house, he felt an urge to cast a glance back into the cart where, except for Paul who was sitting beside him, his clutch was seated together with a blanket over their knees. His eyes instinctively caught those of Jeanne. He noticed they were glazed with emotion, and the fine delicate lines around them were more prominent in the morning light. She had aged as had he, but what she had shed in youthful beauty, she had gained in radiance. All this occurred to him in the instant their eyes locked. Then she blinked, smiled, and gave an encouraging nod that seemed to wave away all doubt. Her regard was now bold and steely. It felt to Jacob as though she had pressed her hand upon his forearm, the way she always did in times of adversity and dashed hopes.

CHAPTER 2

June 1689, New York

THE DARLINGTONS — 10 YEARS EARLIER

Daniel Darlington stood in the lieutenant governor's quarters, surrounded by a dozen New York advisers.

A finely attired man approaching fifty, clad in a frock coat and heels, Jacob Leisler, who had officially received the captaincy of the fort of New York, said, 'Darlington, I shall need you to help organise the work left undone by the previous administration.' Everybody knew he was referring to Lieutenant Governor Nicholson, who had spent the budget on the Jesuit college, and the former mayor Nicholas Bayard, who had claimed expenses for work not completed. Nicholson, though not a Roman Catholic like his predecessor, Thomas Dongan, was no less ardently devoted to the Stuart cause. He also knew that, should James recover the crown, any dissidents would be executed for treason. Indeed, Monmouth's rebellion of 1685 and its suppression were still fresh in his mind.

11

As Daniel gave a resolute nod, he could not help thinking how Leisler seemed to have physically grown; indeed, he had shown a new dimension to his personality by stepping into his new role upon the insistence of the Committee of Safety and the populace. His sound knowledge of defences, his straightforward objectives, and his clear-cut strategy made him a favourite with the people of New York. However, his very down-to-earth manners had quite the opposite effect on the grandees, as he liked to call them. These grandees included Stephanus van Cortlandt, Frederick Philipse, and Nicholas Bayard, the latter being former mayor of New York and one of the largest private slaveholders in the colony.

But despite being well born into a family of German jurists and theologians, Leisler was a man of the people, and his premise was that the French were coming and, for New York to remain free, they had to build up the city's defences to keep the enemy out. Inspired by his frank parlance, the people of New York had taken up their work tools everywhere to help secure every part of the city where defences had been neglected for so many years. Now that France was at war with England, every port along the coast feared a French attack. Already, New England fishing smacks had been taken by French privateers.

In Leisler, Daniel now saw a man standing in the light of his own aura, projecting confidence, sure of his step and sure of his words. 'We shall mend the north wall and the main city gates on Broadway and along the East River.' Then he beckoned those present over to the table by the window, where he unrolled a scrolled plan of the future battery of New York. Placing two paperweights at either end of the scroll that covered the table, he said, 'And this, gentlemen, is what we are going to build.'

Around him gathered Darlington, other advisors, and members of the committee of fortifications. Although Darlington had refused to stand as counsellor for any king in order to re-

12

main, as he put it, a truly free man in heart, soul, and thought, he had nonetheless agreed to stand by Leisler as one of his close advisers, the two men having known each other since Daniel was a lad. Leisler had been a regular visitor at the Darlington household. It was Leisler who had encouraged Daniel as a young man to set up as a merchant trader and had helped Daniel overcome the trauma of losing both his parents in the same year.

The two men had a frank relationship built on mutual trust; Daniel, like Leisler, kept nothing back if he had a grudge or a bone to pick about something. Thus, Daniel realised his old friend was using him not just for his organisational capacity, but also as a check to prevent the old man from getting above himself. For it had quickly become apparent that only Leisler, among the five militia captains appointed to guard the fort, had any solid military training and knew what to do.

With a sweeping movement of the hand over the plan, Leisler continued in his smooth, fluent English which bore just a hint of his Germanic origins, 'We shall build a semicircular redoubt bearing six big guns behind the fort on the flat rock westward.' Leisler then swept his hand west of the fort toward the cape of New York, from the Hudson River to Pearl Street. 'So, you see, gentlemen, this half moon will defend the landing stages of both rivers.'

'I see,' said Darlington. Pointing a finger, he then said, 'And the half moon battery itself will be protected by the fort. Simple but ingenious!'

'Hear, hear!' said the committee members in unison.

'It is a known recipe for defence,' said Leisler modestly. 'So, gentlemen,' he continued, raising his voice above the echoes of approbation, 'with the repairs of our defences, we shall be in a far better position to hold our city should the need arise. Be they French, French-allied Mohawk, or Jacobite!'

'Hear, hear!'

'Furthermore, now we have water inside the fort,' said a member of the committee on fortifications, nodding his head toward the window that looked onto the quadrant.

'Aye, might not be the best, but it is essential,' said a Dutch New Yorker in a baritone voice. 'Needless to say, it is the first supply that any fort needs to ensure in case of a siege.'

'Can't think why it's been sealed for so long!' said Leisler with a note of irony.

A fellow German New Yorker said, 'I suspect that, as long as the Stuarts were on the throne, Louis of France wouldn't give the order to attack, so in some ways, we were preserved!'

'That may be so,' said the baritone, 'nonetheless, I prefer freedom of speech and of religion to the ways in which Louis has subjugated his people.'

'Well said, sir,' said Leisler, bouncing on the upper soles of his feet with his thumbs behind his lapels. 'And if the French want to try their luck, we shall be ready to entertain them... For King William and Queen Mary!'

'Hear, hear!' were the calls from the room.

'For the freedom of New York!' added young Darlington, which gave rise to an equal measure of approbation.

In truth, Darlington thought it slightly bizarre to be standing in the lieutenant governor's office with the committee led by his friend, who just a month earlier had been a merchant among many, albeit a respected one, a former court-appointed arbitrator, and a church deacon. Now the man found himself directing the defences of the city against an imminent foreign attack.

The increasing urgency of the situation had come about through Lieutenant Governor Nicholson's lack of willingness to proclaim the new monarchs. He gave the pretext that no law empowered him, as lieutenant governor, to step in for Governor Andros, who now found himself imprisoned at Castle Island in Boston harbour for being pro-James Stuart.

Rumours had it that Louis XIV had ordered the governor of Quebec to attack New York and drive out all the Protestants. So the people of New York, including Darlington, demanded an official clear-cut stance. Any dithering would send out the wrong signal to the enemy.

They received the stance they desired from Leisler, the sole militia captain among the five stationed at the fort who appeared capable of organizing defences. Moreover, he was a staunch Protestant, vehemently opposed to the French concept of 'one king, one law, one faith'—in stark contrast to Nicholson, known for his admiration of French customs and culture. Consequently, Leisler was elected by the Committee of Safety and tasked with overseeing the government, to serve as captain of the fort and subsequently as commander in chief.

Later that day in his study, Daniel put down his quill and searched for the address that Jacob Delpech had left before departing for England, where he hoped to reunite with his wife.

From a mahogany box on his leather-topped desk, he brought out a stack of *cartes d'adresse*—an excellent idea initiated by his French grandmother-in-law, whose late husband always carried a visiting card on his person. Nowadays, if a contact did not have one, then Darlington would make one up and pop it into his card box. In this way, he was able to keep all his contacts at the tips of his fingers. Showing one such card to the light of the oil lamp, he read: *Monsieur Jacob Delpech de Castanet, The French Church, Threadneedle Street.* Darlington recalled Jacob explaining that this was the main Huguenot church in London and that it would be his first point of contact upon arriving in the English capital. 'Yes, that's it,' Daniel said to himself, over the six o'clock ping of the beautifully made lantern clock.

He wondered if Jacob was with his wife now; it had been four months already since he left back in February to escape the French blockade. However, little did Daniel know then that it would take Jacob another half year and a war campaign in Ireland before he would finally meet Jeanne again. Just then, a woman's voice calling out playfully interrupted Daniel's thoughts.

'Mister Daniel Darling!' It was Marianne who often liked to tease whenever she called her husband's name. 'Dinner is served!'

A short while later, after her husband was seated opposite her grandmother and the maid was serving leek and chicken soup, Marianne asked, 'But why does Mr Leisler want to hold the fort in the first place?' Of course, she was referring to the fort of New York, where merchant and militia captain Jacob Leisler had remained since he had taken his turn to stand guard on June 2nd. She knew that he had done so in part because of the rising fear of an imminent French attack, now that Protestant William of Orange, the French king's sworn enemy, had taken the throne of England. But she couldn't quite fathom why Leisler would want to substitute Lieutenant Governor Nicholson.

'The problem is,' said Daniel, who had agreed to support Leisler in his captaincy from the start, 'even though Governor Andros is confirmed to be held in prison in Boston, Lieutenant Governor Nicholson here refuses to stand in and make an official proclamation regarding the change of king, even though we all know now that William has taken the throne of England.'

'Perhaps,' said Madame de Fontenay, Marianne's grandmother, a French Protestant noble, fidgeting in her seat, 'it is because he hopes that King James, God forbid, will recover it!'

'He claims there exists no law that would allow him to stand in for the governor, for Governor Andros is neither absent from the province, nor is he deceased.'

'I dare say it is a valid enough reason, though,' said Marianne, 'otherwise, every lieutenant governor would be making up his own laws.'

'I agree,' said Daniel, 'but it does not change the fact that our defences are in a shambles. Why, it would not be difficult for the French to saunter right in and take over our cherished city here and now!'

'My goodness,' said Madame de Fontenay, 'and where would we run then?'

'That is why I must join Leisler now. Under his captaincy, we have the chance to make amends. He is a man of action and, in his younger days, he trained as a soldier. I know no better man to take up the challenge!'

'What about you, Daniel? You were born here!'

'No, Marianne, I would oppose any king who tried to curtail our freedom, you know that. Leisler, on the other hand, is a firm supporter of William. Although I will be too until we can do better; he is by far the lesser of the two evils, not to mention a sworn enemy of your King Louis.'

'Not my king!' said Madame de Fontenay, sitting stiff as a plank in unyielding defiance. 'I shudder at the very name.'

'So when will you start?' said Marianne.

'This afternoon, we meet again...' Daniel paused before saying the new appellation of the fort previously named after James, the Stuart king. 'At Fort William,' he declared.

Madame de Fontenay said, 'I suppose the quicker we repair what has been neglected, the safer we shall be.'

'That is all very well, Grandmother,' said Marianne, 'but our house is on the wrong side of the city wall.'

'Then we must make good our own defences here,' said Madame de Fontenay defiantly. 'If the French take us, we will certainly be tortured before being put to death.'

'Alas,' added Daniel, 'along with two hundred other Huguenot families here in New York, having fled persecution in France.'

'I say we load guns and rifles and put them at the ready should the need arise,' said the old lady, her knotted hands patting the table in time with her words as if to give them more weight. 'And have a defensive outer wall built around this very house.'

'I agree,' seconded Marianne. 'To yield is not an option.'

'Hmm,' said Daniel dubiously, 'but that could invite more danger of invasion. If the house fell, then we would be as good as giving the enemy the stick to beat us with.'

'But we shall not be fighting to lose, Daniel,' said Marianne. 'We fight to win; we have no choice.'

'If we become overpowered,' said Daniel, 'then we shall have to set fire to the house and take refuge within the city wall.'

'And that,' said Madame de Fontenay, 'will be our last stand.'

'Indeed, I fear so too, which is why I shall be joining Leisler in securing our defences.'

'Well, I have spoken with Mrs Ducamp, our new neighbour,' said Marianne. 'Her husband, who was once a French lieutenant no less, agrees our households should join forces.'

'I have heard about him: a recent convert, they say, and a man who has seen plenty of military action.'

Daniel spent the rest of the day at Fort William in further discussion, and then helped organise work teams of carpenters, builders, and labourers.

In a spirit of defiance, New Yorkers of varying origins were preparing for an imminent attack, all intent on defending their home. Sawyers cut timber, carpenters fortified palisade segments, builders reinforced the blockhouses, labourers consolidated earthen fortifications, and even children were enlisted for the collection of stones.

Marianne, meanwhile, bolstered and reassured by her beloved grandmother, who always knew what was right, set about organising the defences of their home. The garden boundary had already been cleared of its bushes and flowers. Now Ben, with sweat pearling on his black brow, was digging the trench where a high fence was to be erected. 'Are you quite sure we are being reasonable, Grandmother?' said Marianne as she stared at the old lady standing with hands on hips in her dress and boots.

'Well, it's either we become fearful and prey to defeatism, or we defend our home with true grit, my dear. Why, we have not come this far to give it all up without a fight.'

That evening in the upstairs bedchamber, his limbs aching from the afternoon's toil, Darlington stooped to gaze dotingly into the cradle where his baby son was sleeping snugly, fists clenched.

'Daniel,' said Marianne in a low voice as he joined her in the four-poster rope bed. 'I have something to tell you.' She sat in her summer nightdress, propped up against her feather-filled pillows, the glow of the bedside oil lamp giving her complexion a soft sheen.

But the gravity of her voice made him contemplate her with concern. 'What is it, darling?' he said, trying to read the change of expression on her face.

'Well,' she returned with a coy smile, 'there is another one in the oven.' Daniel momentarily failed to connect her meaning until Marianne dabbed her belly with both hands.

She had barely gotten over the last pregnancy, and baby Samuel was only just beginning to sleep through the night. But never mind that. Marianne, despite her noble upbringing, was no stranger to hardship. After all, she had been arrested with her grandmother in France for being a Huguenot, had been sent in atrocious conditions across the ocean, and had ended up in a mosquito-infested slave colony before managing to escape with Jacob Delpech, the man who had saved her honour on more than one occasion. She wondered fleetingly where he could be now, what he could be doing.

Then her thoughts circled back to the new baby in her belly. Becoming a young mother might have radically changed her perspective on life, but it had not blunted her love of religious freedom. Nevertheless, what with the threat of invasion from New France and the recent internal wrangling in New York, she felt more than ever the need for protection. The house was fine enough; she had gotten used to its cosy rooms and had made it hers with some finer French furnishings. But why, for the love of God, did it have to be located outside the city wall?

Then she felt her husband's long arm wrap around her and pull her close to his body so that no distance remained between them. He did not say it would be awkward for a second baby to come now; it was hardly possible to stop nature in her tracks, was it? Instead, after kissing her cheek and breathing in her light fragrance of rosewater, he said, 'I was thinking, would you mind if we moved into town? At least until these troubles are settled and we've got the defences secured. I've said it once, and I'll say it again: given the current state of affairs, there is no better time for your former countrymen to invade.'

Marianne pushed herself slightly away, enough to look him sternly in the eye. 'This is our home, Daniel, and Grandmother is right. We must prepare to defend it,' she said resolutely. 'We have been driven from our home once like vermin by the French. It will not happen again. Not here. Not in America!

And I am not going to take our child to a place where there are still reports of the pox.'

CHAPTER 3

June 1699, Dublin

THE DELPECH FAMILY — 10 YEARS LATER

Turning in his seat as the cart rattled up to the north gate, Jacob met Jeanne's eyes again and gave her a nod that expressed his admiration and love for her more eloquently than any page of prose.

If God was the bedrock of his inner strength, she was the central pillar of his continued belief in their enterprise—an enterprise that some had gone so far as to qualify as foolhardy. Night after night, he had lain with his pulse pounding in his right ear and opposing thoughts wreathing and snapping like conflicting serpents through the ducts of his mind, keeping him from finding sleep until the darkness began to pale through the cracks of the shutters.

On the morning of every one of those restless nights, with unaltered purpose, Jeanne had set his doubts to rest. 'We have taken that decision, Jacob,' she told him with reassuring resolve. 'Now let us keep our sights firmly fixed on that resolution and not let any sudden squall come to throw us off course.' In her way, she made him whole and allowed him to stride out to embrace their life-changing project; he was fortified by the knowledge of her unfailing support.

As they passed Saint Andrew's church in Dame Street, his glance fell upon Pierre and Isabelle before he turned back to face the road ahead. 'Nearly there, children!' he called out in a deliberately cheerful tone of voice as if they were on just another Sunday trip to Dublin, where they were used to spending the day at the Protestant church. Here they would exchange news and views with fellow Huguenots. Like Jacob and Jeanne, they had escaped their persecutors in France. Many of them had been given a place to settle by King William in return for their services rendered during the Irish campaign against the dethroned James Stuart. Partly thanks to Huguenot fervour, the Catholic king had failed to retake the English throne despite the backing of Louis of France.

But today was Tuesday, and they had said their farewells the previous Sunday to their friends and acquaintances at Saint Andrew's. Instead of stopping off at the church, they rolled onward in the direction of Merchants Quay, where Jacob had arranged for a boat to ferry them further down the River Liffey to Ringsend. Here they were to board the packet boat to Pennsylvania; from Pennsylvania, they would travel up the coast to New York. That was the plan.

'I wish Jess were coming with us,' said Isabelle.

'I wished I could stay here with her,' said Pierre, as they trundled from Dame Street through the ruins of the city gate at a walking pace, into the beating heart of the city.

Jacob and Jeanne said nothing but nevertheless shared young Pierre's angst as they slowly drew closer to the embarkation point.

Jeanne almost wished now they had hired the car man to take them across the boggy tidal-river floodplain to Ringsend. From here, they could have waited to board the ship anchored in the river channel. At least it would have allowed them a lengthier farewell before they stepped off this fair land of Ireland forever. There again, wasn't her refusing to have her church friends see them off the reason why she wanted to avoid any prolonged farewell? Didn't she just want to get the task in hand over with?

Long had they debated whether to take the bumpy passage to that neck of land at Ringsend. But then late one morning, after his return from town, Jacob showed Jeanne a news report in *The Flying Post* that persuaded them to take the waterway instead to Ringsend. The paper had reported yet another robbery by so-called reparees, lost men who had fought in the Irish campaign on the side of James Stuart. Jacob had heard that they were sometimes notoriously led by sons of Catholic nobles, whose families had been stripped of land and estate after the Cromwell war. These fallen noblemen had only become known to Jacob since settling in Ireland, and he had since become well informed of the atrocities and hardships imposed on Catholics—hardships that he could well identify with, having lived through the heinous persecutions in France, and having been stripped of fortune, home, and his estate in his birth town of Montauban.

So it was, they would take the barque to Ringsend and, after a short halt at Cork without making landfall, would embark on a long and perilous voyage across the great vastness of the ocean.

Wedged between her two youngest children, now Jeanne recalled that, adding to the balance in favour of a departure from Dublin by gabbard, she had said, 'Furthermore, I know you have paid for our passage, Jacob, but even so, I won't be reassured until we have claimed our place aboard midship. You know what some people can be like. It would avoid any unpleasantness.'

'True,' Jacob had conceded, 'better sail down the river then, and board before anyone else.'

'Yes, the tide would not allow an embarkation from Ringsend until low water.' That was the clincher, for neither could Jacob envisage spending the long voyage at the ship's extremities. The mere thought of it brought back the traumatic experience of his first crossing of the Atlantic. He had voyaged with eighty other Huguenot prisoners, crammed like sardines in a barrel, in a cell situated at the prow, the worst place of all. For not only was the pitch and roll much greater there, but it was also situated under the kitchen and often became an unbearable, flea-infested hothouse with hardly a breath of air, let alone room to lie down straight, so packed were they. Well he recalled one poor woman who, in her quiet suffering, had suddenly leapt up, ripped off her blouse to reveal a hideous red ribbon of flea-bitten flesh, and tried to dive through the gun port hole to find solace in the sea. By the grace of God, she was hauled back in by the ankles.

And yet, here he was again, ten years older, about to embark on a similar sordid voyage. Only this time would be the last, he had promised himself. And this time, he would be travelling as a free man with his family around him, their fate in his hands. But was it worth it? he wondered as the bay mare pulled them along Dame Street. Now that he had diligently built up his finances, why couldn't the children go to England? But to go to England would very possibly mean setting his progeniture against their ancestors. Surely no man, albeit in generations to come, would want his offspring to be at each other's throats, would he? Or perhaps men were incapable of thinking so far ahead. But that was the problem, for both he and Jeanne did. They did think of their descendants. They did value their own place in their descendants' history and heritage. They did inculcate the values of family belonging in their own children, values that meant so much to him and to Jeanne, who, in terms of heritage, had forsaken so much more, having been born into nobility.

Neither did Jacob want to be part of any intolerance like that which had forced him to leave behind his home country forever. He did not want to be part of any societal machinations that indulged in restricting liberties for reasons of choice of worship. For was that not what the government in England was trying to do by banning papists from parliament and confiscating their ancestral lands? It would only lead to frustration that one day would ferment into anger and violence, wouldn't it? Not least as most of the population was Catholic, and all the more stubbornly so now that the authorities were against the old religion. In turn, did this not only supply further pretext for the descendants of the Catholic gentry and the victims of Cromwell to become rebels, reparees, and highway robbers?

No, neither Jacob nor Jeanne desired their descendants to become inured to any sort of persecution and injustice. So, to the New World it was, despite the possible hardships, despite the heartache of leaving their eldest daughter, Lizzy, to live her own life in France in the old faith.

As the cart trundled along Dame Street into the narrow-congested heart of the city, Jeanne watched her eldest son sitting broad-shouldered beside his father up front.

What adventures awaited a young man in the wilderness of this America? she wondered. It had taken all their powers of persuasion throughout the previous winter and spring to get him to adhere to the venture. He had remained adamantly intent on joining the English army, and they only managed to sway him by, as a last resort, appealing to his sense of family loyalty. Jeanne said, 'Your father is not a young man anymore, Paul. He, indeed, all of us, would be deeply impaired without the support and aid, both physical and intellectual, not to mention organisational, of his eldest son. Pierre is too young to help in the first years.'

A week later, Paul had conceded. He gave up his bid to join the army in England, and now, without acrimony, he threw himself wholeheartedly into the venture; such was his character. Jeanne well recalled when he first joined her in Geneva all those years ago, having journeyed across perilous France with a guide just to join her in place of his elder sister, who had refused to leave her hometown.

Jeanne recalled how he and she had run through the burning streets of Worms, where they had saved the life of their boatman, shot down in cold blood by marauding French soldiers sent to torch the medieval city. Then how he had suffered in silence as they trekked across the hills of the Palatinate to the port town of Bingen on the River Rhine. She had thought she had lost him once after a bad fall from a racing sley in Switzerland. And how he had walked proudly, unflinchingly by her side, as they walked out of a military camp with a rifle pointed at their backs. Her boy of nine had more mettle than many a man. No, she would not suffer a separation, even years later, not after all the trials and tribulations they had been through together.

He had grown into a young man, strong and of even temper like his father, determined and sometimes blinded by righteousness like her. But once his decision was taken, he got on with the task at hand. And Jeanne hoped that to do so on the grounds of family loyalty would galvanise his feeling of importance and of being a partner in this venture to America, instead of a child tagging along with his parents.

Her thoughts were interrupted by the growing hullabaloo of the cobbled lane as they continued deeper into the city, where a street country seller was singing out her wares, and a dandy street musician was deftly playing the fiddle to the thronging shoppers on the rickety paving. Soon, just one row of timber houses separated them from the pong of the Liffey. The sound of seagulls now melled into the smells of poultry and horse manure as Jacob waved to a book seller along Wood Quay. Jeanne turned her head to another hawker, a man with a weathered face in a flat-brimmed hat, selling rabbits for the pot. 'When were they caught?' she called out to the countryman.

'Fresh this mornin', madam,' was his answer.

'Two for a shilling?' said Jeanne. The exchange was made, and the rabbits were given to Paul as they trundled on without stopping. Paul then directed a cleaner-looking city man with a winning smile and a sharp wit toward his mother. The man handed her a pamphlet. 'All the news, views, and tasty titbits for a tuppence, me lady!' he said with a silver tongue as lithe as a Liffey eel. Jeanne knew in it she would find news of the latest highway robberies, crimes, hangings, publicity, notices of absconding servants, and other local gossip. It was her little pleasure. She usually counted on Jacob or Paul to bring one back for her whenever they went into town. She handed over a coin and opened the pamphlet. 'There's an auction at Dick's Coffee House, Jacob,' she said, raising her voice above the din as she perused the publicity on the first page. 'That would explain why the going is so slow today.'

'Oh yes,' returned Jacob, 'it completely escaped my mind. There's a sale of books, if I remember rightly. Same chap I met at Pat's. Name of Dunton. Over from London.'

Their exchange fell away at the mention of the English capital where they both had lived hand to mouth independently, until they were at last reunited when Jacob had taken leave from the atrocious war in Ireland in the winter of 1690. Their pause was further prolonged as the next moment, they could barely hear themselves speak over the deep, powerful calls of the town crier. 'Oyez, oyez, oyez! Take notice!' he bellowed, astutely taking advantage of the milling crowd before Wood Quay to broadcast his news to the greatest number of people per square yard. 'Auction of books from London. Starts at two hours past noon at Dick's Coffee House in Skinner's Row. Oyez, oyez. St James's gate closed for repair works. Oyez, oyez...'

'I would have gone had we...' continued Jacob between *oyez*, but then he gave up. There was no point in trying to compete with both the ambient din and the town crier, whose booming shouts bounced off the river wall and Newman's Tower. Besides, there should be only one topic on his mind right now, he reminded himself, and that was to get Jeanne, Paul, Isabelle, and Pierre along to Merchants Quay and into the single-masted gabbard which he had arranged to take them to Ringsend. They were still in good time, although the tide would be high at noon, and already the sun was beating down at barely an hour short of its pinnacle.

So instead: 'Coming through!' he hurled out with urgency, and the street seller, standing by her wares on the edge of the curb, stepped out of the way to let the cart roll past.

'Careful o' me cages!' she hurled.

'I will, madam, but you should not be selling on the side of the road. It is against the law.'

'Aw, and where am I s'posed to sell 'em then?'

Jacob rode on, careful not to knock over her baskets of eggs and cheese and her urns of milk. And on they trundled toward Merchants Quay that lay before Essex Bridge, where gabbards and lighters had to strike their masks if they were to go any further upstream.

The quays of Dublin were the busiest place young Pierre had ever seen, and he stood, all agog, while his mother and sister alighted from the cart in their turn.

His father and eldest brother were well used to it: they often came to oversee barrels of goods and wine sent from France being unloaded and rolled to their warehouse further along the quay. As for Isabelle, not only had she been accustomed to town life in France, but she had also travelled to Bordeaux and across the sea to Ireland only the previous year. The busiest place Pierre had known until then was the church of Saint Andrew's on Dame Street, where everything had its place and where he knew what to do.

Here, before the web of masts and rigging, the boy could sense an urgency in the iodised, gull-shrieking, foul-smelling, riverside air. All about, malodorous men, drenched in sweat, were rolling barrels and unloading crates ferried to quay on the shallow-draft gabbards from the packet ships anchored at Ringsend. Here, the gruff baying of dockers was alarming as they hauled hundredweight sacks on their backs. 'Mind yer backs!' grunted one. 'Coming through there!' called another close on his heels before the boy realised there was a whole trail of them following suit.

'Mornin', Mr Delpech!' said a voice from another direction. Pierre caught sight of his father giving a wave to familiar voices here and there. Then they were met by church acquaintances Mr and Mrs Devanny, whom Pierre had known all his life. The dignified though moist-eyed adults gave each other farewell amid the milling quay.

'I cannot say I envy you,' said Mrs Devanny to Pierre's mother, 'but I will bear testimony to your courage.'

'I sometimes wish one could wear courage like one wears a coat, my dear Charlotte, for I do not always feel so courageous.'

Too preoccupied with processing all the smells and the colourful hubbub, Pierre gave not a thought that he would never see these people again. He obediently said goodbye in his turn, to let the adults continue their outpourings of good health and Godspeed above his head.

Ten minutes later, while Jacob showed Mr Devanny a cart wheel that would require some attention, Jeanne insisted that she board the gabbard in good time, as much to settle her nerves as to settle the children. Paul, meanwhile, helped the boatmen bring aboard the extra provisions his mother had packed which, she had insisted, would complement the meals aboard, at least, during the first weeks of the long voyage. These included: three salted hams in moist muslin towels, five country loaves, three salted ox tongues, three large, ripened cheeses, a long black pudding, a hogshead of wine and lemon water, a barrel of ale, a crate of biscuits, and a barrel each of potatoes and apples. Jacob and Paul had already taken care of loading the items for cooking and cleaning aboard the packet ship, as well as tools and instruments for their installation in America.

As Jeanne settled on the plank with her children at the stern on the one-masted boat, the pungent smells of timber, tar, and bilge came to her in a flood of memories. She now recalled crossing the Narrows from Amsterdam to London with Paul. To think, he was barely older than Pierre at the time. In her mind, she saw herself and Paul crossing the Irish Sea with Jacob to start a new life in Ireland. How she had loathed the swell in the pit of her belly and the perpetual feeling of angst during the tumultuous weather. Nonetheless, she had indeed twice travelled by sea before and had each time come out none the worse for wear. But this time, she thought to herself, they would have to endure it in the cramped environment of the gun deck for two months solid—provided the sailing was good, that is.

Jacob was the last to take his place aboard while one of the boatmen used an oar to punt the rivercraft from the quayside further out into the river breeze.

The other boatman unfurled the sail, and soon they were sailing against the current to join the *Mary-Ann*, just a few miles further downstream. The sound of a winch seemed to echo from the quay over the chilly River Liffey like a farewell call amid the screeching cries of ravenous gulls. Casting his gaze toward the busy quayside, Jacob felt moved but relieved that this departure signalled the end of his affair with Ireland. He would nonetheless forever keep a place in his heart for the pleasant and hospitable people here, and the emerald hills that had been the backdrop of his existence for the past nine years. But too often he had found himself chasing away horrific scenes of the Williamite war, of disease and destruction, from his mind's eye. Perhaps now that he was leaving the lands that had spawned them, the nightmares would stop haunting him.

Paul was standing with him at the prow. Turning back to stern, Jacob gazed at Jeanne, who was placing a blanket over the children's knees. He sensed the same restlessness in her to be on their way at last, perhaps so that the anguish of inaction would give way to the fulfilment of at last being in the thick of the new challenge.

With just a few miles to spare before they would approach their passage to America, Jacob felt around in his leather bag to prepare a little extra coin for the boaters who, over the years, had so often ferried his goods ashore. Nudging his correspondence pouch to one side to reach his drawstring bourse, he caught a glimpse of another letter from New York that he had been meaning to read. This one was written by the hand of a young woman. It was the hand of Marianne Darlington, née Duvivier.

CHAPTER 4

January 1690, New York

THE DARLINGTONS — 10 YEARS EARLIER

The 17th of January, 1690

Dear Jacob,

    I take up the quill from my darling Daniel who is absent, having joined the campaign in defence of our beloved city.

    New York is threatened by all sides, it would seem. By the French, who are said to be bent on marching upon New York from Canada as I write, which is why Daniel has joined the militia to head them off. I pray every instant he comes back to us safe and sound. Then there are the northern Indians who would raise the hatchet to all Christians whatever their nationality; indeed, they slaughtered two hundred French settlers in their beds last summer in Lachine on Montreal Island, and I have heard such horrific tales of death by torture of the hundred or so who were taken alive.

    My grandmother, baby Samuel, and I are still at the house where we have dug a defensive ditch in case of a French attack at night. And the city, thanks to the constant efforts of Monsieur Leisler who has built a half moon battery, is a safer place now.

But I write to you to advise you to put off your voyage to New York with your family, in case you did not receive the previous letter sent in June from Daniel.

It has become a dangerous place here, what with the French, the Indians, and the internal battle for the control of New York. Indeed, since the governor left, Leisler has been promoted to captain and then, in the absence of Lieutenant Governor Nicholson who sailed to London back in June, has now been sworn in as lieutenant governor of New York until King William sends news of another appointee which, I believe, Leisler is expected to secure, given his loyalty to the throne and his achievement of holding the city for the king thus far. I only hope Monsieur Bayard does not stir things up again, jealous as he is of Monsieur Leisler's success. I fear this as he was, after all, mayor under James II, who was friendly with France.

How the world has gone mad, and it does not help matters, there having been such a drought and a poor harvest this past year, not to mention illness. I sometimes wonder whether it is more dangerous within the city walls or without. In any case, I have chosen to live without, here in our little family abode. I must still be a country girl at heart.

So you see, my dear uncle, you must put off your voyage until New York becomes a safer and more secure place.

To end on a more positive note. You will be pleased to hear that Monsieur Leisler, faithful to his word, purchased the lands in New Rochelle for our Huguenot brethren from La Rochelle. That land has now been signed over to them, which is surely yet more proof of Monsieur Leisler's devout and righteous character, despite the rumours and stirrings of his detractors here in New York, who, though few, are nonetheless vociferous.

I do hope you have found happiness in your family, my dear uncle, as despite these terribly trying times, I find happiness every day in mine, with our baby Samuel, and a second on the way.

Yours affectionately,

Marianne Darlington, née Duvivier

P.S. I do so miss your guidance and wisdom, dear uncle, but I would feel even more anxious should you come without being forewarned of the dangers of this day and age in New York. We shall write to you once the dust of chaos has settled.

Sitting at Daniel's writing table before the snow-white window view, Marianne blotted her postscript with satisfaction. 'There, another job done,' she said to herself as she mentally ticked it off her list of things to do.

That list had been growing in the back of her mind, but she had been busy with baby Samuel and fatigued by her new pregnancy. What with the constant worries of attack from the north and the risk of contagion from the city, and now the weather turning to snow, her only moments of peace were when she gave milk.

There being no wet nurse because of the outbreak of smallpox, she had no option but to give the breast herself, which nonetheless gave her an unending feeling of peace, knowing that the endless fountain of life, as Daniel called it, was forever being replenished.

Looking up from the writing desk through the lattice window at the falling snowflakes, she now felt a tightening and a heaviness of her breasts as she adjusted her woollen shawl. Her milk would leak out at the brush of a hand against her nipple. But baby Samuel must still be soundly asleep, she said to herself, otherwise Claudine, the young maid, would have brought him by now.

As the thought entered Marianne's mind, Claudine did appear, slightly agitated, and wrapped up and bonneted for the chill despite the fires in the hearths. She stood at the study door that Marianne had left ajar so she could hear the movements of the house. 'There is a carriage coming, Madam Marianne,' said Claudine, nodding anxiously toward the window. 'In the distance, there.'

Marianne focussed her eyes on the distorted view of the crown glass windowpanes, into the mid-distance. Through the heavy snowflakes, she could now clearly see the front silhouette of a dark horse, steam rising from its muzzle. It was pulling a covered sleigh carriage. 'Fear not, Claudine,' returned Marianne, continuing to peer through the study window as she pulled her woollen shawl more snugly over her shoulders. 'I doubt the French would attack in a solitary horse and sleigh.'

The afternoon sky was a cold purple, and a thick layer of snow had settled on every surface. The front garden, the hedgerow, the ditch, the fencing, and the lean-to where the wood was kept, were all immaculately white. She felt glad for the kitchen wood burner and the lumber of which there was seemingly no end. Although she had noted during the past autumn how the great forest of Manhattan, that she recalled once stretched from the top of the cultivated fields outside the wall, seemed to be receding to such an extent that they had found it cheaper to buy this year's firewood rafted into New York market from Long Island. Daniel had brought in a cord which he and Benjamin had chopped neatly into logs of two different lengths and stacked in the lean-to. Of course, the arduous chore now was bringing them in by the basket daily, long ones for the chimney, short ones for the wood burner.

Shifting her gaze back to the track past the front gate, Marianne could now more clearly make out the carriage approaching the house from Broad Way city gate. At the same time, there came a piercing cry from the other room, where baby Samuel was manifesting his hunger. Peering through the window with more focus, she clearly recognised the sleigh carriage as belonging to her new neighbour with whom she had struck up quite an affinity. Given the present state of crisis in New York city, it had flowered into female solidarity, as both their husbands were often away from home. 'It is Mrs Ducamp,' she said, turning to Claudine. 'Go fetch baby. I will be in the front room. And ask Martha to prepare the tea service, will you?'

'Yes, Madame,' said Claudine with a note of excitement in her voice. Afternoon tea was becoming something of a habit between the ladies and always gave cause for excitement in the house. Making a brew from the dry leaves was such a ceremony, especially since the beautiful porcelain teacups and saucers had arrived from Europe. Claudine never tired of looking at the intricate scenes from the exotic lands of China.

Marianne still preserved some of the airs and graces of her class from her former life as a duchess in France, despite the distance between the domestic servants being much closer here in New York, where everyone came with a dream of improving their lot. Marianne had already experienced that some servants did not stay long, for it was not rare, partly due to lack of women, partly thanks to new money, for a young woman to be a maid one day and the spouse of a wealthy merchant the next. In the same way, it was not rare for a newly emancipated indentured labourer or even a former soldier to become a trapper and self-proclaimed fur trader. She had heard the latter was partly how Jacob Leisler had become a respected and influential merchant in New York. But with wealth comes jealousy, and with power comes allegations and falsehoods, both from peers and from family.

Through their acquaintance with Mrs Elsie Leisler, Marianne and her grandmother were well aware that things had turned sour, partly due to family relations. It did not help matters that a leader of the grandees, as Leisler termed them, Nicholas Bayard, former mayor of New York under James II, also happened to be part of Leisler's extended family.

Everyone in New York knew Mr and Mrs Bayard harboured a longstanding rancour over Leisler's wife's inheritance from Govert Lookermanns, her wealthy stepfather. Lookermanns, a self-made man from the Spanish Netherlands, had amassed a considerable fortune in the fur trade, an inheritance which the Bayards had time and again contested in court, only to find that time and again the court rejected their claim. Marianne could but conclude that it was partly rancour and jealousy that had taken Bayard north up the Hudson River the previous August to Albany, where he had joined another grandee, Stephanus van Cortlandt—also related to Leisler by marriage—who had taken New York's charter and seal with him to try to limit Leisler's authority. From here, Bayard was able to orchestrate a propaganda campaign throughout New England and the surrounding townships to belittle and discredit Jacob Leisler, the elected governor of the people of New York, and fervent representant of the new Protestant king.

Ten minutes later: 'Where have you been in your condition?' said Marianne playfully as May Ducamp followed her into the main room, where they made their way to the three armchairs by the fireplace.

May Ducamp was ten years Marianne's senior. Charming to a fault, pretty, level-headed, and sometimes quite ruthless in her thinking, May had recently settled into the adjacent house with her new French husband and her young daughter from a previous marriage. It was clear to Marianne when she first set eyes on her that her new English neighbour was a sharp woman of means, and she had immediately taken to the older woman. Taking baby from the maid who had followed them in, Marianne said, 'Claudine, please bring in the tea, will you? There's a dear.'

'I have been to town,' said May, easing herself into the armchair next to Marianne's while holding her lower back with her left hand. 'Can't just sit and wait. You're lucky, you have your hands full with the baby, although I must say, I don't envy you. Anyway, I have some interesting news, my dear Marianne.'

At that moment, the door leading from the passageway opened, and there tentatively appeared the end of a cane, followed by the spry person of Marianne's grandmother, Madame de Fontenay, an aristocrat born and bred. 'No, no, stay seated,' she said imperiously in French to May, who had been edging her way further into the seat rather than out of it. 'You must remain seated in your condition, you know.'

May Ducamp, always the rebel, and always averse to anything that signified a supposed hereditary right to look down upon others, returned in impeccable French, '*Bonjour, Madame de Fontenay.* Actually, I was fidgeting.'

The old lady continued on her way to her chair, where the cat was purring. 'You are entirely within your rights, Madame Ducamp,' she replied, with a very slight emphasis on 'Camp' of Ducamp, which unflatteringly translated as *'of the camp'.* But the verbal joust was but a jolly tussle, some light banter between the two ladies, one a countess, the other a self-made woman. For, after all, they were all in the same boat of insecurity, moored as they were outside the newly reinforced wall of New York.

'How is your leg today?'

'Oh, still half asleep. How is your bump?'

'Having a frolicking time, I should say. There he goes again...' Shameless and without a complex, May held her belly.

Madame de Fontenay picked up the passive puss by the scruff of its neck as she said, 'How do you know it's a boy? You do carry it high, my dear.'

'Old wives' tales! Everyone said Lily-Anne would be a boy, whereas she was quite low.'

As the old lady dumped the cat onto her lap after taking the seat, while it stretched and yawned, Marianne snatched the moment to end the jousting. She said, 'Grandmother has been keeping watch all night again, haven't you, Grandma?'

'Well, someone has to,' replied Madame de Fontenay sharply, her old, knotted hand stroking the length of the outstretched cat. 'It would seem everyone else has given up.'

'You needn't worry,' said May, 'according to some, we are out of danger now, at least until the thaw. Although I confess, I still asked Winden to keep watch when it was our turn. Didier had insisted upon it before he left with Daniel and Monsieur Wendell to Albany. So you may put your two legs to bed this evening, Madame. Winden will keep watch tonight.'

'That is a reassurance, but what if he falls asleep like our Benjamin did? I found him slumped over the spyglass.' The spyglass in question was set up in the upstairs room that looked over the farmers' fields, northward between the two rivers. The watcher could use it in case of any movement under the moon or of any light of an approaching lantern or torch. It was perhaps not very efficient—something that Benjamin must have realised—but it reassured the old lady.

'You cannot blame him, Grandma,' returned Marianne. 'He had been digging the entrenchment around the house all morning.'

'But dark men are supposed to be strong as oxen. That's what we pay them for.'

'That's a very insult, if I may say so, Madame,' said May. 'On what do you base such unfounded nonsense?'

'I have seen their children. They are positively wild and fierce.'

41

'And ours are unnaturally restrained. Let the children play, I say.'

'Anyway, Grandma,' said Marianne, showing her baby her breast, which had the effect of suspending all antagonism as May and Madame de Fontenay watched the infant lunge for the dripping teat. 'May has come to deliver her news. So let us hear it before she delivers her package instead!'

After a slight pause that signalled a change of tone, as Madame de Fontenay sat patiently stroking her purring cat, May said: 'I went into town to find out if there was any news about our husbands' expedition up the North River.'

'And did you?' said Marianne.

'Not much, but I did get confirmation that Lieutenant Rust's expedition to destroy Fort Frontenac has definitely been abandoned. The French had apparently already demolished it in retaliation for the Iroquois siege last August.'

'It's sad to say, it was hardly surprising really,' said Marianne, 'when you consider how the French destroyed all their corn crop the previous year. I wonder how they even got through the winter.'

'That's true. Didier told me they even captured friendly Indians and sent them back to France as galley slaves! If that is not a betrayal of trust, then I do not know what is.'

'The problem is, they wield their trust like a double-edged sword,' said the old lady. 'So they got their comeuppance.'

'That's one way of putting it, I suppose,' said May caustically with a short laugh. 'I do hope we don't get *our* comeuppance!'

Re-grounding the conversation, Marianne said: 'Then why go sending our men up the river just to deliver commissions instead of keeping them here?'

'If you remember, there was talk of them going to watch the trail from the north initially,' said May, 'to spot any French forces before they could attack.'

'But surely no one can move in this cold, let alone be expected to walk hundreds of miles through the snowdrifts, can they?'

'True,' said May. 'Counsellor Van Brugh insists it will protect us until the thaw. But there again, Alderman Van Brugh is a fat, middle-aged merchant unused to discomfort, so he would say that, wouldn't he?'

'Quite,' said Madame de Fontenay as Claudine carefully brought in the tea tray.

'But at least we know they really did go upriver to deliver commissions for Governor Leisler. I was worried there was something we didn't know.'

'My dear, all that way in the snow in your condition,' said Madame de Fontenay.

'Not to mention the pox,' said Marianne, who had hardly approached the town since the first outbreak the previous autumn. It was common knowledge that smallpox would disfigure you if it didn't kill you, the former quite possibly being Marianne's ghastliest fear.

'I quite enjoy a sleigh ride, actually, as long as I've got my muff warmers. But there's more,' said May, edging forward in her seat as if to further captivate her audience. 'Nicholas Bayard has been arrested for high misdemeanours against His Majesty's authority!'

'No...' said Marianne, taken aback. 'Why, isn't that treason?'

'More precisely, he has been arrested and thrown into the fort prison for conspiracy and plotting against the governor.'

Madame de Fontenay added, 'I heard he had come back from Albany because of his sick son.'

'I expect Mrs Bayard is furious,' said Marianne, 'and you know what a vicious cat she can be!'

'But how can they possibly know he was plotting against Leisler?' said Madame de Fontenay.

'They discovered an incriminating letter in one of his companion's pockets, threatening Leisler and his posterity with annihilation by poignard, poison, or pistol. Not only that, if you remember, they had also previously interrupted Bayard's letters.'

'Doesn't surprise me,' said Marianne. 'When they took in Mrs Bayard after he fled to Albany, they found her carrying letters for the opposition too.'

'Strange,' said Madame de Fontenay, 'I didn't put him down as a papist.'

'Actually, he's the son of a Huguenot,' said Marianne.

'It's not a question of religion, more of politics with Bayard,' said May. 'And he hates Leisler to death, as does his wife. They are related, you know.'

'Yes, yes, it goes back to his wife's stepfather's fortune,' said Madame de Fontenay.

'Well, by all accounts, it apparently made Leisler a wealthy man, which certainly must have raised eyebrows since he was already comfortable from his fur trading business.'

'You know so much; how do you do it?' said Marianne, looking up from her baby, who was voraciously sucking at her teat. 'You have only been here a few months, and you already know more than we do.'

'That's what comes of venturing into the thick of things and not taking sides, my dear: you get to know both sides of the coin. Be it Mrs Leisler or Mrs Bayard, I have no quarrel with either of them.'

'Yet,' said Marianne. 'But you wait and see. Judith Varleth Bayard is not an easy woman.'

'Maybe, but she's a man-maker. She made Bayard what he is today.'

'She has the advantage of age, my dear,' said the old lady.

'Fifteen years his senior, no less,' said Marianne. 'Anyway, what's the point of arresting Bayard just because he has different opinions?'

'Because the people have elected their leader,' said May, 'and Bayard would go against the voice of the people of New York, that's what.'

'That is the mindset of new money,' said Madame de Fontenay.

'New money, new land, new rules apply, dear Madame de Fontenay,' said May. 'You will have to get used to it. This is America! A place of opportunity for all. Look at Mrs Leisler. A self-made woman with a fortune and a husband with power.'

'Nonsense,' laughed Madame de Fontenay, 'she already came from a wealthy family.'

'Wealthy, but still not born a lady, because you cannot be born a lady. What nonsense is that?' said May.

'There, I entirely agree,' said the old lady with a self-satisfied smile. 'Indeed, it is all in the breeding, my dear.' May gave a cheeky nod in recognition of the fact that the old lady was in fine form this afternoon. 'In all my years, I have never heard of subordinates electing their leaders,' pursued Madame de Fontenay. 'What a strange New World this is becoming. Why, if we all had the same rights, then even the Silly Sallies and Simple Simons of this world would vote, and if there were enough of them, what would the world come to?' Meanwhile, Claudine carefully prepared the exquisite porcelain teacups and saucers on the tray that she had placed on the gueridon table. 'Thank you, my dear,' said the old lady.

'Madame,' said May, with a false tickle in her voice, 'Silly Sallies and Simple Simons are not reserved for the poorer classes.'

'Ah, that is true, I shall have to concede. Although I am told that being poor can make you stupid,' said Madame de Fontenay. 'Believe me, I have experienced it. It almost made me quite mad.' May gave an indulgent chuckle. The old lady continued: 'And if you ask me, putting your political adversary in prison cannot bode well. In fact, my husband used to say you are better off shooting them rather than giving them the chance of stabbing you in the back.'

'Grandmother!' exclaimed Marianne. 'Whatever will Mrs Ducamp think of us?'

'A little extreme perhaps, my dear, but your grandfather was a passionate man. And the truth is, a political adversary in your midst may prove to be more dangerous than the foreign enemy planning an invasion.'

'You have a point,' said May, conceding, but then added: 'Although you would hope that, faced with a foreign invader, at least people will put their differences to one side and defend the community for the common good.' While the baby suckled his mother's breast and Claudine poured out the afternoon tea, little could the ladies know what was unfolding three hundred miles to the north.

CHAPTER 5

January 1690

VILLE-MARIE, MONTREAL ISLAND

In the frozen city of Ville-Marie on Montreal Island, the governor of New France had arrived back from Versailles with orders to conquer New York.

The highly revered and flamboyant Count Louis de Buade de Frontenac, the re-appointed governor general of New France, had arrived in Quebec the previous October, only to find the Canadian colony besieged by an outbreak of smallpox and reeling from a series of Iroquois raids.

These raids had culminated in the horrific August massacre of Lachine situated on the island of Montreal, which put a temporary halt to the all-important, lucrative fur trade. According to the initial plan previously put forward by the governor of Montreal, a certain de Callière, French raiders were to travel across land, river, and lake, by way of the Richelieu River and Lake Champlain. Once they had taken Albany, the French were to find enough vessels there to travel down the Hudson River to

New York, where a seafaring force would be waiting to attack from the bay.

However, by the time Frontenac had arrived in Montreal, the season was too far gone for a full-scale invasion of New York by land and sea. Yet he knew he had to act swiftly to restore the prestige of New France and regain the Indians' respect. So, believing that it was the New Englanders that had roused the Iroquois to massacre Lachine, Frontenac had approved a plan to send out three raiding parties across land.

Two of the three expeditionary corps were to set off from Quebec and Three Rivers to attack border settlements of New England. Another party was to set out from Montreal to Albany. According to de Callière's initial plan, it was here that the French strike force would find rivercraft to take them down the Hudson River to storm New York.

'But the question is: will the river still be navigable at this time of year?' Frontenac had asked a week earlier as he pored over the map of the region. He was standing, glass of Armagnac in hand, around de Callière's study table with Jacques Le Moyne de Sainte-Hélène and Nicolas de Manthet, whom he had commissioned to lead the party.

'We'll see how the ground lies once there,' had returned Le Moyne, a large and powerful leader, as all eyes watched his large digit run the length of Lake Chaplain and then across Lake George to its southern tip. Le Moyne, a ruthless campaigner, having proven himself in the Hudson Bay raid a few years earlier, had agreed with Frontenac that nobody would be expecting a land attack in the midst of winter.

The Montreal party consisted of 114 hand-chosen *coureurs de bois* used to the great outdoors. These were the worst kind of frontiersmen who lived by blade and bullet, and who were chosen for their capacity to sustain the tough march southward as well as to inflict maximum calamity on the English settlements.

Like Le Moyne, they had learned the ruthless tactics of their native counterparts. The group was completed by ninety-six Sault and Algonquin Indians, totalling 210 men who set out on Indian snowshoes on January 17th, 1690.

They soon reached Lake Champlain and then Lake George. Frozen solid at this time of the year, the lakes offered the raiding party a flat, open pathway instead of having to struggle through the thick, snowy undergrowth, six feet deep in places. Despite being laden with their heavy muskets, provisions, and ammunition, it took them a mere six days to reach the southern tip of Lake George, where the French officers and Kryn, the great Indian leader, held council.

'So what is it to be?' said Le Moyne, sitting on his back pack and bringing out his block of pemmican from his leather pouch. He bit off a chunk of the dried meat and fat to thwart his hunger until the fire was ready. Then he would cut off another piece and boil it in snow to make a hot tin cup of soup. Chewing on the pemmican, he continued: 'Either we take Albany or Schenectady.'

Standing and looking into the bright orange orb of the sinking sun, in a low deep voice, the Indian chief said: 'Scout say many soldiers from Connecticut and New York sent to Albany to stand watch.'

'We have the element of surprise,' returned Le Moyne. 'We attack before sunrise, destroy the sleeping garrison, then burn down the dwellings.'

'That is if we are able to enter through the palisade,' said Nicolas de Manthet, a man of slighter build who was leaning on a rock, filling his clay pipe while waiting for a light. 'At night, the gates will be closed and guarded.'

Le Moyne, tired and cold from another day's march across the ice, but relieved at having reached the southernmost bank of the lake, let his gaze fall momentarily on the Indian brave clad in deer skin and furs, making a fire. He would be forty next month, Le Moyne thought to himself. He had spent the past twenty years learning the ways of the native Indians. He had learnt their cures, to be at one with his surroundings, and he had also learnt their cruelty against those who trespassed against them. Hardly Christian, and yet, somehow, he saw how it made sense to kill and scalp swiftly to save retaliation, breed respect in this life, and put the foe out of suffering, unless, of course, they were to be made an example of to others and were tortured and eaten.

Le Moyne watched smoke quickly appear from the hearth wood as the Indian stopped twisting the wooden stem into the bore hole. Carefully, he then set the wood dust that had turned to embers to the tinder bark. Cradling the tinder in his two hands, he blew gently as he carefully placed the kindling fire into the hollow of the little tepee of dry sticks set against a rock. Le Moyne never failed to be engrossed by the sight of the miracle of creating fire. Turning his gaze back to the Indian chieftain, he said: 'I suppose taking vessels down river is no longer an option.'

Kryn gave a slow, thoughtful shake of the head.

Manthet said, 'There's a good chance the river will be partially frozen. And anyway, without backup, New York will be too tough to take on just one front. Our sources inform us they have reinforced their defences and have built a solid battery by the fort.'

'I say we attack Schenectady instead,' said Kryn. 'It will not be as well guarded as Albany, and by the time the alert is given, we will be faraway.'

'Provided no one escapes from the compound,' said Manthet. 'And there's always a slim chance we'll be spotted by a trapper on the way.'

'Hmm,' said Le Moyne, gazing at the vulnerable flame as the Indian brave set thicker sticks in a tepee fashion around the kindling fire. 'Our mission is to strike at the heart of the English province, to dampen their spirits and blunt their keenness to trade for pelts. And to remind the Iroquois Confederation of our courage and determination.'

'But they are Dutch in Schenectady, not English,' remarked Manthet.

'It matters not where they are from, but who they answer to,' said Kryn. 'And they swear their allegiance to the English king.'

'Who also happens to be a Dutchman, no less,' said Manthet as if it were a joke.

'Fair enough, wherever they come from, it is still an English colony,' said Le Moyne. 'Although Albany would be the greater prize.' His eyes suddenly lit up as the fire bit into the cedar faggots in the early evening, making the rock against which it was set and the snow on the evergreen branches glisten. 'We shall consider our options and come to a decision once we reach the fork where the road splits into two,' he said, 'one road leading to Albany, the other to Schenectady.'

The big Indian chief gave a nod, then crouched down before the warming fire.

CHAPTER 6

January 1690

ALBANY

At the same moment, further south just outside Albany, Daniel Darlington was warming his hands over the chimney fire in a little Indian house where he and Didier Ducamp were lodged.

A cauldron of mutton broth prepared by the Protestant Indian keeper was simmering on a hook in the hearth. Situated outside the south gate, the lodge was one of a number of outhouses for Indians to stay in when they came to town to trade beaver pelts from June to August. During the summer season, the township of Albany became a hive of activity with Mohawk and Mahican traders, and white fur traders from the valleys of the Hudson and Mohawk rivers.

But since the English had taken control of Albany from the Dutch, these allied Indians were banned from staying within the city walls at night—which nonetheless did not prevent some of them from remaining with their Dutch trader friends as in the days of old. Some of the English deemed Indians could no longer be trusted, especially in these times, what with the French never far away, ever courting them for their trade.

This evening, there were only two Indian visitors. They represented Mohawk warriors bivouacked outside Schenectady. From what Daniel had gathered, they had come to petition the Albany aldermen for gunpowder, lead for making musket balls, and axes, in return for sending four Indian scouts to watch the northern trail from the tip of Lake Champlain near Otter's Creek.

Daniel had been invited by Albany fur trader and alderman Johannes Wendell to take a room at his large house inside the stockade on State Street, opposite Pearl Street. But Darlington, always a man of the people, had decided to remain with Ducamp, his travelling companion and new French neighbour from New York. Besides, Daniel knew from experience that Wendell's house was always full of children; the man had an impressive capacity to make them, all ten of them, no less, with another one apparently on the way.

But at least he and Ducamp were off the cold and draughty ketch that had carried them, and Jacob Leisler's commissions, the 150 miles up the tidal river from New York. The voyage back would be quicker, Daniel thought, for it would be a simple southbound run with no commissions to deliver and family to visit, and hopefully, no more run-ins with pans of ice that made the Hudson River so treacherous at this time of the year. To prevent the boat from running aground again, he decided they would only travel by daylight this time. Hopefully, the river ice would not have spread from bank to bank. Now, just a horse ride to Schenectady and back to visit his aunt, and soon, he would be sailing back to Marianne and his son.

Fatherhood, he thought to himself, was quite an enigma. Although it had made him more mindful of the intrepidness of his ventures, it had also sharpened his keenness to succeed.

Now he had someone to raise and to pass his enterprise to. Such was the gift of a son that Marianne had given him, he realised with pride. And now she was expecting another. Counting the months in his mind, he realised it could be born soon. 'Will it be a girl or another boy?' he wondered. He suddenly saw himself in a home full of little feet; he hoped to God his household would not become as populated as Wendell's. His proud brow then winced with concern: what would happen to them all if he was killed? Pushing the needless thought away, he cast his mind's eye back to his recent meetings with his extended family downriver in Ulster County.

When asked, he had told them that his new wife, whom he had met quite by chance on an improbable island en route from the Caribbean, was French. It had caused more than one brow to be raised, but then he would say she was a Huguenot, and nothing more needed to be said on that score. French Protestants were numerous in the valley, where they had found refuge from the terrifying persecution of the king of France. New Paltz, where one of the commissions was destined, was founded by Huguenots. It had pleased him to tell his cousins of his new life in New York now that he had given up his voyages to the Caribbean.

Looking through a tear in the oil-paper window into the encroaching darkness, he felt at peace with the world, despite his present rudimentary lodgings. It was just a darn pity, he thought, what with hostile Indians, the French, and the small-pox in town, that the world was not at peace with him.

His introspection was interrupted by the muffled noise of marching boots on snow. Moving closer to the tear in the window, he watched the tail end of a battalion of troops marching through the south gate, already illuminated by lanterns. He then pictured them marching up the frosty hill to Fort Orange, which dominated the stockaded township of Albany.

'They Staat's men or Bull's? I wonder,' said a deep voice beside him.

Half turning, Darlington said to Didier Ducamp, 'Must be Captain Bull's. The convention refused to hand the fort over to Captain Staats.' He was referring to the commission sent by Leisler and read out to the Albany Convention of aldermen by Wendell, who was probably the best advocate of Leisler's authority and who also happened to be Captain Staat's brother-in-law. But even he had failed in his plea to win over his fellow townsmen. 'The eighty-odd men plus Staat's are still under Bull as far as I know.'

'Less the twenty-four sent to Schenectady.'

'Yes,' said Darlington, as Ducamp left Daniel at the window to warm his back against the inviting fire.

Looking up through the tear, Daniel contemplated the first stars appearing through the thickening darkness. He remembered wondering as a child whether the same spangled spectacle graced every part of the globe. Of course, he had since travelled across the world, which had taught him that it did not, that it all depended on where on the globe you stood. He knew from experience that the sky at night in New York was very different from that of the Caribbean Islands. And he certainly remembered it looking different when he went on a visit to England with his father. He recalled hardly seeing it at all there for the fog, the haze caused by coal smoke, and the night cloud cover. Turning back into the sparsely furnished room that contained bunks, benches, rudimentary three-legged stools, and forgotten charms of past Indian traders, he said, 'Is the sky as clear as that in France?'

Ducamp drew on his pipe, then said slowly in his thick French accent, 'It is so in the south, at least, especially in the summer, and just before the storms of August, the sky is filled with...' Didier searched for the word, then gave up and said in French, '*étoiles filantes*.'

'Shooting stars,' said Daniel.

'Yes, shooting stars,' repeated Didier as if to anchor the words in his mind. 'I recall being on duty there once a few years ago...' Didier's eyes suddenly glistened, and his expression became numbed as he popped his pipe back into his mouth as if to stop it up. He turned his body, rubbing his hands together energetically toward the fire.

Daniel let the abrupt ending of his companion's conversation go. He knew the memory of a soldier was sometimes best left to slumber. 'Marianne tells me the same thing,' he returned after a moment, refraining from catching Ducamp in the eye. 'But tonight, looks like there are some clouds sliding in from the north. It's as black as pitch over there.'

'Aye, I seen,' said Ducamp. 'Wouldn't be surprised if we're in for another snowfall before the week's over.'

'Anyway, we're done here. Best we make for Schenectady at first light; we don't want to be caught in another snowdrift. We'll receive a better welcome; my aunt and uncle have settled there.' Daniel was referring to the suspicious glances they had received from part of the population in Albany. After all, Ducamp was French, and Daniel was a Leislerian. He continued: 'I used to take the sloop up to here with my ma and pa and then ride over to Schenectady and play with my cousins when I was a lad.'

'Oh? Thought they were Dutch there too,' said Ducamp.

'They are, mostly. I'm English by my father, but my mother was Dutch.' Didier gave a nod, and Daniel continued: 'Anyway, ship should be repaired by the time we get back from Schenectady. Leak's stopped, they replaced the old timbers, and I've given instructions for the shipwright to do some caulking around the cabin, so she'll be less draughty. He's none too happy about it because of the cold, but he's agreed to make it good for our return.' Daniel was referring to the cold nights they had spent on the icy water and the wind that whistled through the cabin, taking away with it any natural body heat. He had meant to take the ship for seasonal repairs anyway to Turtle Bay, a cove of Long Island in the East River where ships from New York were moored for the winter, out of harm's way of floating ice.

But Governor Jacob Leisler had asked Daniel to carry out a special delivery. Since the usual messenger had died of smallpox, and with the regular monthly sloop only operated from April to October, Daniel, a trusted member of Leisler's team, had been approached to ensure the delivery of commissions for Ulster and Albany counties. Darlington, having traded his oceangoing brigantine for a shallow-draft river ketch last year, he was the ideal person who knew the North River well enough to navigate the treacherous ice cakes. Indeed, more than once, the ketch became grounded, and on one occasion, it came dangerously close to the rocks where the river flowed faster and was free of ice.

They had been gone since the end of December, leaving their pregnant wives in their homes outside the city wall and their servants to see to any heavy work and chores. After delivering commissions along the way at Kingston, they had arrived on January 11th and had handed the Albany commissions to Johannes Wendell. Daniel knew them to contain Leisler's appointment of Captain Jochem Staat's as Albany County justice, and instructions for him to take possession of the fort and to hold a free election for mayor and aldermen. The convention that consisted of prominent Albany townsmen had again refused Leisler's authority and voted to contest what they considered to be Leisler's illegal proceedings. It had not helped Leisler's cause that Nicholas Bayard, who now found himself confined to Fort William in New York, had initiated an anti-Leisler campaign the previous summer.

But Daniel, who was not into hard-line politics and did not care for any king, be he Catholic or Protestant, let it go. All he cared about now was visiting his family connections in Schenectady and then heading home as soon as his ship was river worthy again. The mayor, despite his resistance to the German-born rebel lieutenant governor of New York, and especially with word out of French intentions to conquer, took the risk of a French attack no less seriously. He offered payment to anyone capable of travelling north to keep watch of the trail from New France. There were no takers from the colonists in such cold, and besides, didn't the recent snowfall create a natural barrier to any foray before the thaw come spring? Only the Mohawks at Schenectady welcomed the offer, and the convention accepted their proposal with gratitude.

Daniel nonetheless had sensed a stiffening at the mention of Schenectady, whose townsfolk were supportive of Leisler. Indeed, Leisler had promised the town a licence to trade furs with the Indians, which did nothing to help relations between New York and Albany. Despite the flats of Schenectady being upstream of the Cohoe Falls on the Mohawk River, and therefore closer to the Mohawks from the west, Albany had managed to maintain its monopoly as it was the only trading post licensed to trade in beaver pelts, hence its former Dutch name of Beverwijck. Sure, everyone knew there were clandestine exchanges in the woods surrounding Schenectady, but giving the settlement a licence to trade would remove the protection of Albany's economic growth. Daniel knew settlers from the same families in both towns, but despite the family ties between them, the rivalry was now palpable.

'All right,' said Ducamp, carrying on from Daniel's mention of the ship's repairs for the homeward bound voyage, 'sooner we leave, sooner we're back.'

'We'll be heading out with the Indians.'

'Guess more's the merrier.'

'And safer.'

'True,' said Ducamp. 'And I still reckon we should be sending white frontiersmen with their scouts to watch the trail from the lakes. That's where they should have sent us with Lieutenant Rust instead of just abandoning the mission to the French fort.'

'Don't worry,' returned Daniel, joining Ducamp by the fireside, 'Mohawks will be watching. Besides, no one in their right mind would march down from the north in this cold...'

'There's nowt madder than a fighting man,' warned Ducamp.

'Maybe, but the Indians'll be watching.'

'I wouldn't trust 'em, though,' insisted Ducamp as there came the sound of footsteps outside the front door. 'They're inconsistent, and who's to say they would go scouting for the sake of the white man's skin?'

'The way I see it,' said Darlington, 'they need the white man to trade their beaver skins for the guns and ammunition that make them all powerful among the Indians.'

'Maybe, but if there's no white men with them, who's to say they're not just taking the arms?'

At that moment, two Mohawks, both cloaked in moose blankets and wearing buckskin tunics, entered the room as Ducamp finished his question. The Mohawks, a grave man and a younger, stronger man, gave a peace salute to which the two white men answered with the same. These were the Indians who had negotiated weaponry in exchange for scouts. They moved to their bunks, where birch-bark mats were laid down, and removed their fur turbans in the dimly lit lodge, then approached the table.

A few minutes later, the old Indian keeper came back from peeing outside and closing the shutters. He proceeded to ladle the stew into the large trencher of the roughly hewn trestle table, around which the men each took a perch on a log stool cut to equal height. Then the old man got down on his knees on the rush-covered floor, brought his leathery hands together, and began to pray. Ducamp felt compelled to bow his head and address his own silent prayer to God. Darlington, surprised to see his gruff and seasoned ex-military companion pray, did likewise. The Mohawks watched, respectfully impervious to the old man's show of white man piety.

After giving thanks to God for their meal, the Indian keeper gesticulated to everyone to tuck in. 'You pray as does the white man every night?' asked the elder of the two Mohawks while shovelling with his fingers into the trencher.

'I pray when God moves me,' said the old man. 'And God moves me every day. I also pray when I feel the need to banish woe and bad spirits from the people around me.'

'A noble gesture,' said Ducamp gruffly, chewing on the soft meat. 'People sometimes need help to reach through their obstinacy and confusion in order to reach God, especially when their lives have not been saintly.'

'You speak from experience,' said the old Indian, bringing the ladle to his mouth to drink the soup.

'I was a soldier in the French king's army,' said Ducamp, as if that answered everything. Darlington listened while picking out another chunk of meat from the stew. He knew Ducamp had recently converted from Catholicism, but he had not before fathomed the depth of his conviction.

'God forgives,' said the old man. 'God is the birth of all goodness. Let his hand continue to appease you as you pray, friend.'

Ducamp answered with a simple nod that showed his tacit respect. The Mohawks supped up their soup and dug out lumps of meat and potato, while Daniel said, 'Indians too pray to one God, don't they?'

Before the lodge keeper could reply, the elder of the Mohawks in fluent but accented English said, 'Yes, we have one. All Indians in these lands believe in the Great Spirit, the one we call Kickeron.'

Daniel said: 'I asked an old Indian once where he thought he came from. From his father, he said. So I asked him where he thought his first father came from. He told me everything came from the great tortoise that brought the world on its back. In the middle, a great tree sprang up where a man grew from. Then another tree appeared which a woman grew from. And so, men and women from different branches were spread across the world.'

'That is true,' said the Mohawk elder, 'but it was Kickeron who made the tortoise!'

The Indian keeper added piously, 'Like the Christian God, he is the origin of all.' Continuing as though it were a revelation, he added, 'But the Christian God brings forgiveness for past deeds and eternal life to those who live by his teachings through Christ. It is written in the book of God.'

'Then who made Kickeron?' asked Daniel, picking up from the Mohawk's previous remark.

'Who made God?' replied the Mohawk Indian.

Ducamp said, 'Man is not capable of knowing. We are only responsible for our own soul. Let that be enough burden for one man to bear. And it must suffice to say it is the task of every man to be at one with his soul.'

The Mohawk elder agreed that the white man's God was a great spirit, and the old Indian was a wise man. 'But the white man, being from the outside world, is of a mixed and therefore troublesome race,' he said. 'For this reason, their God gave them a book to provide guidance and taught them to read it. But we Indians are of a pure race. We have no need of a book to tell us who our maker is. We know it from birth. It is written in our hearts. We have sufficient power of judgement to know good from evil. We do not need a book to guide us.'

'What if one from your tribe goes astray in life's meandering paths?' said Daniel.

'Kickeron will bring him back because the guiding spirit is in his heart. Although it is true, since the Christians came, there has never been so much death and sickness. Is this the way of Kickeron or of your God?'

The men looked around at each other as if expecting an answer. But a silence fell over the little Indian lodge, leaving only the crackle of the fire and the sound of men slurping up their stew.

After a few moments, Ducamp said, 'I think we should let such questions rest. They serve no purpose other than to torture the soul.' Everyone agreed, and after sharing a noggin of spiced rum to keep out the cold, they hit the sack fully clothed.

Ducamp wondered about these people's belief in the afterlife, then he fell into a dreamless sleep, which for a military man was a godsend.

Daniel, however, tossed and turned in his bunk, trying to keep the cold air from seeping in through the edges of his blanket.

They awoke to a stone-cold hearth as the Indian keeper was making a fire to heat up the leftovers of the cauldron of stew.

Ducamp was used to roughing it better than most. As for Daniel, the cold night had left his body stiff and his knees aching from keeping them tucked tightly to his chest. Nevertheless, by eight o'clock, he and Ducamp were both riding out in their hired saddles in Indian file behind the Mohawk Indians, with their pack horse harnessed to a sleigh.

With heads sunk into their collars like cold coots, Daniel and Didier were clad in pelts and cloaked in waxed leather hides which created a warm airlock with the heat from their horses. Instead of the sandy cart road of Daniel's summer trips, it was a muffled winter wonderland they had to ride over, and a treacherous one too, as the two-foot-deep snow could hide ruts and snags for the horses' hooves. So, they rode easy, alert in case of enemy or beast, carefully keeping in line with the Indians on the snow-covered trail to Schenectady. Now it skirted immaculate, snow-white fields, now it cut through frosty woods of seemingly endless evergreens, while the winter sun stayed hidden behind the purple clouds.

Daniel still felt the chill and aches of a sleepless night as onward they pressed without incident, only stopping along the way to rest and water the horses. Six hours later, as they approached the place where the rest of the forty or so Indians were bivouacked, the elder Mohawk halted his mount to let the two white Christians arrive at his flank.

'We stop here,' he said, nodding to where the trail branched off into a clearing a few paces further to the left. 'You continue on this path,' he said, looking straight ahead at the trail before them as he pressed his mount into a slow, four-beat gait. 'It will lead you to the township.'

'Yes, I've been here before,' said Daniel, he and Ducamp riding at the Indian's flank, 'although it is true that the snow, like water, can disrupt a man's bearings.' Then he coughed and spat as a welcome party of Mohawk braves came riding out to meet them.

'You will send scouts north, will you?' said Ducamp, not beating about the bush. The question had been burning on his lips since the previous night.

'We will,' said the elder sternly. With a dubious glance at the sky, he continued: 'But first, we return to our village before the weather turns bad. Then we choose the scouts. The trail will be lost under the snow; there will be no one on it in such cold.'

'But we are, though, aren't we?' said Ducamp, 'which means others might be too.'

'Yes, and thankfully, we arrive before the storm,' said the Mohawk.

At that moment, the Indian braves came galloping through the shallow snow with chilling hoots and calls. Daniel and Ducamp remained outwardly calm on their mounts. They could now hear rumbunctious singing and shouting coming from inside the wigwams, thirty yards into the clearing to the left. It was clear that the Indians had been drinking. The young braves on horseback too were still in high spirits.

The elder Mohawk snapped at them in Iroquois, the language of the Five Nations, and ordered them to take care of the packhorse. But one of the riders reached into the sleigh and cheekily took a keg of rum, which he carried away under his arm with celebratory shouts and hoots toward the wigwams.

'That is what can lead men astray, and keep him even from Kickeron,' said Daniel, referring to their conversation of the previous night.

'It is the Christians who bring us their poison and sickness from their mixed-up world,' said the Mohawk. 'Before, we had only a milder sort of spirit artfully made from what Kickeron has given in nature around us.' Daniel refrained from asking why he had taken the white man's liquor in the first place, but it would be like rubbing salt into a wound, for he knew the elder had no choice if he wanted to appease his troops. The Mohawk pressed his horse into a slow trot toward the Indian camp on the left, leaving Daniel and Didier to follow the snowy trail onwards.

At last, ten minutes later, with the pang of hunger in their bellies, they came to the south gate of the stockaded town of Schenectady, where kids were playing in the snow. They had built snowmen near the entrance, one of which stood carrot-faced like an icy sentinel, keeping watch with stony eyes.

CHAPTER 7

February 1690

SCHENECTADY

Aunt Millie's kind face, with its expression of unreserved surprise, reminded Darlington of his mother's. 'My word! Daniel!' she declared, 'what brings you?'

If it weren't for her streak of grey hair that had grown wider, she would have looked the same as when Daniel had last seen her. Reassured by his smile that banished any contemplation of bad news: 'Never mind,' she continued, 'come in out of the cold.'

After stamping the snow from their boots, he and Ducamp followed her small person inside the two-storey stone house. He figured that she must now be at the age that his mother had died. But as always, she wore a welcoming smile that radiated her special fondness for her nephew, her sister's only child.

Stepping into the large, flag-stoned room, Daniel introduced Didier Ducamp. 'My travelling companion and French neighbour recently moved to New York with wife and child,' he said. Ducamp tilted his upper body in the guise of a bow.

'I was thinking about you only yesterday, wasn't I, Alfric?' said Aunt Millie to her husband, a large-shouldered, taciturn, and forthright man who had risen from his rocking chair beside the hearth.

'Sit yourselves down,' he said, giving each a short, firm shake of the hand while directing them with his other hand to the rush-seat chairs at the table. 'You'll soon thaw out.' The visitors put their outer garments on a vacant chair and sat down.

'I've got some salted pork in the pot,' said Aunt Millie with enthusiasm while fetching wooden spoons and bowls from the dresser. Daniel saw that she must have been seated at the spinning wheel near the fire where she had left her knitting, some child's socks.

The comfortable abode was solidly built and situated on Front Street, off Church Street. The deeply glowing embers of hardwood took the chill off the room and made the butter on the sideboard soft, and a couple of three-inch pine branches, cheerfully enflamed on top, gave the room a pleasant fragrance. Daniel also took in the familiar objects, especially the vase at the windowsill, a relic from the old country. The emblematic object of Aunt Millie and Uncle Alfric's had followed them from Albany to here in Schenectady. It never failed to bring back memories of visits to his cousins as a lad with his parents. It contained dried lavender branches as did his mother's vases in his childhood, no doubt a custom passed down from his grandmother.

'So, what brings you?' said Uncle Alfric, unhooking a half length of *droge worst* from a rail hanging from a beam.

'Yes, you're the very last person I'd expect to see in this cold, now that you've got a family of your own,' said Aunt Millie.

'We brought commissions up the river from New York to Albany,' said Daniel, taking something from his leather pouch that he had hung over the chair with his coat. 'So, I thought I'd take the opportunity to bring you this.' He brought out a book of prayer. 'It was Ma's. She would have wanted you to have it.'

'Bless you, it could have waited. But I'm glad of it,' said Millie, taking the prayer book that had belonged to her mother.

'How are my cousins?'

'Doing well for themselves. Cornelius is in Boston now. And Gerrit has gone down to help at the landing stage. But I expect he'll be over as soon as he knows you're here.'

'So,' said Alfric, pouring out four wooden mugs of apple cider at the table. He paused to shift his weight slightly and let out a vibrant fart, then continued pouring and said, 'This Jacob Leisler really is the lieutenant governor of New York then, is he?'

'He is that, Uncle.'

'That is not what they say in Albany,' said Millie. 'They won't have him. They say he's a usurper.'

'I know, Aunt Millie, but they have been misinformed by bigwig Nicholas Bayard. One thing's for sure: England does have a new king, a Protestant and a Dutchman. Leisler is holding the fort and keeping it from Jacobites, given that Lieutenant Governor Nicholas up and fled to London at the first sign of trouble.'

'That's not likely to make relations with the French any better,' said Aunt Millie. 'It's worrying...'

'They'll be on the warpath, that's for sure,' said Alfric, now slicing the *droge worst*. 'Any pretext is good for them to try to take over the fur trade.'

'That's why, thank God, Leisler is holding the fort. He has restored and improved the city defences. And that's why they've sent a garrison from Albany.'

'Not so sure,' said Alfric. 'I sometimes wonder if the grandees in Albany have sent their guard to watch over us rather than keep watch over the town in case of French attack. No offense meant to your friend.'

'None taken, sir,' said Ducamp, speaking for the first time. 'My wife and I are Protestants.'

Alfric gave a short nod of understanding, then pursued, 'But to tell the truth, I can't see them bothering with us here: we're but a small community. And all these soldiers do is drink at the tavern. Then they have to be herded every night into the fort.'

Millie added: 'There have been altercations with our men who won't have their girls looked up and down.'

Ducamp knew too well how men could become riled if left without a vent for too long. And in an instant, he recalled the days of the Dragonnades in France, in Berne and Montauban, when King Louis used soldiers billeted in French Protestants' homes to pressure them into converting so there were officially no more Protestants in France. With a conciliatory sigh, he said: 'It is unfortunately the nature of military men to cheer and brag when together, madam. It takes a strong hand to continually keep them in check, which is probably why they are allowed to spill into the tavern. But should it come to it, you'll be glad to have them garrisoned here to defend you, mark my words. Then the roughest soldiers are embraced as heroes.'

Alfric said, 'Not likely until the thaw. And things will evolve between Albany and New York by then. We all hope here that Leisler's Milborne will keep his word and give us free licence to trade with the Mohawks. We are ideally placed to do so after all. Better so than Albany, which is downstream of the falls.'

'If we have licence, it will make our fortune,' said Millie. 'Schenectady will be a thriving centre of trade.'

'But then Albany will decline,' said Daniel, who, in the warmth of the house, suddenly felt a heavy brow. 'So, I wouldn't bank on it happening any time soon.' Then he sneezed.

'No, but I've thought it through,' said Alfric eagerly. 'There can be a quota. That way, both settlements prosper, you see?'

'It's nonetheless always more acceptable to receive something you don't have than to have part of something taken away from you,' said Ducamp. 'Expect the Albany convention to cling to their licence as if their livelihoods depended on it. And they have the advantage of being closer to New York city.'

'Aye,' said Alfric, 'that's what we fear, that Milborne's talk is just that: talk. And talk has a tendency to vanish into thin air, unless you set it down in words on paper.'

'Anyway,' chimed in Aunt Millie, 'I expect you boys are hungry. I'll fetch the broth.'

'Aye, welcome, lads. I'll show you around our flats later. You'll find a few changes since last time you came here, Daniel, when was it?'

'Must have been before Mother passed,' said Daniel, without sorrow. For it had already been three full years, and now he had his own family. Then he sneezed again.

CHAPTER 8

February 1690

WILDERNESS

In the bleak morning of the frozen wilderness, Jacques Le Moyne had gathered his officers around him before the camp-fire.

There had been flurries of snow, a blizzard, ice under foot, and freezing marshes to cross as, indefatigably, they had proceeded southward like a relentless procession bent on one goal: revenge. Revenge for the massacre of Lachine. Revenge for something that, in their blind rage to find a culprit, the French of Montreal accused the perfidious English of instigating. It mattered not to Le Moyne whether the English had such power over the Mohawks as to commandeer the massacre of Christians. No matter how it had come to pass, revenge there must be, not only for honour but also to regain the sheen of prestige among the Indian allies. Without reputation and honour retrieved, the native allies might direct their trade towards the English. Any such thought had to be nipped in the bud.

'So, the time is now. What is it to be?' said Le Moyne to the party of officers, leaning forward with one foot on a rock. 'To Albany, and we take the Hudson. To Schenectady, we fork off southward along the trail to the Mohawk River.'

'Our initial target was Albany, then we decide whether to take New York,' recapped Nicolas de Manthet. With a dubious look up at the winter's sky, he added, 'Schenectady is not such a great prize.'

'You know our stance,' said Krya, speaking for the other chiefs. 'The march in this season is tough. Our braves resist, but there are not enough of us to take Albany. It will be a loss of honour. Better to choose smaller prey and eat today than aim for big game and risk getting eaten.'

Le Moyne slapped his thigh decisively, then stood up straight and said: 'Then, gentlemen, Schenectady it shall be.'

Ten minutes later, the war party, having rested and with a new spring in their snow rackets, proceeded in a relentless procession southwestwardly toward their goal of revenge. Revenge that the new war between England and France made lawful. Walking up front beside Kyra, Le Moyne said, 'I doubt there will be enemy Indians watching along the trail in this. But keep up a scouting party, just in case.'

The chief gave a curt nod. 'They are already far ahead,' he said.

'Good,' said Le Moyne, pressing his hat more tightly on his head. 'Despite this bloody cold, we should be at the Mohawk River within a week.'

CHAPTER 9

February 1690

SCHENECTADY

The morning after arriving in Schenectady, Daniel was hardly able to get up from his sopping paillasse that he had laid down in front of the hearth in the main hall.

Thoughts of the worst were soon cast aside as it became visibly clear that he had not brought with him the dreaded pox from New York. There was no rash, so Aunt Millie concluded he must have caught a seasonal ailment. She gave him chamomile and honey in hot water. Then Ducamp helped him up to the calmer, isolated room of the first-floor attic that benefitted from the warmth of the brick chimney conduit.

It had been a long winter already, and, visibly itching to get out of the house, Alfric kept true to his word and showed Daniel's companion around the settlement. Didier discovered that the township itself consisted of around fifty or sixty dwellings, built in a rectangle that was surrounded by a palisade of ten-foot-tall pine logs. Two main streets met in the centre of the town and ran east-west and north-south. The north side of the stockade was planted parallel to the Mohawk River, and the north gate opened onto the small harbour and an array of boat-yards that stretched along the riverbank. The stockaded fort, where soldiers from Connecticut via Albany were garrisoned, was also located on the north side near the gate which led out to the river road to Niskayuna.

Didier and Alfric saddled up despite the bitter cold and rode out of the south gate, past the dwellings along the road outside the stockade, and across the frozen creek where the ice-dripping waterwheel of the mill stood still and powdered over with snow. From there, they followed the south shore road to Mohawk country. Under the leaden sky, Ducamp could clearly see why they called the land here the Great Flats. The expanse of flush, crusty snow extended along the shore, with not a single tree to disturb the monotonous view or to shade any crop once the fields were sown come spring. It was a bleak sight to behold in the bareness of winter.

'Well, a fitful place it must be come spring,' said Ducamp, trying to look on the bright side.

'Aye, doesn't look like much now,' said Alfric, 'but the soil is pitch black and six feet deep in places. And come springtime, we cultivate these fields without manure, and yet year after year, they yield a fine crop.' Ducamp gave a slow nod of appreciation, even though in his mind, he told himself he was glad to have his little family settled outside New York city rather than out in the sticks. Alfric continued: 'The wheat we grow may not yield as well as that raised around New York, but here it makes a whiter flour.'

'True, bread here's the best I've tasted,' said Ducamp as though coming back to himself. Then, to be obliging toward his host's efforts in his praise for the land he loved, he turned in his saddle, levelled his eyes at Alfric, and said, 'I do believe that outside of the cold months of winter, you have a fine life here, sir.'

'Aye, it's a place for the future, a place to raise a family. Our Mohawks come this way up the river from the west with pelts to trade. They pull up their canoes nearby as the river downstream is unnavigable beyond the falls, then they take the trail to Albany, see? If we had a licence, this place would thrive.'

'As Daniel says, they won't tolerate it in Albany, though.'

'Depends. It will still be an important trading centre in the summer for folks coming up from New York and around. We will simply take the role of an outlying trade post. And we'll build a better road to Albany.'

On their return from their tour of the flats, as the day was ending, Ducamp insisted on stopping at the tavern by the south gate to find a bed space for the nights to come. In this season, there were no other travellers, so he laid his bedding in the warmest upstairs room by the chimney wall. He told Alfric that this was where he would spend the nights until Daniel's condition allowed them to head for home.

Home: the term was strangely becoming anchored in his mind now when referring to his house in New York. He had purchased it with his new wife, May, whom he had encountered on the high seas in bizarre circumstances, to say the least. But this was the New World, and the extraordinary was part and parcel of ordinary life. He thought no more of it, only that once upon a time, he had lost his bearings in life and had fallen into piracy, and by saving May and her fatherless child, it turned out that he had saved himself by the same token. Now they formed a family outside the wall of New York, a stone's throw from Daniel and Marianne's house. When talking about the return journey, Darlington would say, 'We shall be home before next moon,' and, 'When we get home, we'll have a right royal supper with the ladies.' Or when talking about the fresh snowfall, 'It must be white as lamb's fleece at home too,' he would say.

A few days after the tour of the flats, stopping by to enquire about Daniel's health, 'How is he?' said Didier when Millie opened the door. It was a frosty morning, and the smell of wood smoke filled the air as the small town was beginning to wake after another ice-cold night.

'He's taking soup,' she replied, 'and a man with an appetite is a man on the mend. But he sure won't be riding back before the end of the week.'

'Ah, we were expected home by Candlemas already,' said Didier, the mention of home filling him with warmth in his heart. 'Never mind, the journey back will be made all the easier as the river thaws.'

'Come in for something warm.'

'Thank you, Aunt Millie, but I had a bowl of mutton stew at the tavern, so I won't stop. I'll be down at the harbour with Alfric and Gerrit if you need me.' Ducamp had been keeping himself busy by helping down at the boatyard outside the north gate. Canoes and an assortment of river craft had been hauled ashore so they could be repaired and maintained for the coming season.

Later that day, as the light was beginning to dwindle, Ducamp said to Gerrit and Alfric, 'Beats me how you can work in such cold.'

'It's been a cold year, but it's already past Candlemas, my word,' said Alfric.

Gerrit added, 'Aye, spring will soon be upon us. So, we like to get a step ahead of the march of time. That way, when the time comes, we can devote the God-given waking hours to the land, see?'

Ducamp had struck up a friendship with Daniel's uncle Alfric and cousin Gerrit, and the three men were standing over a fire, warming their hands, having just finished caulking a shallow-draft cargo craft. Gerrit had explained that, in the summer season, the boat carried rum west and pelts back east. The men usually ended the day's toil over a jug of ale at the tavern, and today was no different.

It was already dark outside when they pushed the door into the warmer, dimly lit atmosphere of the tavern. Two men were sitting on stools at each side of the chimney smoking their clay pipes, their thoughts visibly lost in the glowing embers of the fire. A cat ceased grooming and looked up for an instant to see the three burly men walk in and latch the door behind them. Alfric gave a nod to Hans, the smithy at the caged counter, showed three fingers to Hendrick, the pot-bellied tavern keeper, and then sat around an empty upturned barrel with Didier and his son, Gerrit.

Between them and the fireside, another barrel served as a card table for three young soldiers from the fort. Soldiers were granted permission in turns to pass the time at the tavern, where they played dominoes or cards. Ducamp well knew, as did the soldiers' commander no doubt, that otherwise, with no escape to look forward to, the men would be like cats on hot bricks, for they had been stationed at the small fort since November. A turn at the tavern would be an event, especially if there was feminine company to look forward to. Sometimes, the taverner hired a lady reader to announce the latest news to the illiterate. But this was midweek in small-town Schenectady, and the tavern was hardly busy, most folk preferring to stay by the fire in their own homes. Moreover, in this dead of winter, of late there had been nothing to report, no news about the conflict between Leisler and the Albany Convention, and nothing either about the war with the French. So, tonight, there was no lady reader, and the service was limited to Old Indian Joe and Hendrick, the tavern keeper, who did not like to leave his counter unmanned with the cage up.

A moment later, one of the soldiers slammed down his losing hand on the barrel top and called out, 'Another jug of ale here, taverner!' Hendrick had already filled a jug, and Old Joe now set out across the room with it and three tankards to serve the newcomers. The soldier pushed his stool back, supposedly to allow the Indian to fill the tankards on his table, but Jo passed behind him. 'Where you going?' said the soldier, confused and becoming exasperated. He hadn't seen Alfric's silent order. 'Oye!' he called out as the old Indian carried on to the next table, indifferent to the young soldier's outburst.

'You'll have to wait a minute, lads,' growled Hendrick in English, as Joe put down the tankards and the jug on the barrel around which Alfric, Gerrit, and Ducamp were seated.

'Where's your girl then, Hendrick?' said Alfric in Dutch.

'Down with the chills, leaving poor Joe running around like a headless chicken!'

'Ah, I see.'

Meanwhile, Ducamp reflected that he once harboured ambitions of opening a tavern in France after finishing as a lieutenant in the French army. He was glad these ambitions had not come to fruition, and he realised now that they had probably come about through not knowing what else a retired soldier could do. But that was before he had come to this land of opportunity.

'So, what's in the pot, Joe?' asked Alfric in English, interrupting Ducamp's moment of introspection.

'Mutton today,' said Joe.

'Mutton yesterday too,' said Gerrit with a laugh in his voice.

'Yes, and the mutton's got another two legs!' returned Joe enigmatically. This made the newcomers laugh out loud. Joe had a reputation of being a mine of disarming sagacity.

'Fetch us over some broth as well then, Joe, will yer?' said Alfric cheerily.

The old Indian gave a proud nod of the head, then shuffled back to the bar, where he picked up some wooden bowls that Hendrick had lined up on the counter. Joe then made for the hearth, where a cauldron was suspended on a hook.

'Eh, where's our beer?' called out the exasperated English soldier, looking to his brothers in arms as if he were the victim of a tragedy.

'With you in a minute, lads,' said Hendrick from behind the counter.

'I asked first, I want my beer now!' insisted the brash soldier.

Hans, the smithy, who had been watching the soldier become increasingly curt, turned on his stool. 'Did you not hear the man, laddie?' he bellowed.

Seeing he had the support of the smithy, Hendrick said boldly, 'Aye, and I won't be ordered around in my establishment by any English lackeys! Even if you were sent by the king of England himself. Who speaks Dutch, by the way, ha!'

Ducamp, with heightened senses, detected the soldier was looking for a quarrel, looking to vent his frustrations, which were no doubt exacerbated by the beer. It turned some good men boisterous, especially when they were losing. But the smithy and the men at the hearth were wary, their collective sense of defending one of their own heightened. It did not matter that the soldiers had been sent to protect them. The ironsmith, a big, square man, was pushing his large hands on the arms of his chair, ready to stand up as Ducamp got calmly to his feet, took the jug from his table, and ambled to the card table, while Hendrick behind the bar lowered the wooden cage.

Placing a big hand on the young Englishman's shoulder, Ducamp said, 'Soldier, here, you're a long way from home. Have a drink on me.' He then proceeded in filling the soldier's tankard. 'Then I suggest you get back to your quarters.' The soldier looked up at the gruff-looking veteran. As a former lieutenant in the French army, he had led men to war and mercenaries during the dragonnades, and as a bosun on a privateer ship, he had taken charge of a rebellious body of men. Ducamp needed no words for the English soldiers to sense this. The depth of his accented voice, the practical cut of his short hair, his broad torso, and the bullish stench of the male sufficed, and instilled in Ducamp sovereign force and a calm sense of authority.

'Come on, Ed,' said the more affable-looking soldier opposite him. 'Let's drink up and leave these vagrants to close their flipping gate themselves.'

The third soldier to his right retrieved his deck of cards while the exasperated trooper swept up his tankard and drank down the beer defiantly. Then he slammed down the tankard. 'Suit yourself, old man!' he growled, and he rose heavily.

Ducamp steadied him as he got to his feet, clenching the scruff of his long red coat. 'Whoa, steady there, fella,' he said, then let go of the soldier's coat. The youth made his way unsteadily to the door with his comrades in arms.

With a final glance back, he drunkenly hurled out to the room, 'And you can close yer flipping gate yourselves!' His exit was accompanied by a spluttering of laughter while Ducamp walked calmly to the door, closed it, and replaced the latch. Hendrick pushed up his wooden cage as the Indian ladled the three bowls of broth at the cauldron. The cat continued to groom its underside.

'We need a man like you here,' said Alfric as Ducamp took his seat and poured out three tankards of ale from the jug.

'Aye, I second that,' said Gerrit.

'Nice place,' said Ducamp, 'but wouldn't work for a Frenchman here.'

'French, Dutch, German, English... no matter, here, we are Americans!' said Gerrit, bringing the tankard from his lips.

'Yes, but now they're bringing the war over from Europe,' said Ducamp.

'For sure, doesn't bode well. The French will use any pretext to take hold of the fur trade.'

'But it's fair to say that in New York at least, there truly be people of all nations, including French Huguenots. Anyway, the way I see it, we're all opportunists or castaways really, looking to improve our prospects. Here, we are honest and hardworking folk, trying to make the best of this land that God has given us to behold.'

'Well said,' Ducamp declared, and the three men knocked their tankards together.

A little later, after leaving Alfric and Gerrit to amble up Church Street back to their respective abodes, Ducamp went for a pee against the stockade. As he shook himself after the event, he noticed the south gate had been left ajar and remembered what the English soldier had said on leaving the tavern. He knew the lad could be in trouble if it came to light that he had deliberately left the gate open. So, turning his collar to the cold night air, he ambled over, closed, and barred it.

Having walked off their immediate vexation, the soldiers would have taken care to make sure the north gate was closed, he thought to himself. He looked up the length of Church Street toward the opposite end, which he could not easily see in the dark. Besides, he, Alfric, and Gerrit had closed the north gate behind themselves when they came in from the boatyard.

The cold was penetrating, and the thought left him the moment he pushed the door open into the tavern and climbed the rudimentary stairs to his room. A few moments later, lying in his bed sack, fully clothed, the thought occurred to him that if he were a lieutenant in the English army during times of conflict, he would have positioned a guard and kept a fire at each gate. But this was the midst of winter in a faraway outpost; the lieutenant must have had his reasons.

Two days later, oblivious to Ducamp's adventures, Daniel rose at last from his tick mattress, his limbs having recovered most of their litheness.

Ducamp had passed by the house early that morning and reported that some Mohawks in town, who were wintering with their Dutch hosts, were predicting more snow on the way. So, not wanting to be hemmed in, Daniel and Ducamp bid farewell after some broth and cider to Aunt Millie and Uncle Alfric, amid a profusion of thanks and good wishes. 'I want you to give this to your pretty wife. It's for the baby,' said Aunt Milly, handing Daniel a knitted outfit for an infant of nine months that she then wrapped in a burlap bag. It would fit Samuel, then could be passed down to the next one on the way, if it were a boy. Aunt Millie was moderately suspicious like that; she did not like to offer gifts that could bring distress if the baby did not arrive at its term.

The New Yorkers then saddled up, taking with them for the journey some blood sausage, a loaf of the excellent white bread made with corn from the flats, and a gourde of hard cider drawn from the hog's head that sat on a chair in the hall. It was past ten when they set out through the south gate of the little town, where children, now at Dame school, had made more snowmen that stood like sentinels outside the stockade. As they proceeded at a slow trot past the line of houses along the road, Ducamp gave a salute to someone by one of the houses outside the palisade.

'You seem to have made an impression,' said Daniel with a cheer.

'That'll be Peter, met him down at the shipyard with your uncle and cousin. Your Dutch people are good folk.'

'I wager they tried to talk you into settling here.'

'Hah, too far off the run to New York for me. And I know May wouldn't like to be so far out of the way, that's for sure.'

A few moments later, on reaching the trail where it entered the dark pine forest, Daniel said, 'What day is it, by the way?'

'Saturday.'

Daniel jerked back his head and gave a pause for thought, then said, 'That's bloody February the eighth, already.'

'Ha, you've been out for a week, Daniel!'

'A week!' returned Darlington in disbelief. 'We'll be out of pocket.'

In a consoling voice, Ducamp said, 'You know, as you get older, you realise that sometimes, you just have to give time to time, man. Because time is life. Anyway, there's nothing doing in this season except for the cold.'

'Guess you're right, and I'm thankful you waited. All being well, we'll reach Albany by early afternoon, then we can prepare the ketch; and if we don't stop at Kingston on the way down, we'll be back home for the events.' Daniel refrained from stating what those events were, perhaps as if to distance them from thoughts of a tragic outcome. For it was well understood between the two men that sometimes, babies did not make it into life outside the mother's belly. And when they did, sometimes, the mother did not survive. Ducamp preferred to remain evasive on the subject too, for if such a tragedy should arise, what would he do with May's daughter? It would not sit well with folk for him to bring her up alone. And yet, he loved the child as if she were his own flesh and blood.

They now reached a long stretch of flat, shallow snow that glistened between the dark pine trees. 'Well, time waits for no man!' exclaimed Daniel, and the two men clicked their mounts into a steady canter, chasing away any intrusive thoughts of home.

The grey afternoon light was turning dark when, around four o'clock, the New Yorkers left their horses with the stable boy at the tavern of Albany.

Fatigued from riding six leagues through the ice-cold wind and the hardened snow, and still feeling the effects of his recent illness, Daniel agreed with Ducamp to let the tide go and stay the night in town where they would be warmest. Ducamp would inspect work done on the ketch, make sure the hull was not trapped in ice, and ensure the cargo of timber was secured aboard. Then, come first light, they would cast off down the great river with the morning tide.

CHAPTER 10

February 8, 1690

SCHENECTADY

Meanwhile, the party of 210 French and Catholicized Indian soldiers were arriving at the mouth of the Alplaus Kill, on the north bank of the Mohawk River.

They were just three leagues from the township on the south bank that Darlington and Ducamp had left six hours earlier. The soldiers, though hardy they were, came to a stumbling halt and sat, leaned, or squatted wherever they could find a perch or a dry place in the riverside clearing around a fallen tree.

After a short consultation between the leaders, the proud Indian chief climbed onto the trunk of the fallen tree, careful not to slip on the snow. 'Men,' he said, holding up his hand to quash all utterance. He spoke in French Iroquoian, the Indian language that the frontiersmen understood too. 'Men, we have trekked hard and far over lake, through rivers of ice and snow. Despite the hardships that have come to try us, here we are, so close to our goal. Across and further along the river behind us, that Providence has trapped in ice, is the reason for our brave trek. So now, the time has come to recall our strength and perseverance that brought us here, and to leave all fatigue behind in the mists of the past. The wet and the cold are mere memories. Now is the time to rekindle the fires of wrath that raged when you heard about the massacre of our people in Lachine. This was carried out by the Indian Mohawk but commandeered by the English dogs! Here we come, here we carry out our duty, here we cross the river that will lead us to wash out disgrace, injury, and injustice with the blood of the treacherous people. This we do in the name of our ancestors, in the name of God Almighty, and in the name of our bloodline so they may take example from our rightful duty.' There was a deep, controlled hum of approval, muffled by the snow all around. Anyone nearby would have nonetheless heard the rousing call to arms and to vengeance. But there was no one. Once the voices settled, all was a wintry silence again across the expanse of the frozen Mohawk River that would allow the party to cross.

As Kryn stepped off the tree trunk, Le Moyne stepped onto it, held up a hand, and gave his orders in French. 'Men, three leagues westward across the river is Corlear.' This was the name by which the French still called Schenectady; it was the name of the settlement's Dutch founder, Arent van Corlear. 'We cross now while there is still light. We will halt and eat when we get closer to the prey.'

A few moments later, Le Moyne singled out Jean Baptiste Giguieres, a hardy and level-headed frontiersman. He said, 'Take a detachment of Indians. I want you to check the trail for lookouts, then report back.' Giguieres gave a nod, then swaggered away with two of his Indian comrades to pick out a few braves. It wasn't quite the military fashion, but there again, Gigueres was not a military man. He was a free-loving frontiersman, dressed in hide and shod in knee-high moccasins, and he knew the Indian ways better than those of the rigid military bluecoats.

The thick ice across the river bore witness to the degree of cold, for it held, as had the frozen great lakes on their way down from the north, as two hundred men silently filed over it, with every man lending an ear to the cracking noises to guide their footsteps.

Tips of toes and fingers felt like frozen blocks of wood, and yet the morbid procession marched on westward along the frosted riverside trail. In the waning light, only the small winter birds chirped their surprise as the men marched on. If the birds could speak, they might have given warning. But neither did their chirping agitation raise the alert to the four squaws sitting by the fire inside the hide-covered wigwam erected along the route. It was too late to escape when the sudden sound of many footsteps arrested the ladies' fireside chatter. They were closely followed by the appearance of a big Indian with a leathery face who calmly parted the overlaying hides of the entrance.

'Peace,' he said in Iroquoian as white men poured into the small, heated space behind him. 'We do not come to hurt you,' continued Kryn, sternly but reassuringly. The women noted from his accent and that of a white man, who also uttered reassurances, that these men must be enemies from the north. Krya persisted, 'We only come for the warmth of your fire and knowledge of the white man's town yonder along the river.'

There was no chance of escape, nowhere to run in the freezing cold night. The leading squaw, a proud woman in mid age, invited the men to warm themselves by the fire, which the men did one by one. Meanwhile, Le Moyne and Krya drew out the information they needed for their assault: a stockade, two gates, a palisaded fort inside the north gate, and four score houses. It meant victory was imminent, for there were enough men to potentially put three soldiers to a house. But the first problem was the fort. Even a small garrison of well-trained men could hold it if it was well armed. That given, Le Moyne knew of bands of buccaneers to take bigger forts with fewer men. But the main concern was that the garrison could potentially hold out until the attackers went blue in the face with cold.

Nevertheless, now with insight of the fort and knowledge of the defences, Le Moyne eagerly led the march in the dead of night, a thorn removed from his side now that he knew where to strike first. It was surely a sign from heaven.

But the elder squaw did not see it that way. She knew some of the white people and some Mohawks who were there too. So, once the file of men from the north had disappeared into the night, she consulted with the other three squaws and decided to send Chaya to the township to give warning.

Chaya was the most stubborn, but also the most resilient, and she knew the way in the dark through the woods. 'Hurry, child,' said the elder squaw to her daughter, 'these men do not mean any good. They will take the river route that winds like the snake; you can easily overtake them if you make haste.' Not being from these parts, she reasoned that the foreign men would not know the Indian trail, and the pitch darkness would only lead them astray where the route forked left to join the Albany road. So, they were bound to follow the surest route along the river.

An hour later, shivering with cold and glad to emerge from the dark woods, Chaya at last perceived the glow of a fire within the stockade and right before her, the riverside gate. She wondered how she would get through it as she could see no fire outside and no guards other than the children's snowmen. But as she approached, she was relieved to find the great gate had been left ajar enough for her to slip inside and scurry through the silent town, each house snugly shuttered from the glacial chill and giving off the smell of firewood smoke amid the swirling, silently falling flakes of snow. Leaving a trail of footprints in the snow behind her as she scurried down Church Street, she could sometimes hear the sound of voices and laughter, shouts and grunts, but most of all, she could hear snoring. Midway down, she was heartened to perceive dim light filtering around the shutters of a large house she knew, having sold baskets there with her sister earlier in the day. She banged at the front door with her benumbed clenched fist as she went over in her mind the words she had prepared in the English language, which had become the trade language these days.

After a short time: 'Who goes there?' called the indentured Dutch servant girl from the other side of the door.

'I am Chaya. I came earlier.'

'What do you want?'

'I need to see the mistress.'

The door was unbarred and opened with caution. 'Come in quick, before you let out the warmth,' said the servant girl. In a flurry of snowflakes, Chaya stepped into the warm environment of the wood-heated house and shook off the snow with a wheeze of a sneeze. Candles of the pendant light over the table had not yet been extinguished in the comfortable common room, where the embers still glowed in the hearth. But the family had visibly already prepared for bed; she could hear a loud snoring from the alcove bed, where she deducted the master of the house was sleeping.

No sooner had the servant barred the door behind her than Mrs Philipsen, in her nightdress, had hoisted herself through the curtains of her bed to see who could be calling at this late hour. 'Ah,' she said, seeing as it was only an Indian girl, which did not put her in a good frame of mind as she had already traded a 20-pound pumpkin to the very same girl and her sister earlier that afternoon. In fact, it was the main ingredient of the soup that Chaya had eaten with her sisters and mother three hours earlier, the leftovers of which they were saving for the cold morning. That is, until the Indian and the soldiers from the north had come and eaten it.

'What do you want, girl?' said Mrs Philipsen in Dutch, trying to keep her voice down so as not to wake the whole house. But Chaya found her mouth numbed by the cold, her jaw locked, her tongue tied. She was unable to respond to the request with the prepared words that had left her head, especially as she was not expecting a quick-fire volley in Dutch. 'Come on, girl, cat got your tongue?' pursued Mrs Philipsen. But before Chaya could respond, the sight of her wet moccasins caked in snow made Mrs Philipsen forget all discretion as she bemoaned, 'And look at you, you've brought in the snow, you savage creature! Now look what you've done to my clean floor!'

Chaya did not like being shouted at in any language. She was proud, a trait she inherited from her mother. So, firing back a volley of her own in Mohawk, a volley that carried the message of warning, she turned on her heels, unbarred and pushed open the door, and stepped out into the cold night, never to return.

'What in God's name did the girl want?' said Mrs Philipsen as her young servant pulled the door shut.

'I don't know, something about soldiers eating her soup.'

'Soldiers eating her soup? What does she expect, me to pull out another pumpkin from my hat at this time of night? Good heavens above, what is the world coming to?'

Enraged with the lady, mad with herself, Chaya retraced her footsteps back through the gate and ran as fast as her freezing legs could carry her, back through the woods to the warmth of her wigwam as the blizzard began to blow.

Jean Baptist and the Indian scouts were silently crouching within the edge of the pine forest that overlooked Schenectady. They had taken it in turns to lead the way through the snow, the first passage of snowshoes up front packing it down level, making it flatter for those following behind.

A starless night was falling over the township situated over the flats further below. The Frenchman finished tightening the leather straps that secured his moccasined heels to his snowshoes. Then, all nine men began to slowly stand in one dark mass to get a clearer view of the town surrounded by a stockade of ten-foot-high pine posts. From the slightly higher viewpoint, Jean Baptist could make out the small, palisaded fort in the northwest corner and the glow of the campfire within it. Across the town over the stockade, smoke from the multitude of chimneys of the small timber-built homes gave out ghostly shapes, made perceptible by the faint glow from firelight in the streets here and there. To their surprise, little other movement impacted the strained eyes of the nine onlookers.

'I see no one out,' whispered one of the Indian warriors in the vernacular.

'And there are no sentries...'

'No patrols either,' returned Jean Baptist in a rasping whisper. 'This might be easier than we thought.'

Jean Baptist imagined the settler hibernating in the dead of winter, smoking his clay pipe beside the fire before heading for the alcove bed where he would curl into the warmth of his wife's body, who in turn slept soundly with her children beside her.

'We go now to report to the chiefs,' he said, pulling up his fur-lined hood and thinking that the journey back would be easier given that they had already packed down the trail.

But their advance was made slower against the arctic wind that seemed to grow in strength with every twenty strides. At last, three miles later, through the beating specks of snow that now fell fast and heavy onto his face, clearing his eyes with his mittened hand, he perceived the flickering flames of campfires through the trees. They had reached the main attack force.

Moments later, Jean Baptist was standing outside the makeshift lean-to put up by Le Moyne's attendants. Raising his voice against the jaw-numbing weather conditions, Giguere said, 'No one encountered en route, not a soul.' He was careful not to mention that, for whatever reason, they had not seen any watchmen on duty, for there might be by the time the attack force arrived at the gates of the township.

'Well done, Giguere,' returned Le Moyne, his tall frame sheltered by the hides that served as a screen against the wind and snow.

Jean Baptiste, brushing the ice from his dark beard, pursued, making an extra effort to form his words with numbed lips: 'I do believe they are not expecting visitors.' Some of the men standing within earshot chortled at the remark. But Jean Baptiste did not mean it in jest; rather, his joyless tone of voice echoed the resignation of a man about to carry out a terrible deed against his natural will in the name of duty and patriotism.

'Good,' said Le Moyne. 'Inform the Indian chiefs we head onward immediately until we have the township in view. Then we attack at first light.'

Jean Baptiste knew as well as any woodsrunner that the only way to keep out the cold was to keep your blood pumping. Stop, and your heart slowed; you fell asleep, never to wake up. So, what would they do to keep warm till dawn once they came in sight of the target?

Fire would betray them. Even if its light could be masked, the swirling wind could carry the smell of campfires over the settlement and alert the garrison guards. It would spoil the French element of surprise, and even ruin their chances of storming the stockade successfully. For even a small but well-armed garrison could hold out a fort until fatigue and hunger set in among the attackers, or until the settlement's allied Iroquois Indians got wind and came to relieve the siege. Jean-Baptist knew like everyone else that these Indians allied to the English would give no quarter, and only take prisoners for a torture worse than death. Without a swift victory, the mission would be suicide.

The answer to his question came an hour later, when the attack force arrived at the edge of the pine forest that overlooked the dark stockade. The pastureland leading up to the north gate lay under a blanket of snow, and above it, the cold darkness was flecked with snowflakes whipped up in frenzied flurries by the howling crosswind. The night sky was not visible enough to read, and Jean-Baptist did not have a pocket watch, but he reckoned it was not past midnight, which meant a long, cold night ahead. Or so he thought.

He had pushed back his fur-lined hood to better appreciate any ambient noise as he stood under the pine trees. Le Moyne, stepping to Giguere's side, said in a low, rasping voice, 'Take two Indians. Creep in closer to the palisade to assess the guard situation, and report back without taking action.'

Jean Baptist moved half crouching across the blanket of snow where he had seen the path earlier that evening. The snow was falling heavily as he and his two Indian comrades completed their mission under the cloak of the whiteout in the dark night.

A short while later, he was standing before Le Moyne again. Catching his breath, he said, 'There... is no... guard. And yet... the gate is open... Don't get it...'

'Uncommon,' returned Le Moyne, at ease in the knowledge that there was no enemy within earshot, or even lurking nearby to overhear his voice raised to compete against the rush of the wind through the trees. 'They might have gone for a crap, though.'

'But the gate had not even been cleared of snow, at least since the blizzard. So, it will stay open.'

Turning to his captains standing expectantly around him, Le Moyne said to one of his men, 'Xavier, do you have your timepiece?'

'Can't see the face of it, sir. But must be around eleven, I should say.'

'We wait until they are in the depths of sleep. We begin our assault at two. We shall show them the cost of selling guns to our Indian enemies. If there is a guard, we'll know by then if he's merely gone for a crap or not.'

Jean Baptist sensed it was the right decision to bring forward the attack. But the men had been marching; they would by now have built up a sweat under the exertion, just as Jean Baptist had done. The cold would freeze their skins in this blizzard without the warmth of a fire. He feared less for the Indians and the woodsrunners—who were better clad in furs and deerskin, rendered impermeable by numerous coatings of bear grease—than for the bluecoats, some of whom wore only their regimental winter uniforms. Other, more experienced soldiers—recruited from the rank and file who raided Hudson Bay four years earlier under Le Moyne—wore Canadian-style clothing, which included a worn Canadian capot of blue cloth, a red cloth shirt, and mitasses leggings, along with winter moccasins. They were nonetheless still not as well equipped for the extreme weather as the Indians and the woodsrunners.

But then he sensed a powerful presence approaching the circle of captains in the person of the big Indian chieftain. Jean Baptist assumed Krya had been sent after conferring with the other Indian chiefs. He was held in esteem by both Indians and woodsrunners. Jean Baptist instinctively moved aside as the imposing Indian chief stepped before Le Moyne and spoke Giguere's thoughts out loud. 'The men will freeze to death before three hours with no fire,' said Krya. Then he followed through with a morbid plan of action. He said, 'It is already late. What else will these folk be doing in the dead of night but sleeping in their beds? We strike now!' His reasoning was supported by grunts of agreement from men who had gathered around the captains and chief—men cold, hungry, and eager to snatch the loot so often talked about along the way and in their shelters at night before sleep, perhaps to disguise the fact they were going there not just to loot, but to kill.

This was the way of the first nations people. A way that woodsmen and Canadian-born French soldiers had adopted, one that would shock the European officer who would deplore it as savage and cowardly. A French soldier must stand and fight bravely, face-to-face, hand-to-hand, with bayonets affixed and colours flying. But here, in the harsh wilderness of this New World, any European soldier soon realised that these tactics were useless against the enemy, who employed tactics of ambush, surprise attack, and hiding to kill. Le Moyne was no different. Indeed, he had adopted the savagery of the Indian. He was an old hand, and the men around him knew what was expected of them.

Le Moyne bowed his head in ponderation. Krya was not wrong. This blizzard made the cold wind all the more penetrating; the men at best would be stiff and less alert. It was also un-likely that anyone would be expecting a raid in such conditions. No one would be looking across the expanse of pastureland, and if they did, visibility would be too low to see them coming. The surprise would be total.

At last, Le Moyne looked up. Resolute, he said, 'Alright, we go now.' Turning to his captains, he said, 'Iberville, and you, de Montesson, you'll lead a detachment to the south side to control the road to Albany and enter through the south gate.'

De Montesson gave a curt nod. 'Yes, sir,' said Iberville.

Le Moyne continued: 'I will lead the woodsrunners to the north gate by the river,' he said. Then he turned back to Krya, whom he told to convey the move to the Indian chiefs so they could despatch their warriors north or south to either join Iberville and Montesson or Le Moyne.

A short while later, after a brief trek through the pastureland headed by Jean Baptist, Le Moyne filed his men against the east stockade wall that took the full brunt of the roaring northeast-erly wind. They took off their snowshoes, which they tied to their backpacks, and took out their flintlock muskets from their protective bags. This should give time for the south-gate par-ty to position themselves before entering the township. Then Iberville and Montesson's men would surround it on the south side with three or four men to a house. Le Moyne would po-sition his men likewise on the north side, the two parties thus creating a cordon around the town.

However, ten minutes later, as Le Moyne was about to gestic-ulate the silent order to move to the north wall, a stirring along the silent line alerted his attention. Then he saw Iberville and Montesson wading through the snow toward him. The three captains moved away from the wall to let the wind carry their voices away from the township. Catching his breath as he stood before an expectant Le Moyne, Iberville said, 'Blizzard's too thick, snow too deep. There is a line of houses where the wind has built up a blockade of snowdrifts against the north-facing walls. Too deep to get through.'

'Couldn't find the south gate, let alone reach it,' added Montesson.

'Never mind,' said Le Moyne. 'Better we enter the north gate together. Gate's still open. Then we split up to surround the town. Same plan as before, three men to a house. Except, you two go left, I go right. We surround each half of the town and meet at the south side, then we let the Indians give the signal to attack.'

'Haven't seen a soul. They won't even know what hit them!' said Iberville.

'Precisely, let's make sure they don't!'

Under the pretext of war declared in Europe, 210 men carrying an assortment of knives, tomahawks, primed muskets, and sabres at their hips, crouched silently and swiftly along the boatyard on the north side of the stockade where freshly caulked river vessels sat on trestles.

No one saw them. No one heard them, except the dogs whose masters turned over in their beds and fell back to sleep. Nothing could be stirring on a night like this, could there?

Meanwhile, in the name of the Lachine settlers who were slaughtered by Mohawks with English-made weapons the previous summer, these raiders were primed to maim, kill, scalp, and loot, even though this township of Dutch descent had nothing to do with the powers that be. But in the mind of Jean Baptist Giguere and the rest of these men, there had to be a sacrifice to balance the books. It did not matter if there had been twenty-four or 224 Lachine victims: there had to be revenge for the loss of face. Jean Baptist told himself that theirs was a mission of honour.

The raiders followed their respective captains and chieftains past snowmen that must have been made by the children who lived near the north side of town. Had Iberville and Montesson found the south gate, they too would have found similar phantasmagorical silhouettes made by the young children of the south end. Passing by one of the snowmen, one woodsrunner popped his dead clay pipe into its stony mouth. And there it seemed to stand, a dumb sentinel, blithely smoking while behind, a massacre was in preparation.

Jean Baptiste followed Le Moyne and Montesson silently through the gate left ajar, into the relative calm of the stockaded town protected from the blizzard. He imagined families relaxing by a warm fire in the wintry weather. But at this time of night, whole households would hopefully be sound asleep, making the arduous task less troublesome.

One of these families was the Schermerhorns. Symon and his wife lived with their two young sons, his younger brother and sister, and his slaves. They lived in a timber house much smaller than the one they had in Albany. Schenectady being an upcoming burgeoning frontier town, practically all the timber dwellings were one and a half storeys high and two-roomed. Like the Schermerhorns', some dwellings had extensions and outbuildings added as the needs of their dwellers had grown.

In orderly military fashion, Le Moyne gesticulated to Montesson, who had preceded them. He and Iberville would lead the bluecoats one way, and Le Moyne would take the woodsrunners the other. This enabled them to effectively encircle the town, each taking their allotted half that would thus be separated by Church Street running north to south. The Sault and Algonquin Indians followed their own chiefs, who in turn joined either of the white captains one way or the other. In this way, the expedition commanders could place men as they had planned in front of each house before the signal to attack was sounded.

Symon Schermerhorn had a great dog and, as Symon was slipping into a snorting slumber, the dog began to growl and gave a deep-sounding bark.

'Negar, what is it, boy!' called Symon in a hoarse whisper so as not to wake his wife and children, and his brother and sister in the recently built annexe room. The slaves were sleeping soundly in the basement kitchen and had not stirred. But the dog kept gruffly growling. Could it be soldiers returning from the tavern? Symon had been reading by candlelight until past ten o'clock showed on the pendulum clock face, which meant now it must be well past eleven. What could soldiers have been up to at such a late hour? His curiosity increased with the dog's insistent bark at the shuttered window. Symon swiped the layers of blankets aside, climbed out of the alcove bed, then laid the covers back over his two young sons and their mother. He slipped his stockinged feet into his clogs, then scuffed them over the cold flagstones to the frosty front window. It was then that, while patting the dog to keep it calm, he distinctly heard the crunching sound of snow under feet.

Despite the chilled air, Symon gently pulled open the window and peered through a horizontal crack in the shutters. His eyes widened at first with suspicion and then with horror, as in the faint light of night, he focussed his sight on the silently moving silhouettes. Then came the bearer of a torch, the flame-light of which confirmed his worst suspicions. As his eyes adjusted, the terrible shock of seeing not just soldiers, but French bluecoats and Indians filing by in the falling snow, set his pulse racing. 'My God,' he let out under his breath as he closed the window and then fumbled for his day clothes which he put on in haste. He snatched up a sliver of dry wood hanging by the hearth, plunged one end of it into the fire embers, and then lit two candles. 'Willempie, wake up,' he hushed, nudging his wife. 'The French are outside! Dress the boys, quick!'

He handed her one of the candles in its holder, and then he hurried into the annexe where his twenty-two-year-old brother and his sister slept. 'Cornelius. Cornelius, there are French soldiers in town. Come on, wake up!'

'What?' said Cornelius, who suddenly sat bolt upright, rubbing his eyes.

'Shhh, keep your voice down. There are French soldiers in town. Get everyone up while I prepare to ride to Albany to give the alert.'

'What shall we do?'

'I want you to take everyone out of the stockade to one of the outlying farms. God knows how many there are. I suspect they will want to take the town.'

'All right, yes, yes, of course,' said Cornelius, already with his two feet in his breeches.

On the other side of the small room, Jannetie, their younger sister, was waking. At the same time, wrapping her gown around herself in the doorway, Symon's wife asked, 'What's going on, Symon?'

'My dear, you must get the boys dressed. French soldiers are in town!'

'My God,' said Jannetie, jumping out of bed. 'But it's dark and freezing out!'

'I fear we have no choice, my sister,' said Symon. 'Now make haste! Get dressed and go with Willempie while I go down and tell Solomon to saddle the horse.' Then Symon hurried to the basement to wake the slaves.

Minutes later, two groggy-eyed boys, one of six, one of four, were standing near the alcove bed, one dressed, the other in his nightclothes. Their mother, now dressed, was hurriedly pulling blankets from the bed, knowing the cold could be the death of them. Three of the slaves followed by Symon came climbing up the steps from the basement to join in the bustle. Solomon, a middle-aged black man, was hurrying to the back door to access the stable when there came a dreadful Indian cry that rent the air. Jannetie was still dressing Arnout, the youngest boy, while Johannes, the eldest, ran behind the dog that surely no one would challenge. The next moment, there was a dreadful roar that stopped everyone except the dog in their tracks: *'Ouvrez la porte! Ouvrez!!'*

Seconds later, the door was thrust open under the force of two men at arms and two Indians. As they stormed the dimly lit room, they saw three body shapes and a massive attacking dog. The intruders gave fire with their ready muskets. The great dog let out a brief yelp before collapsing lifeless on the floor, and two slaves fell under a merciless blade.

'Stand down, or we kill you all,' shouted the soldier in accented English, a language that the Dutch family and slaves understood.

'Take whatever you find,' returned Symon, realising their lives were in extreme danger. Then there came a gut-churning wail as Symon's wife found Johannes, her son, lying motionless on the bloodstained flagstones near the dead dog. The boy had taken a shot.

'Dear God! You've killed him, you've killed my boy!' cried Symon, crouching beside his wife with a candle after checking the boy's pulse. Cornelius went to check on the slaves, who were dead too, both having been savagely sliced at the neck.

'Get out, or we kill you all!' hurled the soldier brandishing his sabre while kneeing Symon aside, as the other soldier and the brave began ransacking the house.

'Leave him, Willempie, he's dead,' said Symon firmly. 'We have to save ourselves.'

The Schermerhorn household bundled out the back door to the frightening sounds of gunfire, screams of terror, and piercing Indian whoops, which Symon knew meant people were being scalped.

'Dear God, they are everywhere!'

A few minutes earlier, De Mantel, one of Le Moyne's captains, stood ready with a platoon before the small, garrisoned fort. Some men were positioned with a pine log ram, which they had found at the shipyard and planned to use to batter down the door. The captain's best shots stood ready, their flintlock rifles aimed at the blockhouse defence where English heads might appear.

Then came the signal: a bloodcurdling war whoop that split the cold, blustery night air. '*Frappez*!' cried De Mantel to the battering gang. '*Tirez à vue*!' he ordered the riflemen. Soon enough, the French platoon managed to break through the fort door while the panic-stricken English lieutenant tried to organise his defences, but all too late. The raiders stormed the garrison, swiftly dispatching the waking English soldiers with bullet and blade, and then set the fort ablaze, signalling to all that the town's only defence had been defeated. The town-wide massacre could follow unhindered.

Men, women, and children came running out of burning houses only to be invariably met by Indian warriors who promptly butchered them indiscriminately, then scalped them as they lay dead or dying in the blood-drenched snow.

Only a few settlers came to their senses in time to offer resistance. One of the French captains, a Monsieur de Montigny, suffered two thrusts of a spear, one in the body, the other in the arm. Luckily, Le Moyne arrived in the nick of time. Without mercy or remorse, he skilfully wielded his sword with utmost efficiency, focussing on the fatal blow, the blow that delivered no pain, just a clean, sudden death, one that any soldier, merchant, or maid should favour. De Montigny was taken to the nearby house of a widow with six children. Others did not know panic, silently slain as they were in their sleep.

But at one house off Church Street, an old lady unable to sleep had been cleaning an old family vase. While doing so, Millie reminisced about her grown-up children, their children, and her sister, who had passed away, leaving just a boy who was a fine-looking young man now. Her thoughts were suddenly interrupted by a terrible whooping scream that rent the night air and disrupted the comforting crackle of the fireplace embers.

The next moment, she heard voices coming from the street. 'Alfric!' she called out. At the closed door, she yelled, 'Daniel, that you?' But the reply was brutal. The door was forced open, and soldiers erupted into the room just as Alfric emerged from the adjoining room, holding an unprimed musket. Wielding swords, the three intruders rushed at him, slashing and thrusting until he fell in a mire of blood that seeped from his neck and spleen. The raiders then searched the bedroom and inside the hearth for loot. The old lady stood still in shock and horror as they unearthed a drawstring pouch of gold coins under a loose brick in the fireplace. Then they torched the house and left cheerful, having found the loot, leaving the old lady standing in a petrified stance, still holding the vase.

Coming round to her senses, she put down the vase and dragged her husband of forty years from the burning room and pulled him outside into the cold. An appalling thought struck her as all around, she saw her neighbours screaming and being killed as they ran into the snowy, bloodied street in their night-wear. Of her children, only Gerrit had stayed in Schenectady with his wife and their children. Millie asked for God's grace before leaving Alfric lying dead in the frozen street, in a trail of blood that led from their home on fire.

Still in her nightclothes and clogs, but oblivious to the cold, she scurried around the corner into the main street, where she nearly stumbled on a dead dog. Trying not to look at the terri-fying scenes taking place, instead, she gathered up her shift and nightgown till she came within ten yards of her son's two-room wooden house. Terrified shouts and screams suddenly ceased and made her slow down as she instinctively brought her hands to her mouth, feeling sick inside. Arriving level with the house, she saw flames from a spilt oil lamp spreading through the open door, then met soldiers exiting, carrying bread and ham and a sack full of loot.

Closing her eyes, she fell to her knees, brought her hands together in prayer, and prepared to die. But the soldiers filed past her as if the little mouse of a woman were invisible to them. Meanwhile, inside the house, fed by the cold draught, the flames were spreading fast. She quickly found her son, his wife, and their children lying in their own blood. With all her might, she pulled them out of the burning room, all four of them in their nightclothes, as further down the street scenes of hell were playing out. Indians were scalping their victims who lay dead or dying, having been grabbed and hacked to death as they ran screaming out of their houses. With dread, Millie saw one French-allied Indian holding her neighbour's abundant long hair with one hand. It could only be the beautiful hair of

Mrs Latourette. Making swift incisions deftly with his knife, the Indian then yanked the scalp free from her head and gave a death cry while brandishing his trophy, which he then placed in his belt.

Shock and horror now overwhelmed Millie's sense of grief. A survival instinct kicked in. Should she lie down with her loved ones and play dead? But then the savages might seek to scalp them too. She had heard that the French paid a high price for scalps. She told herself she had to get out of sight, but looking around, she was too petrified to move, which would only attract attention to her. But then a brown hand shimmering in the firelight grabbed her by the shoulder. Before she had time to scream, he spun her round, and she saw it was Senchi, a Mohawk trader from the west valley who had been staying with her son and had been spared by the raiders.

'Come, you can do nothing for them now,' he said, raising his voice through the slanting snow. He took her hand and pulled her into a nearby passageway between houses that were not yet in flames. 'Crouch down here,' he told her, his index finger touching his lips. Shivering with cold and fear, she did as he said and let him crouch beside her. Then he placed a blanket over them both to camouflage them as one unidentifiable dark mass soon to be covered over by the falling snow, while Blood-curdling screams and death cries echoed from either end of the passageway.

'Indians coming this way!' said Symon's wife, making a conscious effort to draw her mind from her murdered son.

They could easily make out three Indians on the backdrop of a blazing house, whereas they were still cloaked in darkness beside their stable. 'Give me the blanket and take Arnout,' said

Symon, passing the boy to his wife and then wrapping him in the blanket that Willempie had taken from the house. 'Quick, hide in the snow,' he said. Catching on, Cornelius joined his brother in hollowing out the fresh snowdrift built up on the north-facing side of the stable. 'Not a sound, Arnout, my boy,' said Symon as Willempie, the boy, and Jannetie pressed themselves into the snow while Symon and his brother quickly covered them over. Then the brothers buried themselves likewise from foot to face. Here they lay as moments later, they heard the Indians passing.

A short time after, Symon brushed the snow from his face, and Cornelius did likewise. 'They've gone,' said Symon softly, and the other escapees lifted themselves from their snowy hiding place.

'They won't be back,' said Cornelius.

'No, but you must get away from here,' said Symon. He then could not help bringing a hand to his forehead at the memory of his fallen son, left lying in the family abode that would no doubt be set alight like many others around town.

Willempie, resolved not to let her grief be master of her and determined to escape with her youngest son, passed the boy to Jannetie. She then turned back to her husband and held his forearms tight. 'Be strong, husband,' she said steadfastly. 'Take the horse, and fetch help.'

Symon released his forehead from his cold grasp and placed his hands on his wife's arms. Together they stood, toe to toe. 'Yes, yes,' he said, locking eyes with her momentarily before encompassing his sister, his son, and his brother. 'Listen, all of you. I will attract their attention so you can run out the gap through the wall by the south gate.'

'We will seek refuge at a farm along the way,' said Cornelius.

'Yes, brother, but don't take any chances. Once through the gap, head for our brother's mill to get out of the cold.'

'But what if it is taken?'

'Then we shall hide in the woods,' said Willempie resolutely, 'until we are able to reach one of the outlying farms.'

'You will freeze.'

'Rather that than burn, Symon,' said Willempie, letting her hand fall into Symon's hand. 'You must go now. It is the only way.'

Symon fleetingly tightened his grasp on his wife's hand and clasped that of Cornelius. Then he grasped his sister by the shoulder and stroked the head of his son, before turning and running for the stable.

Moments later: 'Master,' said a low voice in the darkness as Symon entered through the stable door.

'Solomon...' returned Symon, whose thoughts turned to the fallen slaves, Joan and Kanta, but there was no time for explaining.

'Horse's ready, master.'

'Follow me, then get out of town with the others.'

Under the cover of the night and pummelling snow, Symon cantered with Solomon running behind him, toward the south gate tavern where a horde of villagers were running for their lives to escape Indian tomahawks.

Symon pointed to a small group led by a young man holding a child, with two women running behind him. 'There they are, go with them and stay together,' yelled Symon. Solomon took off toward the side gate to catch up with them as Symon kicked the horse onward and galloped at the approaching Indian warriors. With no weapon, he could only ride into them to draw their attention away from the fleeing escapees.

He galloped the opposite way up the main street, attracting gunfire from those who still had a lead ball in their barrel, while his wife and Solomon were the last of the group to sneak through the side gate that led onto the Albany trail.

Symon galloped through the flattened and blood-stained snow up the main street between burning houses. He witnessed fellow townsfolk being put to the blade. There was nothing he could do, and he pushed on through the open north gate under a volley of shot. The horse gave out a groan as a lead ball sunk into its flesh. 'Come on, boy!' he roared, desperately. 'Run on! Yaha!' There came another dull thud, and Symon writhed in pain as a lead shot ripped into his thigh. But he was out of the stockade, and he pushed his horse in a canter, keeping to the snow-covered road where the snow wasn't so deep, until he reached the pine woods. Onward he cantered along the road to Niskayuna.

For two hours, the killing spree continued: men, women, and children cut down in the first wave of fury with no regard for age or gender. Only the Iroquois Mohawks staying in town were given grace, Le Moyne having been instructed that it ironically was French policy to show they had no war with these Indians. On the contrary, Le Moyne knew that back in Montreal, the French were negotiating peace so that their fur trade could continue unhindered. 'Ironically', because it was these English-allied Indians' massacre of Lachine that had supplied the motive for the massacre of this Dutch township.

In all, Le Moyne counted sixty inhabitants savagely killed during that first furious wave of the raid. White men too killed at random, embracing the legitimised opportunity like a secret pleasure to test their blade and their skill at the kill, a sport that for some was like relieving a sexual itch after a long wait in celibacy. And this was easy picking, like stalking the turkey. But out of the 210 men, not all of them had the killer instinct. One of these was Jean Baptiste. Giguere took prisoners. A few of them in their nightclothes escaped his vigilance, and he let them go. But he knew full well it was no gift of mercy. 'Bah, they'll die from exposure anyway,' said one soldier beside him, formulating his very thoughts.

After the massacre and the looting, Le Moyne ordered all houses still intact, barring a few, to be torched in case the Indians found liquor, which would only slow down their getaway come morning. One of these houses was the one where a widow and her six children resided. It was the house where they had taken De Mantel to be cared for after his injuries. In one sense, the one who inflicted the injuries on De Mantel saved the lives of the woman and her children.

Le Moyne and his captains gave the rest of the night to placing sentinels and to rest so that, the next morning, they could load fifty or so horses from the township to carry the loot back to Montreal.

Such was the revenge the French had sought against these Dutch villagers for the massacre of Lachine by Indians, which they had put down to English incitement.

CHAPTER 11

February 9, 1690

ALBANY

Next morning in Albany, the groggy-eyed tavernkeeper shovelled wood ash from the fireplace into a bucket to make a fire for the two early birds.

'God forbidden hour, this is!' he grumbled with a chuckle in his voice.

'Bloody cold this morning,' said Daniel, who was seated on the nearest bench, and turned toward the hearth. The muffled ticktock from the pendulum clock that stood between shuttered windows, and the air that was almost too chilled to breathe in, made him suspect that it had continued to snow during the night.

'Sure you boys are heading out today?' said the tavernkeeper.

'So long as the river isn't completely iced over,' said Daniel, ending with a cough provoked by the cold intake of air.

'Here, let me get the fire going while you dump your ash,' said Didier Ducamp, who proceeded to layer brushwood, faggots, and thicker sticks in the grate.

'Aright, I'll get rid of this, and I'll put the broth on the hook then,' said the tavernkeeper. He then lugged the full bucket of ash to the back door.

Ducamp, meanwhile, brought a flame to the kindling that soon crackled with nascent flames drawn into the cold rush of the chimney conduit. 'Sure you're up to it?' he said, casting a dubious glance at Daniel's fatigued eyes.

'Oh yes,' said Daniel. 'We both need to get back home, don't we? Some hot broth to start us off, and we'll be casting off as the sun rises. Get a good day's sailing in with the tide.'

'Fine by me, as you like,' said Ducamp, who was piling thicker branches at the back of the hearth as the back door was unbolted and pushed open.

Standing on the threshold, the tavernkeeper called out, 'Good heavens!'

Daniel suspected what had caused his exclamation. 'Snowed?' called out Ducamp, who had the same thought.

'Ground level's risen by two feet, my word!' returned the tavernkeeper. After some clanking sounds as he emptied his load of wood ash, he pulled the back door shut and bolted it. Returning to the room, he said, 'Don't know why there's soldiers everywhere.'

'Probably called out to clear the gates,' said Daniel, re-membering the snowdrifts at Schenectady that blocked the gate, while the tavernkeeper crossed the flagstoned room. The tavernkeeper then set down his bucket beside the fire-place and picked up the cauldron, which he hung on the hearth hook. 'There,' he said, 'won't be too long once the fire gets cracking. Nothing better than warmed-up stew, is there?'

The early birds agreed, although they would have eaten stew nine days old, so hungry were they both. The tavernkeeper ambled to the caged bar, unlocked it, and moved round to prepare two tankards of small beer.

In the first light of day, there came a lone rider, his steed visibly fatigued, riding through the deep snow along the crooked road that led to the north gate. As he approached in the half light, the guard clearing snow from the gate said to his companion, 'That looks like Symon Schermerhorn!' The Schermerhorns were well known in Albany. Symon had grown up there and still possessed, with his brothers, his late father's house in Pearl Street.

'Looks like there's something wrong,' said the other guard, who then called out to the sentry, 'Open the gate wider, it's Mr Schermerhorn.'

Symon arrived at the gate; his head leaned over the horse's frozen mane. He let himself slide with his good leg onto the stirrup and let his weight drop him to the ground, where he lay prostrate, his wounded leg drenched in blood. Moments after, the poor horse let out a short, excruciating scream, then dropped dead beside him.

'For the love of God, speak, man!' said the crouching guard, holding Schermerhorn's head up. 'What happened to you?'

Symon used his last remaining strength to grab the guard's lapel, and in a weak voice, he said: 'French... Indians... attack... many killed... town burned.... They killed my son.' Then he passed out.

The waking town soon began to stir to the news of the tragedy hailed by the night watchman. Lanterns in homes were being lit, and folk were pushing open shutters to the sound of marching soldiers. Of these, two were sent down to the port side where the ketch from New York was about to cast off, as the morning sun edged its way through clouds over the far bank.

'Can you hear?' said Ducamp, holding a punt ready to push the ketch to the middle of the river, where the water flowed with more vigour away from floating ice. 'What's all that din about?'

'Looks like we're about to find out,' said Daniel from the dockside, looping his head to the two soldiers making their way from the riverside gate.

'Mr Darlington?' called out one of the soldiers, looking important.

'I am he,' returned Daniel, with a hand on the rope over the mooring post.

'We are sent by Alderman Wendell. You are not to cast off, you are to follow me as a matter of urgency, sir.'

Daniel said, 'Can you be more explicit, soldier?'

'Schenectady, sir. It has been attacked by the French,' said the soldier. Daniel froze, momentarily stunned by the soldier's news. How could this be? He and Didier were only there yesterday. Thoughts of Millie and Alfric went reeling through his mind.

'When?' said Ducamp, stepping into the conversation from the ketch.

'This last night.'

'How many dead?' said Daniel.

'I cannot say. Alderman Wendell will inform you, sir.'

Daniel left Ducamp to secure the ketch. He followed the soldiers through the east gate and into the main street, where troops in thick woollen coats and bonnets were taking position and horses were being mounted. They proceeded into Pearl

Street, where the footfall was less and the snow thicker. Then they came to the house of Schermerhorn. Inside, Daniel encountered a servant girl carrying fresh linen and a black man bringing hot water from the fireplace. Daniel was shown into a study where Wendell was in conversation with another alderman.

Interrupting himself, Wendell looked toward the door and said with a note of relief in his voice, 'Daniel, glad we caught you in time.'

'Schenectady,' said Daniel with no nonsense. 'What's the news?'

'Not good. French and Indians attacked last night. Set the place on fire.'

'How many dead?'

'We do not know. Symon Schermerhorn managed to escape and give the alert. That is why we are in his house. They killed his son, burnt down his home.'

'My God,' said Daniel. 'I have family there too.'

'Yes, I know,' said Wendell gravely. 'Many of us here do.'

'We must muster an attack force.'

'We don't know how many there are, and they might not stop at Schenectady. There could be thousands. Captain Bull is preparing a task force, but the snow is deep. He suggests we assess the situation before leaving ourselves open and running into battle. In the meantime, we need to get word to New York. I want you to wait while I collate everything I can in a letter to Leisler. You must get it to him as quickly as humanly possible. There's a good chance we'll be needing reinforcements, provisions, and clothing for the survivors.'

Tight-lipped, Daniel said, 'I must help my aunt. I cannot just walk the other way.'

Wendell stepped toward the young man, and with gravitas, pressed him on the shoulder and said, 'Come with me.'

Moments later, Daniel was standing before the pale-looking escapee in his bed. The surgeon was cleansing the thigh after extracting the lead shot. The patient was sitting up in his bed. In the voice of a man battling against grief, Symon Schermerhorn gave the same account as he had given Wendell and Captain Bull of his terrible adventure: how he had created a diversion so his family and others could get through the wall, how he had alerted the outlying farmsteads and the village of Niskayuna along the way.

'How many?' said Daniel.

'I do not know,' returned Symon, becoming increasingly weary. 'All I can say is they were everywhere. French and Indians.'

Turning to Wendell standing next to him, Daniel said, 'I must go with Captain Bull's men. Even if the enemy is gone, the survivors will need help.'

'Daniel,' said Symon with feeling and in short breaths. 'I saw... scenes of hell... I'm afraid... I saw your uncle lying dead... in front of his burning house.'

'Aunt Millie?' returned Daniel, suddenly deflated as he realised the worst.

'I don't know... I don't recall seeing her... but I dread to think... But I saw Gerrit too... and his wife and child lined up in a row... being scalped as they lay dead.'

'My God,' said Daniel.

Symon pursued, 'I saw some people running through the palisade... barefooted with nothing on but their nightclothes. They will surely have died from cold... if they were not able to find shelter quickly.'

'I am sorry, Daniel,' said Wendell with compassion. 'There is nothing you can do for them now. The best you can do to help now is take word to New York.'

Daniel looked down, giving himself a moment to register the loss of his family, then looked up and gave a short, resolute nod.

CHAPTER 12

1699, Aboard the Mary-Ann

THE DELPECH FAMILY — 9 YEARS LATER

Slicing the raw cured ham that she usually kept hung up on a hook in a hessian sack, out of reach of rats, Jeanne wondered how those first pioneers had managed their provisions without knowing when, or even if, land would appear on the horizon.

They were three weeks from Cork Harbour, where they had stopped over briefly after leaving Dublin Bay. To Jeanne, distance and time seemed blurred by the dreary blues and greys of the rolling sea and the cloud-muffled sky that she viewed from the upper deck during calm weather. At least now, she was inured to the nauseating stench of bilge water, she thought to herself, and had even become used to the creaks of the moving timbers that at first made her lose sleep.

Snapping herself from her ruminations, she looked up with empathy at Jacob, lying listlessly in his hammock. 'Jacob, you'll have to get over your seasickness, or you'll be nothing but a sack of bones,' she said, handing him the last crust of homemade bread with a slice of ham on top. 'You must try to eat something.'

'Yes, my dear Jeanne,' returned Jacob in a faint voice. Groggily sitting up astride the hammock and carefully planting his feet on the deck, he reached for the morsel. Jeanne complemented the ship food in this way with bread and ham and anything she could cook herself. It kept her occupied during those days of monotony, only broken by the religious rituals led by the Quakers from Wales, who had embarked on the ship in Liverpool. They sang in a language she could not understand, but at least it reassured her to be travelling with God-fearing folk in search of freedom to live their lives as they saw fit, just like she and Jacob. Pierre and Isabelle had made friends with the Quaker children as only children can, through play.

Holding his free hand to his stomach in time with the gentle dip of the ship, Jacob pursued, 'I must confess, this mellow heave 'n' sway is worse than my first voyage in the southern seas to the Caribbean.'

'I think you exaggerate slightly, my dear,' said Jeanne levelly. 'Travelling in a flee-infested cabin with eighty other prisoners like sardines in a barrel is not quite the same thing.'

'No, I s'pose not.'

'But be assured, Jacob, this is the last voyage we shall ever embark on.'

'To that I concede, my dear wife. You can trust me.'

'Probably not the last voyage for me, though, I hope,' said Paul distantly, looking up from the chest upon which he was sitting and reading a book about sailing while he finished his ham. 'The bosun's been telling me all about knots and rigging and the amazing places he has been to: Jamaica, Curaçao, Puerto Rico, Dominica, Saint Pierre, Florida...'

Jeanne had noticed how her son, true to his temperament, had taken the voyage in his stride and seemed to be making the best out of the situation, although perhaps a little too well. He spent his days learning the ropes and reading the few books he had brought with him. He was even becoming popular among the crew and captain, who let him climb aloft and stow away the sails on the first yards.

Her fear, however, was that with time on his hands to think over his future, he might get it into his head to become a seafaring merchant or something of the sort. Her fears were about to come true as he said, 'Father has often told how his friend Mr Darlington had made a fortune by simply taking a ship south, and with the proceeds of the sale of European merchandise loaded in New York, was able to buy sugar loaves and spices in the Caribbean: indigo and ginger, and tobacco and coffee. Then he would head back and sell his cargo for a small fortune to a merchantman headed for Europe. Didn't he, Father?'

'Well, yes, I s'pose... but don't forget...'

'There you are then,' interrupted Paul, eagerly looking from his mother to his father. 'You could take care of buying and selling merchandise in New York, while I ferry goods back and forth from the Caribbean. We could make a fortune!'

'There's probably more to it than that, Paul,' said Jeanne wryly.

'Of course, there is, Mother, I'm just boiling it down to its simplest notion. And besides, I'm still learning. This voyage is indeed turning out to be the chance of a lifetime in more ways than I could have ever imagined.'

Jacob looked earnestly at Jeanne, who pursed her lips, as he bit a chunk out of the bread and ham, then fell back into his hammock.

However, Paul's promising start to a new career at sea nearly came to a premature end a moment later when, above the song

119

of the Welsh Quakers, someone called from the porthole, 'Dolphins starboard!'

Paul put down his book on a nearby cask and, keeping his head low, shot up the steps for a better view. He zigzagged with the movement of the ship to the starboard balustrade and then, in his exuberance, he climbed the rigging to get a good view of the dolphins making arcs above the water.

Jeanne and the children had followed him above deck and watched him climb agile as a monkey. But halfway up the shroud to the first yard, in his overenthusiasm, not only did he misjudge the ship's cadence, but he missed his step on the ratline. His foot passed through the gap, which made him slip backward, only managing to save himself at the last moment. Jeanne, who had looked up to see her son climb, instead of admiring the dolphins swimming graciously alongside the ship, let out a gasp which attracted the attention of the captain. He yelled out to Paul to keep his focus on his movements and climb down.

'Just a silly slip,' Paul called back while descending. It was nonetheless clear to see his false step had resulted in him spraining his ankle. He hesitated to put his weight on his left foot, using his hands to support his weight every time he placed his sprained foot on the lower footrope.

After easing himself onto the deck, he tried to wave it off to save face, but the sprain made him wince and limp, much to his shame and embarrassment.

'First incident,' said the captain. 'It had to come, and better sooner than later. Puts a man in his place, see.' The captain's words were meant to reassure, but Paul nonetheless felt slightly ridiculous, for he knew he was victim of his own brashness to vaunt his newfound sea legs and head for heights.

'Come along, Paul, lesson learnt,' said Jeanne in a tone that made him want to disappear between the cracks in the decking. 'Your father will sort you out.'

Practical as ever, Jeanne quickly realised that her son's rather frightening false step could serve a purpose.

For all his being a strapping young man a head taller than she was, she insisted he lean on her shoulder to help him limp down the hatch steps to the half light of the lower deck. She suspected that treating the ankle would also serve to help her husband find his sea legs. On seeing the pair of them and on the news piped out by Isabelle, Jacob was instantly alert and swinging out of his hammock. He examined his son's sprain, which he then bound to give it support. 'Stay away from the shroud for the next few days, my boy, and you'll be right as rain sooner than you think,' he said to his son in a cheery tone of voice.

As Jeanne had suspected, sure enough, the next morning, Jacob was up as the first light seeped into the chilly gun deck through the gaps around the closed gun ports. Famished he was too. 'I say, I could eat a horse,' he said cheerily, as Jeanne and the children still lay under the blankets in their space that they had curtained off to preserve a minimum of privacy. 'But I daresay some rabbit stew should do to fill the gap.'

'The rabbits have all gone, Jacob,' said Jeanne in a waking voice. 'You surely didn't think they would keep for three weeks.'

'Oh, has it been that long?'

'All our extra provisions for the voyage are almost depleted.'

Jacob optimistically said, 'Oh, some bread and cheese should tide me over in that case.'

Jeanne returned deadpan, 'Cheese is gone too.'

'The three loaves?'

'I gave you the last of it yesterday, have you forgotten? All we have left is another ham.'

'A bit salty; what about the sweetmeats?'

'The children finished those ages ago. You'd better have some ham.'

'Yes, quite,' said Jacob, holding his stomach with growing concern. Jeanne rose, reached for the ham swinging on the hook above them, removed it from the hessian sack, and sliced pieces off for Jacob to fill his face.

Always the man to bring people together, as the morning wore on, Jacob made small talk with the Welsh neighbours, who did not mind speaking English to a man with a foreign accent. Their conversation revolved around their mutual hopes and what they would find in this new promised land. He learnt that these Welsh folk had been lured by the promise of William Penn.

'Says he wants his colony to be a place where anyone can worship freely, see?' said one Mr Evans, an evenly tempered man with an evenly measured way of talking, full of the good sense of a master builder. 'That's why he named the city Philadelphia, which I'm told means brotherly love in the language of the ancient Greeks.'

'Yes,' said Jacob, glancing up while thinking back to his Greek learning. 'Didn't make the association before, my word, but yes, *philos* means love and *adelphos* means brother. Quite ingenious.' Jacob then told him of his plans to settle in the province of New York, where he had been before.

'I heard there were some difficult times in New York with rebellion and the French breathing down their necks. And the Indians always on the fence, wondering who's the worthiest to side with. We don't have those problems with the Indians in Philadelphia, as the whole colony is based on tolerance and as I say, brotherly love, it's in its name.'

'I believe you make reference to Jacob Leisler.'

'That's the name.'

'Actually, I found him to be a very upright and no-nonsense type of fellow,' said Jacob.

'Oh, you met him, did ya?'

'Yes, I was there just before the troubles in New York began.'

'Right awful what they did to him, so I heard. And his son-in-law, forget his name.'

'That would have been Milborne, Jacob Milborne.'

'Hah, everyone's a Jacob in New York then, are they?' said the Welshman in jest.

'Just like most of you are either Evans or Williams,' said Jacob, in an equally jestful tone of voice. He was referring to the fact that in the Welsh party, there were half as many people called Evans as there were Quakers.

'Anyway, we plan on getting a plot outside the town. Create our own community for the Welsh, like, and we'll call it Gwynedd, which means North Wales. That's where we come from, you see.'

'I heard Mr Penn talk once in Ireland,' said Jacob. 'He did speak then about the Welsh Tract.'

'Well, let's say there's plenty of our people settled there now, and they conduct their affairs in Welsh, which suits us fine.'

It soon became clear to the passengers that Jacob Delpech was a man of means and experience, proof of which was soon to come in a series of events most would rather forget.

In the meantime, the ship was making slow but certain headway in a fair sea interspersed with calmer days, sailing along to the titillating sightings that filled the Delpech family, the Evanses, and the Williams with wonderment. It was as if they had come across a unicorn in a prairie, or with dread, like beholding an ugly troll by a mountain spring.

One of these sightings consisted of a whale, a sea beast that even Jeanne could barely believe existed until she saw it with her own eyes, filled as they were with childlike wonder.

'Don't surprise me,' claimed Mr Evans, 'it's clearly described in the Bible.'

'Yes, it's frightening,' said Jeanne, thinking of the great fish that swallowed Jonah. 'And this one had a calf.' But surely a man could not be swallowed by such a creature, she thought to herself; how would he breathe?

Passengers in their wonderment scurried excitedly from starboard to port and back again, making the very ship pitch with the rapid displacement of their weight until the captain had to warn them. 'Tread slowly,' he hurled in his gruff voice, 'unless you want to join the beasts at the bottom of the briny! Cause that's what'll happen, you'll tip us over!'

Jeanne wondered about those other sea beasts that supposedly lurked beneath the waves, hidden from the human eye. Sea charts and mariner tales told of the kraken, the giant octopus, serpents, and sirens, although the latter she thought very improbable. But the mere thought of them beneath the ship on the other side of the creaking hull gave her cause for a nightmare that night.

She awoke with a start in the black night and realised that the roll of the ship and the constant knocking were nothing more than the wind picking up and whipping the flopping waves against the hull. She laid her hand over Jacob's chest from behind him. He had forsaken the hammock for the firmer paillasse, having realised that swinging in the air only aggravated his nausea. He felt steadier now, letting his eyes and his belly keep in time with the heave and sway of the ship.

'Are you concerned?' he whispered, echoing his own worries about the installation in New York that had kept him awake. The port township would surely have changed; they would have to work hard to prepare their first winter; and where would they stay while they were building their house?

'Just a silly, childish nightmare,' Jeanne whispered. 'I dreamt we were in the clutches of the kraken,' she confessed lightheartedly.

'Ho, that's old sailors' tales,' said Jacob, clasping her hand. Then, turning his head to her, he whispered, 'I was thinking about our first winter, how we shall get by.'

'It will be fine,' whispered Jeanne. 'We have done it before, and Paul is older now.'

'As long as he doesn't succumb to the lure of the sea!'

'Hmm, I was thinking the same,' returned Jeanne, reassured that Jacob shared the same concern; then she added, 'As long as we get through this awful voyage, we'll be fine.' She spread the blanket evenly over them both and then curled into his warm body and closed her eyes, reassured by the familiar smell of his person. Listening to the ship as it cut through the raging and fearful sea, she thought to herself that she would never purposefully set foot in it, not knowing what was lurking beneath its surface.

Jeanne noted that the sailors naturally took all the sightings in their stride, even the dorsal fins of the terrible shark. But then, late one afternoon, there came an encounter that would bound the whole ship, captain, crew, and all, in a common concern.

The sky was low and visibility reduced when, as the day was dimming into evening, there came a yell from aloft: 'Ship ahoy!'

Paul, standing at the bow, looked up and followed the direction of the sailor's outstretched arm with his eyes. Seeing nothing, he clambered up the lower shroud until, through the thin veil of mist, just on the faint line where sea and sky became one, he perceived it—a mere speck in the distance: the fore topsail and topgallant.

'By my troth, there she is! All her sails to the wind,' barked the captain, who had exited his cabin and was now standing at the helm, his spyglass pressed to his eye. Young Paul climbed down the rigging, dashed along the deck, and then charged down the hatch steps to relay the sighting to the lantern-lit deck below.

'How far?' said one of the Welsh lads, both hands placed on the cask in front of him.

'Can't be more than three leagues away,' Paul said, recalling the lesson on distance to the horizon. 'Especially since the captain could see it from the quarterdeck.'

'Which direction?' said another man sitting up in his hammock, clipping off Paul's explanation.

'Travelling eastward, and it appears to be heading straight for us.'

'Goodness gracious,' said one woman, holding an infant, whose concern resonated in her voice and echoed that of all present. For everyone had heard of chilling attacks at sea and would rather encounter a pod of whales than a barque of fellow humans.

Pushing a hand onto Paul's shoulder, 'Let's have a word with the captain, then, shall we?' said Jacob. He then followed his son through a covey of fellow passengers, their faces a picture of anxiety, to the upper deck to see for himself.

'What are her colours, Captain?' called Jacob to Captain Wright, who was standing on the quarterdeck with his spyglass still stuck to his puckered eye.

'Whatever she be,' said the captain combatively, lowering the telescope and snapping it shut, 'she'll not take my ship! We've got plenty of firepower aboard, and we shall fight if it comes to it.'

Jacob thought that prognostic a bit rash and said with insistence, 'But what are her colours, Captain?'

Skipping down the steps to the main deck, the captain said, 'One o' yourn, Monsieur Delpech. She be French.'

'Then not one of mine,' replied Jacob with dignity. 'I fought on the side of King William, sir. But anyway, it matters not. We are no longer at war, are we?'

'No, that we're not, Mr Delpech,' said the captain, standing opposite Jacob. 'Which means we're left with some hungry cutthroats because of it, don't it.'

'Ah,' said Jacob, catching on. 'You mean privateers.'

'I mean pirates, sir!' returned the captain. 'At least you knew where you stood with privateers.'

From experience, Jacob knew this not to be always true but kept it to himself as Paul said, 'Why would they show French colours then, Captain?'

'Precisely because we are at peace, lad. Cause that's what pirates do. They try to induce a false sense of security.'

In a calm voice, Paul said, 'But then, why do they show our colours if they want to cheat and lead us into believing they are friendly?'

'Cunning devils, pirates are,' said the captain. 'It would be too obvious, see? What chances are there of passing an English ship from the New World in this great watery expanse wider than any desert?'

'That is true,' said Jacob thoughtfully as he recalled his past episode as an indentured ship's barber-surgeon aboard the ship of the infamous and terrible Captain Brook. An unscrupulous man whose only goal was winning by any deceit imaginable, including hoisting colours to mislead the prey.

'Harry,' bellowed the captain to the gunner at the main mast. 'Make good the gun deck. Prime the cannons. We'll not let 'em take us if they try. We'll be ready to fire a volley into her belly, and then we run like the wind, for they'll give no quarter.'

'My God,' said Jacob, stunned and dumbfounded as the captain strutted toward the hatch. Was the man truly intent on leading this band of Quakers into battle?

Moments later, standing on the lower steps of the dim gun deck, the captain gave a rousing speech. To Jacob's dismay, even young Paul was suddenly filled with a fighting spirit, just as were many of the young Welsh men, small in stature but thickly set and tenaciously supportive of the captain's intentions.

'We will not let the rascals take this ship nor your earthly possessions, nor your wives and daughters,' pursued the captain to the cheers of outrage from the men and the cries of shock from the women. Captain Wright was a man who knew his audience, thought Jacob as the captain pressed on. 'They will not take away your livelihood nor your dream of a new life!' Again, there came cheers of support and outrage. 'Hit 'em hard and run with the wind, that's what we'll do!' After more cheers had died down, the captain then gave his orders to the gunner.

Soon casks were being rolled out of the way to clear the deck. Chests and baskets that seemed to have multiplied in clusters where families slept and ate were cleared away from the vicinity of the two-tonne gun carriages, as men sworn to the Christian doctrine were riled and ready to kill or be killed.

In the glow of lanterns placed on casks or hung up on hooks around the deck, as the ship sailed inexorably towards an encounter, Jacob intermittently watched the gunner showing Paul and other young men how to prime and fire the instruments of destruction. Meanwhile, the women arranged their living quarters and prayed for a miracle.

Crew members joined the volunteers whom the gunner—a solid and forthright northern man of experience—organised into eight teams for eight guns. But even so, there was not enough time to train the male passengers how to prime a cannon while under fire, men who had never seen battle, let alone battle at sea. But the captain's plan was to fire only one round and then take flight. The gunner allowed one practice blast with no shot in the barrels while the oncoming ship was still far enough away and out of earshot. Otherwise, the sound would travel to the ears of those aboard the distant eastbound ship, which meant, if it really were a French merchantman, its captain might take them for pirates and think the westbound ship was preparing for attack. The thunderous sound of the blasts put terror into the hearts of the women and made the small children bawl. One man, not standing far enough clear of the violent cannon recoil, broke a toe as the truck wheel hit his foot. The swirling smoke, the smell of gunpowder, and the cry of pain from the victim signalled a radical change of atmosphere that the gunner felt was needed. After all, this was serious warfare.

Then there came practice runs with no blast, just so the teams could go through the motions of swabbing the barrel, reloading, ramming, picking the flannel cartridge, and firing should the need arise. At last, under the supervision of the northern gunner, a final cartridge followed by a cloth wad was loaded into the guns, then rammed with wood rammers. The touch-holes were prepped, and cannonballs were pushed into muzzles, followed by more wadding so the shot would not roll out if the ship's roll caused the muzzle to dip downward. After conferring with the captain, the gunner decided not to run out the cannons through the gun port, which would only give away their intentions should it come to it. Instead, the men would have to heave the cannons at the last moment until the carriages touched the ship's bulwark, then take aim. All a bit tricky, but any pirate crew would not be expecting such a welcome, and the captain estimated they would still have the upper hand. Once the gun was fired, they would run onwards while the enemy was left behind, licking their wounds. The captain was adamant his ship would outrun the eastbound ship if it came to it. The teams then sat ready for the hit and run.

Jacob, meanwhile, lent his organisational skills to help relocate some of the family areas—which included bedding, hammocks, baskets, chests, and curtains—out of the way of the cannon areas and the probable trajectories of the cannon team manoeuvres. This meant people often found themselves with new neighbours or that the Welsh clan was fragmented over the gun deck. Curtains were reerected for privacy.

All this took up the whole evening, but once the initial brouhaha was calmed and men's blood was not quite so high, Jacob, chewing on his pipe, sat on a chest to marshal his thoughts. Now, he thought to himself, the so-called pirate ship was three-masted, and much larger than the usual shallow draft sloop that pirates tended to use in their endeavours so they could niftily escape to shallow waters. And besides, what would pirates be doing in the middle of the northern hemisphere sea anyway, where there were so few pickings? Wasn't the improbability of meeting the villains one of the reasons why they were taking this northern Atlantic route to the New World? He had to clarify his thoughts with the captain, so up he got, pocketed his pipe, and climbed up to the main deck to have a word. The wind had dropped to a breeze, and the black water lay calm. Jacob fleetingly wondered how they would get away if the wind dropped off completely. He climbed up to the quarterdeck and, turning his collar to the damp night chill, he knocked on the captain's cabin door.

'Yep, they could well be bona fide,' said the captain moments later, sitting at his desk before his charts under the tallow light of the slowly swaying lantern. 'And let's hope that be the case. But if it ain't, then better to be ready than sorry, am I right, Mr Delpech?'

'You are,' said Jacob dubitatively, 'but if these seafarers are truly who you suspect them to be, what chance do a band of Quakers and a handful of merchant mariners have against an overcrowded craft of bloodthirsty rovers, sir?'

'Not a great deal,' conceded the captain straightforwardly, 'but I wager my honour and everything I possess that this ship can outrun 'em. We have the advantage of running downwind, while they are beating upwind. So, a quick blast and run should do the trick.'

'What happens if the wind drops off and they stalk us?' asked Jacob. He got the impression that his question had nettled the captain, who gave a stage smile.

The captain barked out a short laugh and said, 'Then at least we go down fighting and meet our maker earlier than expected, sir, don't we! They'll not take this ship, so help me God.'

This was not encouraging, thought Jacob; the captain was prepared to put his passengers' lives at risk to save his honour. There again, if they were caught by pirates, it would not only be the captain's honour up for grabs, but there were also plenty of young ladies on this ship, a feast for an unscrupulous crew. Yet, if he mentioned all this to his fellow passengers, they might have all their winds of blustery bravado knocked out of them. Then they would stand no chance at all. There again, this could very well be what it seemed at face value, couldn't it? A French merchantman sailing from New France. New France which was no longer at war with New England. Despite the terrible tragedies they had inflicted on each other, tragedies like the Schenectady Massacre that Jacob had read about and received firsthand news of, the French captain would have no bones to pick with an English merchantman. Like the English captain, the French captain would most likely just want to continue his course and deliver his load of goods and people safely to the port of Bordeaux or Marseille. Jacob concluded there was a good chance that this was not a pirate ship. But there again, what if it wasn't?

Filling the silence and perhaps anticipating Jacob's next question, Captain Wright said, 'Anyway, whatever her intentions, she's on a trajectory to the Bay of Biscay. Could be rounders, see.' He then explained to Jacob that rounders were pirates who took what was known as the Pirate Round, which went from New England to the north of Spain, down the coast of Spain and Africa, and round the cape, stopping at Madagascar before sailing onward to the Indian Ocean.

'Ah,' said Jacob, now better understanding the captain's reasoning.

The captain continued, 'With this sluggish wind, we could come broadside to broadside by first light, or if the wind picks up, it could be at night. We'll double up the night watch to keep eyes on her lights.' Captain Wright let out another bark of a laugh. 'There, that be the long and short of it!' he said, as if to end the conversation.

Paul had made new chums. His cannon team, to Jeanne's horror, situated starboard bow and full of bravado, savoured running the gauntlet and welcomed the chance to get in the first strike should it come to it.

Jeanne put her effects in order in their new emplacement, while Jacob found new subjects of conversation with the usually taciturn Welsh Quakers who ordinarily liked to keep themselves to themselves. As the interminable afternoon had sunk into evening, they analysed any news from above deck, discussed wind direction and velocity, and spoke of secondhand experiences of run-ins with pirates. 'They normally just take the valuables, I heard it said,' said Mr Evans senior, a bald and stocky man with an anxious brow.

'Sometimes, they take captives,' said his brother, a younger version of the former.

'Only the rich,' said Evans the elder.

'Could be worse,' said a farmer named Gareth. 'I heard barbary pirates force all the passengers into slavery, no matter who.'

'That is indeed true,' said Jacob with a little cough of authority. 'I knew a man in New York who had suffered such a humiliation, in fact his entire family, when the ship they were travelling on was taken by barbary pirates. Sold them into slavery in the Maghreb. A ransom was eventually paid, but he lost a son, and his remaining one is scarred for life, so terrible was the experience.'

'What became of him then?'

'A remarkable man,' said Jacob, 'he rose to become the lieutenant governor of New York, no less.'

'You mean that one who came to a tragic end, didn't he?'

Jacob's mind turned to a letter from Daniel Darlington in which Daniel described Jacob Leisler as a former slave. It had come as a surprise and had stayed with Delpech for some time after. It perhaps explained why the man had been so eager to help Huguenots fleeing persecution and a life in slavery on a galley ship if they were caught and sent back to France. But Jacob shook his head and dragged his mind back to the present.

'Yes, it did not end well for him.'

By the time the ladies had finished arranging their new spots, the buzz of the evening had died down into anxious whispers.

Women's voices became more audible as male bravado dissipated. Jeanne had exchanged slices of cured ham for a chunk of hard cheese with her new Welsh neighbour, who said, 'Is this to be our last supper, Mrs Delpech?'

Jeanne sensed the jovial remark was a poke in the eye of fear. In an equally jocular manner, she returned, 'I hope not, Mrs Evans, it would be a pity to let all this ham go to waste.' Then reassuringly, she said, 'But worry not, I am inclined to believe like my husband that the ship is nothing more than a merchantman from New France.'

'But there's no knowing for sure, though, is there?'

'That is true, Mrs Evans,' said Jeanne in a calm voice. 'That is why I don't know why we don't just set a different course and avoid the encounter altogether, be it friendly or hostile.'

'Well said, Mrs Delpech, my thoughts exactly,' said the lady as the watch bell sounded above deck.

But the ship kept its course. Men took turns to accompany the watch so they could relay the alert down below when the enemy came close enough.

Along with the four bells of the morning watch, just before daylight began to pale the sky, there came a banging on a cask. It was Garreth Williams who, having placed his lantern on a beam hook, was standing on the bottom steps as the captain had previously done before him. In a powerful Welsh bass, he repeated: 'Oyez, oyez, I have news!' There was an audible gasp, followed by a hum of mutterings from the gun deck, as waking women held their young close to their bodies and instinctively pressed their lips to their infants' skin. Sleepy-eyed men near their attributed cannon woke their neighbours with a shake of the shoulder.

'Good or bad?' called out one impatient woman standing near, holding a three-year-old child on her left hip.

'Neither,' said the Welshman. 'The fact is, either they've extinguished their lights, or they've gone and taken a different course.'

'If they've extinguished their lights, it can only mean one thing,' said one man. 'A surprise attack!'

'That is the fear, so we need to be vigilant.'

'What if they've just plain taken a different course?'

'Then we would have lost some sleep, that's all,' said the young Quaker, 'but we'll have the consolation of a peaceful slumber come morning.'

'Unless the weather has hidden them,' said Delpech, sitting up fully clothed next to Jeanne.

'That's the other alternative I was about to mention,' said the Welshman, more a man of the fields than of the sea.

With a flat palm on his left side rump to avoid making his bones click, Jacob got up from his paillasse and, upon Jeanne's insistence, put on his great coat that he had slung over their blanket to add extra weight. 'Let me have a look,' he said, as he made his way past the messenger and climbed the steps to the main deck, where the night was just beginning to pale behind the ship's stern. Emerging onto the main deck, he immediately noticed the big sail above him had been trimmed taut so that what breeze there was would pass over it at an angle. He cast his eyes westward in the chilly air, which was filled with suspended particles of water, over the bow to try to pick out the lights of the oncoming ship in the darkness. He could not. Not even the glow of the cabin lights in the dark sea. He surmised it was because the mist had thickened so that the lights were no longer visible.

'The mist is a camouflage,' he said as he climbed toward the captain, who was standing stiff as a board on the quarterdeck, having just come out of his cabin.

'Aye,' returned Captain Wright, his hatted head sunk into his coat collar. 'T'is thicker than expected, for them... and for us.'

'Which means the French merchantman might still be there, and closer than we think.'

'It does that, Mr Delpech,' said the captain. With his hands pressed into his pockets and a slight bow of his body, he said, 'There again, we too will be camouflaged until the sun rises and dissipates our cover.'

Catching on, Jacob said, 'You mean we could make a run for it in the mist.'

'There's enough time to take us out of harm's way, avoid an encounter, be they French or pirates.'

'I think that would be an excellent course of action, Captain,' said Jacob, hiding his relief that good sense might yet prevail and save the day, indeed their lives. 'And I think there's not a soul aboard that will not regret losing time to venture around a potential hazard.'

While the captain gave his orders to the crew, Jacob agreed to give the news down below, which he did to great cheer. Despite their bravado, it was clear to Jacob that no soul aboard really wanted to risk having to fight to the death, being maimed, or being captured and raped. Jeanne, for her part, wondered why in the world they had not simply opted to change their course from the outset. But at least, she noted, the episode had broken the ice, brought down barriers, and brought people together into a community spirit. A community that slept the cold and early misty morning away in the notion that they were still safe in their ark.

However, most passengers were still sleeping off a night fraught with anxiety and drama, when later that muffled and misty morning, there came the clomping sound of someone clambering rapidly down the steps. Jacob looked round and saw Gareth the Welsh farmer, who called out: 'Arise, arise! Ship sighted! She'll soon be upon us!'

'How far away?' fired back the gunner in a stern and steady voice.

'Barely a furlong, emerging from the mist!'

'To your battle stations, men!' hurled the gunner, visibly shocked.

'Wait,' shouted Jacob above the sudden din of men scrambling to their stations. 'What are her colours?'

'French. French colours, Father!' said Paul, hurtling down the hatch steps. He had been watching from the first yards and now hurried to his position at the starboard bow cannon, the first to fire.

'Then hold your horses, men!' shouted Jacob, precipitating to the steps. 'Hold fire, wait for the captain's orders!' Moments later, after quickly assessing the situation from the starboard balustrade of the quarterdeck, Jacob saw there was barely a furlong between them and the oncoming ship still partly shrouded in mist, the slanted rays of sunshine slicing across her mainsail. 'They keep the French standard, do they?' he called to the captain, who was staring through his spyglass.

'So far, yes,' he replied. Captain Wright knew as well as Jacob that a pirate ship would hoist the terrible black flag upon approach as if to foreshadow their villainy and so put the fear of death in the hearts of their prey. But as the two men stood side by side, for the first time since the dragonnades of thirteen years earlier, when French soldiers ransacked his home in the quiet township of Montauban, Jacob was relieved to see the white French standard as it continued to float atop the main mast of the oncoming ship.

News was quickly relayed below deck. Soon, instead of cannon muzzles, it was Quaker heads that peered through the gun ports as the French ship passed by.

As they passed slowly at two knots, twenty yards from one another in the calm sea, the French captain yelled into a mouthpiece, 'Bonjour, Capitaine! We changed course, and here you are! But we are truly glad to find you are English!'

'Ahoy, Captain!' hurled Captain Wright, his deep voice sounding like a foghorn in the mist. 'Same for us here. Glad to see you are French. Godspeed to you and safe voyage!'

'Thought we were lost in this cotton until I spied you thankfully with the day in your backs. Allow me to say there has never been a more welcome time for me to encounter an English ship! Where are you from?'

'Liverpool. Where are you headed?'

'Bordeaux.'

'Godspeed, Captain!'

'Fair wind, Captain!'

Jacob reflected on the moment that had passed in a few blinks of an eye as the eastbound ship travelled onward into the mist. Two ships passing at sea, having both tried to avoid an encounter. How rare a thing was that? And yet, he concluded, they were attracted like two drops of water. How often would ships pass in the like manner in ten years, a hundred years' time along these shipping routes, he wondered.

Turning to Jacob, the captain said, 'Oh well, at least one thing: there's nothing like the fear of death to bring people together, is there, Mr Delpech?' For a moment, Jacob wondered if the captain had played such a game before. But there again, he had changed course; the French ship would not even have been visible if it had not changed course too. And indeed, the clans had been scattered by the move, and people were speaking and sharing private food reserves with their new neighbours. It became a wholly different atmosphere below deck now, after experiencing fear entering their hearts together.

But that newfound unity was soon to be put to the test with the capricious changes of the weather.

CHAPTER 13

1699, Aboard the Mary-Ann

Jeanne redoubted the elements even more than the beasts in the sea, and when the dreaded storm came, slowly at first, then with increasing force, she vowed to God she would never again set foot on a seagoing vessel.

The ship with billowing sails roared along at great speed, the captain wanting to take full advantage of the high winds as the vessel dipped down prodigious waves and rose over vertiginous crests.

Knowing the battering to come, Jacob, for his part, had gone round making suggestions that loose baggage and chests be tied down, or they would risk sliding over the deck, crashing into the cannon carriages and possibly splitting open. Who would want their family linen strewn all over a soiled deck and washed over with bilge, seawater, and slops? Then he had arranged it so that the toilet buckets were emptied to save the deck from becoming smeared in faeces. He knew, however, there was nothing to prevent vomit from spilling over the deck, making it treacherously slippery, especially in a rough sea. He recalled once seeing a large Dutchman slip in a big storm and crack open his head on the butt of a cannon. That ship was lost to the sea with the Dutchman still in it. So, he had suggested they all sit as tight as possible and address any calls of nature beforehand to avoid doing so in the midst of the storm.

With the hatches battened down and prayers offered to their maker, the passengers braced for the severe shake-up that reached its peak in the middle of the night. The roar of the wind and sea, the gut-wrenching cracking of timbers, and the pounding of powerful waves against the hull became even more terrifying at night.

Jeanne had wedged herself and her children between a secured trunk and a chest, ensuring they wouldn't roll about the deck like loose wine bottles and thus keeping them from a thousand dangers. She glanced intermittently at Jacob when the dim light allowed her to. He had been through a shipwreck at sea before and kept an ear out to any treacherous sounds of the ship breaking up. Paul had refused to sit and wait; instead, he volunteered aloft to help with the sails in guiding the ship through the tempest. But despite the screams from the women and children aboard, by the end of the night, the ship had weathered the storm. Without realising it, the shaken passengers, fatigued by the long night, had naturally fallen asleep as the ship entered a slower cadence, rocking from wave to wave.

Jeanne and Jacob were both expecting to find the deck in chaos. So, when at last the battens were pulled open, letting in not a dingy light but the bright light of sunshine, they opened their eyes to a scene of heaps of sleeping bodies among their earthly possessions, with their children lodged between or flopped over them. Thanks to the foresight of securing loose objects to ship beams and posts, it all had remained a great deal as they had seen it last before the storm. But Jeanne did not respond to her husband's satisfied beam, and he knew the reason for the furrows of deep concern on her worry-stricken face. But the next moment, his deep and peaceful love for his wife became amplified on seeing her face suddenly transform as a wave of joy spread across it.

Another hatch was pulled open, followed by Paul skipping down the steps like a true seaman. 'Mother, Father...'

'Paul!' she exclaimed, not letting him finish. But the brash young man, not unproud of himself, announced his news. 'We are at Newfoundland! And we have weathered the storm!' Passengers had opened their weary eyes at the same time as the light flooded in from the hatchway. Paul said it again loudly, 'Ladies and gentlemen, we are at Newfoundland!'

The whole deck gave a sigh of relief and joy. And shortly after giving thanks in prayer to God, the ladies grouped together to put their part of the ship back in order, proud as they were that it had carried them safely through the greatest challenge yet.

CHAPTER 14

1699, Aboard the Mary-Ann

The grey outlook from the gun port of the barren island coastline did not live up to Jeanne's expectations.

There again, she was a southern French girl at heart, she told herself, a girl from the midi of France, brought up on the warm backdrop of peach-pink buildings and colourful orchards. She also sensed a natural aversion to this land, it being in the hands of the French. However, neither did the other passengers find much to rejoice over in their first view of the New World. 'It's land all the same, though, init,' said Mr Williams, the husband of her new neighbour.

Gwyneth Williams, a short and buxom lady, in some ways reminded Jeanne of Ginette, the friend she had left behind in the northern Swiss canton of Schaffhausen. Gwyneth, like Ginette, was never short of a quip. 'But hardly my picture of the Promised Land, is it!' she said, peering through the gun port opposite them. 'It's all browns and mucky-baby yellow, looks bloody awful, it does!'

'That's because we're not there yet, are we,' said her husband, trying to be reassuring. 'Our land is further south in the New North Wales sunshine of Pennsylvania.'

'Well, I bully hope it's *green* New North Wales.'

'It will be, won't it,' returned Mr Williams, thrusting out his powerful chest, yet with a hint of reserve.

In truth, the captain had veered. The change of course while passing the French vessel, combined with the storm, had pushed the ship further north than he had predicted. The extra time added to the voyage meant that provisions could soon become low. They would have to begin rationing food and water if they were to survive the voyage to Pennsylvania. But there was a simple solution, claimed the captain, standing at the foot of the gun deck steps. 'We shall simply put in at Boston to water and bring on new supplies for the rest of the voyage down the coast of America.'

Jacob could barely keep a smile from his lips when he turned to Jeanne and said quietly, 'That means we can disembark at Boston and make our own way to New York. It will save us a journey from Philadelphia, passing through Indian territory.'

'Good,' said Jeanne contentedly.

But what happened next soon deprived the whole ship of any notion of victory and plunged its occupants into a drawn-out state of emergency for longer than one night in any storm. In short, the wind ceased to blow.

With rations dangerously low, there would have to be a change of weather soon, or they would starve. But a temporary reprieve to their hunger came when a shoal of fish thousands strong was spotted. The fishing proved good, and cod soup was served which, in the torment of their hunger, many vowed was the best thing they had ever eaten.

With a meal in their bellies and reassured that their catch would at least keep them from starvation, their main preoccupation turned to water, or rather the lack of it. There was, nevertheless, beer and wine in barrels that was watered down to extend the liquid ration with moderation, and after some discussion, was allowed by the Quakers as long as it did not impair one's relationship with the divine spirit.

The lull lasted five days, five days of only sporadic breezes that each time got up hopes and led to shouts of "Alleluia!" Each time, however, the wind would drop off a few hours later. The prayer leaders concluded that the Lord was testing them. 'We shall endure!' the congregation repeated, with faith and conviction strong in their hearts.

Once fully past Newfoundland, with nothing but sea and sky ahead, beneath, and above them, even the lookouts were finding it hard to keep watch in the sun without so much as a sea breeze to cool them down. Jacob raised the question of sighting land during a game of whist with Mr Evans and two others around a chest they used for a table. 'I got my idea,' said the Welshman, slapping down an ace of spades. 'Why don't we set up a pot? First to spot land gets the lot.'

'That should certainly be a fair incentive to the younger members of our ship,' said Jacob, who laid down a nine of hearts, which was the trump suit. Swiping up the trick, he agreed to participate in the pot.

Paul, for one, took up the challenge. But not so much for the stakes as for the pretext to take the place of sailors too hot to go aloft. He was seriously beginning to consider a career at sea; he could become a naval officer, couldn't he? But where should he start? Where would he train? He asked these questions of the bosun one day, a bearded sandy-haired Scotsman with tattoos on his forearms. They were sitting on the forecastle steps. 'The first thing you need to do,' said the bosun, holding his pipe, 'is to know your way around a ship, lad, learn the knots and get to know about the rigging.'

'Yes,' said Paul, 'I'm learning a lot already.'

'Aye, you're doing fine, lad. Then you'll need to learn the different states of the sails, how to trim them to make a vessel go faster than the wind that blows it forward. And you'll need to know how to tack into the wind and how to ride a storm. But first thing's first, eh?'

'Yes,' said Paul with a resolute nod of the head, 'learn the ropes, know my way around a ship.'

'And never forget this,' said the bosun in a low, gravelly voice, his widened eyes looking straight into Paul's. 'One hand for yourself and one for the ship. Always!'

Not only did Paul discover that, unlike his father, he had solid sea legs and a good head for heights from the moment he set foot aboard, he also felt the call of the sea.

Alone on the top yard, without fear or trepidation, he would look across to the horizon and dreamily repeat the exotic place names the bosun and other mariners had told him about and which he would visit during his naval expeditions: Dominica, Guadeloupe, Martinique, Puerto Rico; and then there was Port au Prince, where his father had landed as an indentured servant, and Jamaica, where Jacob had been forced to join a privateer ship. Added to these were the voyages recounted by the sailors, who loved to talk about the old times. It was not difficult to extract yarns from them, Paul found, neither was it too much for them to share their experience and learning with him.

Despite the listless sails, the calm sea nonetheless enabled passengers to walk on the upper deck in the warm air and the light of the sun, and experience in full view, the wondrous spectacle of the gigantic new creatures: great barnacled whales with striated gullets, turtles floating by, a swordfish leaping out of the water, and playful arcing dolphins. Often, the conversation would turn to the many strange creatures that the briny sea must host, given the breadth and depth of it.

But Jeanne for her part preferred to keep her thoughts firmly on land, making plans for their first steps in this New World. Jacob gave unfailing reassurances that he knew people in New York, and indeed in New Rochelle, where he had purchased the plot, and then Jeanne would laugh a nervous kind of laugh about the prefix added to each place name. 'Perhaps we should call ourselves New Delpech,' said Jacob with a laugh, secretly hoping that his friends had not forgotten him. After all, nine years was a long time.

Casting his mind back to those bygone days, he wondered if he would recognise New York at all, especially since the Leisler governance, and the war between New England and New France. And yet, his memories were as fresh in his mind as yesterday's news. But how had the Darlingtons weathered the storm of retribution he had read about? Daniel had been on Leisler's side during that confusing period when the English crown changed heads to that of the Protestant king, hadn't he? And hadn't he been among the first to answer the call of America's first army? Nine years already. Dear Marianne would not yet be thirty, but her grandmother would be quite advanced. That is, if they were still alive.

Alone with his thoughts in his hammock one afternoon, Jacob sat up, reached for his leather pouch, and pulled out the last letter he had received from the friends he had left in New York all those years ago. As he perused the message it contained, he heard a shout that must have come from the high sails: 'Land ahoy! Land ahoy!' *Sounds like Paul has won the pot*, thought Jacob as he tried not to let in any intrusive thoughts of his son up so high in the mast, and of his keenness to learn the seafaring ways. Some of the passengers dozing in their curtained areas arose, some hurrying to the upper deck to see clearly for themselves, others moving to the gun ports that had been left open to clear the deck of the damp and the smells.

Jacob knew that land would not be visible yet from the deck, so he read on. He looked at the top of the letter again, dated February 12th, 1690. Such hard times to come for the New Yorkers, he thought to himself. In hindsight, his seven and a half years in Ireland might have saved his family. Then he wondered about the mention of a certain Ducamp, a name etched in his memory with the many episodes of his life associated with it.

CHAPTER 15

1690, New York

THE DARLINGTONS — 9 YEARS EARLIER

The Twelfth of February, 1690

Dear Jacob,

I take up my quill aboard my ketch as the world about us here in the province has been turned upside down. We now find ourselves in the midst of war with the French in Canada, who have massacred innocent people and destroyed the frontier town of Schenectady. I had just visited my aunt and uncle there but a day before. I have been told they were all killed, and that my cousin, his wife, and their children were slaughtered in cold blood, then scalped, and their house burned down.

I am sailing down the half-frozen Hudson to report the news in New York with my good neighbour, Monsieur Ducamp, one of your countrymen here with his English wife, now converted to Protestantism. I cannot describe my anger and sorrow. But my concern now turns to those who would paint Leisler in a bad light; he has been incessantly vilipended by the grandees jealous of his

rise to power. Marianne and her grandmother said that no good
could come of this infighting, especially when the opposition is a
member of the establishment and now finds himself imprisoned
at Fort William. I refer to Monsieur Nicolas Bayard no less.

My darling Marianne has been a tremendous support to me,
although I have yet to tell her about the terrible killings. I love
her every day more, if that is at all possible, and thank my lucky
stars you took her to the island where we met, surely by the hand
of Providence. She is nigh all the family I have in this world now.

Your friend and servant,
Daniel Darlington

A cold, howling wind pushed the ketch round the impressive half-moon battery still in construction. Ducamp reefed in some more canvas as Daniel, at the helm, carefully steered the ketch into the docking bay in front of the New York Stadthuyse.

While Didier dealt with the sails, Daniel cast a mooring rope toward a big Dutchman named Davey, a docker in his forties, who caught it with his large hands. 'Surprised you made it down the river, it being so full of floating ice, Danny boy!'

'Took a few knocks, but she's none the worse for wear,' returned Daniel, who had something else on his mind.

The Dutchman, who had known Daniel since he was in breeches, cast an eye toward Ducamp as the Frenchman called out. 'You go on, I'll finish up here and unload the lumber with Davey and the lads.'

Davey gave a nod of agreement, while Daniel, stern-faced, gave a curt nod and then leapt onto the quay, where a warming fire burned invitingly in a wrought iron basket. Glad to be back on firm land after a week on the icy river, he rubbed his mittened hands over the fire. 'Governor in town?' he called out, dropping the 'lieutenant' prefix from the title for simplicity.

'Believe so,' said Davey, placing a mooring rope over a post. 'Either at the fort or at his house, unless he's down by the construction. Never in one place for long, is he?'

'Thank you, gentlemen, I'll leave you to it.'

Darlington gave another nod, then set off into the bustling street of New York, where at this time of day he imagined most people were heading for their noon meal. With his duffle collar turned up against the chill, walking alone in the sharp wind, he allowed his thoughts to sail back to his Aunt Millie. But Daniel was a known face; apart from his excursions to the southern seas, he had lived in this city all his life, and everyone had probably known his parents, an English clergyman who had wed a Dutch girl. He walked into the marketplace just a stone's throw from the dock, with its mix of Dutch façades and English-style brick houses, as if into the embrace of an old friend. He flecked away a cold-weather tear from his left cheek as intrusive thoughts of his mother and now of his aunt flooded his mind's eye. With his right hand, he seized a hand thrust out in front of him from the cluster of merchants standing at the marketplace, where market sellers were carting away their wares and others were having a bite to eat—bread, cheese, and dried sausage—before they headed back to their homes in the country.

'Ah, Darlington, see you're back,' said the clean-shaven, well-heeled merchant with an affable smile. 'Haven't seen you for a while.'

'Mr Holden,' returned Daniel, gesturing to his own soiled coat and trousers. 'Just back from Albany.'

'First ray of sunshine in weeks,' said Mr Holden. 'Let's hope we're in for a thaw.'

Daniel sensed he was about to plough into conversation, so with a polite smile, 'Can't stop, Mr Holden,' he said, following into step while calling back over his shoulder. 'I'll be in touch later; I have lumber aboard.'

151

Walking on toward the fort across the thoroughfare, Daniel reminded himself he would have to send word to his cousin in Boston as soon as he got home to Marianne. *Home to Marianne* had become a refrain that had taken up residence in his mind, for home with Marianne was all he had left. He knew what the terrible act of Schenectady meant as he felt for Wendell's message in his pocket to make sure it was still there. He knew he was carrying a summons that would change Mr Holden's, Marianne's, and everyone's lives. For it was a summons to open warfare.

The ketch had been reported rounding the port. The fort guard informed Daniel amicably that the lieutenant governor was waiting for him at his residence on the Strand.

Daniel took long strides to cover the short distance down the narrow streets, layered in sludge and snow, to Leisler's house, built in the Dutch style. Fifteen minutes later, Daniel had been given a chair and a plate at the table and had already announced the tragic news of the massacre to the gathering in the dining room that included Leisler, Jacob Milborne, who was becoming Leisler's scribe and his right-hand man, and two other men of rank. He had visibly interrupted a working meal.

Leisler said nothing at first. He had simply stood up amid the room stunned into silence and approached the garden-facing rear window. This was a test, thought Daniel, who in the past had not doubted Leisler's capacity for leadership. But here, these were lives lost through division and lack of an appropriate watch. The French had simply walked in, looted, and destroyed an entire village. How could such a force travel so far, undetected through English territory? Was it not a direct consequence of all this division between the Williamites and the Jacobites, even though they were on the same side?

At last, Jacob Leisler turned to face the room. To Daniel, he said, 'I am truly sorry for your loss, my friend. I am sorry for the needless loss of all those victims.' Then, staring into the middle distance, he addressed the room and exploded: 'But, God's wounds, it needn't have happened! I knew it, we all knew it; we had all been given fair warning that the French would attack. And yet, the Jacobites resisted. I even signed a commission for Lieutenant Rust to take twenty-five men to watch the northern trails. It was rejected!' His voice was firm and precise, with a hardly perceptible hint of a German accent.

'It is true,' seconded Milborne. 'Darlington's family would still be alive if it weren't for those meddling Bayardites!'

'We must act swiftly. We must stop Bayard's faction from celebrating their constant lies. Why, if he had not stirred up emotions in Albany against me, there would have been better management between Schenectady and Albany. We must stamp out the treasonists before anything. Next, we'll determine what aid we can send to those poor wretches. If ever there was profit made of disunity, here it is.'

'I believe Albany will concede, given their guilt in this tragedy,' said Milborne. 'But I fear the French may be upon them even now.'

'We must call a meeting; then I propose we organise an inter-colonial conference to form a united front against the common enemy. For it is clear, the French are a constant pest and must be eradicated if we are to sustain our livelihood in this place. We cannot wait for news or troops from London. We must act now. It is time we built our own American army, composed of the men of diverse origin who love this, our home, which unites all men and women in the desire to speak freely and celebrate their faith as each man sees fit.'

Lieutenant Governor Leisler left a natural beat as the room let out: 'Hear, hear.'

Turning to Milborne, he said, 'Jacob, I want you to call an emergency meeting this afternoon. We do not want panic on our hands, but we must be seen taking immediate action. We will need to reassure our citizens that we know about the situation and that we are doing something about it. Our first course of action must be to weed out potential traitors. Any Jacobites must be considered friends of our enemy, and as such must be confined accordingly.'

'Yes, sir,' said Milborne. 'And would it be pertinent to inform the town criers?'

'Yes, yes, of course, they must be briefed, but not before we meet with our assembly.'

'Yes, sir,' said Milborne.

'And we shall have to send word to our church leaders.'

'Yes, sir.'

'And Daniel, I suggest you take some rest; I would like you to convey our message to Albany when it is ready.'

'Unless I organise a voyage, sir,' interrupted Milborne. 'It will allow us to see how the ground lies in Albany.'

'We shall discuss that later. In the meantime, gentlemen, we have our work cut out.'

The dreadful news that Darlington relayed hit like a cannon blast over the new battery of New York, to the gates of Broad Street and beyond.

It devastated his own household and momentarily shattered the spirits of its occupants. Even Marianne's hardy grandmother sat mute as a map, her traits drawn and pale when, later that evening, Daniel arrived home and recounted what he knew about the tragedy.

The initial cheer and relief upon his homecoming had become quickly sobered when Marianne sensed all was not well.

'Are you all right, Daniel?' she had said. He delayed his reply, visibly processing how to deliver something hanging on his mind that moistened his eyes and made his usually affable mouth twitch glumly at the corners. At last, he had told her he had something grave to announce. After letting Marianne slide his coat from his shoulders and pass it to Claudine, with gravitas, he had taken his usual chair at the dining table and told of the terrible news and the loss of his relatives.

'Good Lord,' said Madame de Fontenay after a long silence. 'What are we coming to when so-called Christian soldiers slaughter innocent people? And the poor children, the poor angels...' She did not finish her sentence. Instead, she stopped her mouth with her kerchief, clenched in her knotted fist. The only solace was to say a prayer, which Daniel led.

Later that evening, after watching, half-mesmerized, his son suckling at his wife's breast in the lamplight, Daniel slept like a rock the moment his head sank into the fragranced feather pillow.

It was a glorious morning that greeted Marianne as she pushed out the shutters of their southwest-facing bedroom window to change the chilly air in the bedroom. The snow-covered graveyard, and the fields to the right that met the North River, glistened under a crystalline sky. Letting the sunshine into the cold room, she gave a sigh and asked God in heaven why couldn't all in the human world be as well. But it was not.

Daniel was already up. She could hear the metallic sounds from downstairs as he shovelled ash and prepared the fires. She had encouraged him to get some rest, but he told her he would have to drag himself into town and speak with Leisler. 'There will be consequences,' he had said. 'If Albany falls, it will be like a dam breaking upstream, and the beaver run would be lost.'

They did not speak of the massacre. Instead, he talked of selling the lumber he had brought back from Albany, where it was still plentiful and cheaper than in New York. What with the lack of lumber on the market due to the epidemic of smallpox, and the dwindling forest every year pushed further back from their doorstep, demand would be high; it would fetch a good price. Then he would moor the ketch at a safe cove further down river.

'Can't the lumber wait a day or two?' insisted Marianne, holding the baby on her hip opposite him, as he stood booted and cloaked for the season in front of the door.

'Can't, my dear wife. I would very much like to, but this, I'm afraid, is war.' The three-letter word, so short and yet so grave, came like a bolt out of the blue. He then held her squarely by the waist. 'And this is my family, the most precious thing I have in this world, and I won't let them come here!'

Wasn't that how his uncle and cousin must have felt about their family, she wondered. 'But Daniel...' She was about to say something about going to church, but she let it go.

'This is no time for me to be sitting still,' he continued with a reassuring smile. After making sure no one was looking except the baby in her arms, he then kissed her on the lips before putting on his fine felt hat and striding out to face the cold, sun-filled air. It was a fine morning. He did not take his horse, preferring to continue at a brisk pace to the city gate and down the broad thoroughfare.

The street was crowded near the market square, despite the recent outbreak of the pox. People still had to eat. As he walked, to steer his thoughts away from the massacre, he mulled over how the town had changed since he was a boy, running through the muddy lanes of New Amsterdam, as it used to be called, that were flanked by houses largely made of wood. Nowadays, with fortunes in the making or having been made, bricks made from River Hudson clay were increasingly used. Cobbles were no longer restricted to Hoogh Street, which some had termed Stone Street, as it was the first to be paved in stone. He recalled how his mother would go off in Dutch about the quagmire during the thaw as he made his way past the fort and the marketplace to his first port of call.

Ducamp was already at the docks. When they had moored the ketch, while Daniel was giving news to Leisler, Didier oversaw the offloading of the noble logs for beams, the rough-hewn planks, and any firewood. He ensured they were properly stacked, and today, he had brought in extra hands to store the good planks in the lockup, taking care to stack them with aeration layers between each plank.

Meeting Daniel at the brazier, rubbing his large hands over the embers, Ducamp looped his head toward some timber merchants who were inspecting the quality of the arrival and said, 'Told them you would be down this morning.'

'Good. They must be keen,' said Daniel with a winning grin as Mr Holden, cane in hand, came up to shake his hand.

'Darlington, there you are. Good lumber, it's needed, and there's a demand for firewood more than anything else. This winter seems to have burnt through the equivalent of last year's worth already.'

'We have plenty,' said Daniel.

'And most importantly, there's the city walls repaired and being reinforced with double layers of hardwood,' said Holden. Then, almost as an afterthought, he added, 'Did they have a wall at Schenectady?'

'Yes, they did,' Daniel replied, wondering to himself too how the French had gotten inside so easily. Schermerhorn had told him they had entered and surrounded the houses before anyone had given the alarm. The stockade must have been too low or in want of repair, he thought to himself, as he tried to recall how tall the palisades were at Schenectady. Would an uncleared snowdrift have raised the ground? But he would soon come to learn that the north gate had not been closed during the night, and that the French simply walked in like a breeze without any resistance at all.

'Mr Darlington?' said Holden, as Daniel dragged his thoughts back to negotiating a good price for the wood for the sawmill owners and master builders who were completing the wall reinforcements. They might be in the midst of a war, but Daniel was still a merchant, capable and obliged to make some coin from any event or situation. 'Mr Darlington, do you have a price in mind?'

'No,' said Daniel, almost absent-mindedly. 'Do you?'

'Well,' said Holden, touching his chin, 'I should like to purchase the whole lot. What do you say?'

'And where will it be stored?' said Didier Ducamp, stepping in, seeing that Daniel seemed slightly absent. Daniel had once previously told Ducamp that the last time Holden made a purchase, he left the wood at the warehouse longer than he said he would, which had caused Darlington to rent extra space.

'We'll still need to store it till Mr Holden can take it away,' said Daniel, again dragging his thoughts back to the present negotiation. 'But I expect it will be removed in a timely fashion by the time we need to fill the warehouse again.'

'Hope so,' added Ducamp, 'because storage costs money.'

'I can arrange for it to be taken away by the week's end,' said Holden. 'Anyway, they are saying the whole town was burnt down to the ground. Is it true?'

Daniel was about to reply when a sergeant came up to him with a summons from the governor. 'Pray, excuse me, gentlemen,' said Daniel, turning back to Holden and Ducamp. 'I must go.'

'I say, must that Leisler make everyone hop?' said Holden, slightly narked. 'Pray, just give me a price before you go.'

Daniel stated his price. Holden responded with a merchant's dubious jeer, prompting Daniel to start leaving. 'All right, hold your horses, one moment,' Holden called out. 'I will take it.'

'Good,' Daniel replied. 'Now, I must be off.'

The ground was still hard and crunched underfoot despite the spell of sunshine, as Daniel made his way toward Fort William.

This interminable winter would soon be reaching its end, he thought to himself, and the thaw would properly begin. The two rivers and the bay beyond the battery, now so barren and bare, would soon be filled with a forest of masts and billowing sails. The river traffic of sloops, ketches, yachts, frigates, and flouts would reach its peak from June to August during the beaver trading season. At that time, when the Five Nations Indians came with their castor sec and castor gras pelts, every conceivable shallow-draft vessel would join the ebb and flow from Albany to trade for the precious pelts, the profits of which made this city a thriving trade counter today.

The beaver was everywhere in New York society, from the name of the transatlantic ship—in which Daniel had once travelled to Holland—to Albany, previously known as Beverwijck. All in the name of the beaver, men would kill, massacring women and children, and now, things were about to get even nastier, if that were possible, to protect the trade routes to the beaver-rich regions to the north and west. All in the name of the beaver—was it ethical? Daniel wondered.

Beaver was not the only fur traded, but to New Yorkers, beaver pelts were like gold dust to the Spanish in Peru. On his only trip to his mother's birthplace near Amsterdam and then to his father's hometown in the south of England, Daniel was able to gauge the popularity of the pelts in England and Europe, particularly for the manufacture of felt hats and such like. This demand had turned modest traders into rich merchants. All in the name of a creature that would probably become extinct before demand for its pelt fell, just like its European cousin, the Baltic beaver.

A single pelt could buy you passage up the river, and each pelt had a value that the connoisseur could determine as well as a vigneron grades the worthiness of a wine—considering the thickness, size, and colour, which indicated whether it was a castor gras or castor sec. Darlington knew that the castor sec was a recently skinned, stretched flat and dried pelt that still retained the guard hair, the long hairs that had to be removed, leaving just the soft felt. The castor gras was the most coveted sort. It was thicker, its guard hairs fallen, and its felt was made glossy by the constant friction against the skin of the Indian who wore it for a year, and whose sweat added sheen.

Was this the only reason that most people came and stayed here nowadays, just to tap into the beaver's misery? Now was the time for the spring hunt. He recalled that as a boy, he went with Uncle Alfric and his cousins Cornelius and Gerrit into Mohawk country to see Indians and trappers searching for beaver washes in the iced-over rivers west of Schenectady. He had learnt that spring beaver pelts were more valuable; they still had the heavy winter coat, and the further north, the thicker the hide. It possessed all the properties, and more, that the other skins did not have: it had sheen, softness, flexibility, elegance, and was watertight. That was almost twenty years ago. He remembered the Indians' delight at receiving steel knives for one beaver pelt, or precious fishhooks, shirts, and even hatchets. Daniel now wondered, as had that Indian back then, whether the white men were in their right minds. Had this lucrative trade blown up out of all proportion? Is this what nowadays encapsulated the American dream, where once it was all about getting a boat to a freer way of life? To a New World made up of men and women of all nations with the common faith in freedom for all, thought Darlington as he saluted the guard at the open gate of Fort William.

'He's expecting you,' said the guard, waving him into the fort, outside which soldiers were being drilled.

So, here he was, striding to the lieutenant governor's house on his left, intent on enlisting in the army. Ultimately, this would serve not only the security of his own family but also, by protecting the beaver trade, the crown in England. That is why he had made it clear to Marianne that he would not be joining the king's army for the sake of pelt tax, but the first American army for the sake of his family and the people.

Or was it Leisler's army? He admired the man very much, but wasn't he becoming dangerously close to abandoning the very fundamentals of the Charter of Liberties and Privileges of 1683, previously disallowed by James II, which Leisler had reinstated as the basis of his government? After the recent wave of arrests of Catholics suspected of vindicating the former Catholic king, wasn't he becoming too big for his boots, as the grandees and their followers suggested? And yet, Leisler always had the people's safety in mind, going as far as paying out of his own pocket to finance repairs to the city defences. But would the usurper of the established grandees become king of the castle? He did not know. All he knew was that Leisler was the only man he trusted to secure this town, and who had the know-how to do so. The battery was proof. It made New York impregnable by sea.

Darlington knocked on the door and went into the large room, the right side of which looked onto the quadrant. Leisler was sitting at the head of the large oak table.

'Ah, Darlington,' Leisler cried out, 'come in and take a seat.'

'Gentlemen,' said Daniel with a nod to the aldermen, composed of Milborne and other members of the committee of safety. Darlington had walked into a meeting and offered an apology.

'Nonsense, we were expecting you,' said Jacob Milborne, grave and cordial. He was sitting to Leisler's right. Daniel sat in one of two vacant chairs opposite him. The other, he was told, was empty because of smallpox. There had been new but, mercifully, milder cases of late, and one of the aldermen had it in his household.

'We have been discussing our defence and attack strategy, given the recent perfidious attack,' said Leisler. 'I intend to unite the sachems and call a general assembly with two representants from every county under my jurisdiction. After that, we intend to hold an intercolonial conference to create a larger colonial fighting force.'

'I agree, in union there is strength,' said Daniel. 'And I would gladly be among the first to sign up to defend our homes and liberties.'

'I know that, Daniel, but the reason I have asked you here is not for you to see action; rather, I need you to continue the river run. The thaw has not properly set in, and I need someone I can trust to convey a writ along with goods to Albany.'

'Given the state of the river,' added Milborne, 'I don't expect to be able to leave myself before early next month. But it is imperative that we send supplies earlier.'

'When?'

'The sooner the better,' said Leisler.

Milborne added, 'We need to be seen as reactive and caring.'

'Otherwise,' said Leisler, 'Bayard's faction will try to use the tragedy against us. We cannot bring back the dead, but we can and must bring solidarity and humanity to the survivors.'

Milborne gave a neat little cough and added, 'Then the Albany Convention can but admit to our goodwill and intentions and rally to the central governance of New York.'

'Hear, hear!' said the other members in unison.

Leisler continued, 'I want you to help source an initial supply of cloth, stockings, and other items for the Schenectady survivors. Also, the Albany garrison needs duffel blankets, and gunpowder along with horns to hold it in, hourglasses, and so on.'

'We have drawn up a list,' added Milborne, sliding a sheet of paper over the table to Daniel, who placed it in front of himself with the tips of his fingers.

'Can we count on you?' said Leisler.

'Of course.'

'Then I suggest, once purchased, you store the goods somewhere dry, anywhere but near the waterfront. I was thinking of the church here in the fort.'

'Yes, good idea,' said Daniel, 'I will ask Pastor Daillé. And what about finances?'

'Tell the suppliers to charge anything to my account,' said Leisler. 'I will sort out reimbursement later when we have more time. It's rather *act now, think later.*'

'I'll get to it right away.'

'Good. Then that's settled. We have already made out the list, as you can see.'

'You might add to it as need befits,' said Milborne.

'I will try to leave before the week's end, weather permitting.'

'Thank you, Darlington,' said Leisler, 'I knew we could count on you.'

Since it was Wednesday, Darlington stopped at the small fort church, located a few steps from the governor's office in the southeast corner of the fort quadrant.

Domine Daille, a mild-mannered and learned Huguenot with a caring brow, preached to the Walloons and Huguenots there twice a week. Marianne preferred his service for the same reason Leisler had not suggested the new French church of Saint Esprit, located on Petticoat Lane. It was not so much because painted ladies would gather there to offer their seductions on the infamous street, but more because Pastor Peiret, who preached there, was an outspoken anti-Leislerian influenced by his affiliations with the established New York oligarchy.

Pastor Daille willingly agreed to allocate space for storing supplies to help the refugees. He had led prayers that morning for the Schenectady minister who had been burnt alive in his lodgings. Indeed, the names of the deceased and horrible details of the massacre were now being divulged as further word followed Daniel and Didier from settlement to settlement in their wake, all the way downstream to New York.

After taking leave of Pastor Daille, Darlington left the fort and turned his feet toward the docks, where his warehouse was situated. Didier was finishing up along with a docker who was sweeping the wood debris into the street, which caused a street hog to come sniffing. Ducamp had served as a lieutenant before deserting the French army. His military training had left the warehouse full of stacked timber, stacked per type, easily accessible, and neatly arranged. Daniel peeked inside the lockup to see the glow of the hewn timber in the streaming sunlight of late morning that gave the place a golden sheen, as if it were a fabulous treasure vault.

'We just need to put the ketch in dry dock, and we can stop for a bit,' said Ducamp as he closed and locked the doors with a big iron key, which he then handed to Daniel. 'May says she'd forgotten what I look like. I expect your wife is no different, Daniel. And you'll be needing some rest, more than me. You need to beef yourself up, man.' Ducamp, the elder man, gave Daniel a pat on the back.

Daniel let out a laugh; he appreciated Ducamp's forthright and dry sense of humour. He might lack airs and graces, but he was a good man of the world, and Daniel found that, especially after the ride from Schenectady, they got along more and more. 'We must treat our wives,' said Daniel. 'You, May, and the littlun must come over one day for tea.' Daniel realised it sounded a little absurd and rather too delicate to ask a former seasoned French lieutenant to tea. 'It's apparently all the rage in Europe,' he added, almost apologetically.

'*Avec plaisir*,' said Ducamp, slipping into his native tongue with a wry smile. 'I'll tell May that we're invited to the Darlingtons. She'll be pleased. She's been trying to teach me the finer things in life.' Daniel chuckled at Ducamp's humour.

'And by the way, might not be necessary to put her in dry dock,' said Daniel, turning his head to indicate the ketch, anchored a stone's throw from the landing stage.

'Why's that?'

'They want us to transport supplies to the victims and the Albany soldiers for their defence in case of another night attack.'

'She'll still need a few repairs, though,' said Didier levelly. Daniel noted that he did not question the return journey. Ducamp continued, 'We took a few knocks, remember?'

'Too true. You'd better sort it out with old Stephen, the shipwright, while I fetch in the supplies.'

'We'll need space for storage while the repairs are being done, though, won't we?'

'Yes, and I just had a word with Pastor Daille at the fort church. We can store the supplies and cooper them there.'

'And there was me thinking you were going to the fort to join Leisler's army,' said Ducamp.

'So did I, but they prefer to use the ketch until the river becomes navigable for deeper-draft vessels.'

'I'm not fussed,' said Ducamp, 'told you, personally, I'd rather do this than enlist. I've done enough of army for one man.'

'Good man. We need to be weighing anchor before the week's end. Can it be done?'

'Can it not be?' said Ducamp, playing along. He knew there was another reason why Daniel wanted to get back to Albany so quickly: he needed to honour his dead. He needed to kneel before their graves if they had one. Ducamp continued, 'I'll talk to Stephen straight away.'

'Good man,' said Daniel, glancing up at the sky, where a cold cloud was now covering the sun past its zenith. 'He'll probably be over at the tavern. Old Mavis does a good soup.'

'Come on, then,' said Ducamp. 'It's bloody freezing down here by the water.'

The following Friday after the midday meal, despite the prodigious size of their bellies, Marianne and May insisted on marshalling the supplies that were to be carted into the cold quadrant of the fort in front of the church.

A handful of ladies from their circle of acquaintances had joined them, along with Mrs Elsie Leisler, no less, the provisional lieutenant governor's wife. An unaffected yet mild-mannered woman in her late fifties, Elsie was nonetheless a forthright and astute Dutch New Yorker. True to her Dutch heritage, she was accustomed to partnering in running the business of her busy spouse. The ladies had moved aside benches and set up trestle tables on either side of the central aisle of the small church. This arrangement allowed items to be more easily checked and prepared for packing into barrels outside.

Madame de Fontenay, who refused to be left out, was given a chair, some paper, and a quill and ink at the end of the table nearest the door. She was tasked with listing all items that were called out to her as they left the church. Content in her role at the head of the table, she embraced the opportunity. 'It will allow me to practice some new vocabulary of the *vernacular*!' she said, referring to the English language, which made the ladies laugh.

Madame Leisler, her twenty-year-old daughter, and their team of ladies checked and folded incoming ells of linen and serge, while Marianne and May took charge of the opposite tables of stockings, Penistone—which was a cheap wool fabric—and items for women which they knew that men would not care to even contemplate. Thus, rags and cotton wool were also discreetly prepped and packed on their stretch of trestle tables.

To the tune of the latest topic, the exode of more Catholics, the cold vernal sunshine flooded in through the church door, which was wedged open to allow the comings and goings. Meanwhile, outside, the cooper and his black mate, on loan from the brewery, packed everything into barrels for dry and practical storage during the voyage. Marianne noted that, in keeping with the reputation of former New Amsterdammers, the ladies naturally created an efficient work chain. They checked the length and refolded the fabrics and other items, then dispatched them to the end of their set of tables. There, a lady took them to the threshold, where she handed them to the cooper's mate, thus keeping the church flagstones free from muddy boots.

'Another six stockings, Grandma,' Marianne called out as Domine Daille sailed into the open church, carrying a hog's head of beer under one arm and a dozen wooden nesting beakers in a basket.

'I must say, well done, ladies!' he called out heartily. He was genuinely surprised at the progress, which he judged by the number of barrels lined up outside, waiting to be carted to the dock. There, Daniel and Didier oversaw the loading onto the main deck of the ketch.

'Many hands make light work,' Madame de Fontenay said in French to Pastor Daille, glad for the opportunity to express herself properly in her native tongue.

'Indeed, Madame de Fontenay, indeed,' the pastor replied as two Dutch ladies relieved him of his beer, basket, and beakers, which they spread out on a table like soldiers in a row. 'Thank you, ladies. I have brought some refreshment for you,' he continued. 'Lieutenant Governor Leisler told me you'd be thirsty.' Then, turning to Elsie Leisler, he said, 'Ah, Mrs Leisler, I have just been speaking with your husband about freedom of worship, something we all cherish so dearly here in New York, don't we?'

Anticipating the pastor's thoughts and shifting the conversation to English for all to understand, Mrs Leisler said, 'We do, Pastor Daille, we do, and no less so than my husband!'

May Ducamp turned to Mrs Leisler, whose forthrightness May particularly appreciated. Shrewdly giving Elsie a chance to further develop her point, she said foxily, 'And yet he has imprisoned rather a lot of Catholics, hasn't he?'

'That may be so,' said Elsie evenly, 'but only those papists caught conspiring to take control of New York or plotting against the new king.'

'There 'as to be order to reign over the chaos,' said Madame de Fontenay in her accented English.

'But the temptation,' said May, purposely provocative, 'is to go a step too far, and before you know it, you have a tyrant running the show.'

'And we from France all know what that can lead to, don't we?' said Pastor Daille, who then added, 'But of course, I have no doubt this is far from the case.'

'My husband is well aware there is a very fine line between religion and politics,' said Elsie in an affable tone.

'Indeed, indeed,' said the pastor.

'And let us face it,' continued Mrs Leisler, now becoming quite stern, 'if the papists did get in, they would certainly let in the French Catholics, and we don't want that, do we?'

'We certainly do not,' seconded Madame de Fontenay. 'We would be skewered and roasted in no time.' She reached over the table with the plate of biscuits to Elsie. 'Have another biscuit, Mrs Leisler, my own recipe.'

Interrupting the discussion, the distant sound of an iron door being clanged shut came from across the quadrant. All chatter suddenly ceased. Everyone but Mrs Leisler looked toward the outer door that led from the fort prison into the court as it creaked open.

'Thank you, Madame de Fontenay,' continued Mrs Leisler, nonchalantly taking a biscuit from the plate. Even Madame de Fontenay had turned her head and now stared through the open church doors to the far side of the quadrant, some forty yards away.

It was an upright woman, dressed in a black fur coat and sporting a flat-brimmed, high beaver hat, who stepped out and proceeded toward the fort gate. This was Mrs Judith Varleth Bayard, and she was accompanied by a slave girl. Even the cooper watched the lady, who an hour earlier he, like everyone else, had eyed as she had stepped into the fort prison. Everyone knew she had been visiting her husband, Nicholas Bayard, a high officer of New York and Jacob Leisler's archrival. With eight slave ships to his name, he was also one of the biggest slave owners in New York.

Mrs Bayard stopped her progress midway to the fort gate and glared across the quadrant where barrels were lined up outside the church. The doors of the church stood invitingly open to the sun-warmed day, bringing a gentle respite from the cold and frost, and an uplifting feeling that spring was not too far away.

The ladies turned their heads back to their toil and resumed their business as Mrs Bayard marched toward the church.

'Watch out, the witch is on the warpath!' said Mrs Stevensen, a large lady wearing a brown serge dress and in her mid-forties, old enough to know something of Judith Varleth's infamous past.

'I'll have none of that, please, ladies,' said Pastor Daille. 'That nonsense in Salem was dismissed many moons ago.'

'She was still found guilty, though, wasn't she?' insisted Mrs Stevensen.

'Lucky for her,' murmured May to Marianne, 'the then-Governor Stuyvesant stepped in and saved her from a dunking. Then he set her up with Nicholas Bayard fifteen years her junior, would you believe!'

'Yes, I remember you saying so,' said Marianne hurriedly. Like everyone else, she was curious to see what was going to happen. Would Judith launch an attack on Elsie, whose husband had incarcerated Bayard for plotting against him?

The cooper's black boy flashed the whites of his eyes at the oncoming dark form and became visibly more agitated. With an excess of diligence, he set about carrying the effects to the cooper, who was hitting the last wooden hoop to seal another barrel head.

'Ah, Mrs Bayard. Have you come to help?' called Pastor Daille, at a loss for words but trying to sound naturally affable.

Immediately realising his error, he stepped awkwardly out of the church to greet Judith Bayard. Not one of the ladies inside pretended to be occupied now as Judith sharply gave her reply in Dutch.

'Pastor, I cannot stop or disrupt your little get-together.'

'No, no. We are preparing goods to help those in distress following the terrible massacre at Schenectady,' said Daille, almost apologetically. But then he regretted saying that too.

'Well, you can pass on my husband's message of sincere sympathy for the sufferers of this tragedy. And please tell those usurpers to stop pointing the finger at him. He had nothing to do with the incident,' Judith pursued, steeling her eyes at Elsie Leisler and tightening her lips, which in the old days would have meant a prelude to an outburst or even a physical attack. However, Judith had decided she would keep her composure; she would not be ruffled or drawn into a common hen fight. In a sharp voice that pierced the crystalline air, making the seagulls flap and squawk, she said, 'Neither you nor your husbands will break us Bayards! Mark my words, the tide will turn as it always does. The time will come when some rogues will pay dearly for creating distrust and division in the king and queen's colony. For the true governor sent by the king is on his way!' With resolve, she then stamped down a foot and stood upright and righteous. 'Good day to you, ladies.' The cooper tipped his hat, the pastor humbly dipped his upper body, and the ladies in the church responded with an equally affable 'Good day, Mrs Bayard.'

But before she could stomp away to the gate, Mrs Leisler surged forward from behind her table. Now standing poised on the church threshold, she said sternly in a raised voice, 'Your husband owes his current position to himself, Madame. He scandalously set out on a campaign of defamation and slander, caused division even in Albany, and is the root cause of division in Schenectady, which has been destroyed. Have you people no sense of shame?'

'Shame?' squawked Judith. 'Huh! I beg your pardon, you petty thief. Your husband arrested my husband when he came to see our only son on his sickbed! And though he pleads his innocence, your usurper husband shows no humanity.'

'You talk of humanity? Your dealings in the town are not clear, and your ships transport slaves in appalling conditions...'

'And you are no better than one of them! Being the slave that you were, Elsie Leisler!'

'You nasty woman!' said Elsie. Everybody knew that Jacob Leisler, along with his stepsons and crew, had once been captured by Algerian corsairs in the English Channel. His ship, the *Susannah,* along with two others, was taken to Algiers, where Leisler was put under house arrest and the others sold into slavery before a ransom was paid. It had happened thirteen years earlier, in 1677, and her surviving son still bore the psychological scars of the terrible experience, which was never mentioned in the Leisler household.

'And I would be more humble if I were you,' insisted Judith, more calmly. She knew she had struck a nerve that could spark a frontal attack. High-minded, Judith pursued, 'What with another case of the pox around, anyone can be taken at a moment's notice.' Judith knew that her past of being accused of witchcraft was still in the minds of people and that this would put the fear of death into the onlookers. She knew that some would take her words for a spell. It was a genuine laugh that she let out. She was enjoying herself.

'She's going to cast a spell on us,' said one woman fearfully under her breath to her neighbour, standing at their trestle table.

Judith continued, 'Before being scurried off to their day of judgement, you will be judged like your usurper husband, Elsie Thymens Leisler!'

'Ladies, ladies,' said the pastor, stepping between the two women, both of whom had taken steps towards each other, reducing the distance between them to no more than twelve yards.

But then, as May Ducamp also approached, Judith abruptly turned on her heels and haughtily said to her maid, 'Come, Maisie, let us not linger within the reach of the devil!' She then stomped across the quadrant and out through the fort gate toward Hoogh Street, where she lived.

'What did she mean?' asked Marianne.

'Don't pay the slightest bit of attention to her,' said May. 'I've known horrid old birds like that before. Just smile back at them. And if you want my opinion, she ought to try standing in line with the girls on Petticoat Lane once in a while. One night or two would soon calm her nerves!'

'Oh, May, you do come out with the most outrageous things!' said Marianne, who had always been curious as to how those ladies performed their acts. She went on, 'Why ever do they do it?'

'All for money, no other reason,' said May, 'or else they starve.'

'I think I would rather eat worms,' said Marianne.

'You'd be surprised how many girls say the same thing, but then when faced with their imaginable bowl of worms, they take the coin.' No sooner had her remark left her lips than May told herself she must be careful in future not to let down her guard with such frivolous talk. But it was fun shocking the younger generation in this way.

However, her naughty smile quickly turned to a look of anguish when she saw Marianne suddenly freeze. Her lips drooped and her face grew livid as she tried to stabilize herself by placing her palms flat on the trestle table. Marianne was about to faint. 'God, quick, help!' May cried out as she positioned herself behind the young woman, holding her by the waist to prevent her from slumping to the hard flag-stoned floor. Four ladies dropped what they were doing and rallied to the two pregnant women. May relieved herself of the weight as Marianne collapsed into the arms of the ladies. They were able to gently lay her down on the floor, one woman unravelling a roll of linen beneath her, and another cushioning her head with a stack of woollen cloth.

Madame de Fontenay took charge, and despite her lame leg, she managed to kneel down using her cane, by her granddaughter's head. 'Loosen her corset,' she said, 'and move away so she can get some air.'

'We must get her home,' said May, recovering, with one hand holding her rump and the back of her other pressed against her forehead. At that moment, there came the jangle of a horse harness and the rumbling of wheels approaching the church for the last batch of barrels. 'Jack,' called May to the cooper outside, 'tell the carter to come in.' But it was none other than May's husband who appeared moments later at the door, wearing a look of deep concern as he viewed the scene before him, with ladies congregated around the nearest table to the right.

'What happened?' said Didier Ducamp, striding to the trestle table where Madame de Fontenay was holding a beaker of beer to her granddaughter's lips.

'We need to get her home to her bed,' said May, ignoring the question.

Didier gave a nod of mutual understanding to his wife. 'Are you all right?' he said.

'Yes, yes,' said May as the ladies made way for the burly frame of the former French lieutenant, who then dropped to one knee opposite Madame de Fontenay.

'*Oui, doucement, s'il vous plaît*,' she said with a nod of concern.

Ducamp placed his arms beneath Marianne's back and knees and gently scooped her up. 'Don't worry,' he said to the young woman, limp and pale in his arms. 'I'm going to carry you to the cart, and we'll get you home.' Marianne blinked once to show she understood.

'I'll come with you,' said Madame de Fontenay.

'Me too,' said May.

'I shall send for the doctor right away,' said the pastor as Didier proceeded with the young woman to the flatbed cart, where ladies had quickly laid a bed of fabric. Didier gently placed her down. He then helped her grandmother and May up the step, while the other ladies covered Marianne in a blanket made of coarse wool.

'What's up with her?' said Ducamp as he slid into the driving seat and took up the reins.

'I told her not to come,' said Madame de Fontenay, sitting with May on the bench behind the driver, with Marianne carefully wrapped up and lying at their feet. 'I have noticed she's been under the weather lately. But she insisted.'

'We shall see,' said May, in response to her husband's question, keeping her true thoughts to herself. For she had witnessed similar symptoms the previous autumn while tending the sick who had contracted the pox. Didier turned and fleetingly caught May's regard but said nothing. Instead, he turned back to Madame de Fontenay and said, 'I'll be going slow.'

Madame de Fontenay nodded to Ducamp and gave a look to May that needed no words. It read: *She is all I've got*. Neither lady mentioned the baby; there was no point stating the obvious.

As the cart trundled toward the fort gate which Mrs Bayard and her girl had walked through twenty minutes earlier, Ducamp half turned in his seat and looped his neck toward the old cooper. 'Jack,' he called out, 'better get your boy to run over to the dock and tell Mr Darlington to get himself home.'

The old cooper tipped his hat. 'Will do,' he called back.

'I told you she were a witch,' said Mrs Stevensen, speaking of Mrs Judith Bayard to the remaining cackle of ladies, as they saw the cart off through the fort gate.

'Don't know about that, but she certainly has power over folk,' said Mrs Leisler, standing next to her.

'Yes, power to do ill,' Mrs Stevensen returned. 'I would not cross her for all the silver in the world.'

CHAPTER 16

1690, New York

That afternoon, Marianne's temperature soared.

Having taken ownership of the patient's room, May insisted from the outset that Daniel neither approach his wife nor enter the marital bedroom. It would do her no good and only potentially spread the malady. For, as incomprehensible as it might seem, May had the intimate conviction that somehow, the devil could spread the disease through the air. After all, though you couldn't see the wind, you could still feel it, couldn't you?

But Daniel insisted. 'I want to see her,' he said, having stepped over to greet May and his wife's grandmother from the hall window, where he had been contemplating the encroaching darkness.

The ladies had just returned from the upstairs bedroom where May had instructed Madame de Fontenay to keep her distance. 'She is resting, Daniel,' said May, gently but firmly. 'I'm very sorry, but you'll have to be patient, I'm afraid.' For good measure, she then reiterated what the doctor had said earlier: 'He says she has symptoms of the flu.' However, she refrained from telling him the doctor had also mentioned it could be symptoms of the pox. Only time would tell. She continued: 'She is strong; she will get through it, Daniel.'

'But...'

Cutting short Daniel's remonstrance, the old lady added, 'And Marianne said she wants you not to fret, and to deliver the goods to the victims of Schenectady. She doesn't want their hardship on her conscience.'

Daniel, caught between his duty to the survivors and his deep concern for his beloved wife, still insisted, 'But I cannot just leave without knowing how she is...'

'We will take good care of her, Daniel,' said May. 'There is nothing you can do to help here. She is not in danger, just fatigued. She needs rest.'

'And the victims of Schenectady cannot wait, Daniel,' said Madame de Fontenay.

'Aye, we'll soon need to be catching the tide, man,' said Didier, who had risen from his chair before the fire that crackled in the hearth. He did not mean to sound unfeeling. Apart from the urgent matter of relaying the bare necessities to the victims of Schenectady, his intention was to bring Darlington away so that May, who had already proven her worth in such cases, could do as she thought fit.

After kissing his son, who was asleep in his oak rocking cot in the study, Daniel, heavy of heart, at last dragged himself away with Ducamp toward the harbour.

Trying to steer his mind away from intrusive thoughts of calamity, Darlington noted that the ice in the thoroughfares had lost its sheen and was turning grey. Rows of icicles under the eaves of houses dripped in the intermittent sunshine, and the bare trees along Broad Way glistened as the frost melted from their branches and boughs.

An hour later, Daniel and Didier cast off with the turn of the tide and set their course up the shimmering North River, now less cluttered with ice floes.

CHAPTER 17

1690, New York

May gave her a preparation of dried willow bark steeped in hot water to reduce the fever. Experience had taught May that the worst was yet to come, and she insisted that she was the only one who could sit with the patient with the dabbing sponge.

On the fourth day after Marianne's malaise at the church, May's worst fears proved to be justified with the appearance of a nasty rash. It was confirmation of May's initial dread: the poor thing had indeed contracted smallpox. May ordered her chaise longue to be brought from her house and placed in Marianne's bedroom, so that she could put her feet up and nap from time to time.

Madame de Fontenay initially resisted the take-over by this strong-willed English commoner, endowed with enough wealth to make her infuriatingly impertinent and overly confident. 'Madame Ducamp,' she said in a higher pitch than usual. 'You have been more than helpful, but I cannot have you risk the life of the child inside your belly to endlessly care for my grand-daughter. I shall stand in so that you may get some proper rest.'

'Impossible, Madame. And you know it.'

'I would rather risk my life than have you risk that of your child, Madame!'

'You wouldn't be much good to Marianne dead, would you? It would only complicate matters.'

'But you said yourself her case is relatively mild compared to those in town before Christmas.'

'True, but it would probably still kill you.'

In the end, Madame de Fonteney had to begrudgingly concede to May's infuriatingly implacable reasoning. In a final bid to have the last word, she said, 'But if it's a mild case, at least it means she won't get the scars, doesn't it?'

'Unfortunately, not, neither does it mean she is out of the woods. I only hope she does not miscarry.'

'I see. And if you lost yours, I would never forgive myself. And I don't see why only you can tend to her.'

'Madame, let me tell you; it is a gift sent to me from heaven,' May said, to reassure the old lady. 'I was five years old when I contracted the pox. Like Marianne's case, it was during a second wave, so it was not so virulent. I prayed to God with all my heart, and I survived. It is for this reason that I am immune to the disease today. My skin hardly shows any trace of scarring, at least none that powder cannot obscure.'

Subdued, the old lady replied, 'I admire your sense of community spirit, Madame.'

'I was lucky, let's say.'

But Marianne's condition grew worse as the rash developed into bumps. Spots appeared all over her body, including a few on her face in patches, giving her the irresistible urge to cry out in an effort not to surrender to the terrible itchiness.

'You must not scratch them,' May insisted, as Marianne lay trying not to move, trying not to feel her body for fear of it itching so terribly. 'Or the scars will remain, and if you start, you will be seized with a tortuous desire to continue.'

'It's... unbearable, I cannot stand it...' implored Marianne feebly.

'I can bathe you in oatmeal to relieve the itching, but you must keep the cotton gloves on at all times.'

However, the moment she felt calmed, her baby would invariably kick in her belly, making the taut skin tingle and in turn causing her to want to gouge the skin from her flesh.

Judging from their welcome upon their arrival in Albany, Daniel and Ducamp quickly ascertained that the consternation of Symon Schermerhorn's account—which was confirmed by other escapees—had already persuaded the Albany Convention to comply with the Leisler administration.

They also learnt that, at the fort, pro-Leisler Joachim Staats had replaced Captain Bull with just sixty men. To the dismay of the frontier townsfolk, Captain Bull had been recalled with his men back to Connecticut, where Governor Robert Treat feared an attack on his own colony. Daniel hoped that now that Leisler's summons would not be contested, he could ride on to Schenectady to see the aftermath for himself and to properly mourn his relatives who were savagely killed.

As Didier took charge of offloading the supplies, Daniel made his way to the town hall, where he was met by the aldermen. 'This is but an initial token, gentlemen,' said Daniel in response to the burghers' concern that it wasn't enough. 'Milborne will be arriving as soon as the river thaws with a much larger convoy of goods, military wear, and soldiers.'

'Then we should show our gratitude, Darlington, for once again braving the dangerous ice-filled waters of the river in this cold season.'

'Hear, hear,' the room resounded in agreement. Then Daniel presented Leisler's invitation for two representatives from Albany to meet him in New York on April 24th.

'Gentlemen,' he concluded, 'only in union are we strong!'

To Daniel's relief and satisfaction, the aldermen elected Reyer Schermerhorn, the elder brother of Symon, to represent Schenectady, and Jan Janse Bleeker to represent Albany at the forthcoming New York assembly. After the meeting, Johannes Wendell and Reyer Schermerhorn took Daniel aside. They praised and thanked Darlington for bringing the ells of cloth and other goods. Then, changing the subject, Daniel said to Reyer, 'Have you any news of your brother's family?' It was a calculated shift. Daniel desperately needed to face the gruesome facts about his own family so that he could prepare to face up to the charred bodies and scalped crowns.

'Yes,' said Reyer. 'Actually, that is why I wanted to talk to you.' As they walked along the wide and rutted Jonker Street, Reyer shared the news that his sister-in-law and surviving nephew, along with Reyer's youngest brother and sister and a number of slaves, had managed to reach the refuge of a farm, where they remained until the raiders had departed.

Wendell added, 'We sent a war party to give chase to rescue the captives and recover the fifty or so horses the villains took for carrying the loot. According to the latest messenger's report, our Indian scouts got close and watched them confront snowstorms that slowed their progress, making them run out of provisions and even resort to eating some of the horses. Our main party was rapidly closing in and managed to put some of the stragglers to the sword. But alas, the main bulk of the villains managed to escape across the frozen lake on sleds they'd hidden on the bank, prior to their loathsome attack.'

'Pity,' said Daniel.

Reyer sensed Darlington's polite impatience and said, 'But we digress. Anyway, by the grace of God, my brother has since recovered his family, save for his poor eldest boy, shot dead in cold blood. But I am sure you want to know about your own relatives, which is why I want to take you to my house before you have refreshments. You see, we believe we may have found your aunt.'

'My aunt?' said Daniel, stopping in his tracks. The other two men did likewise. 'I was given to believe she died in a fire.'

'We cannot be sure,' said Wendell.

'That is why we want you to tell us,' Reyer said, inviting the other two to fall back into step with him. 'You see, we found an old woman sitting beneath a hide in the freezing cold. That was all she had left. She was huddled next to a fire, beside which she had pulled dead bodies. When asked who she was and who they were, she simply looked up and said: "They are still mine." Then she said no more. She was brought back here and given a room at my house. We were going to send for her son in Boston to identify her, given that she is not speaking. My brother knew her husband but did not know her so well, and besides, it would seem that the death of her loved ones has left a tragic toll on her. Neither Symon nor his wife recall her looking so frail.'

At last, they entered the large house of Reyer Schermerhorn. Reyer walked along the corridor and knocked on the door at the end of it. 'May I enter, madam?' he said through the door as a matter of courtesy. After another knock, he announced, 'There is someone here to see you, madam.' Then the door opened. 'Is this your aunt?' he asked, turning to Darlington as a little old lady appeared on the threshold. Her dark shawl and skirt, obviously given to her, were a size too large and accentuated the fragility of her appearance. The little lady looked up at the tall figure of her nephew.

'Aunt Millie,' he said, as gently as if the mere expulsion of words could puff out the light in her dark eyes.

'Daniel,' she said, tears welling up. 'They have gone.'

'Yes, Aunt Millie. They have gone, the Indians and the French have fled. You are safe here.'

'No, Daniel, *they* have gone, haven't they?'

At that moment, Daniel understood. Cradling her hands, he walked into the bedchamber and led her to a chair. Reyer discreetly left them to themselves and gently closed the door behind him. 'Yes, Aunt Millie, they have gone. They are with our Lord now.'

Daniel sat with her for an hour. He told her he would take her back to New York with him, and she gave two tearful nods in agreement. He would send for Cornelius, her son in Boston, but she would stay with him and Marianne as long as needed. Unable to speak, she nodded again twice.

On the mention of Marianne, the intrusive thought of her flashed through his mind, and he wondered how she was faring. Surely, she would be over the worst by now. But had she lost the baby, as often happened? He realised he must prepare for that eventuality. Soon, however, his mind would become even more crowded with thoughts—too much so to dwell on his personal issues—which perhaps wasn't such a bad thing, seeing as he could do nothing about them anyway.

That afternoon, Darlington and Ducamp were at the tavern when Alderman Wendell burst through the doors with the terrible news of another mass killing.

Darlington had been hiring horses for the ride to Schenectady, even though he lacked the heart for it. Wendell placed his large buttocks on a stool at the table near the fireplace, where the two New Yorkers were spooning down broth and supping beer. He said, 'It's a small settlement north of Albany, in Mohawk territory, about an hour's ride from here.' He explained that there was a fair chance the French raiders did not know the terrain. 'They can still be caught,' he said, his eyebrows crossed like a challenge. 'But the problem is, we need volunteers.'

'Send soldiers,' said Ducamp, who had already guessed Wendell's intention.

'We can only spare five or six at the most,' Wendell explained. 'Our war party is still up in New France, and now that Captain Ball has departed with his men, Captain Staats has only sixty men left to defend the fort here. It would be all too easy for the perfidious French to draw them out and then take Albany by surprise, God forbid!'

'I will join the chase party,' Daniel declared, his voice cold with contained defiance.

'Then you'd better count me in too,' Didier added, sighing softly.

The ruins were still smoking in the clear, cold air when they arrived at the settlement the next morning. Bodies lay frozen stiff outside the cluster of burned-down houses. Inside, Daniel stumbled on the charred remains of children. The scene, which likely mirrored many in Schenectady, filled him with horror and a visceral rage.

As for Ducamp, the sight and the stench of death only brought back scenes that, when recalled from the hidden vaults of his mind, never failed to make him feel bereft of humanity and hope, as if nothing existed beyond death—no judgement, no retribution, no punishment, no hope. What was the point of building a family if it all just turned to dust? This had been his sentiment after the death of his first wife and child, both lost to a distemper back in France. But since teaming up with May, his sense of hope had been reborn. It now lived in his adopted daughter and the child May was carrying in her belly.

Having read the Bible and reflected on the belief of natives in a supreme spirit, he had come to accept the existence of his own soul and God. Regardless of the form God might take, he had come to accept that one day, his soul would face its day of judgement. He desired with all his heart for his child to live in honour, trust, and justice, and in the fear of that divine retribution, so that they might reunite in eternity. Maybe one day, he would also meet his first love and child in the place they called heaven. He fondly remembered her wrath whenever he left for battle, and her sweet, lingering presence in the perfumed scarf she left in his pocket—a scent like that of an angel that soothed his war-weary spirit. It just made sense to him now.

He wondered to himself if these unrecognisable settlers were now in heaven or hell. Not knowing them from Adam, he said a silent prayer for their souls to rest in peace and let the thought go. Then, he heard himself say out loud, 'Their bodies should be buried before the wolves find them.'

Daniel agreed. However, the designated military leader, a young lieutenant, insisted they follow the tracks left in the snow. 'It's fortunate it hasn't snowed since they left,' he added, pointing to the snow tracks with his elbow while cupping his pipe in his hand.

Ducamp knew the younger man was right. It would have been his choice too if he were the young lieutenant he had once been. If they were to stand any chance of catching up with the murderers, there was not a moment to lose. 'They will be laden with loot,' he said, nodding his head slowly. Despite his newfound faith, he was nevertheless still a trained soldier after all. He had not forgotten how to cleanly kill a man. When he had started out with Darlington and this party of cavaliers through the snowy trails, he had questioned whether he could kill again. But now, seeing the disgraceful destruction of life and feeling the strong sense of injustice, he knew with certitude that he could.

Daniel also agreed with the young lieutenant. He said, 'They probably don't know of the pass that cuts through the valley, halving the time to get to the northern side. Instead, they'll likely take the river route. If we ride hard, there's a good chance we will catch up with them.'

'We can head them off if we leave now,' the lieutenant added slowly. 'So, are you with me?'

The sentiment of injustice being stronger than any need for ceremony, they forfeited the burial for the chase and retribution. Having mounted their steeds, they kicked into a gallop, each rider seething with determination to bring these French perpetrators to justice. As they rode out, the squawks of the famished carrion birds echoed in the beautiful snowy scene nestled behind them at the foot of the hills.

However, as they followed the mountain trail, pushing their steeds wherever the path was clear, they soon noticed a fine tendril of smoke rising at a slant on the backdrop of the wooded hill and darkening northern sky. Daniel glanced to Ducamp to his left who, standing on his stirrups, silently gestured for the party of eight men on horseback to halt and rally.

'It could be trekkers,' said the young lieutenant, noting that they might not be the perpetrators of the killing, as the windblown tracks abruptly stopped where they logically should have continued toward the river.

'Whoever they are,' said Daniel, 'they must have seen the fire from the houses ablaze.'

His steely eyes levelled at the lieutenant and his men, while Didier suggested, 'Let's stay in the saddle and get as close as we can, the wind being to our advantage.' The young lieutenant nodded; he didn't need further explanation to know that the north wind howling through the valley would largely cover the sound of their approaching horses. Ducamp added, 'Then we dismount and approach on foot.'

Onward they rode, the slow rhythm of horse hooves muffled by the deep snow; they were confident that their target would not be moving on till morning.

It was an hour to sunset when the party dismounted by a cluster of bare, slender trees near a half-frozen brook. As they secured their mounts to the branches bowing under snow crust, Didier said in a low voice, 'We'll be coming from the high ground on the dark side. Suggest you stay back till we're on them.'

'Signal?' asked the lieutenant.

'Two owl hoots,' replied Didier.

'Let's be done!'

The party then split up, leaving one man behind with the horses to watch for wolves. Didier and Daniel climbed up the wooded, west-facing hillside. The ascent was heavier than anticipated. They endeavoured to weave their way down the other side to the camp through the deep snow, making as little noise as possible. One snap of a stick too many could betray their presence. However, time was on their side; the men below were burrowed in for the night.

'French woodsrunners. Maybe scouts,' whispered Daniel to Ducamp as they peered through the sparse undergrowth onto a clearing set back ten yards from the main mountain trail. Hides had been layered around three poles in the Indian fashion, and in a last blaze of orange dusk, smoke coiled through the apex where the poles crossed.

The French called these men *coureurs de bois*, as they were known for travelling in extreme conditions. Daniel and Ducamp were well aware that their long exposure to nature would have taught them to be astute, rough, and ruthless. They also knew that woodsrunners usually wintered in proper accommodation to prepare for the new season and the trek into the wilderness to trade with French-allied Indians. Darlington was suspicious of their presence here; it was highly unusual at this time of year. Could they have been part of the raiders that destroyed the village?

'I make out three?' whispered Ducamp, bending an ear to the conversation inside the makeshift tent.

'We have no proof against them, though,' Daniel responded.

'They'll know something for sure. I'll go once the sun's gone down. Cover me.'

'Wait,' Darlington interjected, 'why not draw them out first?'

'More control in a small area,' Ducamp explained. 'And woodsrunners might have an Indian. Keep out of sight and cover me.'

As the winter sun dipped behind the trees, Daniel gave the nod. In the purple light, Didier moved to the rear of the tent, crouching as he went, the French voices covering the crunch of his boots on the snow.

'Or I'll be pissing in me boots,' one of them quipped in French. As Didier settled to the rear of the tent, Daniel, from his spying position, saw the west-facing flap push outward from the glowing interior. A broad-shouldered Frenchman stepped out, clad in skins and a beaver fur hat, and took five paces forward while reaching inside his pants.

From the stillness of the shadows, Didier watched the woodsrunner douse the snow with a long, drawn-out pee. He noted the man was carrying an axe at his belt and a knife dangling from a leather thread around his neck. *This will be easier than he expected*, Didier thought, planning his next move. He waited for the man to finish and reach the flap. As the Canadian pulled it back, Ducamp, in one swift movement, swung around from the side of the tent and pressed the barrel of his flintlock against the back of the man's neck. 'Hands in the air!' he commanded in French, aiming his other flintlock into the tent. 'One false move and your friend's dead!' He then ordered the big man to pull back the flap so that it remained wide open.

Sensing that Ducamp could kill on a whim, the other two woodsrunners inside rose carefully, their hands held limply in the air. Ducamp took five paces back. 'You, turn around!' he commanded. The big man complied. 'Now, out! All of you,' he barked, and the two woodsrunners inside followed the big man into the twilight. Ducamp knew from his pirating days he would have the advantage in the dim light, his eyes already adjusted to the encroaching darkness.

As they advanced slowly, Ducamp could see them wondering why a Frenchman was holding them up. Then the elder of the woodrunners, following behind the big man, ventured to speak. 'Look here, friend,' he began in French, trying to sound friendly, 'I don't know where you're from or what you want, but the way I figure it, you got yourself into a pickle.'

'Just keep coming out!' Ducamp ordered, ignoring the man's affable tone.

The old timer advanced while he pursued in French, 'See, you got two shots for three of us. And what if one of 'ems too damp to fire?' Ducamp knew the man was trying to engage, to create

191

doubt, and to distract him so that one of his cohorts could try something on.

'Stop there,' Ducamp commanded, his voice lowering to a simmering threat.

Daniel, looking on from the undergrowth and fighting the urge to leap out, suddenly realised that in their focus on the target, they had forgotten to give the owl hoots. Meanwhile, the talker kept up his parlance. Just then, Daniel perceived a dark figure creeping up behind Didier in the half light, with a tomahawk raised to kill.

'Get down!' Daniel shouted, springing from his hiding place. He quickly took aim with his rifle and fired a shot that whistled over the head of Ducamp, who was crouched down. Ducamp twisted around just in time to see the assailant freeze and then fall on his tomahawk.

Throwing his rifle aside, Darlington drew his sword to confront the two Frenchmen nearest the tent. Meanwhile, Ducamp swung back around to face the big, formidable man who had yanked his dagger from the leather cord around his neck. There was no time to think Christian thoughts of right or wrong; it was a matter of kill or be killed. Didier stood back and pulled the trigger of his flintlock. The big woodsrunner's eyes widened in expectation of a deadly blast. But when the shot failed to fire, he lunged forward, his eyes glaring with relish and malice, his dagger poised for the kill.

At the same time, a loud rifle blast resonated from the thicket that separated the clearing and the trail. Behind it, five men charged into the clearing, hurling war cries and causing a great ruckus and confusion. Taking advantage of the commotion, Ducamp snatched the big man's wrist. Turning into the opponent's body, Didier swung him over his back. As the man hit the ground, Didier quickly delivered a clean, swift soldier's death.

A minute later, the two remaining woodsrunners had five flintlocks pointed in their faces. Beside them on the cold ground lay the big man and the Indian, the latter with three rabbits at his hip, both joined in death. Ducamp and the lieutenant stood before the captives, while Daniel searched inside the tent.

'What are you doing so far from home?' Ducamp growled in French, addressing the affable talker who was kneeling on the ground next to his companion, both with their hands behind their heads.

'We are free souls just like yourself, brother,' replied the woodsrunner calmly. 'And, far as I know, these old hills still belong to Mother Nature.'

'Wrong,' said Ducamp, now levelling his eyes at the talker's mate. 'This is war, and this land belongs to New England!' Ducamp was making it clear he harboured no remorse or nostalgia for the old country where he was born—where a man born a pauper stayed a pauper.

'Who are you scouting for?' said Daniel in accented French, stepping out of the tent.

'Who said we're scouting?' replied the affable talker. 'Woodsrunners, that's what we are, my friend.'

'Really?' Daniel asked, tossing a small jewellery box to the ground before the kneeling Canadians. It had an inscription in Dutch; his own mother had one just like it, and he had retrieved it from inside the tent. 'This came from the settlers you killed!' he declared.

'They were already dead, man! We just went berry picking.'

Ducamp gestured to the young lieutenant to pass him his rifle, which he did. Ducamp then casually looked down the barrel at the captives. 'Who's next?' he said, devoid of emotion. He was in soldier mode; all notions of mercy had left him.

'All right, brother,' said the affable talker, now desperately holding out his hands. 'If I tell ya something important, what's in it for me?'

'Got no silver, but I got plenty of lead,' Ducamp replied evenly, ostensibly positioning his trigger finger. 'Talk, or you die here and now.'

'Tell him, Claude!' urged his younger mate.

'All right, man, all right,' said the elder woodsrunner. 'Just take me to your captain first. Then I might tell him about the two thousand five hundred French soldiers on their way to New York as we speak.'

Daniel glanced at Ducamp. 'He's lying,' he said. 'That many men cannot march down from the north during the thaw. Anyone marching behind the first fifty men would be bogged down in mud and slush.'

'I wager the same was said of Schenectady, my friend,' ventured the affable talker, recovering his chirpy confidence. 'But they still did it, didn't they?' concluded the woodsrunner with a smug smile.

Daniel's eyes flared with anxiety as he imagined an onslaught of more than two thousand bloodthirsty French Canadians and their allied Indians descending on New York. The first to feel the wave of war would be those outside the wall. Darlington gave a curt nod to the young lieutenant and Ducamp.

'There's nothing more we can do out here,' said the lieutenant.

'Once they've buried their dead, tie their hands and arms, Sergeant,' Ducamp instructed. Turning back to the lieutenant, he added, 'I suggest we head back at first light to give the alert, just in case.'

By the time they reached Albany, Jacob Milborne had already arrived at the frontier town with more stockings, ells of linen, and serge, presents for the Five Nations chiefs, and 160 men to add to the sixty already garrisoned at the fort under Staats. The search party lieutenant gave his report and held the woodsrunners in the fort. Daniel and Didier had no time to linger. Once they had loaded victuals for the voyage, they cast the ketch off down the tidal river carrying Albany County delegates Reyer Schermerhorn and Jan Janse Bleeker, and Aunt Millie on their board.

From the stern of the ketch, as they approached the rocky tip of New York's artillery battery, Daniel contemplated the cold grey bay ahead. Port side, he ran his eyes over the old Dutch windmill of his childhood, surrounded by its copse of burgeoning trees now that spring was underway.

A time of renaissance and recovery, he thought to himself. Yet, the anxiety in his heart reminded him that he might need to prepare for the contrary. He, who felt the need of a tender touch, would likely have to comfort Marianne had she miscarried. As his gaze turned back to Ducamp, who was discussing plans midship with Reyer Schermerhorn and Jan Bleeker, Daniel was unaware of the very different, yet tragic, surprise that awaited him. Suddenly, Ducamp called out, snapping him from his train of thought. 'Daniel, I suggest you go with Mr Schermerhorn and Mr Bleeker to report directly to the governor. I can take care of Aunt Millie.'

'Yes, yes, please do,' Darlington replied, glancing toward the cabin where Aunt Millie had taken refuge throughout most of the river journey down. Unfamiliar with how to act around a mourning lady, the men had discreetly left her mostly to the privacy of her own company, curtained off inside the cabin. Here, the men went only to shelter from the rain or to sleep at night. Daniel added, 'Take her to my house.'

Didier gave a nod of acknowledgement as Reyer said, 'Mr Bleeker and I will accompany you to Lieutenant Governor Leisler, Darlington.' Daniel nodded once, then got ready to manoeuvre the ketch into the dock.

Two hours later, in the governor's office at Fort William, Leisler greeted Bleeker and Schermerhorn in Dutch with an appropriate degree of solemnity, then expressed heartfelt gratitude upon their declaration that Albany County had unanimously rallied to his administration. Daniel noted that although he might be blustering his detractors one moment, he was capable of showing a profusion of goodwill and forgiveness the next. Then Leisler listened to Daniel's account and the woodsrunner's claim.

Standing behind his desk, as though he were expecting to leave at any moment, Leisler switched back to his accented English when he said, 'You are right, there is no smoke without a fire. In fact, it probably harks back to the French plan to invade New York last autumn. Instead, however, as we know now, they managed only to send a two-hundred-strong raiding party in the midst of winter to disrupt our trade and dampen our spirits. But the danger is still very present. I believe their strategy now is to raid rather than invade, which is why we must act now in concert, gentlemen.' Here, he paused to acknowledge the delegates' solidarity as they leaned stiffly forward and bowed their heads. He pursued, 'I will discuss more when we all meet on the twenty-fourth. In the meantime,' Leisler continued, pressing his fingers firmly upon his desk from his standing position, 'know that there has been yet another massacre. At Salmon Falls.'

'Good God. Near Plymouth?' Schermerhorn asked, taken aback.

Leisler gave a curt nod. 'They killed the men and cattle, carried away women and children, and burnt down the houses, barns, and mills once they had plundered them.'

'Good God!' Daniel interjected. 'Will they ever cease this savagery?'

'No,' said Leisler, his voice steady, 'not until they have control of these lands and the beaver trade, or until we stop them. That is why it is imperative to unite against the French scourge and eradicate them before they wear us down and wipe us out.'

'It is fair to say,' said Reyer, 'that the French Canadians in their unified and focussed objectives of destruction—even though they are ten times less numerous than we—have shown just how disunified our English colonies are.'

'It puts us to shame and our people in fear,' Bleeker added.

Darlington said, 'And if we do not regroup on an intercolonial level, then we shall be surrounded time and again, isolated like sheep against a pack of wolves.'

'So, gentlemen,' said Leisler, 'you see why I look forward to our meeting. Then I shall meet the other colony governors, but first, our own house here in New York Province must be in order, and its members must speak through me in one voice.'

'We do not disagree on that point, sir,' affirmed Schermerhorn.

'Thank you,' said Leisler, pausing to measure the gravity and importance of the statement. 'Then we have a chance of convincing the governors to form the first American army.'

CHAPTER 18

1690, New York

Daniel had heard enough political spiel and could hardly wait to get back home for a warm meal and some homely solace. He had seen at close quarters what the smouldering aftermath of a massacre looked like, and he had killed a man. But he felt no remorse for saving his friend and would raise that gun again a hundred times, if need be, to shoot down the assailant.

Even so, a darkness clouded his spirit that sombre afternoon as he peered through the window into the main room of the house, nestled outside the town wall. He saw three ladies seated before the fireplace, where the maid was serving tea. He could not fully see their faces, but his mind filled in the blanks, telling him that Marianne was sitting with her back to him, flanked by her grandmother and Aunt Millie on either side by the incandescent fire. From her silhouette, he noted that Aunt Millie had changed into clothes that fitted her petite frame. He imagined her cheeks to have recovered some of their rosiness, and that she had been welcomed and looked after.

'Praise be to God for this blessed house,' he whispered to himself, unable to wait any longer to feel his dear wife's delicate fingers brushing aside his worries from his brow. He crept through the front door, holding a finger to his lips as the maid closed it behind him.

The three ladies paused as he entered the room from the hall and looked around expectantly. He could not help his forced smile drop from his lips as it suddenly dawned on him that Marianne was not among them.

After the initial greetings, desperate to pierce the abscess of anguish, he said solemnly, 'How is she... and the baby?' He stopped short of asking if she had miscarried.

'The baby is fine,' said Madame de Fontenay. 'You have a baby daughter!' But before he could digest the good news, May, who had been sitting in Marianne's armchair, stood up, her bump prouder than when he last saw her. Walking toward him, she said, 'Daniel, about Marianne.'

'I must see her. Where is she?'

'Daniel,' said May softly, 'you cannot go up.'

'What do you mean, May?' said Daniel, with an urgency in his voice tainted with the disturbing chime of fear. The cloud of despair seemed momentarily to cover his soul again, blacker than before. 'Do you mean she is...'

'No,' interrupted May more firmly. 'She is better now.'

He gave a sigh of relief, grabbing the back of a chair to regain his composure. 'You gave me a fright. Then why such drama?'

'Daniel, she recovered from her illness. She had caught small-pox.'

'God, why didn't you tell me?'

Brushing aside his question, May said, 'It was a mild case. She is over it now, but you'll have to give her time.'

'Then I must go to her,' he said, as the meaning of the illness sank in.

'She doesn't want you to, Daniel.'

'What do you mean?'

'It is nothing of your doing. The pox has left her with scars...'

Daniel guessed what May was about to say next. He slumped into a chair, leaving his arm trailing over the back of it, his hand pinching his chin. 'That is no reason for her to shut me out,' he said without conviction.

'Give her time, Daniel.'

'Time is something that is becoming increasingly tight. We only have a little time left before we confront the French in a full-scale war!'

The room fell silent as the ladies absorbed the full scope of his words, aware that in the event of a land attack from the north, they would feel it first.

During those first days back from Albany, he had resigned himself to let his wife, if not fully recover from, then at least become used to her scars.

Thankfully, Jacob Leisler kept Daniel busy with errands in preparation for the provincial assembly and the intercolonial conference. Darlington assisted in finding suitable premises a couple of miles outside the city, where there was no small-pox infection, which would reassure those arriving from other colonies. Securing the Two Mile Tavern, formerly Stuyvesant's country house in the village of Bowery, was made easier as it was currently occupied by old Adriaen Cornelissen—a tavern keeper and recently-made militia captain whom Daniel knew well. All this organising meant that Daniel only returned home come evening to supper and to sleep. Deep down, however, he knew that being thus occupied allowed him to flee a confrontation closer to home—one that he dreaded perhaps as much as the prospect of war. He had seen after previous outbreaks what those afflicted with the pox could look like. It was not a pretty picture.

So, early every morning, he was not discontent to sit in his saddle at the city gates, waiting among a gaggle of countryfolk in their ox-drawn carts, until the fort church bell chimed in a new day and the gates were swung open. Then he would ride down Broad Way between the leafing trees, amidst the rattle of early-morning traffic, to the governor's office to make himself useful.

When Leisler asked him to accompany him to the Provincial Assembly as advisor, he was not averse. At least, this way, he thought that in his absence, Marianne might venture out of her bedchamber. She did just that, according to her grandmother, wearing a veil to cover her face while nursing the newborn baby girl. Yet, Daniel often found himself questioning how long this situation could continue. Each time, he would put the question aside to busy his mind with the pressing state of emergency.

Daniel saw Leisler grow in stature during those first meetings with the delegates from each county of New York Province, which preceded the intercolonial convention. Now bolstered by renewed county allegiance following the Schenectady massacre, and with the pretext of the uncovered network of papists, Leisler was able to cast his dragnet wider, issuing warrants for the arrest of Catholics known to harbour sympathies for the dethroned Catholic king.

Darlington was reassured when the provincial assembly agreed to the funds Leisler needed to support the military amid the looming French-Canadian threat. Threepence in every pound would finance the war effort. The warship

Blessed William had already been requisitioned to join William Phips's expedition against Acadia, where Darlington knew that the French maintained a small but strategic stronghold, large enough to serve as a launching point for French privateers.

Leisler did not, however, have it all his own way. One delegate, mid-forties and balding under his felt hat, whom Darlington knew to be from Richmond County, stood up when the discussion turned to the arrests of papists. 'Gentlemen,' he said, removing his hat and placing it against his chest, 'let us not forget that every man has the right to choose and practice his own religion in this colony. Indeed, the Charter of Liberties and Privileges of '83 grants freedom to choose one's faith, does it not, including the Catholic profession? We must, at all costs, guard against the same religious persecution that we accuse the French of!' Daniel, seated next to him, nodded his head amid the mutterings of support from the room. As a free-born New Yorker and son of a clergyman, he did not want his home to become a place of intolerance. It was troubling enough that certain families with newfound wealth were leading the trend of acquiring black slaves, something his father had been ferociously against.

'I agree,' said Leisler, clearing his throat above the utterances of approbation. 'If the French get hold of New York, many here would be tortured and executed under the edict of intolerance of the perfidious French king. It is not something we shall ever imitate in these fair lands of New York!'

'Hear, hear!' the county delegates exclaimed, one of them a French Huguenot who added: 'No fewer than two hundred Huguenot families, New Yorkers born in France, would surely be put to the sword if the French Catholics got in, heaven forfend!'

Leisler continued: 'However, I put forward these arrests in the name of our safeguard against conspirators. Need I remind you, gentlemen, the Charter explicitly applies to those, and I quote, who do not actually disturb the civil peace of the province? I propose that this is not the case for some of the papists whose support for the Catholic king only weakens resistance against the French foe from New France.'

Calls of 'Hear, hear!' grew louder around the room. Daniel thought to himself that the genius of Jacob Leisler lay in his ability to always predict any opposition and have prepared answers to hand. Meanwhile, Leisler pressed on.

'Let us not forget that since the end of last summer, it has come to our attention that King Louis has been pushing to invade New York Province and take over our fur trade. And that, gentlemen, is what we are combatting in the name of King William and Queen Mary! Is it not?'

While not everybody was in total agreement with the purge, the discovery of the papist network and plot to retake power allowed Governor Leisler the confidence and conviction to proceed with the arrests in the name of the Protestant king and queen of England. As one of Leisler's respected close advisors and a native of New York, Darlington was tasked with accompanying the arresting officers to ensure that no unnecessary harm came to the accused. Per Leisler's order, no one was to be harmed in case of resistance, but would merely be thrown into prison, where they were to be kept safely out of harm's reach.

However, just as fear of death brought people together, so did it breed paranoia among the populace. During this time of heightened emotions, exacerbated by the recent murderous raids, it seemed the enemy was everywhere. Where once a Catholic was just a Christian neighbour, even Daniel became wary now that any Catholic could be viewed as a spy, ready to slit your throat in support of the return of James II to the English throne. Thankfully for many, however, the multiple arrests prompted a rather convenient exodus of Catholics from New York.

In early May, while Marianne remained entrenched in her refusal to see her husband, Daniel attended the intercolonial convention that enabled Leisler to bring together the colony of New York with those of New England—consisting of Massachusetts, Plymouth, and Connecticut—securing promises to supply men for the war against the Canadians. Again, Leisler did not achieve total consensus despite having reconquered the allegiance of the New York counties. There was still the opposition from the former grandees of New York, the most vociferous of whom were locked up in the fort prison.

One Wednesday morning, before leaving for another round of talks, Darlington, forthright as ever, said to Leisler, 'I am not sure it is wise to shut one's enemy in the jailhouse and throw away the key.' Darlington had been approached by Pastor Daille as he entered the fort gate about Bayard's protests of unfair imprisonment. However, Leisler would not listen. In his drive to protect the city and province as a Protestant colony, he refused to spend precious time addressing the Bayard issue, his mind crowded as it was with creating a union to strengthen the English Protestant cause in the face of French-Canadian aggression. Although very different, Daniel could not help but draw a parallel with his own situation with Marianne, who still refused him so much as an audience. It felt all the more unjust as she was not his enemy; she was his wife, whom he loved dearly.

Even though Leisler acknowledged Bayard's condemnation of the shocking raid on Schenectady and his written plea for innocence sent from his prison cell, he did not believe it was the right time to release such a perceived enemy to the cause as Nicholas Bayard. The same applied to William Nicholls, former attorney general of New York Province under James II, and other vehement detractors. Nor did he feel it was time to detract from the conversation about creating an intercolonial military force, so he relegated the Bayard case to the confines of his mind.

As a man whose time was counted, Leisler swiftly moved onto the topic of that morning's intercolonial meeting. He declared, 'The French will exploit any chink in the defence of New York, be it physical or moral. They will do anything to take over the English beaver trade. Therefore, given our superiority in numbers, our greatest means of defence is attack. I propose a two-pronged offensive that will divide their strengths and keep their raiding parties busy and away from our frontier settlements.'

'It will keep the focus on man-to-man battle,' said Darlington, 'rather than allowing them to massacre innocent settlers.'

By the end of the intercolonial convention, Daniel had witnessed how Leisler had brought back provincial control to New York and unified the colonies against the common enemy. Leisler had conquered the allegiance of the New York counties and the New England colonies, although Daniel knew as well as anyone that there were some who still contested his legitimacy as lieutenant governor. Thankfully, regularisation was on its way in the person of Henry Sloughter Ingoldsby who, Leisler himself thought, would no doubt give the German-born lieutenant governor full recognition for his services to the English throne and to the province of New York.

It was a week after the delegates had departed from New York when early one morning, Aunt Millie caught Daniel as he was about to leave through the rear door to the stable.

The previous evening, upon returning home, as per his new habit, he had looked in on Aunt Millie and Madame de Fontenay, who were playing a game of whist. 'Any change?' he had asked with polite enthusiasm. He no longer mentioned his wife's name; over the passing weeks, asking if she was ready to see him had become a cheerless ritual. They had responded with a mournful nay of the head before he went for some broth and then retreated into his study where, every day, he made up his own bed.

'Aunt Millie, what brings you down at this hour?' he asked, reinserting the door bar as he turned to see the frail woman, sombrely clad, standing before him. Millie had nonetheless regained something of her rosy cheeks, in part thanks to Madame de Fontenay, who would not let her new friend wallow in grief. She had also responded well to a letter from her eldest son, who wrote that he would be in New York before the end of spring to take her back to Boston with him. But she was still a pale reflection of her former self.

'Daniel, before you leave, I wanted to have a word.'

'Of course, Aunt Millie,' he replied and suggested they return to the main room. He pushed open the shutters to let in the first light of day as they settled in.

As they spoke, Daniel reached for the tinderbox on the oak mantelshelf to light the faggot prepared in the hearth by Martha, the housekeeper. He kindled the tinder and carefully placed it among the brushwood while continuing the conversation with his aunt, who sat in her usual armchair.

'My Cornelius won't be long in coming now that the apple and lilac are blossoming in the garden,' said Millie, turning her glance from the front window. 'Your mother used to love this time of year.'

'She did that,' said Daniel, now setting the tinder embers to the brushwood.

'Anyway, Daniel, I don't want to leave without repaying your kindness that has brought me out of my torpor,' said Aunt

Millie. They had not exchanged words since Albany about those killed in Schenectady, and Daniel sensed she was keeping down her emotion.

'I can't stop thinking about them, Aunt Millie,' he returned gently, as he reached for the bellows in the corner of the hearth with one hand. With a fondness in his voice, he pursued, 'Ha, I remember like it was yesterday when we used to visit you all when I was a boy.'

'My poor Daniel,' she said fervently, reaching over and grasping his free hand in her tiny palms. 'Mine are sadly gone. And yours is absent, but she is still here. Keep up hope, my lad.' She paused to catch her emotions, then with bravado and a twinkle in her moist eyes, she said, 'After you left for bed last night, Geraldine and I came up with an idea.'

'Geraldine, Aunt Millie? Who's that?' asked Daniel, slightly concerned. A fleeting thought struck him that she had been dreaming again. During those first tentative days of grieving, she had been known to sleepwalk. Since she had not left the house at all, where could she have come up with such a character? Was she dreaming now?

'Why, your wife's grandmother, of course!' she returned brightly, releasing his hand.

'Oh. Is it?' said Daniel. Reassured, he half turned back to the fire, holding the bellows in both hands.

'What do you usually call her then?'

'Ma'am.'

'Ha, it matters not,' Aunt Millie chortled to herself. 'As I was saying, we were talking about this predicament of yours. And she mentioned that in time, according to May Ducamp, Marianne's sores would eventually become flush and less visible. But in the meantime, you are both unhappy, and poor Marianne cannot hide herself away forever behind a veil. And the bedroom door was made for intimacy, not for separation. So, I suggested to Geraldine that we could perhaps make up a patch.'

'A patch,' repeated Daniel, as if to push home the concept while directing the bellows onto the nascent flames.

'Yes, a patch to cover her scars on her face. Upon my proposition, Geraldine stamped her cane on the floor and declared we ought to go a step further and do as they do at court. "We should make beauty spots," she said!'

'Beauty spots?' echoed Daniel, intrigued.

'Yes, you glue them on your face.'

As the brushwood began to smoulder nicely, Daniel rose from his bended knee. While reaching for thicker sticks from a basket to build up the fire, he said thoughtfully, 'Oh, one spot to hide another, then.'

'Sort of. Except we can make them look attractive by using different shapes. When Geraldine lived in France, it was all the rage at the court of the French king, you know.'

Daniel paused from piling the wood and levelled his eyes at his aunt. 'But that is our very enemy, Aunt Millie,' he said, his voice louder than he had intended. He couldn't help pursuing in a more pedantic tone of voice, one he knew Marianne particularly disliked. She would have given him a sardonic grin, but Aunt Millie let him go on. 'He's the very one responsible for the tragedy. He was the one who gave the command to invade New York and try to take the fur trade from us.'

'I don't see what that's got to do with Marianne's spots,' said Aunt Millie in all simplicity. 'We are trying to find a way of coaxing Marianne out. We are trying to bring you two together again as husband and wife.'

'Oh, yes, yes,' returned Daniel quite contritely, 'I am sorry for my outburst. It's that I keep seeing Catholic conspirators everywhere these days.'

'My dear boy,' said Millie in a motherly tone, 'Catholics are still Christians, you know.'

'Yes, I do, Aunt Millie, but some of these would side with King Louis and the pope.'

'Ah, you mean the papists!'

'Yes, Aunt Millie, the papists!'

'Anyway, all I wanted to say is to try not to become too distraught. You looked so down when you came in last night, and I wanted to let you know that we are working on a way of bringing you two together again. One that would not offend your eye or Marianne's vanity.'

'Thank you, Aunt Millie,' said Daniel, cupping her hands in his. He had been secretly hoping that the ladies of the house would endeavour to bring Marianne around, especially as she would not even contemplate seeing him, even though in his eyes he had done no wrong. 'Thank you. If you succeed, it will put the flame back in our family hearth.'

Later that morning, after receiving word, May Ducamp arrived by carriage with ribbons of black taffeta. Once they had applied gum to one side of the strips, May, Millie, and Madame de Fontenay amused themselves greatly with cutting out various shaped patches, some the size of a mole, others large enough to cover a significant blemish.

'The French call them *mouches*, don't they, Geraldine?' said May, sitting slightly drawn back from the table to make room for her bump.

'We do indeed, and it means "flies" in English because they look like flies that have settled on one's face.'

'Very flattering,' remarked Millie. 'I'm not sure which of the two is better, a pockmark or a fly on your face!' The ladies burst into laughter.

May, always one for a saucy remark, smiled and said, 'Let's hope we can get Daniel stuck on Marianne again like a fly to sugar!' Millie let out a nervous trill, while Madame de Fontenay wasn't sure if she ought to be amused or shocked at the covert remark about her granddaughter's intimacy. So, she made a guttural sound in her throat and carried on cutting out another *mouche*.

Marianne usually emerged from her room shortly before noon for the baby's third feed of the day, and today was no exception. As for Samuel, who was romping about the place, Claudine had been assigned the task of feeding him now that he was weened.

Marianne had lost much of her bump and already cut a fine enough figure to be able to wear one of her larger gowns, though she still donned a gauze veil in case someone should pass by, or in case Daniel tried to surprise her. However, he never once did.

When she entered the main room, she was greeted by the sight of May, Aunt Millie, and her grandmother all seated at the dining table. When they looked up at her, she would have dropped the packet she was holding had it not been for the fact that it was her baby daughter, Delphine. Instead, she clutched her bundle to her bust with one hand and brought her other hand to her veiled mouth. In that moment, it dawned on her that they might have been trying to find a way for her to escape her self-imposed confinement. As she fully took in the scene before her, her initial shock gave way to melodious laughter that no one had heard since she had contracted the terrible pox.

Such a spectacle it was, to see her friend, her husband's aunt, and her ordinarily austere grandmother, wearing black stars and crescent moons that stood out against their powdered alabaster faces. On May, who wouldn't be seen dead without face powder and paint, Marianne found them rather novel and even becoming. But on her grandmother's wrinkled face and Aunt Millie's rouge-tainted cheeks, she could only find them more comical than comely, which sparked her uncontrolled laughter. To make matters more hilarious, the shapes were imperfectly cut, although the ladies, as shortsighted as they were, probably hadn't noticed, which explained why May had easily picked out the least imperfect for herself.

Her laughing fit took her to the nearest chair by the table, where she sniffed the baby's bottom, then laid the gurgling baby Delphine on her back and exclaimed, 'I am so sorry, you look like you just walked out of the court of Lady Castlemaine!'

'We are glad you take it so well, my dear,' said Madame de Fontenay. 'Because we made them for you! Here!' She handed her granddaughter a snuffbox, which Marianne opened to find it full of patches.

'Oh. But aren't they supposed to be immoral?'

'Don't be silly, not anymore,' laughed May. 'That was back in the days before miserable old Cromwell yielded up the ghost, and that was when I was but a babe!'

'We have made lots of small ones and a few larger ones too, to cover the most noticeable part near your cheek,' said Aunt Millie.

'It will allow you to lead a normal life until the sores fade,' said Madame de Fontenay, as one of her *mouches* dropped off her cheek.

'And it will allow you to face the world and your husband once again with confidence!' said May. 'Now, stay seated while you are feeding the baby; we will prepare your pretty face and apply the little flies.'

'Let me lift your veil,' said Aunt Millie.

Marianne was going to lift the dark veil anyway, so she could better watch her sweet daughter while feeding, but she let Aunt Millie proceed.

'I don't know why you don't get a wet nurse,' said May. 'I wouldn't compromise my figure when there are plenty of women who are prepared to do it for money.'

'I might think about it later,' said Marianne, as she adjusted the embroidered hem of her dress and brought baby Delphine to her breast by the warmth of the family hearth. She felt content to be fussed over by these ladies who cared enough about her to make themselves look jovial and ridiculous. She could hardly refuse to oblige them, could she? Even so, she said, 'But I can't go out and about looking like a... like one of those tavern ladies.'

'You can still wear your veil outside if it suits you,' said May, 'but at least indoors, these little patches will allow you to receive your husband with confidence.'

'You know,' said Aunt Millie with a tone of solemnity, 'life has dealt us both a terrible blow.'

'I'm mindful of yours, Aunt Millie,' said Marianne, touching Millie's hand, 'and we are glad to have you here with us.'

'But I suppose we must learn to live with it, my dear, mustn't we? That is what you ladies have encouraged me to do.'

'Yes, we must.'

Millie went on: 'Daniel is your husband, the father of your children. And he needs you.'

'I know, I know. It's that I feel I would be... imperfect and diminished under his gaze, like spoilt fruit in autumn or a blight-stricken rose.'

212

'Forgive me, but that sounds like vanity,' said Madame de Fontenay. 'I am sure Daniel knows beauty is more than skin deep, my girl. You should trust him.'

'I have never felt diminished before any man except my pig-headed first husband,' said May loftily. 'Once he was dead to the world, I learnt to stand my ground, and so should you.'

'I honestly wish I could still feel diminished under my husband's gaze,' said Millie sadly. 'But sometimes, you don't know what you've got until it's gone, do you?'

Sensing Millie was about to fall into a sob, Marianne pressed her arm reassuringly and said with resolve, 'You must be strong now, Aunt Millie, for your son, Cornelius, who has lost his father and brother.'

'Yes, yes. You are right to remind me, lass. I promise I will if you promise to let Daniel back into your heart.'

Marianne nodded. 'I suppose I can hardly refuse since you've all gone to such lengths, can I?'

'And more importantly, back into your bedchamber, my dear,' said May, who began to powder Marianne's face. 'Before he comes back from the tavern one day. And then it won't be smallpox to blame for any sores on his face, or anywhere else for that matter. It will be because of you.'

'Madame, really!' exclaimed Madame de Fontenay, quivering on her seat as another patch fell from her chin. 'You do come out with the most outrageous things.'

'That's life, Geraldine! I call them truths. And as you can see, madame, this is New York, not Versailles.'

Marianne said nothing as May continued to apply the powder to her face, but the conversation nonetheless gave her plenty to think about.

Upon entering the family room that evening, Daniel was greeted by the alabaster faces of Madame de Fontenay and Aunt Millie, whose beauty spots had mostly fallen off—though he didn't know it.

He had endured another tough day, and in the glow of the tallow lamplight and the fire's warmth, the pair seemed to have something theatrical about them as they sat in their chairs, each holding a glass of Madeira wine. But then he dismissed the thought when, wordlessly, they encouragingly gestured toward the upstairs bedroom, which could only mean that his wife was at last waiting to see him.

Feeling oily and gritty from his day, much of which was spent in the saddle accompanying officers to another arrest, Daniel momentarily hesitated behind the door of their bedroom. His drive to see her in the flesh, however, overcame his reserve.

'Marianne?' he said gently, as he thought about the young woman he had met on a tiny Caribbean island where he had come to water. It was indeed an extraordinary combination of circumstances that had brought them together, and he recalled how he desired her for his wife the moment he set eyes on her.

He pushed open the door into the conjugal bedroom. The familiar perfume filled his senses before he caught sight of her on the far side of the candlelit room. She was standing by the mahogany dressing table, upon which stood a washbasin, a pitcher, and a snuffbox. She was clad in her green gown and a China-blue shawl, and she wore a veil.

As he approached, prudently at first, he noticed the children sound asleep in their cots. He moved toward her more steadfastly, his arms slightly held out with the intention to embrace her, but she preferred to greet him at arm's length. Facing her veil squarely, he said, 'My sweet Marianne, do you no longer trust your husband?'

'I do, Daniel,' she said, feeling ridiculous and shy to be treating her husband like a mere acquaintance when once in this bedroom, there used to be deep passion. Yet, when their hands touched, she instantly felt that secret and unexpected desire rousing within her. The desire grew stronger as his familiar scent enveloped her, and his deep voice resonated, causing her heart to flutter.

'Then for the love of God, remove your veil and let me kiss you!' He took her hands, gently guiding her to the edge of the bed, where they sat side by side.

She nodded as if to brace herself, then slowly lifted her veil. Her face was powdered, the ugly blemishes that he had only seen in his imagination were absent, or at least, they were concealed by the beauty spots that he now recalled Aunt Millie speaking to him about early that morning.

Smiling, he said softly, 'I don't understand.'

'What don't you understand, Daniel?'

'Such fuss for such little, I was half expecting a hideous, bespeckled, witchy face from the way everyone was going on. But instead, you present me with the face of a young woman, matured and beautiful. I have missed you, Marianne.'

'Sorry, Daniel, but I cannot...'

'Hush,' he said, placing his finger on her lips. 'You must face me as you must face the world.'

'Exactly, and where in the world have you been?' she said, pushing his hand away. 'You didn't even try to see me.'

'You told me not to,' returned Daniel in defence. 'And I had to get back to Albany. Then there were the meetings for Leisler, and more killings.'

Studying his face as he spoke, she noted a new gravity around his eyes. What had he seen? Had he suffered? May had told her what she had learnt about the killings from Didier. 'Are we safe here, Daniel?' she asked.

'As safe as can be,' he reassured her. 'Leisler is building an intercolonial army that will keep the French busy. We just need to become more organised. We outnumber them by far. Now...' he said, his hands slowly approaching her veil again. She gave a short nod, and he gently pushed the veil back fully over her hair.

'Marianne,' he said, as he began peeling away a large patch below her left eye, 'you are still my beautiful young wife and the mother of our children.'

'Daniel, the scars will diminish.'

'I care not. Whether they are scars from life or wrinkles of time, I will love them because I love you.' He then kissed the scars on her face amid her silent tears. 'Be brave, be confident. I never want to see you veiled again,' he continued. She nodded, her hands now cupping his jaw. 'And you don't need to be wearing these funny patches either. This is straight-talking America, not pompous old Europe!'

By the time Daniel arrived downstairs the next morning, Aunt Millie and Madame de Fontenay were already merrily cutting out more patches.

Shortly afterward, when Marianne pushed the door into the main downstairs room, neither veiled nor patched, her grandmother gave a deep sigh of relief while Aunt Millie brought her hands together and said, 'Thank goodness. I was not relishing having to wear them when my son arrives.'

'Millie, my dear,' said Marianne's grandmother, 'now that your idea has done its job, let's throw them in the fire, shall we?'

'Oh yes!' exclaimed Millie. 'In the fire they go, and good riddance!'

As if on cue, there came a rapping at the door. Daniel turned to peer through the crown glass window. 'It's Ducamp!' he exclaimed as the maid handed the baby back to Marianne and went to let him in.

'I wager May must have gone into labour!' said Madame de Fontenay. Moments later, Didier burst into the room. The old lady asked, 'Has she had it yet?'

'No, no, the bun's still in the oven,' said Ducamp, who then turned to face Darlington. 'I've come with a message for you, Daniel.'

'Oh?'

'Leisler's been looking for you.'

'Hah, for once I'm not there at first light.'

'There's been another massacre,' said Ducamp levelly. 'Falmouth in Casco Bay this time.'

'God, that's the easternmost outpost of New England.'

'They murdered the wounded, killed the cattle, and carried away prisoners.'

'Good God!' exclaimed Madame de Fontenay. 'Are they savages?'

'Where will they strike next?' said Marianne.

Daniel asked, 'And where is the new American army?'

'That's what he wants to speak to you about,' said Didier.

As Daniel and Ducamp passed through the city gates, where extra guards had been posted, stern-faced and wary, they could sense the agitation in the otherwise balmy early June air.

News of the French Canadians' third murderous raid had spread through New York like wildfire, overshadowing any feeling of victory from William Phips's recent invasion of Acadia. New Yorkers were agitated, furious, and feeling powerless. Ordinary men were taking up arms at their own cost to thicken the ranks of regular militia. It was clear now that the English crown would not be sending aid any time soon, let alone an army, despite the crown's foothold in this part of the New World being at stake.

Onward they cantered toward the marketplace by the fort, where there were clusters of noisy armed tradesmen and merchants rallying on horseback. Upon entering the fort, Daniel exchanged nods with the blacksmith, a thickset man on a stout steed, and then with a tall, slim merchant on a beautiful bay horse, whom Darlington knew to have a family of six. The sight of such a display of patriotism drove home to Daniel that it was now solely down to the colonists to defend their own livelihoods and their homes.

In the governor's office, Leisler reported the advancement of the two-pronged offensive to oust the French foe from this part of America. A fleet of over thirty vessels was assembling in the bay of Boston to strike Quebec from the Saint Laurence River. Meanwhile, the intercolonial army was rallying in Albany, where the five colonies were to dispatch their quota of soldiers: 140 from New York, 160 men from Massachusetts, 135 from Connecticut, and sixty men from Plymouth. From Albany, the expedition force was to head north to strike Montreal by land.

'The problem is,' said Leisler, pacing up and down before his office window, 'we are down to three colonies now that Massachusetts and Plymouth have redirected their men to Casco Bay.'

'That's calling the midwife once the baby is born,' remarked Ducamp evenly.

'To some extent. But at least they will be able to bury the dead. They also fear the French could continue southward. According to initial reports, the settlers at Fort Loyal were besieged by a five hundred-strong force of Indians and French Canadians for four days.'

'I've been there,' said Daniel. 'The town is in the fort, and it's not very large, surrounded by a gated palisade. Difficult to hold, though.'

'The settlers had agreed to surrender if they were all spared.'

'What went wrong?' asked Ducamp.

'The French lied. They murdered two hundred sick and wounded and took the rest away as captives, and destroyed the fort, barns of grain, and livestock.'

'Despicable!' exclaimed Daniel. 'No free-minded settlers will be safe until the French are defeated and sent packing!'

Leisler paused in his pacing and turned squarely to Darlington and Ducamp, who were standing on the other side of his desk. Pressing his palms down on his desk in a show of determination, he declared: 'We have to take the war to them! As I mentioned, Boston is sending Phips with a fleet of thirty ships to Quebec. Meanwhile, Benjamin Church will lead a small fleet from here to hammer the French and the Abenakis in Port Royal, which has rebelled since Phips's victory.'

'He is certainly the man for the job,' agreed Ducamp. 'He understands the art of Indian warfare.'

'Indeed. And that leaves us to assemble for a land attack on Montreal,' continued Leisler.

'But without the soldiers from Massachusetts and Plymouth,' remarked Ducamp.

'Yes,' said Leisler. 'However, during my meeting with the sachems, the Iroquois pledged their support; the Mohawks are sending three hundred warriors, and the westerly nations have promised to send one thousand braves.'

'A sizeable force,' said Daniel.

'Even so,' continued Leisler, 'we'll still need all the men we can get.'

'Aye,' said Ducamp, 'pledges are one thing; the reality is often very different. With all due respect, sir, weren't the Indians supposed to be watching the trail when the French walked into Schenectady?'

'True, and the Mohawks have since shown their loyalty by pursuing those raiders and slaying twenty-five of them who lagged behind. They have promised to raise a thousand men. In the meantime, we have already dispatched a company of fifty, comprising both Christians and natives, to establish a base a hundred and fifty miles north of Albany at Lake George. This will allow us to be timely advised of any enemy approach. Major Winthrop, currently in Hartfort, will be taking command of the army in Albany. From there, we will assemble at Wood's Crown before marching on Montreal. What do you say, gentlemen?'

'You're not even a royalist,' said Marianne to Daniel that evening in the family room.

'No, but I will be fighting for freedom of speech, for the sake of our children and their children. I am American, and now you are too. Besides, I told you before, I shall not be joining the king's army. I shall be joining the colonial army, the first United Colonies army of America, Marianne. I must defend my home, our house, our future. You are all I have in this world. And our only home is here, in this province.'

'I understand, Daniel, but if war comes upon us here, what shall we do?'

'That is why we must be on the offensive. Even Mohawk wisdom says so. We must take the war to them. It will put an end to their raids and skirmishes.'

'He is right, my dear Marianne,' said Madame de Fontenay, hobbling into the room on her walking stick, having left Aunt Millie resting in their bedroom. Daniel noted that Madame de Fontenay was leaning more heavily on her stick these days.

Marianne had not noticed; to her, her grandmother was still the rock of her existence. As the old lady continued to her chair, she said, 'We cannot just sit and wait to be scalped in our turn.'

'What if they come here?' said Marianne. 'Our ditch seems so pitiful when you think how determinedly they tore down entire settlements...'

'If there is the slightest doubt, then I will be back,' reassured Daniel. Marianne looked into his eyes as a terrible thought suddenly struck her. What if he got killed? But she said nothing as he continued. 'Then we shall go to the plot I purchased in New Rochelle, remember? We were supposed to wait for Jacob, but he cannot come here now under these conditions. I fear we are nonetheless in for a long war of attrition. We may never see him in this world again.'

CHAPTER 19

1699, Aboard the Mary-Ann

THE DELPECH FAMILY — 9 YEARS LATER

Watching Paul so high up in the billowing sails gave Jeanne twists and turns of anxiety in her abdomen.

As the *Mary-Ann* made headway to Boston, one hearty old salt remarked, 'Take a look, ma'am, see how he walks 'long them yardarms with the ease of a ship's monkey.' This offered her no consolation at all. But she could hardly call out to her grown-up son and tell him to climb back down. Therefore, she left her husband on his own to gaze from the portside balustrade and returned to the lower deck to give the bedding a shake before the evening dampness chilled the air.

After five long days of stagnation in the calms, Paul was in high spirits, visibly proud of just having learnt the rudiments of tacking into the wind. Consequently, being so high up, he had been among the first that afternoon to get a clear view of the patchwork of laboured fields that only now caught his father's gaze. He had also been the first to view a native Indian giving a wave. The novice sailor returned the wave while clenching the yardarm with the other hand, in anticipation of the bosun bellowing out: *one hand for yourself and one for the ship, laddy!*

Meanwhile, standing on the main deck with welcome gusts of sea spray intermittently moistening his sun-browned face, Jacob let his gaze roam among the gentle hills of New England, while contemplating how he could perhaps play a role in the birth of this new nation. *Still in the force of age,* he thought to himself as he chewed on his unlit pipe. He reasoned that there were still enough years before him to establish a business to give his descendants a solid footing in the new society in the making. After all, he had done it before in Montauban, where, being a Huguenot, he had been barred by royal decree from practicing his profession as notary. And he had done it again in Ireland, where he had become a merchant-planter. 'I think I know the ropes by now,' he told himself as another spray of sea refreshed his face.

But glancing over the endless forest now made him shudder. How could so few men carve out a society in such a wilderness? Had he set himself and his family too great a task? This was the first time he had contemplated the wild coast of New England; his previous voyage to New York took him from the Caribbean up the coast of Florida and Virginia, where towns and settlements were more common. Here, the weather was grimmer, the woodland seemed impenetrable, and only the rare scatterings of plantations suggested any sign of European life.

He asked himself: How many generations would it take for New York to blossom into a city equal to those of the Old Continent? Or even with Boston? Could New York truly evolve into a major city based on one prevalent trade alone? He had decided against going into the fur trade, which had made so many New

Yorkers rich, and caused much conflict. Besides, competition was fierce, and he would have needed to be a stronger, fitter, and brasher man than his bourgeois upbringing and legal training in France had prepared him for. He was, after all, the soft-palmed son of a physician. But he knew how to run a plantation, understood the powers of irrigation, and how to optimise a water mill. He also knew how to choose a workforce: constant and steady were the key words here, though there was unfair competition these days with the controversial introduction of slavery, which brought down prices. Nevertheless, he also had his grown-up son to lean on for part of the heavy lifting, provided, that is, he did not get it into his head to go to sea. Heaven forfend!

Suddenly, a short, shocking cry rent the air, abruptly disrupting his thoughts. As he turned his head in alarm, an awful cracking thud pounded against his eardrums, pushing aside all other thoughts.

Jeanne heard it too, from below deck. Gathering her skirts and clasping the ball of dread in her gut, she dashed up the steps to the main deck. There, she pushed her way through the crowd already huddled around a crouched Jacob, his brow heavy with thought and concern. Before him lay their son, prostrate and unconscious, with a trickle of blood running from his nose.

'I saw him, ma'am,' said the old salt. 'Finbar up there slipped, and the boy saved him, but then he lost his balance and came a-tumblin' down.'

'I heard such a terrible crack!' exclaimed Gwyneth Williams, the Welsh matron, bringing her hand to her mouth as much in shock as to stifle any further words for fear of stating the obvious—that Paul had fallen again.

Jacob darted a glance into Jeanne's eyes as she crouched beside him, wordless, as if stunned. 'He is breathing,' he said. 'His lower left leg is shattered at the shinbone. I fear his hip might be affected too.'

Processing the information and shaking off her initial shock, Jeanne touched her son's cheek. He moved his head and half opened his eyes. 'Paul. Can you hear me?' she said calmly, true to her practical nature.

'Yes, I... can hear you,' he murmured feebly before passing out again, as Captain Wright broke into the centre of the crowd.

'Fetch a plank, you lads!' the captain bellowed. Then, turning to Jacob, he said, 'We need to get him below, M'sieur Delpech.'

'Yes, yes,' Jacob agreed, realising they were a hindrance on deck. 'I will see to him on the orlop.' Although the captain did not say as much, Jacob knew he wanted Paul moved, not so much out of kindness of heart as from a need for the crew to make as much headway as possible before the wind dropped off again. With rations of liquids worryingly low, they desperately needed to put in to port soon to water.

Moments later, the sandy-haired bosun ushered forth a couple of burly-forearmed sailors to lift the lad. 'Aye, lucky to be alive,' said the bosun. 'I told him: one hand for yourself and one for the ship!'

'Thank God his fall was broken by the crossjack,' said the old salt. But Jacob knew that the body could still give up the ghost, and that there was no way of telling the extent of the internal damage caused by hitting the deck from such a terrible height.

Under the supervision of the bosun, the thick-armed bearers carried the unconscious patient down the steps to the orlop deck. Meanwhile, Captain Wright pulled Jacob aside. 'Monsieur Delpech, your son is twice unlucky.'

'Indeed, Captain, he has a head for heights, but alas, not the legs of a sailor.'

'It is not so much the legs as the grip, Monsieur Delpech. Nevertheless, it pains me to see he may pay the price of a leg for a lesson learnt. Now, as I see it, you are the only man aboard with knowledge of surgery. Will you be able to attend to him?'

'Indeed. I have set bones before.'

'But this may call for instruments for a removal, alas,' said the captain. 'I will bring you the instruments I have for such procedures.'

Jacob remained mute as it hit home that it would be down to him to operate should the need be. The captain continued, 'I do not envy you, especially in these waters. What is good for the ship will not help in your endeavours. Can you operate while we are in motion?'

'A calm sea and a stationary ship would be the best case. But I have no doubt you require the ship to be making headway.'

'We have no choice unless we drop anchor, sir.'

'How long are we from Boston?'

'We could be sighting Castle Island within a couple of weeks, wind permitting. That's where newcomers land and go through customs and checks. Boston is about a mile from there by lighter.'

'I see. So, you prefer to keep sailing?'

'Not my preference. But if we halt, we could be blown leeward, which could put the whole ship in jeopardy of hitting rocks. That be the danger. And I need not remind you our water supplies are low. If the wind drops again, it will only prolong discomfort and suffering.'

'Then I shall not ask you to halt this ship, Captain.'

'Good man. I will fetch the instruments for your use, should need be.'

Jacob gave a nod. Captain Wright hurried up the steps to his cabin, while Jacob descended to the gun deck to fetch his medical bag, which he had kept from the time he practiced surgery on board a privateer ship. He had been forced to amputate on several occasions. Although the decision to sacrifice a limb was each time jointly made between himself and the patient, it was never an easy one. But each time the wound was severe, with bones not cleanly broken and piercing the skin. In this case, the wound was not open, he thought to himself, trying to keep his focus on the wounded limb rather than the patient. All eyes were upon him as he hurried toward his living quarters.

'I will require the assistance of four strong men,' he announced upon reaching his family space, where his neighbours had gathered around.

'Albeit no small presumption to dismember the image of God,' said a Welsh carpenter solemnly. 'I will assist you, Monsieur Delpech, in this endeavour to save your boy.'

Other men stepped forward as Jacob caught the eye of his wife, who had descended to fetch some cloth and was holding Jacob's medical bag. 'Better our son lives with one good leg than not at all,' she said, handing him the bag. He surmised there had been some debate below deck while he had been talking to the captain. He saw the anxiety of a worried mother through her brave face.

'With God's grace, we shall not lose him. And as there is no open wound, there's a chance that the leg can be saved if we are able to properly position the bone.'

'Won't there be an increased risk of death by infection?'

'Indeed, I will not say otherwise, Jeanne.'

'Then isn't the risk too high?'

'I will have to put the question to our son. He is a young man, and only he will answer to his maker should he commit his soul to Him.'

Jeanne brought her hands together in silent prayer as their young daughter asked, 'Will Paul have a peg leg, Father?'

'That will depend, Isabelle,' he replied, as Captain Wright now hastened toward him carrying a roll of surgical tools.

'This is what I have,' said the captain, partially unfurling the surgical roll upon a nearby crate. It was a roll-up leather case with pockets and loops for holding the various grim instruments, including scalpels, saws, forceps, and needles.

'They will need to be sharpened and then thoroughly cleaned in vinegar,' Jacob observed, inspecting the dismembering saw wrapped in an oil-soaked cloth. Jeanne began to roll them up, but Gwyneth Williams intervened.

'I will take care of these with our smithy,' said the Welsh woman, swiftly taking the roll to have the instruments sharpened and cleaned. Although Jeanne had put the lid on her emotions, Jacob sensed that his wife was comforted that the ship's community had come around them in support.

Turning to the four volunteers who had stepped forward, Jacob said, 'Well, gentlemen, once I have prepared the room, time will be of the essence. It will determine whether we set the bone or amputate. The longer we delay, the greater the risk of muscle contraction and swelling, which will only make a possible realignment more difficult, should that be the chosen course of action, that is. Have any of you done this before?' The men shook their heads.

'Oh,' said Jacob with a sigh of disappointment as he saw the risks of a realignment increase dramatically and the argument for amputation grow in strength. 'In that case, we might have to...'

'I have,' interrupted a Scottish voice, as the large frame of the bosun loomed nearer. 'Done both. Helped a few times with bone setting and amputation. I'll lend a hand, if the captain allows.'

The captain, still standing by, gave a curt nod. 'You have my permission and blessing,' he said, then turned and proceeded to the upper deck.

Within the hour, the sturdy table where Paul lay unconscious was surrounded by lanterns casting a yellow light over the shimmering, gruesome instruments laid out on a carpenter's bench by his feet. The late afternoon light seeped in through the port holes and the open hatch.

'He's coming round again,' said one of the assistants, the Welsh carpenter with a square, wooden face and a grim pleat for a mouth.

Jacob, shears in hand, carefully continued to snip away the remaining cloth from Paul's trouser leg to fully expose the wound. 'Steady, Paul,' he murmured as the lad spasmed, becoming aware of his surroundings.

'What are you doing, Father?' he said with trepidation, lifting his head to eye the amputation tools laid out on the bench by his feet.

'Try to keep still, my boy. I am first going to examine the break more thoroughly,' said Jacob, putting down the shears. He then greased his hands and gently placed them around the lump of the left shin to feel for any small fragments of bone, which could necessitate opening the leg to extract them or proceeding with amputation. His diagnosis could mean life or death.

Paul winced and crushed his elbows into the wooden board to raise himself. But as he did so, following Jacob's previously given instructions, two large hands pinned him down. Another pair of hands came crushing down on his lower body, clamping him firmly in place.

Jacob distinctly felt the two ends of the broken bone through the derma, the lower part riding up beside the upper part, pushing against the muscle. The ends seemed symmetric, and there appeared to be no other fragments between them.

'It's a clean break,' Jacob declared, as much to himself as to the assistants he had enlisted for the operation. There was a hint of optimism in the studious tone of his voice. The tibia could be realigned without too much complexity. However, judging from the bulge, some painful and strenuous pulling and twisting would be necessary to align the two ends.

'Paul. Paul, can you hear me?' said Jacob, raising his voice. Now fully conscious, the lad responded with an affirmative grunt as the sharp pain from the exploratory touch subsided.

'Yes, Father.'

'There is a choice to be made, my boy. Your leg has a clean break and can be mended. But there is always a risk of infection, not to mention the possibility of a painful sequel for the rest of your life. Some men prefer to have it removed and avoid the pain thereafter...'

'No, Father. I would rather die than lose a leg,' said Paul categorically.

Jacob had anticipated Paul's reaction and approved, thinking to himself that there would still be time to amputate should the need arise. He forced himself to keep his distance and not let emotion cloud his judgement. He needed to think logically, the way God had ordained everything in life. Jacob concluded that the patient was strong and healthy, and his heart would probably stand the strain of two operations if needed. 'Then you must be strong during and after the operation,' he said, as he prepared the splints, grease, and the clean linen Jeanne had provided.

'Give him a draught o' spirit,' suggested the bosun.

'He is not used to it,' said Jacob. 'It will do more harm than good.'

'It will dull the pain,' insisted the bosun.

'The nausea induced by alcohol will only make him sicker and therefore weaken the postoperative recovery, reducing his resistance to infection. And besides, strong spirits could act like poison to him.'

The bosun looked at Paul dolefully, snorting bullishly through his nostrils, but said nothing.

A short while later, Jacob approached Paul's ear. 'Be brave. It will soon be over,' he whispered.

'Don't worry, lad,' said the bosun, as he thrust a block of wood between Paul's teeth, 'won't take more than a couple of minutes to set yer straight.' Paul nodded, his eyes wide in anticipation of the pain. Then the bosun took his position and placed his strong hands above the bulge of the bone, while the Welsh carpenter grasped the opposite end firmly. The two other men stood ready to pin the lad down as Jacob gave the nod.

'Once the bone is pulled back far enough,' Jacob explained, raising his voice over the strain of the pullers who tugged the opposite ends of the leg, while Paul bit hard on the block of wood and clenched, white-knuckled, the edges of the table, 'I will then endeavour to position it properly.'

Having spread grease over the leg, Jacob slowly set about feeling the broken, serrated edges of the bone through the skin as they were pulled into alignment. 'Twist it to the right slightly—easy does it, now hold it there!' Working with the rhythm of the ship's roll, Jacob pressed firmly as the vessel dipped, while the bosun and the Welshman held the leg steady. With skilled and steady hands, Jacob manipulated the bone ends until he could feel them meet.

Despite Paul's spasms, Jacob remained focussed on aligning the broken bone ends as precisely as possible. With the assistants still steadying the leg, Jacob set about swiftly wrapping it in strips of linen. Next, he secured the splints with ligatures, and soon was slipping the last splint beneath them. For additional stability, he placed a belaying pin on either side of the lower leg. As the pain dulled, Paul fell quiet.

Half an hour later, Jacob surprised himself when he said, 'If he were a horse, he would have been put down.' It was something he would say back in the old days after setting a sailor's broken limb.

'Don't talk such,' Jeanne chided, touching the patient's forehead. Exhausted by the trauma, and now that the pain of movement had ceased, Paul slept peacefully as the body's own soothing powers took effect. Inspecting Paul's neatly packaged leg, Jeanne said, 'I had little idea you were such an artful bone setter, Jacob.'

'I was once a barber-surgeon, remember?'

'Yes, on a privateer ship.'

'Indeed. But my first patient was a little black girl named Lulu, when I was indentured to a cruel plantation owner.'

'You are tired, Jacob. Get some rest; you've done all you can. I will sit with him now.' Jeanne pulled up a stool.

'He won't be running along the sails again,' remarked Jacob.

'Perhaps it is God's way. Perhaps his destiny is on land.'

'Let us not speak too soon. He isn't out of danger yet.'

'We have all been praying for him.'

The fall had deprived Paul of being part of the ship's crew, and now that he was confined to the dim, dank orlop deck, the fever kept him from observing the captain's seamanship.

In his feverish delirium, he saw himself falling toward the lower yardarm, unable to grasp it firmly. He saw himself plum-

232

meting inexorably toward the flat, hard deck. It dawned on him that he lacked the gripping power of a true mariner, one not brought up holding a quill but using his hands as toughened tools. He had to admit he was a product of his upbringing, and perhaps he was not meant for a life aloft in the rigging after all. Had his vision of a life at sea been nothing more than a naive pipe dream, even before he had begun learning the ropes?

Over the ensuing days, while the vociferous captain asserted his navigation skills by making remarkable headway into the wind, Paul lay listlessly swaying in his hammock with the ship's pitch and roll. Jeanne had noted a distinct dejection in his demeanour. The fever had soared the second night after the operation, and now it was as though he was letting it consume him. So, early in the morning, on the third day after Paul's fall, worried that her son was beginning to let the dark humours invade his mind, Jeanne found the bosun, who was busily directing the riggers for a new day of sailing. 'If you had a word,' she said, clasping her shawl against the blustery wind, 'it might buck him up and help him resist.'

'I'll see what I can do, ma'am,' the sandy-haired Scotsman replied gruffly. Then he turned back to the sailors aloft and called out, 'Steal all you can, lads! Keep her sails full and tight!'

Paul heard this too and felt the thrust of another sail being unfurled. Minutes later, it was the captain he heard baying to the helmsman, 'Keep her as close to the wind as ya can!' Paul knew this meant sailing the ship right next to the edge of the wind, just shy of heading directly into it. The trick was to trim the sails to extract every bit of power from the wind in a bid to make the ship go faster. A degree too much and the sails would luff, and the ship could come to a timber-creaking halt, or worse, leave her struggling to sail off a lee shore, which could be very frightening in a rough sea. Paul recalled that the race was still on to reach port before the liquids ran dry. So, time was of the essence if they weren't to die of thirst. But what was the point of taking any interest now? he thought to himself and let his eyelids fall to forget his throbbing headache.

But the next minute, the distinctive smell of the bosun's backy and body odour filled the closed room as Paul lay in a cold sweat in the half dark, with bolts of pain shooting up and down his fractured leg. He cracked open an eye.

Without any prelude, the bosun let pipe smoke filter through his nostrils, and in his deep, low voice, he said, 'I've arranged it with the captain so we can sit you on the poop deck.' Paul's fatigued eyes opened slightly wider, and he acknowledged his visitor with a nod. The Scotsman pursued, his intense blue eyes catching Paul's, 'But only once your fever's abated. So, you know what you need to do, aright?'

Paul winced as he raised a hand and said in a croaky voice, 'But there's no point, is there? Not if I can't learn the ropes?'

'Nah, but you can at least see and hear how we operate, can't ya? Being part of the crew in spirit is just as important as pulling your weight.' Making to leave, he said, 'Better go. All hands aloft. She'll soon be flying into the wind.'

If Paul could not be part of the crew, at least the prospect of sitting near the action gave him a new reason to fight the fever.

However, by the time it broke, the wind had changed direction, putting the captain on edge as they sailed by the lee, fighting the shoreward wind to keep from the shallows. Nevertheless, the poop deck turned out to be an ideal spot for observing the chain of command. Propped up on a paillasse and hessian sacks, Paul carefully made notes whenever the bosun spared a moment and gave a brief account of any given situation—such as why the topsail was reefed to gain back control from the overpowering high winds, and how to read the treacherous uncharted coast as they sailed along it. He loved hearing these accounts and the wind billow in the sails.

Onward they cruised on an even keel along the rocky shore-line of America. Thanks to the captain's navigational skills, they were on course to reach Boston Bay before their supplies of beer, wine, and water ran dry.

On the eve of their arrival, as his father carefully tightened the bandage around his left leg, Paul winced and then, in one breath, asked, 'I won't be able to climb the mast again, will I, Father?'

'Well,' Jacob began, clearing his throat with feigned cheer. 'You are of a fine constitution, my boy. It's a near miracle how well you have come through.'

'But will I be able to walk again? Properly, I mean,' Paul asked, slightly alarmed by his father's evasive answer.

'Do not fear,' Jacob reassured him with a quick glance over the ligatures. He had done his finest work; the splints looked as tightly packaged as a well-ordained ship. Yet he knew the leg could still turn bad and have to come off. To manage his son's expectations, he added, 'Indeed, even if I had been obliged to remove it, you would have been left with one good leg. And I've seen many a good sailor with just one good leg, which is better than losing a hand.' This was not encouraging, thought Paul, becoming even more alarmed. Jacob concluded, 'But you've been making a fine recovery, actually. There is a chance, how-ever, that your bones will not be the same length as they were before. I daresay you will have a limp. It is a common feature among seafaring folk.' As Jacob said this, Paul's shoulders sunk even further, despite half expecting nothing less. 'Ha,' continued his father on a cheerful note, 'I recall seeing one mariner with a limp who still managed quite ably to climb the rigging, even though he had lost something of the nimbleness required of a rigger.'

'So, I will at least walk,' said Paul flatly.

'Yes, my boy, but prepare to do so with a cane.'

'Oh.'

'Time will tell. But I would suggest that you set your sights on other perspectives for your future than the sea. I'm afraid you will have to accept your new condition of mobility, the sooner the better. Then you will free your mind for other pursuits.'

There it was—the final confirmation he had been dreading. He could hardly believe he would never again experience that exhilarating feeling of being on top of the world, harnessing the power of nature's mighty elements. He sat still, wordless, as the reality sank in. Jacob continued, 'And besides, you may have lost your ability to climb like a ship's monkey, but you still have your youth.'

'What is the point if you cannot choose how to spend it?' There was bitterness in the lad's voice.

'When you consider a lifetime, youth is but a fleeting passage. It is a time for learning and building foundations for later life,' Jacob said. As he said this, he realised that his own life's ups and downs had forced him to learn and build new foundations even now. Nothing in his youth had prepared him for such adventures in later life. However, it was not the right time to share these thoughts with his son.

Mercifully, support arrived in the form of his wife, who had brought down some turtle soup in a jug, sailors having caught a couple of the green sea creatures to much hurrah. 'Your father is right, and perhaps it was God's will,' Jeanne said gently, pouring the soup into Paul's bowl.

'I had plans,' Paul replied, taking the wooden bowl and spoon. 'For if you can control the power of the wind, then the world is your oyster.'

'There are other ways to harness it than being sixty feet in the air. He who strikes with the hammer in the shipyard does not become a shipmaster, does he?'

Paul conceded that her gently delivered reply was as cutting as it was true.

CHAPTER 20

1699, Castle Island

The Delpech family stood on the weather deck, Paul supported by a crutch made from an old oar, all with their eyes fixed on the bleak mound of Castle Island, the fortified gateway to the Massachusetts Bay Colony. This was where they would first make landfall for inspection, before being allowed—or not—on to Boston harbour across the glimmering bay.

The year was 1699. It was mid-morning late in September, with sky-blue breaches in an otherwise mackerel sky. The captain having signalled their arrival, two officials from the island had been rowed out to meet the newcomer anchored between two islands among a handful of merchant ships. The officials checked the ship's papers and the captain's intentions, then gave their instructions before returning to their boat.

Captain Wright turned to Jacob, who joined him at the bulwark. 'I have asked for authorisation to water, no more,' the captain said. 'Only you and your family will be disembarking.' Gesticulating toward another ship flying Dutch colours anchored further in the bay, he added, 'Gather your personal belongings, but leave the heavy trunks and crates. They'll be taken ashore on the lighter. Make your way to the longboat. It will ferry you to the other side of the island, where you'll find the passengers of that Dutch ship are assembled, so that you can state your intentions. Shouldn't be more than a mere formality; they'll want to know who's coming into the colony now the war's over and normal traffic has resumed.'

'Understood,' said Jacob, recalling the Treaty of Ryswick that had prompted his own departure from Ireland. 'So, that piece of land is the gateway to our new life in America.'

'Aye, it's all about to begin for you now, Mr Delpech. You keep yourself and your family well now. May God keep you.'

The two men shook hands earnestly. 'And you, Captain Wright,' returned Jacob, 'may the Lord keep you and all aboard safe.'

Jeanne stood beside him, clutching her two young children by each hand, her eyes misty but resolute. This ark, which had been both the vehicle and sanctuary of God's Providence in the watery wilderness between worlds, had served them well. It had kept them safe through terrible storms and amid frightening beasts. Jeanne now realised why the English often referred to a ship as one would a lady. The *Mary Ann* had been a mother amid the element of creation, providing food from the sea when they were desperately near starvation, and wine and beer from her generous hold when water had become scarce.

A short while later, as Jeanne said her last farewells before boarding the longboat, it seemed so strangely unjust to her to leave it all behind, as if she were shedding a part of her like a lizard who relinquished its tail to escape a peril. Her heart missed a beat at the thought that she would never hear the Welsh singers again. Their children, who had endlessly scurried about the ship with Isabelle and Pierre, would be forever young in her memory. She squeezed her own children by the hand more firmly before letting go when she came to Gwyneth Williams, who placed her once chubby hands on Jeanne's forearms. How the Welsh matriarch had grown thinner since she left the Irish Sea! Jeanne wondered for a fleeting moment what she herself must look like.

'If ever you get tired of New York, Mrs Delpech,' said Gwyneth Williams in her big singsong voice, 'know there'll always be a welcome for you in our New North Wales, tucked away in the hills of Pennsylvania.'

'I shall miss you dearly, Mrs Williams,' said Jeanne, almost succeeding in keeping down her emotions. For this was no place for extreme manifestations of feelings. Such a display would only annoy and even infuriate. She had to bear up, although she came close to failing, as the big Welsh matriarch squeezed her against her large bosom.

'May the Lord watch over you and yours, Madame Delpech.'

'And may He continue to bless this ship,' said Jeanne, on the edge of tears, 'and deliver you all safe and sound in your new home in New North Wales.'

Now that the time had come, neither did Jacob feel quite ready to disembark from the relative sanctuary of the ship and the people he had come to know and appreciate. But this was not the time to doubt his own leap of faith. And, thankfully, there was no choice anyway. Being careful to time his movements with the motion of the ship, he peered over the side where a sailor had opened a gang port. It was a significant drop to the longboat below. The sailor approached, unfolding a rope ladder and securing it firmly to the deck. 'This way, sir,' he directed. 'Take care as you descend. Put your feet firmly on the rungs.'

Jacob climbed down, demonstrating to his family how to negotiate the ladder. As he reached the longboat, sailors in the smaller vessel steadied him. Then he turned to receive his wife. 'Take it slowly,' he called. 'I will not let you fall.'

Jeanne looked apprehensively at the swaying ladder, thinking to herself that if she did fall, Jacob would get a face full of her. 'Perhaps you should move aside in case I do fall,' she called back.

'Careful, ma'am,' said one sailor on the edge of the ship as Jeanne approached the side. The rope ladder swung slightly with the gentle motion of the waves. Jeanne hesitated for a moment, gripping the side of the ship tightly. Seeing her apprehension, the sailor offered assistance. 'I've got you, ma'am,' he said, holding her arm firmly as she placed a foot on the first rung. 'Just place your feet firmly on each rung as you step down.'

With a sailor's help, Jeanne slowly made her way down, and Jacob, in the longboat below, assisted her to a bench in the boat. Then the bosun carried Isabelle and Pierre down in his arms. Paul, refusing any assistance, shook hands firmly with the bosun. 'Keep your chin up, Paul, you've a whole life ahead of you,' said the Scotsman, and then Paul clambered down the ladder, carefully avoiding the use of his broken leg.

Jacob sensed a surge of excitement and trepidation as the boatmen navigated across the white-crested wavelets toward Castle Island to the sound of screeching gulls and grunting cormorants.

With her shawl protecting her face from the salty spray, Jeanne was seated behind him in the middle of the barque, with the children on either side of her to keep them from squabbling for a view of the island. Little Pierre stood up, capping his brow with his left hand, to cast his gaze starboard at the grim-looking castle fort as they passed it. It contrasted starkly with the distant view of Boston harbour, where scores of ship masts glimmered in a pool of sunlight. Pointing to the side of the sombre island, he said, 'What if we get attacked by Indjuns?'

Always quick off the mark with a taunt, Isabelle fired back, 'If you're lucky, you'll get your throat slit first before they scalp you and put you in the pot.'

'Sit down, Pierre!' said his mother, yanking him by the cuff. The boy shrank back down onto the wooden bench. It wasn't fair; Isabelle always liked to cut him to the quick. And she could be very cruel. He even caught her once cutting up live worms to feed to the birds. Being the youngest wasn't fun anymore. He had to watch his tongue for a start, especially now that her English was as fluid as liquid silver after a year of living with them.

'You've been reading too many of your father's accounts!' said Jeanne.

'And highly sensational they are too, my boy. You must take many of them with a pinch of salt,' said Jacob, who continued to contemplate the fort-dominated landscape. The grim structure atop the rock face stood steadfastly seaward, resolutely against all elements and foes.

'The letter from Mr Darlington about the massacre at Schenectady wasn't false, though, was it?' said Pierre grumpily.

'First of all, you should not be reading such accounts.'

'I didn't know,' said Pierre. 'You left it on the table.'

'Secondly, it was during the war between England and France, when there were atrocities on both sides.'

'Didn't the French pay for the scalps then?' Pierre asked.

'That's enough, Pierre,' said Jeanne, as Jacob behind her continued to study the fort made of earth and timber, with its formidable walls.

Cannons jutted out from equally distanced points along the fortification, their muzzles aimed seaward, ever vigilant of the threat from the ocean. 'Look!' he exclaimed, pointing to the top of a flagpole where the English flag fluttered gently in the late summer breeze. 'That must be the fort centre.' It was a symbol of the dominion of the crown over this far-flung colony previously controlled by Puritan elites. He recalled reading that it was here Governor Andros had been imprisoned, about the time of Leisler's takeover of New York. He fleetingly wondered how much of New York had changed in the interval of his absence.

His thoughts were interrupted as Jeanne half turned seaward and gave a last wave goodbye to the *Mary-Ann*, as the longboat rounded Castle Island to the leeside. 'We are on our own now,' she thought to herself, a realisation that made her sit bolt upright and tighten her shawl against the salty spray of the sea. They were soon met with a gently sloping shore where wavelets expired on the strand, and where sparce patches of grass and shrubbery sprouted here and there.

As they approached the wharf, Paul, sitting wordless, pale-faced, and lugubrious at the back, contemplated the stretch of low-lying land before them; more propitious for a debarkation, he thought to himself, conscious of his handicap. Smaller buildings served various purposes: sheds, a small chapel, and a garrison building that he assumed served as quarters for the soldiers who manned the fort. Adjacent to these stood a few makeshift structures, where travellers from the Dutch ship were being shepherded for inspection.

So far, he was unimpressed by the rudimentary-looking fort complex, compared to the solid stone edifices he had left behind in Dublin. Even the wharf was built without elegance, merely lengths of thick, roughly hewn timber fitted or nailed together to form a platform that, albeit visibly solid, served only a functional purpose.

'Up you come, Paul,' said his father some minutes later, while a boatman lassoed ropes around the wooden mooring posts and pulled the boat tightly to the wharf. 'Remember, you mustn't even think of putting weight on that leg,' said Jacob, helping the lad up. Paul gave a wordless nod of agreement as he braced himself for the humiliating part. A couple of boatmen unceremoniously lifted him by the arms and onto the gangplank so he could hop ashore with the aid of his makeshift crutch.

'That's what you call setting foot ashore!' said one of the boatmen in cheerful banter. Paul acknowledged the pun and smirked wryly. It was hardly the way he wished to remember first making landfall in the New World, a cripple in a land where pulling your own weight was a prerequisite.

'I'm fine, Father. I can manage,' he said, quite exasperated, as Jacob offered his shoulder.

As he stepped on American soil once again, Jacob felt a mix of excitement and apprehension—there were procedures to undergo and colonial authorities to satisfy before they could proceed to Boston. He led his family from the wharf toward the previous horde of passengers, the air thick with the aromas of sea salt, crushed grass, gunpowder from the fort, and the whiff of cooking from an open fire where rugged-looking soldiers in unadorned uniforms were preparing sausages on a grill. Other men stood with watchful eyes on patrol or posted here and there.

Jacob picked out the colonial officials, who were already busy inspecting goods belonging to the horde of passengers from the Dutch ship. He heard one of them, a stern-faced official with beady eyes, call out. 'Remember, ladies and gentlemen, you are in a Puritan colony. Sabbath breaking, blasphemy, and idleness are not tolerated,' he cautioned, as his eyes seemed to fall on Paul, who had just found a crate to sit down on, guided there by his weary-eyed mother. The children played around them.

But then Jacob recognised one of the officials who had been ferried to the *Mary-Ann* to meet with the captain. The official paused and gave a curt nod of recognition, then turned to a soldier in his wake and said, 'Ensure these folks receive some bread and water, and if we have some available, a bit of cheese or dried meat. They've had a long journey.'

Losing nothing of his rectitude, Jacob gave a subtle bow and thanked the official, who made to move on. Jeanne, quick to step forward, asked him discreetly, 'Excuse me, sir, could you direct me to the privy?'

'Aye, ma'am,' returned the officer with a nod, pointing toward a small wooden structure on the far side of the main buildings through the crowd. 'You'll find it yonder. Just follow your nose. And mind your step.'

She gave thanks, then turned back to the children, who were playing near Paul. '*Les enfants*, come this way, please,' she called out.

Despite its austere and rudimentary appearance, Castle Island was a hub of activity, functioning both as a military installation and a gateway to the Massachusetts Bay Colony. Jeanne, having just returned from a long trip to the privy, now read the furrow of concern on her husband's face. This was where their journey would begin or end.

Here, they would be deemed worthy, or not, to enter the New World that lay just across the water. 'There is no reason for them to turn us away, Jacob,' she said, sounding both relieved and revived. 'I am so glad to simply stand on firm ground again. And I never thought I'd hear myself say this, but this black bread is the best meal I've had in a long time.' She was referring to the pieces of dense, dark rye bread that Jacob had shared out, having received it from the soldier. 'I couldn't eat another one of those sea biscuits!'

He was about to concede when the stern-faced official he had seen earlier at last walked stiffly toward him and asked to see his papers.

'You are aware that this is a Puritan community, governed by God's laws?' the official questioned, perhaps having detected the soft French undertones and the unstressed syllables of Jacob's brief presentation of his intentions. This was always suspicious, given the long and bitter war of attrition with New France. Jacob may well have been a Huguenot with papers to prove it, but he still carried in his voice that accent of the former foe.

'Yes, sir,' replied Jacob, remaining dignified and respectful. 'We seek the freedom to worship God in our own way, and naturally, we intend to abide by the laws of the land.'

'Good. Let's see what you've brought with you, sir. Come, this way.'

'Keep together, *les enfants*,' said Jeanne, keeping up with Jacob who, in turn, was following the officer. He strode purposefully to another area nearby the quay where a line of wooden warehouses had been erected for the purpose of inspection. But the day was turning out to be clement, with a light, refreshing southerly breeze. Consequently, the lighters had placed the crates with many others in transit outside, making loading easier and quicker for the next stage, which, all being well, would take them to the harbour of Boston.

Once Jacob had located the Delpech crates and chests, looking over the notes in his ledger, the official said, 'A merchant and a planter, you say?'

'That is correct, sir,' returned Jacob, standing resolutely upright with Jeanne by his side. 'I intend to cultivate crops for both sustenance and trade, and also to operate a small trading business.'

'Very ambitious. Let us start with the planting. What crops do you intend to cultivate, and do you have experience in this area?' questioned the official sceptically as he measured, in a fleeting movement of the eye, the quality of Jacob's dark clothing. Even though they were somewhat worn at the hems, the cut of the cloth was certainly that of a gentleman of means, which perhaps made the official question Jacob's capacity to farm the land. He had dealt with Huguenots before. Unlike the Puritans, they liked the so-called finer things in life, coming initially as they did from France. Scandalous indeed.

Jacob said, 'I plan to start with corn and barley. I have some experience with farming from my younger days, and more recently in Ireland, where we lived before coming here. Also, on a previous visit, I investigated the conditions in terms of weather and soil quality.'

'And what of labour? Planting can require a considerable investment in time and effort,' cautioned the officer.

Jacob ignored the implied lack of knowledge; he was not born with the last rainfall. But he kept a calm and polite demeanour and said, 'I hope to start small and expand as circumstances allow. At the beginning, it will be just me and my eldest son working the land.'

'I see,' said the officer, marking a pause for thought before continuing. 'Now, regarding your merchant endeavours, what goods will you be trading, and do you have any trade connections?'

'In Ireland, I previously traded in wines and other items from France and Holland, and I plan to establish a trade here, importing goods likewise from Europe. I still have contacts in Bordeaux and Amsterdam, as well as in New York.'

'Very well, Mr Delpech. One more question. How do you intend to finance all of this?' asked the officer, whose entire interrogation was now culminating in the crux of the matter. 'The colony is eager for enterprise but not for paupers,' he cautioned. Jeanne could have stamped her foot but refrained and stood with an impatient glare at the official, who was evidently making a meal of his moment of power.

Standing erect, Jacob said, 'I have brought sufficient funds to get started and sustain my family until the farm and business are operational, sir.'

Ignoring Jacob's stance and Jeanne's tacit remonstrance, the officer side-glanced toward Paul. 'That is your eldest son?' he said dubiously, gesturing toward the young man, who had perched himself on a crate, his throbbing leg bound in bandages and supported by wooden splints and belaying pins.

Without deflating, Jacob said, 'Yes. As you can see, Officer, he suffered an unfortunate accident only a few weeks ago and broke his leg.' Jacob said nothing of his bone-setting skills. It was getting late; there was no need to complicate matters further, especially if they were to find lodgings before nightfall.

The officer cast a concerned look at the young man. 'Sounds serious. How did it happen?'

'An accident. He fell from some rigging. He will be walking again in another few weeks, I should expect.'

'Lost his sea legs, did he?' said the official. Jacob offered half a smile. He could see the official doing a mental calculation that would lead him to conclude that Paul would not recover the use of his limb until well into the preparing season. Apart from the purchase of land, Jacob knew full well they would have to plough the fields, turn the soil to prepare for spring planting, and incorporate manure and perhaps lime to improve soil fertility and structure. Then there was tilling to be done to further break down clods and create a smoother seedbed.

'And you still intend to plant crops and engage in trade, despite your son's handicap?'

'I do, sir,' said Jacob, bending his body slightly, 'although I recognize that we'll be starting at a slower pace. My wife and I are prepared to work harder to compensate.' Jeanne stood with determined complaisance, her expression saying: *We are not shy of toil.*

'Your plans are ambitious, Mr Delpech, particularly in light of your son's condition,' said the officer, raising an eyebrow. 'However, I assume you have factored in this unfortunate turn of events?'

'Yes, indeed, sir. Moreover, my wife also has skill in weaving, which will help supplement our income until my son can join in the labour.'

The customs officer took a step backward and noted down something before closing his ledger. 'Very well, Mr Delpech. Your plans remain largely sound, despite your son's unfortunate condition. I do hope nothing else untoward sets you back in your well-made plans. However, I would recommend a follow-up examination with a physician in Boston to assess your son's progress. And where will you be staying until you get settled?'

'Ah, actually, we have not come to live permanently in Boston. Our final destination is New York, sir.'

'New York, you say? A different colony altogether, with its own set of laws and governance under the jurisdiction of New York Province. May I ask why you did not sail directly there?'

'Our ship was bound for Philadelphia, but as we needed to take on fresh water, we were obliged to put into port here. So, we decided to make landfall here and travel onward to New York rather than travel from Philadelphia, which would have been a longer and more hazardous journey.'

The officer made another note. 'Very well, Mr Delpech. Your stay in Boston will be short then, I presume?'

'Indeed, sir. We shall take the first ship down.'

'There will be no shortage of ships now with the end of hostilities. Trade has never been more vibrant. Let's hope it remains that way. I bid you well in New York.'

'Thank you, sir. God willing, we'll find prosperity there.'

'Many have tried,' returned the official, pausing for effect. With a hint of a smile, he added, 'And some have succeeded. Now, here are your documents, Mr Delpech. You may proceed. Welcome to the colony of Massachusetts Bay.'

The official gave a nod and strode away to the next group, leaving Jacob to gather his thoughts and organise his documents, and Jeanne suddenly bereft of a fight. But then, she felt a surge as the vacant space was filled with an overwhelming emotion, and a desire to cry.

While waiting for their effects to be loaded onto a vessel, Jeanne wasted no time in locating the designated washing area on the island where barrelled water was readily available. She took the children to the basin to wash their hands and faces and give their clothes a rubdown in preparation to meet the sprawling port town over the water. After a short discussion with one prim-looking lady, she found out that the passengers from the other ship were mostly Puritans.

Jeanne asked if they knew where they would be lodging. 'Oh no,' said the lady, 'we are expected.' She then told Jeanne that she and her husband would be staying at her sister and brother-in-law's until they found their feet. 'God does the planning; we do the preparing,' said the prim-looking lady, whose smile then left her mouth.

A little while later, united in prayer, the Delpech family gave further thanks to God for their safe arrival in the New World.

'And may the Lord guide us to a safe haven this night,' concluded Jeanne.

It was late in the day when at last Jacob shepherded his family to the lighter loaded with their effects for the short boat trip to the bustling docks of Boston, the next leg in their longer journey to New York colony.

As the leading lighterman—a lean, middle-aged man with bright blue eyes set in a weather-worn face—tranquilly pushed the boat from the wharf with his oar, a loud boom reverberated through the air, startling the gulls on the wharf and the passengers aboard. Unperturbed, the lighterman turned toward the boat, an amused smile showing his tobacco-stained teeth. 'Hah, don't be skittish of the evening gun,' he said in a gravelly voice. 'They always blow it off just before sundown.'

It was the last crossing of the day. Midway, Jeanne, Jacob, and the children scoured the bay seaward for the *Mary Ann*, while Paul watched wordlessly from the stern. But it was not possible to spot her in the waning light, even if she were there. 'She's gone,' concluded Jeanne, slightly subdued, her hopes of seeing their ocean home one last time dashed. Jacob was quick to call to everyone's mind that they had successfully faced numerous obstacles and delays. All but Paul were buoyed by the promise of the life that awaited them as the sun began its descent over the hilly port town in a blaze of vibrant hues.

Night was encroaching by the time their chests and crates were stored away in a lockup along the busy harbour quay. Jacob obtained the receipt for his stored goods and placed it inside his leather bag, along with some other documents and bundles of seed. When Jeanne had asked him about the latter, he had said he would disclose all later. He recalled her reproach about his secretive side. But he was just having a tease; all would be revealed in due course.

Amid the pong of the tide and the smells of pitch, timber, and fish, he then wove his way through a line of dockworkers, each bowed under a hundredweight, hauling the last hessian sacks of the day's Caribbean delivery into storage.

He found his family waiting where he had left them, along with their essential baggage, near some barrels of Madeira wine from Europe that had yet to be rolled into a warehouse. A bedraggled sight they must have been to onlookers too, he thought to himself with a pinch of anxiety at what he had put them through. Paul was leaning on his crutch, his expression twisted with intermittent pain as he watched the dockers going by. The children dangled their satchels from one hand, and Jeanne, looking gaunt, stood with a wicker basket in front of her and her canvas bag slung over her shoulder. As he approached, he tried nonetheless to pull off a smile, pushing aside the intrusive thoughts to focus on the single new objective at hand.

'We'll need to find somewhere to stay, Jacob,' said Jeanne impatiently, taking the very thought out of his mouth.

'The storeman said there's an ordinary in Red Lion Street further along.'

'Ordinary?' Jeanne asked.

'It's another word they use here to mean inn.'

'How do we get there?' said Jeanne, getting ready to leave.

But before Jacob could reply, a tall, lanky gentleman in his mid-forties, piously dressed in Puritan black, strode toward them from the deepening shadows. He doffed his tall felt hat to reveal a disarmingly shiny crown and bald front, with a thick curtain of hair skirting it. It occurred to Jacob that any gentleman in London or Dublin would have worn a periwig to cover the lost thatch. But this gentleman visibly had no complex about it, which could be equated to having no pretence either, couldn't it? 'Welcome to Boston,' he said congenially, extending his hand to Jacob. 'My name is Robert Marley. You'll be needing a place to stay, I presume?'

'Yes, er, we would,' said Jacob, momentarily taken aback by the offer from the bald stranger.

'Madame,' said the gentleman to Jeanne, making an elegant bow. 'Pray, please do not think me brash or too forward. It is part of my communal duties to assist newcomers. I have just returned from assisting another family.'

'Then thank you for asking, sir,' said Jeanne, accepting the explanation with a polite smile despite her fatigue. Jacob nevertheless sensed she was still on her guard as she picked up her basket.

'We shall only be staying for a short time,' Jacob said, replying to Marley's question while surreptitiously measuring the sincerity of the gentleman who spoke well and seemed appropriately attired. 'We plan to move to New York on the next available passage.'

'That is very well,' said Mr Marley, replacing his hat on his head. Then, more delicately, he asked, 'You are French, may I presume?'

'French Protestants, sir, we come from Ireland,' returned Jeanne forthrightly, slightly put out that this gentleman had recognised her accent in so few words.

After some careful thought, Mr Marley said, 'In that case, I would suggest Mrs Shrimpton's lodging house. Decent rates, and she's known for her hearty meals. I know she has a room freshly vacant. It isn't far; would you like me to show you the way?'

'That would be most kind of you, sir,' said Jacob, feeling somewhat relieved to have a thorn removed from his side. He had not been relishing the idea of taking his family to an inn, especially given the reputation of merry-making sailors, even if this was a Puritan port town. A private room would offer them a more affordable and practical base as they navigated their first days in the New World. It was a more prudent choice than an inn where all the usual services—tavern meals, drink, and washing—would need to be paid for, and there was no knowing how long it would be before they could sail for New York. In a room with a chimney, they could cook their own meals.

'I see the young sir is hindered,' said Mr Marley, with a sympathetic smile toward Paul.

'Broken leg,' confirmed Jacob.

'Would you like me to call a barrow boy?' Mr Marley asked.

'No, no,' said Paul, repulsed at the very idea of being barrowed up the lane like a sack of turnips. 'Thank you, sir, I can manage as it's not too far.'

'Very well then, let us be off!' declared Mr Marley, motioning the way into town.

The Delpech family picked up their bags, bundles, and baskets, and off they set, with Paul hopping at the rear with the aid of his crutch.

'Pray, Madam, allow me to carry that basket for you,' said Mr Marley, turning to Jeanne, who was at first reluctant to give anything to a stranger. 'I have an arrangement with private houses, you see,' Robert explained, as if addressing one of her doubts. 'There is nothing for you to pay for my services. Do let me relieve you of the weight,' he insisted cordially.

Jeanne, reassured, passed him the wicker basket, and they all followed Mr Marley past a boat yard—where workers were finishing caulking a ship for the day—and then into a narrow lane made of beach pebbles that led to the beating heart of the

English port town. The cobbled streets were flanked by brick houses, some half-timbered, with overhanging second floors jetting over the street, and some very fine buildings made of stone, all with glass windows and as comfortable and well-made as those built in London after the Great Fire. 'All very English,' Jacob thought to himself, quite the contrary to what he recalled of New York, which was built in an assortment of styles reflecting the diversity of its population. On they plodded, the smells evolving from seaweed to spices, and then to horse dung as they continued into the bustling centre of Boston where, given the lateness of the hour, shopkeepers and tradesmen of all sorts were closing their lantern-lit premises or preparing to do so.

'Not far now,' called out Mr Marley encouragingly to the group. 'We are rather proud of our town, you know—all in one style, as you can see,' he added cheerily. 'We may not be as grand as London, or indeed Dublin, but we pride ourselves on our modest developments.'

'Very quaint and orderly, if I may say,' Jacob remarked.

'You may indeed, good sir,' said Marley heartily. 'Huh, rather different from New York, I'm sure.' Did Jacob detect a slight snub? 'That's one of our meeting houses over there,' Marley continued, pointing to the large wooden building. 'We have a number of them all over the town where our community worships and debates,' he said before leading them into a side street that sloped upward.

'And what will you be doing in New York, if I may venture to ask?' said Marley to Jacob, after tipping his hat civilly in response to a gentleman and a lady hatted and clad in muted tones as they passed on the opposite side of the street. Recalling from his stay in New York that there was little time for small talk in the New World, where people and places could change quickly, Jacob responded to his guide's affability by letting him know his intentions as merchant-planter. Marley let slip to Jacob that he ran a dry goods store.

'Interesting,' said Jacob. 'I may well pay a visit once we are settled.'

'Do, do, dear sir, yes do, you will get a fairer price here as you won't have to bear the middleman's shipping costs to New York. And then you might be so kind as to tell me any news you might have from Albion. Do we still have the same king, I wonder?'

'We do, indeed, sir, at least, until I departed,' said Jacob, looking back to find Paul lagging behind.

Mr Marley continued, 'I was not averse to King William, quite the contrary. What would have become of us had the papist stayed in, I ask you? My only regret is that in my day, our colony was self-governing, but has since been brought under the crown, which is unfortunate when you consider we came here to get away from it and be free.'

'Ah, indeed,' said Jacob evasively, slowing his stride to let Paul catch up.

Jacob did not want to be drawn into a political debate. He had learnt from previous experiences that one had better keep one's political aspirations to oneself. But he was saved from any further pursuit of the question when Isabelle burst out in surprise. 'Look, Mother! Over there, there's a black man!' cried the girl, pointing to the open window of a joiner's workshop where oil lamps were lit. A young black man in a loose-fitting linen shirt and a leather apron was sweeping up wood shavings while the carpenter—dressed in leather breeches, woollen stockings, and a shirt and waistcoat protected by a leather apron—was delicately leaning a window frame by a wall. Jeanne gave her daughter a stern look, making big eyes at her. 'Well, I've never seen a black man before, have I?' insisted the girl.

'A servant with his master,' said Mr Marley, gently correcting her. 'Don't worry, there are plenty more to be seen; we have quite a few of them here now, though not always as well attired,' he added, quite pleased with himself. Jacob knew what the euphemism referred to, having been condemned as a 'servant'—or rather an indentured servant—himself. He dared not think what would have happened had he not managed to buy his way out of it. But this man was a black slave, bound for life with no way out.

Marley continued his spiel about his town as if he were promoting it, so proud he seemed of its ordained growth. 'Look up there rather!' he said to the girl, pointing over the rooftops in the evening light. 'Can you see the beacon on that high mountain with three little hills on top? We call it Trimountain,' he said as he turned back to Jacob. 'It is armed with great guns, and from its summit, you can get a wonderful view of all the islands in the bay, which, by the way, is large enough for the anchorage of five hundred ships, would you believe!'

The Delpech family followed Marley past more half-timbered houses and workshops, with Paul silently struggling to keep up, until at last they reached a modest but well-kept two-storey timber building.

A few moments later, Mrs Shrimpton, a stout woman in mid age with a warm smile, greeted them at the door. After introductions were made, she said, 'We have a room available with two beds and some floor space for the little ones. Will that do?'

'That would be perfect,' Jeanne agreed, her body aching for a place to rest in privacy.

'That's settled then,' said Mr Marley to Jacob. 'I trust you'll find your stay here comfortable. Don't forget, Mr Delpech, if you need dry goods or have items to trade, my shop is just down the road. Mrs Shrimpton will tell you the way. Now, I will leave as I'm sure you have many things to tend to.'

'Thank you, Mr Marley,' replied Jacob. 'Do not be surprised if you see me again tomorrow.'

Holding out an oil lamp before her in one hand, Mrs Shrimpton showed her new boarders up the creaky wooden stairs into a guest room, sparse but tidy and well-appointed. A large wooden rope bed stood against the hind wall to their right, with the headboard facing the shutters that were still open to the twilit evening. 'You'll find a trundle bed underneath it,' said Mrs Shrimpton to Jeanne, placing the large iron door key on the round table. This table, conveniently mounted on wooden casters, stood in the middle of the room to the left of the bed.

Meanwhile, Jacob took a rolled-paper spill from a holder and proceeded to touch the flame of her lamp with it to light the sconces on the wall. 'And you'll find plenty of linen in there,' Mrs Shrimpton continued, pointing to a storage chest at the foot of the bedstead. 'My husband's often at sea, you see, but I only let the room out to good and respectable people. So, you needn't worry; the linen is thoroughly cleaned.'

'I am sure it is,' said Jeanne, placing her bag down on the rug beside the ever-so-inviting bed. 'Thank you kindly, Mrs Shrimpton.'

'You won't get bitten in bed in my house, my word!' laughed the landlady.

'This will be perfect,' said Jacob with a sigh of contentment, having now lit the sconces that gave a warm glow to the room—a room in a house that did not rock and pitch. How folk can content themselves with such small comforts, he thought to himself.

'Can we trouble you for some water, Mrs Shrimpton?' asked Jeanne.

'Oh, don't you worry, Mrs Delpech. I've thought of everything, my word! I always follow my plan, you see. We can heat some water for you on the fire, but it'll take a bit of time. In the meantime, I will bring you something to put between your teeth. I expect you're all famished, my word!'

The whole Delpech family gawked at her as they realised that the pang in the pit of their bellies and the feeling of faintness was due to nothing more natural than hunger, a feeling they had subconsciously learned to ignore.

'Food. Yes, Mrs Shrimpton, thank you,' said Jeanne, breaking the spell of that moment.

No sooner had Jacob and Jeanne made up the beds and organised the room, with a convenient dividing paravent that they found in a corner, than there came a knock at the door. Isabelle jumped up from the big bed where Paul was lying outstretched, his aching foot being rebound by his father, and opened the door to a young black woman.

Jeanne looked up from arranging the children's paillasse to find her daughter standing there at the door, gaping. 'What is it, Isabelle?' she asked.

'It's a... It's a pot of soup, Mother,' said the girl as Mrs Shrimpton's servant strutted in, dignified, carrying a large bowl of hot pottage thick with turnips, carrots, and chunks of salted pork, its aroma filling the room. She was closely followed by the landlady bringing some corn bread, a wedge of hard cheese, and some apples, all of which the landlady enumerated on entering. 'Apples a little bruised from storage but still good and sweet to eat,' she said as she put down her basket next to the pottage on the table. 'And I've brought a jug of small beer. You'll find beakers, bowls, and spoons in there too.'

'Oh, my word,' said Jeanne, echoing Mrs Shrimpton's favourite saying. 'God bless Mr Marley for bringing us here. We must thank him again.'

Ten minutes later found the Delpech family sitting around the table, joining hands to say a prayer of thanks before diving into their meal, their first in this new land.

'I shall take Mr Marley a bundle of seed tomorrow,' declared Jacob in good spirits.

'Seed, Jacob?' asked Jeanne, then remembering the bundles Jacob carried in his bag.

'Yes, my dear wife. Here, real money is scarce, you know. People often barter. That is why I made up some bundles of medicinal seed, some of which I grew, some I purchased in Dublin, you see?'

'Ah, good, so that's what they're for. So, we don't need to spend so much money then.'

Jacob nodded with a wink. 'That will do nicely, thank you, my dear,' he said, with joy in his voice, as Jeanne served him another helping of pottage. He was relieved to see his family in fine fettle at last, at a proper table, and content to have found a place where they could rest before the next leg of their journey to their final destination: New York.

Chapter 21

1699, Boston

Early the next morning, Jacob walked his thoughts down the gently sloping street toward the belly of Boston: the Town Dock. If only he could be sure that everything would turn out in New York as he had planned, he thought to himself. But of course, that was the trick of life; you didn't know until you lived it.

He was thinking about the plot of land he had told Jeanne he had signed up for when last in New York. But he had not specified to her that he had only paid the holding deposit; he had not paid the full amount. 'And that was ten years ago, my goodness!' he mumbled to himself as he hopped out of the way of the wheel of a barrow. Even if he had the money to pay up, given the tumult and turmoil that New York had been through since then, would anyone even remember?

He joined the flow of early birds going to market, and tradesmen, fishermen, and dockers tranquilly setting out for a long day's toil. It reminded him he was in a Puritan town where principles of hard work and diligence were engrained in the collective spirit of Bostonians. 'Turn left into the meeting house street, go past the meeting house toward the dock, and Mr Marley's general store will be on the corner of Exchange Street,' he told himself, echoing Mrs Shrimpton's directions as he continued toward the dock.

He let a horse-drawn cart, loaded with baskets of fruit and vegetables harvested in the country, pass by as it rattled over the cobbles. As he came in sight of the central wharf, the harrying screeches of gulls and the iodine scent of the sea rushed into his ears and nose in a single wave of sound and smell. Behind him, the distant beat of a drum sounded a change of guard at the grim stone prison. It must have been no later than six o'clock, thought Jacob, going by the position of the shimmering sun in the fresh, cobalt-blue sky. Mrs Shrimpton assured Jacob that Marley was always up with the lark. So, after supper the previous evening, Jacob had scratched down a long list of necessities that he would ask Marley to deliver to the lock-up the following day, if that was at all possible.

From experience, Jacob knew it was always wise to be ready to load goods at the tip of a captain's hat. The weather could become advantageous very quickly, he thought to himself as he now stood before the general store, which was a stone's throw away from the marketplace where vendors were setting up their wooden stalls. Constructed from sturdy oak beams, the exterior of the corner store was weathered from the salt and sea, giving it a silvery-grey hue. A wooden signboard, painted with an emblem of a ship and three barrels, hung from an iron arm and gently swayed in the salty harbour breeze. Jacob peered through the squares of warped glass windowpanes and made out a hatless man without a periwig standing behind his counter, visibly going over his books.

Jacob entered through the half-panelled door, greeted by the confusion of scents of timber soaked in Madeira wine, dried herbs, and spices. The interior was dimly lit, with a few of the windows without glass and instead covered in oiled parchment that allowed in a golden light. Candles in pewter holders provided extra illumination on the counter and aisles. In a sweeping glance, Jacob took in the swathes of fabrics on shelves, including wool, linen, and a few precious imported silks. Baskets on lower shelves contained dry goods like beans, rice, and other grains. In one corner stood a parade of shovels, ploughs, harrows, and other farming implements that reminded Jacob it would soon be time to prepare the soil.

A set of scales stood on the counter, and behind it, a securely locked cabinet, presumably containing more valuable or delicate items such as glass vials of medicines, spices, or imported teas.

Jacob was glad to be the first that morning to enter the store that would soon become abuzz with activity. Pulling out his list from his frock coat, he doffed his hat and bid good morning to the bald fellow behind the counter. The two men fell into easy conversation. As promised, Jacob brought some political news from England and recounted the latest bill affecting Ireland, which forbade foreign-born citizens from serving in the king's army. 'It meant redundancy or stunted careers for a multitude of good men, including my son, who had set his sights on becoming a soldier.'

'So that explains why you seek a new home.'

'One reason, at least. We seek a fair place to verily call home in the name of the Lord. Tell me, do you ever miss your hometown, Mr Marley?'

'Nay, neither my hometown nor my home country, sir. The good Lord has provided me with more than I could have wished for. Apart from peace in this world, what more could I ask? It does get cold in the winter months, mind, but as long as you've wool on your back and wood in your hearth, then it's warm as apple pie, sir. This is my hometown now. I've seen it grow, and I intend to stay around to see it flourish, God willing.'

It wasn't long before a clerk reported for duty. Wasting no more time, Jacob handed Marley his list, which they went over line by line: hardtack biscuits for the voyage down, a sea chart of the coastal areas between Boston and New York, soap and cloth, some nails, hoes and scythes, candles, oil lamps, additional flint and iron for fire-starting, and some blankets.

'You drive a hard bargain, Mr Delpech,' said Mr Marley an hour later, as the store grew livelier with the clerk dealing with early customers and a couple of sailors discussing tackle. 'But leave it with me, sir,' Marley continued; then as an afterthought, he added: 'And, oh, by the way, it nearly escaped my mind, my soul. The *Nassau* moored in the roadstead last night. I know her captain, and I expect he'll be making a run down to New York by the end of the week, as per his custom. You might find out if he can make space for your passage, unless you'd rather settle in Boston.'

Jacob chuckled. 'Oh, I've fixed my sights on New York Province for a number of reasons, and I've already reserved a plot in the country,' he said, and thanked Robert Marley for the excellent news.

'Then I am sure New Yorkers will be thankful for such a fine addition to their colony. But if you feel it falls short of your expectations, I am sure our city elders would be glad to find a plot for you here in Massachusetts Bay Colony.'

By the time Jacob took his leave to amble down to the quayside, the store was buzzing. Locals bartered with the clerk, while sailors browsed the aisles, looking for goods to replenish their ship supplies or personal trinkets to carry with them to foreign lands.

His main task done, Jacob headed toward the quayside and got to wandering back to the same old concern that had kept him from sleeping. What would they do if they had no plot? He had gone over it a thousand times. He would just have to find another one. That was the solution, but how would he explain it to Jeanne?

Jeanne was glad that she was unable to bear another child, her monthly cycles having ceased. A godsend, especially as she did not suffer from it the way some women did, at least not yet.

However, in the first flush of morning, she had woken with a griping gut, perhaps from eating a proper meal the previous evening, and probably too much of it in one sitting. Or was it a sign that her cycles were returning? Regardless, she dreaded the thought of another seafaring voyage, even if it was short. 'Just a few days, a week at most,' Jacob had told her encouragingly, but it did not help her come to terms with the notion of returning to sea. During one mighty storm, she had thought she would die, and she had the fright of her life when Paul fell from the rigging. She had momentarily thought he was dead. Now, watching him sleep on the trundle bed as she tiptoed toward the shutters, she recalled how bravely he had accompanied her every step of the way during their great trek across Switzerland, and then up the worn-torn Rhine Valley to Amsterdam, and then to London. How courageously he had taken everything in his stride, embracing new languages and cultures. It would have been such a cruel and tragic fate had it all ended on that ship deck.

No, she did not relish another voyage on the perilous sea, she told herself as she quietly pulled the shutters ajar to get a peek at the new day amid the chatter of birds. A perfect day greeted her gaze. Over the half-timbered and stone houses, nothing but deep blue skies, and in the bay, she could spy a myriad of masts huddled together, a couple with their topgallants unfurled, airing out in the early morning breeze.

But what about Boston? It seemed quite a fair place to stay, she thought to herself while waiting for Jacob, who had gone down to the quay to find out about a passage to New York. With a new conviction, she decided she would have a look around the town in the full light of day.

After her morning toilette and quietly dressing behind the paravent, she hushed her instructions to Paul about the children, who were still lying as she had left them, asleep in the big bed where they had climbed in with their parents.

Paul had lost his tongue. He could not speak, could not even pronounce the words to ask how his mother was feeling, despite vaguely recalling her groan at first light. It was as if something was impeding him, and he knew what it was: the unspoken realisation that he would have to remain a landsman after breaking his leg. While it might have reassured his parents to consider him no longer seaworthy, it had shattered his dreams of travelling to fabulous places and finding wealth as a marine merchant on the high seas. It was constantly at the forefront of his mind, so much so that he felt unable to engage in normal conversation. So, he answered his mother in grunts and single syllables.

Jeanne descended the stairs that led to a flagstone corridor, where Mrs Shrimpton was changing the candles on the wall. 'Ah, Mrs Delpech. Good morning to you, and a fair morning it is,' she said heartily, gesturing to the open back door where sunshine was streaming in.

'Good morning, Mrs Shrimpton. Indeed, it is. I was tempted to go for a walk.'

'Your husband went down earlier; I gave him directions to Mr Marley's general store. And you'll be glad to know we can wash clothes if you have any to wash. My girl does a very good job.'

'Thank you, Mrs Shrimpton. I will bring them down once I've been to town to fetch some provisions.'

'You'll find plenty of logs up there, but just holler if you run out. I went to New York a few times back in the old days, you know. Awful long trip; the post road will take you all the way down. But at least if you're going by sea, you won't have the worry of finding somewhere to sleep.'

'That's true.'

'Although, I've heard there are taverns all the way down nowadays. If I'm honest with you, Mrs Delpech, I wouldn't trust a Yorker.'

At that moment, there came a knock at the door. Interrupting herself, Mrs Shrimpton went to open it to Jacob, who was carrying some items in a basket. 'Mrs Shrimpton,' he said, 'I have found a passage to New York already.'

'Splendid,' said the landlady. 'And there I was just saying to your good wife I have been there a few times. Not overly keen, personally. Don't get me wrong, I've nothing against the Dutch, but it's not quite English, is it?'

'Indeed, one might say it is full of cosmopolitans,' said Jacob, feeling shamefully pedantic.

'Of course, it is, Mr Delpech,' returned Mrs Shrimpton, which was her set answer to anything she wasn't quite sure of. 'I was in New York during the Leisler troubles, you know. Chaotic, it was, what with all the cosmopolitans, as you call 'em. Glad my husband brought us here with his inheritance; my son couldn't have been an inch taller than your youngest at the time. And we all know what happened to Governor Leisler, don't we?' Jacob's curiosity was piqued. He did know vaguely what had happened to Lieutenant Governor Jacob Leisler and his son-in-law. What he did not know was what had become of the Darlingtons. The landlady could not possibly know, of course, so he let her ramble on. 'At least you know where you stand with the Puritans,' she said, then added, 'That being said, the new governor's gone and reinstated him, my word. I expect his poor wife's relieved, proud woman, from what I can remember. Did you know they went and threw her out of house and home after they killed her husband? She's got it back now, though, at last. It's all kicking up a right stink here, mind, if you'll pardon the expression.'

'What is the name of the governor again?'

'Governor Bellomont. Sent from the king, no less, though they all wanted a local man in charge. He's been sent to stamp out bandits and piracy, and now he's put Captain Kidd in jail, my word!'

'Was Captain Kidd a pirate then?'

'Started out as a pirate hunter, actually, but then he went and joined the bandits, from what I gather. And what with the peace between England and France, the punishment for piracy is death these days. My Albert says his days are counted.'

'How do you know all this?'

'My Albert's a fisherman; everybody knows everybody at sea, my word. He knew a man who was one of the crew, was promised a fortune. My Albert says some of his crew desert- ed—they ain't stupid, are they? Some say they travelled back to New York in another vessel to escape the authorities, but the governor isn't having any of it, is he? My Albert reckons they must have put in at Cape May, south of New York, and who knows where they are now. So, you see, a dangerous place is New York! Anyway, can't stand here nattering; washing won't get done on its own, and the sun don't wait for no one, does it!'

'I shall fetch the clothes,' said Jeanne, who, putting off her walk till later, followed Jacob to their room.

Isabelle and Pierre sat bolt upright, rubbing their eyes as their parents crept into the dim room where a vertical strip of light streamed in between the shutters. Paul, ordinarily so buoyant in the mornings, had fallen back to sleep in his trundle bed behind the screen.

'You might have told me first you had found a passage to New York, Jacob,' hushed Jeanne sharply as she floated noiselessly across the room. She had not yet eaten, her belly was griping again, and she was not ready to leave land so soon.

'My apologies, my dear,' said Jacob, leisurely placing his hat on the table and his basket on a chair. Jeanne pushed out the shutters fully to let in the fresh air. Jacob sensed he might have put a step wrong and that perhaps Jeanne had gotten out of the wrong side of the bed. He had long since learnt to calmly caress her frustrations when she was in this frame of mind. 'But she had asked how long we would be staying,' he said. 'It doesn't really matter, does it?'

'It does matter very much, Jacob,' she said, becoming exasperated as she turned back to face the room. 'I would have liked you to have spoken with me first. Paul is thoroughly fatigued after his ordeal, and the children need some rest ashore too. Must we leave so soon?'

'That was the plan, my darling Jeanne. I have not deviated from it, which is why I ran down early to get a price on the items we shall be needing.'

'We could stay a little longer. We haven't even seen the town properly yet, let alone explored it. I have heard such stories about New York. It might well be safer here.'

'But I have reserved a plot,' retorted Jacob. It was true, although whether it was still in his name was another matter. 'And we will need to prepare the land before winter is upon us. You know how I like to plan ahead. Otherwise, our spring toil might be fruitless.'

'Seeing as it is a plot of unfarmed land, there is nothing that ties us to it, is there? It could be sold if we find it more agreeable here, Jacob.'

His position was based on the supposition that they had land to go to. But what if they didn't? Telling Jeanne would only comfort her in her position, wouldn't it? 'It could, I suppose it could. But it would make things awkward, and I would still need to go there.'

'You could go by the post road to avoid a perilous journey over sea. But the point is, I would have liked us to discuss this matter seriously between ourselves before you committed to anything, Jacob. You are so secretive lately; it's not at all like you. What with these seed bundles for money and now springing it upon us to depart so suddenly. We are in this together. And together we make the decisions!'

'I should have thought better, indeed, I should have,' owned Jacob. Beaten into a corner, he could only cling to his belief in New York. So, he pursued, 'But I do believe New York is the better option for people like us.'

'Like us? We are not lepers, Jacob!'

'No, but perhaps living in a town with people of many nations would allow more opportunity for a French-born family of Protestants. And my contacts happen to be in New York, my dear Jeanne.'

'That was ten years ago. Have you any news of them?'

'You know I haven't,' said Jacob. But so as not to add oil to the flame, he said, 'Come, let us go out after we've eaten to see what this town has to offer, shall we?'

'Yes, and we shall get a new set of clothes. I daresay we look like paupers again,' said Jeanne with a note of pathos. The poignancy was all in the last word, poignancy that Jacob was quick to grasp. For he well remembered her accounts of her long and perilous trek across Europe with Paul, young as he was at the time, and their arrival in London with nothing but the clothes on their backs and what remained of her family jewels hidden in the hem of her coat. In a flash, he remembered too finding her in the little second-floor room in London, trying to make ends meet. Jeanne, who had been born a marquise, was reduced to courageously earning a meagre living at her loom.

'I know, Jeanne, my darling, I know,' he said gently as she steadied herself at the windowsill, her eyes glistening with pent-up emotion. 'But if it helps, remember, nearly everyone here in America has looked like an immigrant at least once in their lives.' Jeanne gave an emotional nod of consent. Jacob went on in a cheerier tone of voice. 'We shall go to town and see what it has to offer.'

'Yes,' she said and went to pick up one of the two sets of worn clothes the children had left on their paillasses.

'The ship won't be sailing for another few days anyway. And we are not likely to receive delivery of my list until tomorrow, let alone have it stowed aboard by then.'

'Then we have time to consider our options, don't we, Jacob,' said Jeanne with finality. Having regained her composure, she began folding up the clothes to give to Mrs Shrimpton.

'We do indeed, my dear Jeanne,' said Jacob, struggling to find words that would not inflame her sense of injustice. He then reached into the basket on the chair and brought out a loaf of corn bread still warm to the touch, butter, a dozen eggs, cooked ham, salted pork, a black pudding, a large meat pie, carrots and runner beans, some apples, a corked jug of cow's milk freshly drawn that morning, and a book. He laid them all out on the wooden table like items of luxury. It brought the hungry children skipping in their shifts to the table's edge.

'And you know what this is,' he said to Pierre, placing a miniature Noah's Ark on the table in front of him. 'And these are the animals, you see?' he continued, bringing out some crude wooden carvings of pairs of animals: elephants, lions, horses, and goats.

'Is it Noah's Ark?'

'Yes, that's right, Pierre,' said Jeanne encouragingly as she folded the clothes into a basket. 'And I think we can all imagine how it must have felt to leave it after the great flood, can't we, children?' she added with a note of sarcasm.

'But how did he navigate it?' said Pierre. 'There aren't any sails!'

'When you trust in the Lord,' said Jacob, 'He leads you along the best pathway.'

Jeanne gave him a stern look. 'And our ark has led us to Boston, hasn't it, children?'

Jacob sensed she knew something was awry with his own plans for New York. But how could he tell her there might not be a plot now?

After a breakfast of delicious warmed-up broth, bread, and cheese, Jacob and Jeanne strolled down into the bustling centre of Boston with Isabelle and Pierre to find clothes for everyone. Paul remained behind.

With no time to have clothes made, they stopped at a draper's, where they found some ready-made linen shirts, stockings, breeches, dresses, shawls, and bonnets. Shifts, stays, waistcoats, and petticoats would have to wait. Jeanne seemed at home here, Jacob observed. While waiting to be served, she caressed the swathes of cloth with the pleasure of a connoisseur and selected the finest of the pre-made garments. The visit to the draper's took Jeanne back to her previous life in Montauban, where she would shop at Monsieur Picquos's store—that was the draper who had found her abandoned by soldiers on the main square right after she had given birth to Isabelle. She wondered what had become of him. No doubt he had prospered, she thought to herself without bitterness, just like the peach-coloured brick town itself, whose one condition to ensure its continued prosperity was to abjure its Protestant beliefs.

She was already assessing the social fabric of this town of Boston, thought Jacob. Next stop, the tailer's, two shops down. When it came to Pierre's turn, Jacob walked a little further down the lane to order some supplies from the apothecary: some bandages for Paul, and some tinctures and laudanum, which would always come in useful. He would meet them at the dressmaker's next door. On the way to and from the apothecary, he could not help wondering if indeed Boston was a good option. Pigs still roamed here and there, and the sewers stank to high heaven just like in New York, but the streets were paved, the houses were tidy enough, and the port was much larger than he had expected. But even so, from memory, he still preferred the more varied architecture and multi-accented soundscape he remembered of New York. He set aside the thought as he entered the dressmaker's workshop, where Jeanne was finishing up. 'Thank you. That is agreed then. I shall pick them up before noon tomorrow,' she said to the dressmaker, and then the ladies bid each other good day.

It was close to noon, and the sky was turning grey over the wharves of Boston. Their shopping done, the Delpech family ambled back from the Town Dock. The children were happily munching gingerbread as they came upon a crowd of felt-hatted men outside a merchant's store. The sharp voice of an auctioneer rang out, punctuated by the thump of his hammer.

'Look, Papa!' cried Isabelle, pointing to a platform upon which stood a topless black man in chains being led off, to be replaced by a woman and a child.

273

'And now for the wife and child, if you will keep them together, sir?' the auctioneer asked the gruff-looking man who had just purchased the young man. But he gave two curt shakes of the head. 'Fine specimens,' announced the auctioneer to the crowd. The mother comes with her fine and healthy child. Starting at twelve pounds.'

'My God,' Jacob murmured, realising that the man was likely the husband and father, and that the family would be separated in slavery.

Isabelle, curious yet shocked, approached to get a closer view. 'But that's horrible, Papa,' she said as Jacob fetched her away.

'I am glad to hear you say so, my daughter,' replied Jacob, stunned and lacking words for the sudden upheaval that the unexpected scene had brought, as they strolled near the wharves of Boston. He wanted to say to his daughter, who was looking back over her shoulder, 'There is nothing we can do; it is the law here,' but the words sounded ludicrous in his head. They would have sounded cruel in his mouth. In either case, they left him with the sour taste of cowardice on his tongue.

Jeanne recalled Jacob's haunting account of his time at a plantation on Hispaniola, and of the horrific scenes of slavery he had witnessed. As the cruel reality hit home, she realised that their present struggles paled in comparison to the grim fate of those auctioned like cattle, and that Boston was not at all how she had imagined it to be. Speechless after having viewed people being sold like livestock, Jacob led his family away from this dark side of Boston. 'We must shop at the apothecary,' he said after a few moments of awkward silence, as if to divert their thoughts away from the scene they had just witnessed.

The meetinghouse bell tower chimed noon and resonated through the lanes and over the wharves of Boston, as the apothecary shop door rattled, and another customer entered. 'Ah, Mr Delpech, I have prepared your tincture and everything else as you ordered,' said a greying, methodical, and bespectacled man once he had finished serving the previous customer. Placing the items atop the polished hardwood counter, in a more confidential voice, the apothecary said, 'I might add, you do well to depart so soon. There's talk of a suspected case of bilious fever.'

It sounded quite startling, and Jacob saw Jeanne stiffen in the corner of his eye. He said, 'You mean yellow fever?'

'I do,' said the apothecary with a slow, grave nod of the head.

'Are you certain, sir? I thought that was a disease of the tropics.'

'Indeed, sir, and it is suspected that a ship brought it from the Caribbean. I daresay if you don't leave soon, you could very well be required to quarantine. At this time of year, if there was a period of quarantine, you would be unlikely to get a passage until the spring thaw.'

Jacob thought that the suspected presence of such a terrible disease could only add substance to his argument for a rapid departure. After catching Jeanne's eye, he asked the apothecary, 'Yellow fever is as bad as the pox, isn't it?'

'Without the marks. You can still die from it, though, which equates to the same thing in my book. But as we say in my profession, prevention is better than cure.'

'Indeed, sir, indeed,' said Jacob, concerned at such news, while hoping it would enable Jeanne to agree to a swift departure, especially as Paul was still weak, and it could be fatal to him if he caught the disease.

'I am sure you agree, there is no point fleeing a contagion if it is to take it with you, isn't that so, sir?'

'Yes, yes, indeed.'

'Perhaps you'd be interested in my preventive tonic. Composed of nature's finest medicinal herbs, it is composed to keep the plague at bay.'

'I might.'

'I do have a few more bottles, sir. How many of you are there?'

Jeanne made a noise in her throat and stamped her foot hard on the floorboard as she closed the space between herself and the counter. 'Thank you,' she said to the apothecary, placing the items in her basket. 'We shall think over your offer, but we really must be getting along.' She then turned to Jacob. 'Mustn't we, my husband?'

'Yes, yes,' said Jacob, remembering himself, not to mention his wife. 'We shall discuss the matter. Thank you for letting us know.' Then he followed Jeanne and the children out into the street.

'Couldn't you see he was preying on your fear?' said Jeanne as they turned the corner.

'Fear?'

'Fear of there being yellow fever and of us contracting it.'

'With good reason, I might say, my dear Jeanne. And moreover, even more reason to depart as swiftly as we can, or risk being stuck here in a disease-ridden town till next year.'

'And how do you know it isn't already in New York, Jacob?' Jeanne said simply.

'That is a fair point,' said Jacob, feeling stumped and slightly foolish, 'but I should be dishonouring the well-being of my family if I left you all here, whereas we can depart now.'

It was past noon. Jeanne gave him a hard stare and led the way up the hill, with the children running ahead.

Pierre and Isabelle had rarely witnessed their parents lacking words at the table, nor had they often sensed such tautness in the air during the after-meal nap.

The silence was only broken later that afternoon when Jacob announced he would be going down to the docks to oversee part of the goods he had ordered from Marley's. They were being shifted into the lock-up where the crates from Ireland were stored. While the children played and Paul read, Jeanne went downstairs to the room with a large hearth to neatly fold the clothes that had dried outside that morning.

'I have a new washerwoman coming,' said the landlady. 'She can take care of any ironing you want done, Mrs Delpech.'

'All right,' said Jeanne, who did not relish the thought of standing before a flaming fireplace, pressing clothes with hot irons in the late summer heat. 'Just the shirts, skirts, and chemises then, if you please.' There was no point in spending service money on clothes that were not visible.

'They say the weather's set to spoil tomorrow,' said the landlady, 'though you might say that depends for who. I expect the sailors and the fishermen will be glad for a bit of breeze.'

'I am glad the washing was done this morning.'

'And bone dry this afternoon. If you don't mind me saying, I do hope you stay longer, Mrs Delpech. It is always lovely to have respectable company, especially you being French and used to such a life, I'm sure.'

'Oh, very kind of you, Mrs Shrimpton. We were fortunate to have found your residence.'

'I hope you found Boston to your liking this morning.'

'Very charming, and we managed to find everything we set out for,' said Jeanne, keeping the slave auction to herself.

'You could always winter here, you know, until you find your feet.'

'We have a plot to go to,' said Jeanne, but thanked the landlady all the same. 'Have you heard about the case of yellow fever?'

'Oh, I wouldn't worry about that, Mrs Delpech. They're always trying to give people the jitters, what with contagions and witchery. And it gets folk to buy all sorts of quackery. I hope you didn't, did you?'

'No, no,' said Jeanne, refraining from mentioning their trip to the apothecary shop.

'Anyway, it's just one case aboard a ship. As long as it's isolated, we'll be fine ashore.' Jeanne hid her surprise that the landlady was even aware of a case. It might be confined to a ship; but it was a confirmed case, nonetheless. Perhaps Jacob was right. Perhaps they should take the first ship out—a prospect she dreaded wholeheartedly. Memories of surviving a shipwreck on Lake Geneva during their flight from French persecution haunted her still.

The following morning, as she thrust open the shutters, an ink-stained sky greeted her and cast a duller sheen over the wooden shingles of the roofs and Boston Bay than the previous day.

Once Jacob had dressed Paul's leg, he accompanied her, along with Isabelle and Pierre, to the dressmaker's. There, Isabelle and her mother were to try on their altered dresses and coats. Jacob continued to the Town Dock; he would catch up with them at the tailor's once he had finished at Marley's general store.

'Your remaining goods are ready,' Marley told Jacob a little later. 'I managed to get you a sea chart from Boston to New York, brought up by a ship from Virginia the other day.'

'Excellent news. I was about to ask.'

278

'And I have news of sailing. You should see the wharf master and the captain. He might well be making sail on the morrow, so you might be prepared.'

'Ready as ever,' said Jacob. 'I shall discuss the matter with my wife.'

'I recommend you don't dally none, sir. There won't be many ships like this one setting sail southbound now. What's more, I have heard it said that there is a case of yellow fever.'

'Yes, I know, aboard a ship.'

'No, this case is in town. They have already isolated the victim's house and the entire family to boot.'

Meanwhile, back at the room, Paul sat alone reading the book Jacob had brought back on his first outing, which was titled *A New Voyage Round the World* by William Dampier.

He was reading the descriptions of places whose names resonated through his mind like an incantation—Magellan, Brazil, Mexico, Nicaragua, Costa Rica—when his gaze fell upon the crude toy ark, reminding him of his brother's remark about the lack of sails. Pierre did not lack a sense of observation, he thought to himself. How indeed did Noah navigate his ark without sails? He then pondered how nowadays, it was possible to harness the invisible might of God's element. He could see himself atop a yardarm, the wind battling his ears, and spotting the contoured coast of Madagascar with its spine of mountains running north to south. So, he decided to hop down on his crutch to the quayside to view the tall ships. There, he soon got talking with a nautical man and then a sailor, and then one thing led to another...

Jeanne was in merrier spirits, knowing that soon they would no longer have to resemble the French *réfugiés* that she and Paul had once been when they arrived in London more than a decade ago. But not so merry as to be blind to Jacob's furrowed brow, despite his friendly banter with the tailor. Jacob was either trying to charm the tailor into reducing his price or merely pretending to be jolly. Either way, he was putting on a show.

'I wouldn't want it to fit too close to the wind, mind!' he said playfully when it came to his turn to try on his new waistcoat that had been cut with some play. 'You know what three months at sea can do to a man. Why, I've quite lost my comfortable padding!' he added with a chuckle and two brisk taps on his belly.

'Don't you worry, sir. It soon returns,' said the glum tailor, a long, thin man with a downturned mouth and large feet. 'Once back on land, one's true nature soon comes galloping back.'

Jacob wanted to pay partly with medicinal seeds, but the trim and wiry tailor, aware that Jacob had come from the Old World, insisted on payment by coin. 'It's not every day you find a client with coins in his purse,' he said with a glum grin. Then the family—minus Paul—marched back across the busy town and up the hill toward the house, where they knew a slice of savoury cooked ham and some crusty corn bread awaited them. 'Is there anything wrong, Jacob?' said Jeanne as Pierre and Isabelle ran along ahead.

'Nothing wrong as such, my dear,' Jacob replied, looking a bit stiff in the leg. 'Things might become just a little... er... precipitated, perhaps.'

'What do you mean?' returned Jeanne, levelling her eyes at Jacob's.

'Well, dare I say it, but Mr Marley says that ship is likely to set sail tomorrow. I checked with the wharf master, and he expects everything to be stowed aboard by the afternoon tide.'

'There will be other ships, Jacob. And I would rather not risk another voyage immediately. Need I remind you—Paul is still with a broken leg!'

'But my dear, there's been another case of yellow fever. We might not get out before spring if it spreads.'

'Then we could winter at Mrs Shrimpton's. She has been very kind. She told me she would allow us to use the large room.'

'Certainly, she would—for a price!'

'We always said we would have the means to do so if all did not go to plan. And you have your seeds. And the air is turning cold. I dread to think what it would be like at sea now!'

'But we have a plot to tend to. It's in a pretty area north of New York Province along the East River, all rather picturesque,' said Jacob, trying to conjure up a picture of paradise.

'I know, Jacob, it's called New Rochelle, which frankly doesn't bode so well—the old one was taken over by papists!' reposted Jeanne, perhaps in bad faith, as they passed a couple of Bostonians.

'That's the whole point,' said Jacob, lowering his voice while doffing his hat to the couple. 'They want to make it like a New Jerusalem.' The couple returned a furtive glance, something between a salutation and a frown.

'Hush, Jacob. Someone might hear you and accuse us of being blasphemous.'

'I can't see how when that's what everyone wants here.'

Quickening her stride, Jeanne said, 'Besides, the case probably hasn't been verified.'

'They've isolated the family,' said Jacob, keeping up with her.

'Let's discuss this in the privacy of our own room, shall we,' said Jeanne stubbornly as they stopped at the front door of Mrs Shrimpton's boarding house.

Isabelle had already knocked. The door opened. Jeanne stood speechless on the threshold for a moment, her thoughts in a tumult, as she saw a new black maid standing there subserviently. It suddenly dawned on her that this wasn't just Mrs Shrimpton's new washerwoman: it was her slave. It was the same young lady with her child whom she had seen the day before, being sold under the auctioneer's hammer.

They entered the family room; Jeanne, confused and dissatisfied, placed the bread on the table, her sense of values in turmoil, while Jacob, frustrated and flustered, set down the basket of clothes. But their conflicting views were promptly forgotten when Isabelle cried out, 'Where is brother Paul?'

Paul was gone.

Moments later, the landlady knocked on the door and confirmed that Paul had left the house. She had watched him slowly hop down the hill with his crutch under his arm and turn left at the bottom. 'I'll go down and fetch him,' said Jacob, tearing off a piece of corn bread. Jacob then thundered down the stairway and hurried down the hill in long strides toward the port, the only place the lad was likely to venture. It would not be difficult to pick up his trace, given his identifiable crutch, or so he thought.

He was soon crossing over the Town Dock. The absence of vagrants to compete with the pigs scavenging for squashed leftovers was surely a testimony to the wealth of the port city, Jacob thought, as he threaded his way between the market vendors who were clearing away their stalls.

He continued to the main wharf, where much of the usual activity had been suspended for the largest meal of the day.

Jacob found the nearby tavern abuzz with dockers, sailors, and merchants eating broth, some drinking ale, others cider while they waited for the afternoon tide. But Paul was not there.

He asked the wharf master, who was smoking his pipe outside his office, and a couple of fishermen mending their nets among the gulls on the quay, if they had seen a young man with a crutch, but none had.

However, there was at least one person he knew who might help him uncover the increasingly mysterious disappearance of his son. He stopped at the general store where Mr Marley had served his last customer of the morning. Standing at the counter, Jacob explained to the merchant that his son had walked into town and was nowhere to be found. Marley hadn't seen him either.

'He has no friends, is not one to frequent taverns. I don't know where he might be,' said Jacob, who had lit a pipe to ward off hunger and to keep his thoughts from wandering.

'There's nowt so queer as folk,' Marley remarked. 'Let's just hope he hasn't been drafted aboard a ship.'

'With a broken leg? No,' said Jacob, his face showing alarm as the notion took hold. 'I don't believe Paul would do such a thing, even if he weren't in his right mind.'

'That is perhaps the crux of the matter,' said Marley. 'What frame of mind was he in, if I may ask?'

'Perhaps he was slightly downcast since his fall, I suppose. But from there to abandoning his family after coming so far...'

'The problem is, some of 'em aren't given a choice, sir. You see, there are no lengths to which some unscrupulous captains would not go to recruit new crewmen who know their way around a ship. And his leg was on the mend, you say?'

'You mean he might have been coerced onto a ship? Outrageous!'

'If there's still no sign of him after dinner, you should report his disappearance to the authorities, in case he's been taken aboard a ship ready to sail.'

'My wife would be devastated.'

'But he's a strapping lad. I'm sure if he's still in town, his stomach will lead him back to his mother's apron strings soon enough.'

'Yes, yes, he's probably gone out for some fresh air. He hasn't put his nose outside since we arrived.'

'I'll let you know if I hear of anything, Mr Delpech. If he's still in town, I will know.' Jacob thanked the general store merchant and marched back to Mrs Shrimpton's in the hope that Paul had already returned.

As he pushed the door into the room filled with the aroma of cooking, upon meeting Jeanne's expectant look, Jacob shook his head. 'Marley says he will send word if he hears anything.'

'What do you mean by "anything"?' Jeanne asked as she poured out an earthenware jug of beer into Jacob's wooden tankard, which stood next to a bowl steaming with stew. Pierre and Isabelle broke from playing with the toys at the table and looked with bated breath at their father. Jeanne was no dupe. Jacob would have said if there had been a sighting of him. So, what did he mean by 'anything'?

Jacob took off his frock coat and hung it up behind the door. Taking his seat, he said cautiously: 'Marley says it's unlikely but possible...'

'What?'

'He could have been recruited on a ship, Jeanne.'

'With a broken leg? Nonsense!' said Jeanne. However, a flush of alarm swept over her face as she sat down opposite her husband with a heavy sigh.

'That's what I said,' returned Jacob. 'But he might have been coerced. And he's still not back yet, is he?'

Jeanne absorbed the sinking notion that Paul might well be missing for a very long time. 'But it's out of character,' she said.

'I know, but he hasn't been himself of late, has he?'

'Well, one thing's for sure, Jacob. Yellow fever or not, I will not be leaving here without my son, so help me God!' said Jeanne resolutely, her elbows planted on the table, and pressing together her hands.

'I would not expect you to either, my dear Jeanne,' said Jacob, cupping his wife's hands across the table with his.

'What do we do now, Jacob? We cannot just sit here.'

'Once I've eaten this, I shall continue my search. If by three o'clock, he has not returned, I shall inform the authorities and ask them to search the ships that are due to head out with the next tide.'

Jacob released his wife's hands and reached out to his children, seated on either side of him at the round table. Jeanne did likewise. 'Come, children,' Jacob said, 'let us pray for your brother's well-being and prompt return.'

Jacob spent the afternoon checking public areas, inns, wharves, and docks, and asking constables and watchmen if they'd seen a lad with a crutch. 'Oh, aye,' said one of the watchmen, a man in his thirties dressed in a brown set of clothes and black shoes with a buckle. 'I seen a lad with a couple of sailors helping him out of a longboat.'

'Out of a longboat, you say?' said Jacob.

'Aye, they must have come across the bay from the roadstead.'

The situation had become grave. Paul had actually been with sailors to their ship, although there was a glimmer of hope. It would have been worse if they had been helping him into the longboat, as it might mean he was already stowed aboard somewhere. Nonetheless, Jacob felt deeply shocked: he would never have guessed that Paul could do anything so out of character. At what point had his son started behaving so unlike the son he thought he knew so well?

Exhausted and morally fatigued, yet with a racing heart, Jacob passed the meetinghouse he had previously noticed on the way to the boarding house up the hill. As he approached the entrance where two watchmen stood, he could hear an authoritarian voice expounding 'measures for the safety of the town and its good people,' followed by a mighty brouhaha of cheers and jeers.

It being a public meeting, Jacob entered the large, crowded room unimpeded. It was headed by a stage where the speakers stood with a handful of the crown's guards surrounding it. The brouhaha had died down, and he now heard a man's deep, flat-toned voice, endowed with a measure of good sense, calling out, 'With all due respect, if we close the port, there'll be no trade, and we'll all starve by the first frost, sir.' It was followed by great cheers and loud 'hear-hears' as, from the flank, Jacob observed the main men on the stage. He asked his immediate neighbour, a well-heeled merchant with a well-trimmed beard and no moustache, who replied prosaically in a northern English accent, 'Fat one's Town Constable Gibbs, and the tall one with the periwig's the governor.'

The fat town constable, a middle-aged man dressed in black with white frills and buckles on his shoes, made a calming motion with his hands. 'Pray, ladies and gentlemen, let the governor speak.'

So, this was Governor Coote, the Earl of Bellomont, the governor of both New York and Massachusetts, thought Jacob to himself as the tall, grey-faced gentleman in the periwig stepped forward, clad in a deep red justaucorps adorned with gold tassels and buttons. 'Ladies and gentlemen,' he said in the measured way of someone accustomed to being listened to. 'I did not say this measure was to be implemented directly. I clearly stated that it would only occur, as is common practice in any of His Majesty's ports, if the situation became out of control.

'But... But... Please let me finish,' he said, raising his voice to be heard above the groans, now silenced with the help of the town constable's gesticulations. 'Thank you.' The governor pursued unperturbed, 'But we seem to have contained the contagion at the early stages. And we have detected the victims and confined them to their houses until they recover, or till death doth carry them away. We shall pray for their salvation during evening prayer. The port, therefore, will remain open for the foreseeable future, unless the outbreak spreads inexorably—a situation, I am reassured, that is rarely the case with yellow fever during the coolness of our New England autumns.'

The town constable, visibly used to compering, quickly stepped forward and said in his deep Lancashire accent, 'Are there any more questions, ladies and gentlemen?'

'Where's it come from then?' came a shout from the crowd.

'If only we knew, madam,' said the governor. 'But by God's grace, we shall be spared if that be His divine will. And we must pray that it is so. I will add, that to aid the Lord in His divine will, I believe it is preferable not to provoke matters and advise staying away from the infected area. All we know is the ship's carpenter, who the house belongs to, probably brought the contagion from the south seas. It is highly unlikely that it was meant for our northern ports here in New England.'

Again, the town constable stepped forth amid the 'hear-hears' from the congregation and said, 'That will be all, ladies and gentlemen. Peace be with you, and may God bless your homes. Evening prayer will commence at six o'clock.'

The milling crowd began to hum like bees and make for the exits while Jacob endeavoured to wade against the oncoming stream of townsfolk. At last, he made it to the stage where the town constable was descending the steps, followed by the ageing governor.

'Goodman Gibbs, might I have a moment of your time?' said Jacob with formality. Leaving no time for a refusal, he pressed on, 'My name is Delpech, and I am a Huguenot merchant and planter, newly arrived.'

'Where are you from, monsieur?'

'From Ireland, where I served in King William's war with the cavaliers. Before that, I came from Montauban, which is in France, naturally.'

'I have known many Huguenots from Ireland. All fine fellows, and resourceful too. You won't get a better education than from a Huguenot, I have heard it said many a time. I expect you are concerned about the bilious fever, Master Delpech?'

'Well, yes and no. Or rather, I am deeply concerned about my son, twenty-one, disappeared.'

'Disappeared, you say? Do you suspect any foul play, sir?'

'I have no proof of it. But he was last seen down at the quayside in the company of sailors.'

At that moment, the governor stepped stiffly forward into the conversation.

'Ah, I think that should reassure the public, as long as we can contain this contagion.'

'I believe your speech served its purpose, Your Excellency. They might have railed against your sympathies regarding the Leisler legacy, but keeping the port open has certainly won you some support. Let us hope we won't have to close it.'

'Is there any other problem?'

'No, except the gentleman here,' said the town constable, turning to Jacob. 'Monsieur?'

'Delpech, Your Excellency,' said Jacob, taking the cue with an appropriate bow. 'I beg your pardon for the interruption.'

'He's newly arrived and has lost his son,' added Constable Gibbs.

'I am indeed in great distress, and I seek assistance in learning his whereabouts.'

'That is indeed unfortunate,' said the governor.

'If I may, Your Excellency, I wanted to inquire whether there has been a navy recruiting campaign recently. I fear he may have been taken aboard a vessel.'

'Pressganged, you mean?'

'Yes, Your Excellency, I believe that is the term.'

'There has been no such recruitment as far as I know. You might ask the harbour master.'

'He said that he hasn't seen any such recruitment and has no knowledge of my son.'

'Then you must take him at his word, sir.'

'Indeed, I have no reason to doubt it. But my son is still nowhere to be found. I fear he might have been coerced by a merchantman in the roadstead.'

'Ah, we can inform the constables. If you could give a description, it would help. Any distinguishing features?'

'Certainly. He's recovering from a broken leg and walks with a crutch.'

'Broken leg, you say?'

'Oh,' said Gibbs, 'I might add, alas, that some of the less scrupulous merchants are not so considerate, Your Excellency.'

'Former pirates, rogues, I wager. Wouldn't be at all surprised if they were some of Kidd's crew.'

'Could well be,' said Gibbs complaisantly.

'In that case, Monsieur Delpech, you must prepare for the worst. They are such slippery eels! We can send out a search party, but we cannot extend the search beyond the roadstead. You understand, I trust.'

'I do, Your Excellency, and thank you for any assistance you can give. I pray to God he is still ashore. My dear wife is most distressed.'

'I understand. Children can indeed pose challenges to matrimonial bliss. My wife was the same, you know. Lost all our sons. Please give the details to the clerk here. The town constable will then organise a search party and inform the watchmen. Where are you staying, sir?'

'At Mrs Shrimpton's, midway up the road to the beacon, Your Excellency.'

'Note that down, will you?' said the town constable to the clerk.

By the time Jacob had finished describing Paul to the clerk, who then relayed the information to the town constable, extra candles for evening prayer were already being lit inside the meetinghouse. He gave thanks for the support but wondered how the town constable could possibly assemble a search party before the next tide, even if he promised to address the matter during evening prayers to guard against the spread of the contagion. Would it not be too late by then? The next high water when ships usually took to the sea was in less than two hours.

Jacob walked at a brisk pace through the dimming streets of Boston, tipping his hat whenever he passed the district's Puritans as they headed in droves to the meetinghouse for evening prayer. He might well require their support at some point. And if there was going to be discussion about the disappearance of Paul, he perhaps ought to be there too with his family. At any rate, he would have to check back first at the lodgings to see if Paul had returned or not.

He wondered how he would break the news to Jeanne and soon found himself climbing the stairs light-footedly to avoid alerting the talkative landlady and wasting time. He paused momentarily behind the boarding room door; his heart skipped a beat when he heard the voice of a man inside. His hope was quickly dashed, however, as he realised the voice did not belong to his son, but he did recognise its distinctively loquacious affability. He pulled the latch string and stepped inside.

Jeanne stood before the window with the children at her side, all of them dressed in their new clothes. His admiring look told her she had regained her former distinction, but she did not let the moment linger. 'Ah, at last, Jacob. Mr Marley has just arrived,' she said, gesticulating to the figure of the general store merchant, who was sitting at the table with his hat placed before him.

He got to his feet and said, 'Mr Delpech, your son has been sighted. My nephew, a fisherman, stopped by earlier at my store for some tackle and mentioned seeing a lad with an oar for a crutch being coerced by some unsavoury characters.'

'Scoundrels!' exclaimed Jacob, feeling suddenly helpless to prevent what seemed to be his son's inexorable flight. Regaining his composure, he said, 'Please excuse the outburst, Mr Marley, and thank you for coming.'

'I came as soon as I found out.'

'Where are they?'

291

'Down at the King's Head tavern.'

'But I was there earlier myself.'

'You were probably at the King's Arms by the harbour. This one's by Scarlett's Wharf, further along to the north. My nephew often stops there for his pint,' said Marley, giving a say-no-more look that Jeanne, still standing by the window behind him, did not see. From Marley's expression, Jacob guessed that the northern wharfs—further from the centre of town and with less official oversight—were probably a haven for less-than-Puritan behaviour. But what would Paul be doing there?

He acknowledged the discretion with a knowing nod and then briefly explained where he had been, what the town constable had suggested, and that he feared they would act too late.

'We'd better inform Constable Giggs now, then,' said Marley.

'There's no time, sir. They could embark at any moment; the tide will be high within the hour. Pray, take me there now.'

'Please, Mr Marley,' Jeanne said, stroking the heads of her children, who now stood in front of her. 'I could not bear to lose my son to the sea.'

'All right, all right,' said Marley, shifting his eyes toward Jacob. 'But be warned, sir, it is hardly a place fit for a gentleman.'

'Have no fear, sir,' Jacob said, reaching under the bed to take up his sabre—a weapon he preferred over the rapier that most gentlemen wore. 'I have surely seen worse.'

'I shall inform the town constable,' said Jeanne. 'The children can stay here.'

'I should rather you remained here together, Jeanne. I don't want to risk losing anyone else.'

CHAPTER 22

1699, Boston

The two men rushed to the northern wharf as fast as their middle-aged hearts would allow. The district, seedier, quieter, and darker, was less than half a mile from the Town Dock. After pausing to catch their breath in front of the red brick building with crown glass windows, and observing that the place was relatively quiet, they entered the side door of the King's Head tavern, all aglow inside, a roaring fire at the hearth, and lanterns on tables giving off a mellow light.

Jacob's senses were instantly overwhelmed by the smells of alcohol-soaked timber, tallow wax, tobacco, and a savoury whiff wafting from the great iron cauldron hanging from the hook inside the chimney. It did not take him more than a few seconds to scan the shaded faces of fishermen, sailors, dockers, merchants, and tavern girls, engulfed here and there in their cocoons of conversation. On the way, Marley had described the tavern as a place of less reputable dealings—duty-free tobacco, spirits, games, 'and dare I say it, the carnal touch of *filles de joie,*' he had said between breaths. Proud of his Puritan city, he did not want the Huguenot newcomer to think the place he was about to enter was typical of Boston taverns.

'Over there!' said Jacob to Marley, with a discreet nod to a high-backed settle bench further down the long tavern interior to his right. Paul sat flanked by three sailor-types on one side of him, while a tavern girl was stroking his temple on the other side. His crutch was leaning against the end of the bench. The three men were clashing tankards with Paul who, Jacob ascertained by his exaggerated gestures, had visibly had more than his fill. On the table in front of the lad, Jacob perceived an inkwell, a quill, and a scroll. 'We arrive just in time to spoil the party,' he said, undaunted.

'Careful, sir,' Marley muttered in Jacob's ear, 'those men are dangerous—some of Captain Kidd's crew no less. Let us fetch the constables. They will know how to deal with them.'

Ignoring the patrons at the bar, frolicking couples, and smoking gamblers, Jacob, stern-eyed, made a beeline for the settle bench and planted himself squarely before the oblong table. Marley knew the Huguenots could be a stubborn lot, but he did not know they could be so heedless. Despairingly, he threw out his arms but followed closely behind, despite the trembling sensation of walking into a lion's den. Aspiring to become a selectman, Marley felt duty bound to keep the man out of trouble.

'Paul,' Jacob called sharply. 'Paul, take your crutch, we are leaving!' The lad could only stammer something unintelligible about a 'bootiful ship' he had visited.

'And who are you when you're at home?' the sailor scowled, a flat-nosed man with a bullish forehead, who was sitting between his two mates. The ale slopped over the lip of his tankard as he slammed it down on the table.

'I am the boy's father,' returned Jacob, unmoved and unimpressed by the sailor's show of impulsive anger. 'Now let him go!'

'You hear that, Stu?' said the bullish sailor, playing dumb as he turned to his pal on his right.

'Ha, too late, da!' said the sailor named Stu, a man with a good-looking face, ferreting eyes, a goatee, and a missing front tooth. 'He's just signed up.' Leaning forward, he then looped his head to his left, toward the third sailor, who was sitting next to Paul. He said: 'Show 'im, Jack!'

Jack, with thinning straw-coloured hair, pushed aside the ink holder from the top of the scroll on the table and held it up for Jacob to see. 'Look, there! See?' he said, indicating a signature scratched at the bottom of the articles.

'Under duress!' snapped Jacob, ignoring the brandished agreement. 'Let him go now, or you'll be headed for the same place as your former captain!'

'Oh yeah, and who's stopping us? You?' jeered the bullish sailor cockily, with a sardonic laugh. He looked invitingly at the surrounding tables, where patrons remained aloof in their clandestine cocoons.

'Constables are on their way now,' replied Jacob, unperturbed. He had not come all this way to let his son be snatched away by these halfwits. But he nonetheless knew all too well from experience that such mindless scoundrels could snub out the life of a leading light without so much as a second thought, especially when goading each other on in their drunken pack. Such were the insidious ways of pirates, as Jacob had previously experienced. The scourge of the seas, villains of every nation, these men would willingly do the devil's deeds.

'Yes, yes, gentlemen, they have been sent for, so let us have no fuss,' seconded Marley good-naturedly, knowing it was a blatant lie, as he tried to calm the volatile situation. But he was not expecting Jacob's next stubbornly bold move, which Marley would have called heedless and irrational.

'You're coming with us, Paul, me ole mate,' said the sailor named Jack, draping his arm fraternally around the lad's neck. 'We'll show you a piece of real freedom, my man!'

His paternal pride piqued to the quick, Jacob instinctively drew his sword. The moment he did so, he realised the rashness of his action. But too late for second thoughts, he stood his ground in a posture of solid defiance.

The three sailors' smiles vanished. Suddenly becoming alert, lithe, and cunning, they rose to their feet in unison, slowly pulling out their daggers from the sheaths dangling from their necks. The bullish sailor stood half a head taller than Jacob.

'Come, come, gentlemen, let's be reasonable,' insisted Marley. 'I am sure we can resolve this unfortunate misunderstanding like civilized men of honour.' However, his pleas fell on deaf ears.

Jacob gripped his sword firmly with fierce conviction. It was the way the French lieutenant he once knew had taught him. 'Lose your sword and lose your life!' he recalled Lieutenant Ducamp telling him before having to stand behind the line as the barber-surgeon of an attacking privateer force in Cuba. He had also honed his swordplay and self-defence skills during the brutal war in Ireland. Nevertheless, these sailors possessed an innate sense, and as a lion assessed its prey, so they discerned this man was no predator.

'Stand down, gentlemen!' cried out Marley with insistence. 'We have sent for the authorities, I say!'

'He's coming with us,' said the sailor with the scroll. Turning to the drunken recruit, he said, 'Come on, Paul, my man, or we'll have to spike the old fart!' Bewildered, Paul shook his head, staggered onto his good foot, then fell back onto the bench.

'This old fart is not leaving this place without his son!' said Jacob defiantly, raising his voice into a loud growl. He drew back his sword and swiped the tankards from the table with the back of it, sending them, along with the ink pot and the lantern, crashing to the ground. He knew full well that with any show of weakness, these men would pounce like a pack of wolves.

The neighbouring tables fell silent, and the tavern girls stopped giggling as the bullish sailor booted the table into Jacob's legs, forcing Delpech to step back. Faces flashed around to see what all the fuss was about. 'Come and get him then!' taunted the pirate as his pals moved a step forward. Jacob stood ready, hardly believing that no one was coming to his aid. In fact, it seemed all eyes were eager for a fight.

A gravelly voice then came rolling in like a landslide, breaking the silence. 'Hold it, lads!' it rumbled. The sailors turned their heads toward a thickset man approaching from the counter, his knee-high boots marking his unhurried, swaggering step.

Jacob sensed a commanding presence as his eyes ran over the man's attire—a black leather jerkin under an open great coat that must have been taken from a high-ranking Spanish official. 'Stand ye down, lads. Let the boy go,' said the man in a calming, sovereign growl.

As the man's face emerged in the yellow light of a wall sconce to the left of the high-backed settle, Jacob, still in a defensive stance, locked eyes with the commander's unforgettable piercing blue eyes. He immediately recognised the face—despite a new scar slashing diagonally from above the right eye across the cheek to the jawbone—of the pirate he had encountered over a decade ago on a buccaneer ship. His name was Cox, Captain Cox, a pirate prisoner who had been freed when Jacob had been taken with him aboard a ship in Port Royal. Jacob, then an indentured barber-surgeon, had been working off a debt incurred while he had fallen ill. In a fleeting instant, Jacob wasn't sure whether to thank his lucky stars or Providence for sending this man into his path again. He quickly realised that Cox must have been recruited by Kidd, making sense of this seemingly fortuitous encounter.

'Doctor,' Cox acknowledged, prompting the three sailors to obediently stand down and sheath their daggers. 'Take your son,' he said, tearing up the scroll that sailor Jack had placed in his open palm. 'You will come to no harm.'

Jacob wondered what he really meant, because he knew this species of rover had the custom of cunningly lying by omission. Did he mean, *You will come to no harm... yet?*

'There will be no reprisal,' said Jacob, more for Marley's sake than for his own welfare.

'Respect the code, and all will be well,' said Cox, steely-eyed. He had evidently heard Jacob and Marley speak of constables on their way. Jacob gave a nod before the pirate turned to usher out the three sailors.

The four men filed out of the tavern, leaving Jacob with a flashback of his days on a buccaneer ship. He recovered Paul, who had fallen unconscious on the bench.

'And what about me?' said the tavern girl, a pert, blond, painted lady.

Jacob tossed her a coin. 'Now be gone with you,' he said, as Marley called for a barrow to transport the lad back to Mrs Shrimpton's guest house.

Ten minutes later, as the two men walked on either side of the carter, pushing the handcart with Paul slumped inside, Marley said, 'Odd, the way he called you Doctor. Did you know him?'

'No,' said Jacob, 'he must have thought I was someone else.' It was his second lie of the evening.

'Well, he certainly showed you respect,' said the dry store merchant from Lancashire, who was unfamiliar with the instruments of warfare. 'I must say, you handle a sword admirably, sir. Very bold indeed. Admirable!'

'No less admirable than you standing by me, good sir,' said Jacob. 'I am eternally grateful.'

'I suppose I did, didn't I?' returned Marley, rather pleased with himself. But then his brow creased under the concern of seeing these men again.

It was with a pounding heart that Jeanne gave praise to God when she heard the rumblings on the stairway, as Jacob and Mr Marley helped Paul up the stairs. 'We've got you, me boy, just keep hold of your oar.' But it was less comforting when she smelt her son's breath when they brought him into the room. 'They must have spiced his drink with strong spirit,' said Jacob as he and Marley laid the lad on his bed, to the sound of unintelligible mutterings about freedom, paradise, Martinique, and Providencia. His brother and sister awoke and broke into giggles before falling heavy-headed back to sleep.

Marley left under a volley of thanks. Dreary-eyed and extenuated, Jacob supped on bread and broth as he told his wife about the stand-off with the rovers and the intervention from the pirate he once knew more than he cared to avow.

'But if this Captain Cox is found out, then he might well accuse you of piracy too, Jacob,' said Jeanne.

'That was yesteryear. It's a long time since I was bound to that horrid indenture,' he said as it dawned on him that Paul had uncannily also been taken aboard a pirate ship against his will. But there again, was it against his will? In any case, the difference was that these days, pirates could no longer sail in the guise of privateers under the banner of a letter of marque. Piracy these days was punishable by hanging.

'But what if he gets caught, Jacob?' insisted Jeanne. 'He might think you told the authorities and tie you into his murderous past.' There was no chance of that, Jacob reassured her, but he did know that a man like this would seek retribution.

Paul spent half the night bent over the chamber pot, and by morning he was bringing up nothing but bile. He voiced a timid apology for the inconvenience caused, but most of all, he felt ridiculed for having succumbed to the parlance of these sailors who had tried to coerce him into going to sea.

'I don't understand it, Paul,' said Jeanne, standing at the window with the morning sun alighting on her back and shoulders. Jacob sat at the table opposite Paul. She continued, 'It is totally out of character for you to go sauntering off like that, unable to run, onto a ship of thieves.'

'I don't know, Mother,' sighed Paul softly, holding his pounding temple in his left hand, trying not to let the words make his aching head feel worse.

'What made you do it?'

'If you must know, I suppose I was fed up with hearing you two arguing over where to settle.' He raised his head and squinted toward the bright light of the window where his mother was standing. 'I do know one thing, though. It is actually not the case of where to settle, is it?'

'What do you mean, Paul?' asked Jacob.

'You don't see it, Father, do you? It is not that Mother doesn't want to go to New York. It is that she does not want to go by sea. She was the same after the shipwreck in Geneva. She only boarded the riverboat because it was the only route.'

It was the first time Jeanne had heard Paul speak of that tragic event. Paul's bringing it to the surface made her realise he had kept it inside all these years. And so must he have kept everything else they had suffered locked away in a dark place that perhaps he had only now had the courage to open. He was just a young boy of nine during those times of extreme hardship; it must have had a huge impact on him, and still did. She realised that she had not dwelled enough on his suffering, especially since he had kept it locked inside that dim place. She had only really coped with her own feelings. Had she been a good mother?

'Yes, of course. I see. I have been so stuck on my own sights,' said Jacob contritely, echoing Jeanne's very thoughts. It seemed Jacob too realised their son was opening a secret door, and he listened carefully and spoke with tenderness and modesty.

'And I am the one preventing you now from going by the post route.'

'No, Paul, that's not the case,' said Jeanne levelly. She knew he would be embarrassed by any show of the emotion she now felt inside. 'I wouldn't want to take that route anyway. It would mean seven weeks in the American wilderness. So, you must not see it as your fault.'

Jacob saw an opening. Gently, he began, 'New York would suit people like...' Then correcting himself, he said, 'Would suit *us* better, and....'

'I know, we have a plot there,' Jeanne interrupted, her eyes welling despite herself as she reflected on her evaluation of her son.

'I was going to say, I have contacts there.'

'So you said, and yet they have not replied to your letters for many a year, Jacob.'

'I believe they are still alive, Jeanne. The old lady might have passed by now, but Daniel and Marianne were young and

301

strong. They had children. Surely, they could not both have succumbed, could they? At any rate, we must decide today whether to stay or go. It will be too cold to arrive in New York in eight weeks' time or to wait for the next ship.'

Jeanne, wiping her eyes on the backs of her hands, pulled up a chair next to the one where Paul had put up his leg, after Jacob had dressed it earlier that morning. She could no longer speak; she just needed to coddle him. After a moment straightening his splints, she looked up at her son with a bright smile and whispered, 'You are right.'

As soon as she spoke, there came loud voices from downstairs that broke the moment: Mrs Shrimpton sounding overly loud, polite, and falsely jovial amid male articulations. Then they heard boots clomping up the stairs. Jeanne shot a glance across the table at Jacob; her eloquent stare needed no words. In it, he read, 'You don't think they're coming to arrest you, do you?'

Jeanne and Jacob stood up smartly. Paul jerked his head toward the door but remained seated with his leg on the chair. There came three raps at the door. 'Monsieur Delpech, I present His Excellency, Governor Coote, Earl of Bellomont, who wishes to speak with you,' bellowed a guard. After a moment's pause, he articulated again in no uncertain terms, 'Please open the door!'

At last, Jacob unbolted the door and opened it wide to find the governor of New York and Massachusetts, whom he had met the previous evening, standing tall in his periwig and inch-high heeled, buckled shoes. 'Monsieur, or should I say, Lieutenant Delpech,' said Governor Coote, who stepped with aristocratic poise into the room while the two guards posted themselves at the door left open.

'Your Excellency,' said Jacob with a slight inclination of the head, while Jeanne curtsied respectfully, a clear demonstration of her breeding.

'I have come about the incident last night that has been the subject of much talk in town.' The governor's cheerful tone of voice told Jacob he had probably not come to arrest him, but Jacob remained on his guard. The earl turned to Paul. 'Ah, young man. You can be proud and thankful to your father. He searched frantically high and low and yet methodically until he found you *in extremis,* I hear. He boldly rescued you from the clutches of pirates we have been hunting for the past year. Dangerous men. Yet he stood up to them as no man ever has.' The governor seemed to observe Jacob's expression, which did not change. 'I wanted to congratulate you in person, Monsieur Delpech.'

'Thank you, Your Excellency. I did what any father would.'

'You, sir, have left an indelible mark in the collective spirit by showing how one man can stand up to such rogues. For that, I am exceedingly grateful. Sir, you are an inspiration. Your show of bravado will undoubtedly inspire others to act likewise.'

Jacob thought it would be foolish to try such a thing, though he did not say so, knowing that anybody else would have been sliced and run through in the flicker of an eye. He was unsure how or exactly what the governor had heard. But one thing was for sure: the governor was certainly angling for something, and Jacob wished he would get to the point.

'You see, we are ferociously intent on eradicating this scourge of the seas, and we rely upon witnesses to help us bring them to justice. In short, according to our investigations, we have reason to believe these rogues were members of Captain Kidd's crew, led by an unscrupulous scoundrel by the name of Cox, one Captain Thomas Cox. He should have been sent to London a decade ago but managed to jump ship and escape.' The governor paused. Jacob remained silent and impassive, although he could hear his beating heart in his ears. The governor went on, 'Now, would you recognise him if you saw him again? And, more particularly, do you recall any distinguishing features?'

Jacob now understood what Cox had meant by 'respect the code'. He had read those articles aboard the *Joseph*, on which he had served under the terrible and infamous Captain Brook a decade ago, the same ship on which Captain Cox had embarked as a pirate prisoner in Port Royal only to be taken to Caimen Island, where his ship and crew had been waiting for his deliverance. Jacob knew that a lie, or rather, his sworn silence guaranteed his safety, as well as that of Marley, who would unquestionably have been recognised by anyone present in the tavern as the dry goods merchant of the Town Dock.

Without wavering, he said, 'I am very sorry, Your Excellency. The tavern was dimly lit, and, alas, my eyesight is not what it used to be in such poor light.' Jacob assured himself inwardly that this was the truth.

'I am told the commander spoke with familiarity to you,' said the governor. Jeanne saw he was carefully assessing Jacob's reaction.

'I believe I was very lucky, Your Excellency,' returned Jacob. 'He must have mistaken me for someone else.'

'Yes, for a doctor, I believe,' said the governor, with a fleeting glance at Paul's leg.

'I am a merchant and planter, Your Excellency. I have served as lieutenant in the king's army, and as a notary in my home-town. A doctor, I am not.'

'Ah,' said the governor, looking pensively at his feet as if a rug had been pulled from under them. 'Never mind, you have done well. All there is left for me to tell you is to stay away from the Northern District from now on. There is unfortunately another danger lurking there.'

'Rovers, Your Excellency?' inquired Jacob, feeling that a critical moment had passed.

'No. Another case of the contagion,' said the governor. Jeanne raised her hand to her mouth, glad for a pretext to hide her own face and to gulp freely. The governor went on, 'But pray, don't let that deter your installation here. You have the backing of the constables and the selectmen of Boston, you know. You would be made most welcome.'

Mrs Shrimpton had followed the governor up the stairs and was standing outside the open door between the soldiers. She clasped her hands together as the governor took his leave cordially and was visibly somewhat reassured. Judging from the Huguenot's replies, the governor's secret as to his prior dealings with Captain Kidd and his crew was as safe as the infamous Boston gaol in which Kidd was being held.

Jacob bolted the door behind the soldiers and turned back into the room; his shoulders deflated as the strain of the moment fell away. Moving back to the table, opposite which Jeanne was still standing, he said, 'Well, you heard what he said. An invitation to stay is not something we can easily turn down, is it?' He gave her a subdued smile in anticipation of seeing her bat her hands in joy. But she did not. She remained standing, her palms face down on the table, searching into his eyes.

Jeanne knew deep down that Paul was right. Her fear of another sea voyage had perhaps prevented her from clearly seeing their goal and their dream. Travelling to New York was something they had planned before their departure from Ireland. If they remained in Boston, not only would they be putting themselves within reach of the contagion, but Jacob would also be forever concerned that one day he would have to justify his past life and explain that he had been an innocent captive of a system that had tried to corrupt him. But he had resisted in the name of his faith and for the sake of his family. And now, they were together again.

Isn't that what she had constantly prayed for in that secret recess three yards wide and two yards deep, where she had hidden with nothing but a stool and a bucket, during the waking hours every day for sixteen months solid? Isn't that what she had prayed for on the perilous journey with Paul across the war-torn hills of the Palatinate? Hadn't she risen above humiliation in London and kept herself and Paul from poverty thanks to her faith, her loom, and her belief they would all be together again? One more step to freedom.

One more voyage to the new life they had dreamt of. Why was she unable to embark on this last trip that would take them to that final victory? Was it only that she feared the dreaded sea? Or was she afraid of failure, that it would not turn out to be the place they had dreamt about after all?

'Mother,' said Paul, bringing her out of her introspection. 'If we stay, I will be pointed at in the streets as the one who was naïve enough to be taken in by rogue sailors. But we have been in far direr straits, and I will live it down. You have my blessing as well if you wish to remain here in Boston.'

After a moment of thought, Jeanne, with renewed spirit, slapped the tabletop with her palm and exclaimed, 'No, Paul. Your father was right. We had a plan. We have a dream, and we have a plot!'

Surprised and joyous yet contrite, Jacob took his wife's hands across the table. His shoulders, weighed down like his conscience by his secret, sagged.

'My dear wife,' he said with a note of guilt in his voice. 'You are the bravest woman I have ever known.'

'No, Jacob...'

'Let me finish. I am the most wretched of men. I should have seen your strife, but instead, I was blinded by my own course.

I must confess, I have not been as forthright as I should have with one as honest and courageous as you have proven to be. Accepting to embark on this final voyage means that you are capable, for the love of your family, to overcome a deep-rooted fear, and the terrible memory of that tragic event on the lake of Geneva. And yet I stand here, such a feeble soul in that I have not even had the strength and honesty to share my doubts with you.'

'What do you mean, Jacob?'

'Sit yourself down, my dear wife.' Jeanne pulled up her chair while Jacob sat back down opposite her and continued in a tone of penitence. 'That plot of land I have been using as a reason to leave here, I must confess, I do not know for certain if it is ours to claim.'

'What do you mean, Jacob? You showed me the letter of reservation.'

'Yes, I put down a payment to reserve the land, but I did not complete the purchase of the deeds at the time. I took the money back with me to England to join you in London. But as you know, that money was stolen on my very first night there.'

'Are you saying you brought us all the way across the world,' Jeanne said evenly, 'through storms that still give me night-mares, and on a ship that brought us close to starvation and nearly killed our son, on the mere hope that we had a place to go to?'

'Yes, I am sorry, I am afraid so.'

'But surely the reservation must still hold, Jacob.'

'Dare I say it, that is my hope. But I confess, I cannot guarantee it. After I left, there was a revolt in New York. The man I entrusted with my reservation payment has since died, and Darlington's letters ceased thereafter.'

'It's no wonder you have been behaving so secretively since we left Ireland!'

'I'm afraid so. I must confess it had continually clouded my judgement, hampered my sleep, and made me blind to the anxiety of those I love most of all in this world.'

Folding her arms, Jeanne sat back in her chair. Her mouth tightened; her eyes steeled. Her determination returning, she said, 'Then, my dear husband, we shall sort this through once we get there. There's nothing we can do about it here, is there?'

'No, I do not believe so.'

'I wish you'd told me before, Jacob,' she said with empathy, seeing that, now more than ever, Jacob needed her faith in him. Having uncovered his weakness and dilemma, and having reconnected with her role as one of the two founding pillars of the Delpech family in this New World, she had by the same token recovered her faith in her husband. 'Then we shall be strong together, and if need be, we'll rent rooms in a lodging house until we find a plot to our liking,' she declared. Then, beckoning to Isabelle and Pierre, who were sitting on the big bed, she called out, 'Come, children, let us pray together for God to bless our house of Delpech.'

'Isn't this the house of Mrs Shrimpton, though?' said Isabelle saucily as she jumped off her parents' bed.

'Never forget, children, wherever we are, that we make up the house of Delpech. Just as a church is made by its congregation, not its building, so too our family makes up our house. As long as we are together, we are the house of Delpech, built on strength, founded on faith, joined in love, and kept by God above.'

'Amen,' said Jacob in earnest as they all joined hands around the table.

Paul, quietly listening, wondered how that could make sense if not all of them were present.

A little later that day, with a lighter step, Jacob sauntered down to the bustling quayside to oversee the loading of their effects onto the *Nassau*, a two-mast, square-rigged brigantine of 125 tons. But there was still the awkward question of what they would do when they arrived. Did they have a plot? And what had become of the Darlingtons? 'Only time will tell,' he told himself and then pushed the thoughts to the back of his mind as the stevedores began hauling the crates and chests from the lockup to the hold.

Meanwhile, standing before the lodging room window that looked over the bay, Paul reminisced about the ship he had visited and the taste of freedom he had sampled. With that taste in mind and despite his handicap, he distinctly remembered feeling a desperate desire to sail away, so desperate that he would have gladly sailed right out of the bay with those sailors, even if he had known they were pirates. It was, he thought to himself, recalling the words of his mother, 'out of character,' and it quite frightened him.

Jeanne spent a frantic afternoon preparing for the imminent departure, which had thankfully been put off till the morning tide.

By the evening, she was reassured to learn that Jacob had arranged for a carter to pick up their belongings in the morning, and especially that he had reserved a private cabin aboard, albeit for the hefty sum of five pounds. The extra comfort of privacy helped her process her anxiety, but she was nonetheless conscious they were leaving a threatening situation in Boston only to be heading toward an uncertain future in New York.

Mrs Shrimpton had her maid bring up the evening meal. The landlady was sorry that Mr and Mrs Delpech had finally decided to depart for New York. Having settled the bill earlier, Jacob understood why she had been so keen to encourage them to stay longer. It reminded him of the exorbitant rent he had been obliged to honour once when he fell ill in the perfidious town of Port Royal. It had forced him to become indentured to a privateer ship to pay it off.

'A short stay, this time,' Mrs Shrimpton remarked perfunctorily.

'This time, yes,' Jeanne returned and thanked Mrs Shrimpton for her warm welcome.

'You know where to find us should you come back, me loves.'

'Thank you,' said Jacob.

'By the way, I heard them rats are gone, my word.'

'Rats, Mrs Shrimpton?' said Jacob, quite surprised.

'Pirates, that's what my Albert calls 'em. And I wager the governor ain't 'alf glad to see the back of 'em.'

'I thought he was on their heels.'

'Put it this way: they are out of his periwig now, ain't they! If the truth be told, he doesn't want them stirring up his past dealings with Kidd and his crew. Saw them in a completely different light not so long ago, didn't he, my word, before Kidd turned pirate. I imagine he probably thinks everyone's forgotten about it, and it won't do him any favours if someone breaks the silence about the captain's lot. I'm sure he's quite happy to let them go, long as they remain as mute as a prison door! Bad enough with his settling the Leisler score. Many were against it here in Boston, you know. And he doesn't want any more bad air, does he? Anyway, I'll see you in the morning before you leave, me loves.'

After dinner, Jacob raised his head from the letter he was reading in the lamplight and pondered what Mrs Shrimpton had said about the previous night's episode. He conjectured that if he had not met Cox in a previous life, his journey might have ended last night. How strange was the journey of a man, he thought to himself as he headed for an uncertain future in New York. But perhaps it was fate.

'What are you reading, darling?' asked Jeanne, pouring a hot, calming herbal infusion into his cup.

'Oh, just an old letter from Darlington, my dear,' he said, folding the letter away as the soothing fragrance rose from the chamomile flowers steeped in the pot. Taking up his cup, he wondered if his young friend had survived the commotion of the day. However, he did not think it necessary to tell Jeanne that, at the time of writing, things were turning pretty sour in New York for Daniel Darlington.

CHAPTER 23

1691, New York

THE DARLINGTONS — 8 YEARS EARLIER

Darlington perused the letter he had been writing earlier to Jacob Delpech.

So much has come about since I last wrote, but I shall try to be brief.

The Canadian campaign was a disaster. The allied Indian sachems had pledged to supply a thousand warriors to add to our first American three-colonies army, but their tribes had been severely affected by the contagion, and they were unable to send a single brave.

Last August, I and my neighbour, Didier Ducamp, whom I mentioned in an earlier letter, along with four hundred men, followed Major Winthrop northward, only to watch our rank and file being decimated without seeing the face of a single Canadian enemy. I could only helplessly bear witness to the unstoppable demise of scores of men who dropped like flies as they succumbed, not to enemy fire, but to a terrifying onslaught of the smallpox!

Nobody complained when Winthrop ordered our retreat, except Leisler, who blamed Winthrop for the failure to attack Montreal and had him arrested upon our arrival in Albany. With hindsight, I realise now that Leisler must have fathomed the consequence of leaving Montreal without a battlefront. William Phips's strategy relied on our land attack on Montreal to support his raid on Quebec from the St Lawrence River.

Indeed, Phips fared no better with his thirty or so ships that sailed from Boston, tasked to destroy the French in Quebec. Phips had been waiting for reinforcements from England that did not come, and so, he did not sail into the St Lawrence River until October. The tardive season, the lack of a secondary battlefront, and the early onset of cold weather took a terrible toll. You know how cold it can get here in the fall.

With no other battlefront to defend, given that we had already retreated to Albany by then, the French under Frontenac were able to force the fleet out of the St Lawrence River with the loss of thirty-seven New Englanders against seven Canadians. The only consolation being that Jacques le Moyne de Sainte-Hélène, the infamous commander of the Schenectady massacre, was among the dead. But then a further one thousand men tragically died on the return journey to Boston from illness, dysentery, and shipwreck. Again, Leisler was furious.

Daniel paused and wondered if he should send the letter. Was there any need to burden a man three thousand miles away with his own frustration? Moreover, it gave him nausea to review the events of the previous months. It made him feel even more republican to think that two kings on another continent were in many ways the root cause of this war in America. Couldn't New Englanders and French Canadians have sorted out their own disagreements by themselves? If Frontenac had not obeyed his king, there would have been no massacre, his cousins would still be alive and going about their daily lives, and his aunt would not be in Boston.

But there again, wouldn't the Catholic Canadians have still set their sights on capturing the totality of the fur trade anyway? It was hard to know. 'More, always more, such is the greed of the white man, wherever he is from,' he recalled that his pastor father used to say. And didn't he himself strive for more wealth, more success, more importance? Was it even possible for so many who had come to this world with burning ambitions just to live their lives content with their lot? Manifestly not, for after all, this world they were building was founded on a dream of success, come what may.

By the winter of 1690, Leisler's plans of a two-pronged attack to eradicate the French had irremediably gone awry. However, he remained adamant in his self-imposed duty to defend the territory and hold office until the king's new governor, Henry Sloughter, arrived from England. Leisler remained focussed and steadfast even in defeat. During a meeting at the fort one day, Leisler said, 'Failure is only part of the story, gentlemen. For did not Columbus discover America by failing in his endeavour to reach the Indies?' Daniel had heard the refrain before as a reason to fight through setbacks and accomplish that all-important dream of success. But he had nonetheless agreed; at least the French had been driven back to a defensive stance, for the time being. And, all said and done, had the land expedition not encountered the invisible enemy of disease, the French would have stood little chance against the Boston fleet, occupied as they would have been with the battlefront south of Montreal.

Leisler knew he had been right, that he had been cheated of success, and Daniel soon noticed the acting lieutenant governor becoming more and more distrustful of all but his closest circle. Darlington saw the man gradually acquire an increasingly guarded attitude toward anything that challenged his power, including one of the king's appointees named Major Richard Ingoldsby, who arrived one day in January ahead of the incoming governor.

Even Marianne was beginning to say that Leisler was becoming unreasonable. But Daniel remained steadfast in his support for Leisler. He only hoped the price of his commitment to the man would not be too costly. But never in a thousand years would he have foreseen the events that would lead to the inexorable demise of Jacob Leisler.

He perused the last lines of the letter again, then picked up a fresh quill, which he dipped delicately into the ink well. He wrote his name at the bottom, followed by the date: January 29th, 1691.

Darlington had been writing the letter earlier that morning when his flow of ink was interrupted by a messenger with an invitation for Daniel to meet Leisler urgently at his house on the Strand.

In the large hall, he had found council members seated around the table. Jacob Milborne—having recovered his vibrant tenor voice after the tragic death of his wife and daughter from smallpox—was rereading out loud a note sent by Major Ingoldsby, who demanded that he be admitted into the fort with his stores.

'That is correct,' had said Chidley Brooke, the messenger, a lean English gentleman with an accommodating rictus.

'This is a direct affront to our governor's rank and honour, no less, sir,' Milborne had remarked with indignation at the show of such insolence from a representative of Their Majesties. 'An absolute outrage!'

Leisler had distanced himself from the table and had taken his usual stance before the rear window that looked onto the frost-covered garden. 'But let us first see his orders,' he had said, while holding an official letter. 'Milborne, I want you to kindly remind Major Ingoldsby that this letter means that, until the newly appointed governor arrives to relieve me, he must obey his acting lieutenant governor.' Daniel had surmised that the letter in question was the one from the king received back in '89. At the time, Leisler had interpreted it as an endorsement of his position as acting lieutenant governor, following the flight back to England of the appointed Lieutenant Governor Nicholson. This was the letter upon which Leisler's authority as acting lieutenant governor had been founded and subsequently validated by his counsellors.

Chidley Brooke had glanced over the letter that Leisler had handed to Milborne to lay out before him. 'I do believe we have a copy. But I will convey your message to the major. In the meantime, I am to hand you this. It is the new composition of the king's council for New York.'

Leisler's face had seemed to set in a mask of passivity as he perused the names of his enemies on the note that was handed to him. With hindsight, Daniel reflected now how courageously Leisler had kept his composure when everything inside must have been a maelstrom of disappointment and disillusion. Besides the name of Chidley Brooke, who was sitting at the table, the names on the list included William Nicholls and Nicholas Bayard, whom Leisler had kept in jail for almost a year for trying to sabotage his rule. But Leisler's name was absent. Was he to understand that there was something special reserved for him? But how could he work with these Jacobites who would have left the gates of the city wide open for the French to march in like a sharp winter gust? There again, maybe Their Majesties were wise in thinking that to rule, one must deploy one's enemies in positions of importance and so have them become dependent on the authority that gave them their rank in society. Alexander the Great deployed such a method very well. There again, it could all be a Jacobite ruse, couldn't it?

Brooke had taken his leave by the time Leisler had turned to Daniel, and explained that it was best to hold Major Ingoldsby at bay until they understood his orders and the authority under which he intended to carry them out. Leisler counted on Daniel as one of his most trusted men to convey Milborne to the *Beaver* anchored at Gowanus Creek off Long Island. 'We only know that our detractors were seen headed toward the island and no doubt have polluted the major's mind one way or another.' Could this all be a ploy to take the fort? It was a delicate matter, and Daniel was not only a trusted friend, but he had also shown his worth on a number of commissions before. He also had a boat. Daniel could hardly refuse the man to whom he had sworn allegiance, so he had accepted and had sent word to Didier Ducamp to prepare the ketch so they could be out with the rise of the morning tide and arrive at the *Beaver* by noon.

Marianne now entered the study with a basket of victuals. She said, 'I don't like it, Daniel. Why can't he send someone else to do his begging? Or better still, why doesn't he meet the Englishman here in New York?'

'He is suspicious.'

'He's afraid of his own shadow, Daniel.'

'That's because of the papists and the Jacobites who are dying to cook his goose, and he knows it. I'm the only one he trusts with a suitable vessel.'

'Anyway, here's your basket. There's plenty in there for May's husband too.'

'Thank you, my pretty wife. Truly, I am a lucky man.'

'Yes, and don't you forget it! You have a wife who loves you and two littluns who haven't seen their daddy very much of late. So don't you go taking any risks for that Leisler, or Ingoldsby. You hear me, Daniel Darlington? There's enough to worry about with the French threatening to attack, and more and more men willing to risk their lives. What is this world coming to?'

'The weather is cold enough to freeze the fringe of the sea in places, but the wind is blowing a stiff breeze; we will be back by nightfall. But you're right, we should really be rejoicing that more men have come to defend the colony.'

'That's not what I meant, Daniel. A soldier far away from home often loses the moral compass that binds him to virtue.'

Daniel immediately realised that, in his natural inclination to win her over, he had made an insensitive blunder. He had not forgotten that she had undergone the French dragonnades in '85 at her ancestral home in France, where soldiers were billeted with the order to pressure Protestants into converting to Catholicism. Marianne, like her grandmother, had resisted despite the soldiers' shocking and unruly behaviour, and then had been arrested, tried, and sent into confinement with her grandmother in Marseille. From there they were sent to Toulon, and then to a prison island in the Caribbean. He had encountered her, a beautiful young lady of good breeding, at the island where he had come to careen his ship before his onward voyage back to New York. He literally stole her away along with her grandmother.

'I am so sorry, my darling,' he said softly. 'Please forgive my thoughtlessness. Kiss our children for me.' Making sure no one had approached the study door left ajar, he then took his wife by the waist with his two hands and kissed her on the soft, warm skin between her jawbone and the crook of her neck.

'What if they really are papists?' she said soberly.

'Worry not, Leisler doesn't believe it any more than I do. He's just being magnanimous and procedural. I will be back by nightfall. Promise.'

Half an hour later, Daniel found Ducamp and Davey the Dutchman making good the ketch to set sail, with the yardarms dripping melting ice in the thinly veiled sun. He would rather have let her go to the relative safety of Turtle Bay to pass the remaining winter as he had planned. Her sodden timbers had made her more sluggish than usual, not to mention that she was in need of some robust repairs. But these were trying times for everybody. She had nonetheless served him well so far, so Daniel tried to let the thought go as he put down his basket of provisions inside the cabin.

Returning on deck, he said, 'Why is it, every time we plan to put her into dry dock, we are sent on a commission?'

'Probably because Leisler knows he can trust you,' said Ducamp. 'And believe me, trust is more precious than gold when you're at the top.' Daniel shrugged his shoulders to confirm what he knew already. Ducamp went on, 'So, what's it to be this time with Milborne and company?'

'We'll be carrying them to Major Ingoldsby's ship, anchored at Gowanus.'

'Right. In that case, might be worth fetching in some lumber while we're there to make it worth our while.'

'You'll have to be quick, though. I'll be stuck with Milborne.'

'That's why Davey's coming with us,' said Ducamp. The big Dutch docker kept his silence, just showed a large, mittened palm, and continued to unfasten the moorings.

'Fair enough,' said Daniel.

'So, why's Ingoldsby anchored at Long Island? That's King's County. Won't they give him a pilot to see him in?'

'No, he's demanded admission into the fort, that's what.'

'Ah, I'm sure Leisler will love him for that,' Ducamp said ironically. 'On whose authority?'

'That's what Milborne wants to find out. They fear he's already been approached by Bayard's clique and had poison poured into his ear. God only knows what they've been telling him about the situation in New York. And that van Cortlandt is a cunning as an old fox! He'll have gotten his foot in the door already. In my opinion, Leisler shouldn't have waited, should have got in first.'

'Then it is wise to bring the major over to our way of thinking,' said Ducamp. 'I only hope poor Milborne's the man for the job.' He nodded toward the very man approaching on the quay, looking official in his greatcoat and livery, flanked by two guards in full regalia.

A moment later, Jacob Milborne was stomping over the gangplank, looking like a man entrusted with an important mission. After a brief exchange with Darlington, he dived into the cabin, 'to review my notes,' he said.

A steady northwesterly breeze filled the two main sails to a pleasing curve, enabling the ketch to slice through the blue-grey waters of New York Bay with greater speed than usual, despite her sodden timbers. As the sun, obscured by a thin veil of winter clouds, ascended to its highest point, Daniel, with a practiced eye, discerned the distinct opening of Gowanus Creek where the *Beaver* lay at anchor.

Shortly after, he could clearly make out her English colours floating above the forest of bare trees that screened them from the creek, a clear visual indication of Their Majesties' frigate even from a distance. 'Prepare to ease the mainsail and brace the yard,' Daniel instructed, his voice carrying on the wind. Ducamp, standing nearby, nodded in understanding, their seasoned camaraderie needing no excess words. Davey was already scaling the rigging to reef the topsail and drop their pace as they neared the inlet. Meanwhile, Daniel observed the current, a subtle but crucial factor in their approach. 'Mind the ebb flow,' he said to himself as he held the helm, aware that the outgoing tide could subtly alter their course. 'Steer a point closer to the wind, and let's take advantage of the back eddy near the southern bank.'

As the ketch adjusted its approach, harnessing the wind's power while countering the creek's outward flow, it glided with a mariner's precision towards the anchorage upstream. The crew, well-versed in the language of sails and seas, worked in unison, trimming the jib and mainsail to maintain a controlled, steady advance. Daniel felt a surge of satisfaction in his good old ketch. Here was the true reason why Leisler had summoned his skills—skills previously honed by years on the open sea, now guiding them safely to their destination.

Joining him at the helm, Didier Ducamp suggested, 'Let's drop anchor before we come into sight; then we can *casser la croute* before the meeting.' He often used the French expression that Daniel had come to know meant *break the crust of bread*, which basically meant *stop and have a bite to eat*.

But Milborne, who did not care much for sea travel and had remained below deck for most of the hour-and-a-half-long voyage, now emerged from the cabin, no doubt having noticed

321

a reduction in the ship's pitch and yaw as she decreased speed. 'I say the sooner we put in, the sooner we depart,' he said sharply. 'We can eat on the way back.'

Ducamp, in his slow, deep voice of reason, replied, 'As an old soldier, sir, I'd abide by the saying, "A hungry man is an angry man." So shouldn't we let the major fill his belly first?' The two guards, who had stood up from their sitting positions as Milborne stepped from the cabin, gave a knowing smirk. They knew Ducamp's frank-talking reputation, a reputation also borne out of the fact that English was not his first language.

Milborne eyed the frigate's top masts above the remaining strip of leafless trees, whose trunks still screened them. He straightened his coats as if he were about to go somewhere and said, 'As an envoy of the king's representative in New York, I would say, until the newly appointed governor gets here, the major is under our dominion and should show us respect. Whatever his bodily needs!'

Daniel felt that Milborne had a strong point. Why should they bow down to a military leader who had never set foot in their world until this week? But he knew that Ducamp's experience and knowledge of military matters made more sense, especially given the delicate circumstances surrounding Leisler's assumption of power. This authority was only confirmed if one read carefully between the lines of that letter sent by the king in late '89.

But of course, Jacob Milborne's hastiness trumped the former French lieutenant's caution. Daniel kept their course sailing between the last of the treacherous sandbanks of Gowanus Creek, still with four hours to spare until low tide.

Finally, they rounded the wooden bend in the creek to find the anchorage that sheltered the magnificent frigate, a three-masted might of two hundred tons along with its storeship still in tow.

Daniel also recognised the pilot boat Chidley Brooke must have travelled in and figured he must have left New York directly after the meeting with Leisler. On the south-facing shore sat the Symon farmstead, where he and Ducamp had purchased lumber the previous autumn. In old George Symon's image, it was a sight of tranquillity, with the stone chimney smoking and the surrounding laboured fields that lay furrowed, hoary, and glistening in the raw winter sunlight, while a raucous chorus of caws from carrion birds echoed from their rookeries over the misty, brackish water.

'Darlington, you come with me,' said Milborne imperiously, as the ketch gently lined up against the starboard flank of the huge frigate after they had received the signal to approach. To Ducamp and Davey, he said, 'You two keep the boat prepared for sail.' Cupping his mouth and raising his head to the gunwale ten feet above them, he then called out, 'Ahoy. I am Counsellor Milborne. I come from His Excellency Governor Leisler.' Daniel couldn't resist a glance to Ducamp, who must have thought the same thing, that this was probably not the most diplomatic approach for one seeking to appease.

Five minutes later, Milborne was standing on deck, flanked by his two militia soldiers, while the taller Darlington, naturally reticent to position himself next to Milborne, hung back two steps behind them. Daniel looked around the deck where sailors were completing their chores, visibly making the ship impeccable to parade into the port of New York: checking rigging, swabbing the decks, and inspecting timbers. He then detected sounds of scraping bowls, gruntles, and laughter coming from the berthing deck hatch, where he supposed groups of men were indulging in fresh provisions after the long voyage fed on salted beef and hardtack.

They were greeted by a well-attired gentleman in his mid-thirties. 'Major Ingoldsby, I presume,' said Milborne, addressing the younger man standing before him.

'Oh no, sir. I am Shanks, first lieutenant. I shall show you to the Great Cabin where the major is dining with the captain and... er... others.'

Milborne could have kicked himself for not recognising the absence of a uniform, remembering now that the navy did not recognise the new trend for army men to wear one. For unlike in the navy, instantly recognising one's enemy in the army was paramount during hand-to-hand land battle. Milborne stood erect, and rigidly, he said, 'Yes, yes, carry on.'

The New York delegation followed Shanks along the main deck to the stern, passing crew members changing a sail, and up the steps to the quarterdeck. The first lieutenant knocked smartly on the door, and then pushed it open to reveal a sumptuous meal taking place in the plush captain's cabin, where another surprise awaited Leisler's messenger. 'Visitors, sir,' said Shanks, then retreated, leaving Milborne standing in the doorway of the bright and well-furnished cabin with Daniel standing at his shoulder.

'Ah. To whom do I have the honour?' said Major Ingoldsby quite bombastically, without introduction, then forked a piece of meat into his mouth. Around him sat the ship's master, Chidley Brooke, and none other than Stephanus van Cortlandt, a prominent colonial administrator, and the wealthy merchant and slave importer Frederick Philipse, these last two being sworn enemies of Jacob Leisler.

Milborne adroitly took no notice of these men and instead addressed the middle-aged major in full military attire, which consisted of a red coat with gold buttons and braiding, a white shirt and cravat, and a red silk sash. He said, 'Major Ingoldsby, I presume?'

'You presume rightly, sir, unless I am wearing another man's uniform!' quipped the ruddy-faced major. Daniel did not fail to notice the smirk forming at Cortlandt's thin-lipped mouth.

'I am Counsellor Milborne,' said the messenger, 'sent on the authority of Lieutenant Governor Leisler to inspect your orders before your admission is considered into New York harbour.'

Stephanus van Cortlandt rose and nodded discreetly to Philipse, and the two grey-haired gentlemen tactfully took their leave. The major then turned on his chair, reached into a writing bureau, and brought out his orders. 'There, sir,' said Ingoldsby, handing the parchment scroll to his servant, who then delivered it to Milborne, who had edged further into the room.

Daniel, in the meantime, observed the faces of the two men. Ingoldsby did not invite Milborne to eat at his table. There again, he suspected that Milborne would not have sat at a table where his enemies had been seated.

'These are orders that grant you authority over your men, sir,' said Milborne. 'Do you have any others?'

'That should suffice in the presence of the appointed members of the council, to grant admission to me and my men into the fort,' said the ruddy-faced major.

Calmly, Milborne said, 'Those members have not been sworn in. Therefore, as I understand it, they have no bearing over the fort.'

'Governor Sloughter will not be long in arriving!'

'Indeed, and until then, Lieutenant Governor Leisler has advised that you take up residence at his house in New York. The officers will be offered quarters in burghers' houses.'

Ingoldsby stood up and pounded the table. Barely keeping his composure, he said, 'It is the fort I have come to take. And if there be resistance, then he who resists is no friend of the king and queen, sir!'

Daniel sensed the two men both digging into their positions, both of them too stubborn, too stuck in their pride to reach any mutual terrain propitious for an agreement. Raising a humble finger, Daniel turned to Milborne and said, 'Might I suggest we return with the major's message and seek our governor's response?'

'I still see no orders to support your request, sir,' Milborne continued, remaining infuriatingly stern yet calm.

Ingoldsby exploded. 'And I see no orders that authorise you to display such cavalier behaviour against an appointee of the king, sir!'

'I see no point in continuing. Sir, I leave you with the invitation. Good day.'

'Sir, I am sure you can find your own way off this ship.'

Milborne clicked his heels, turned, and left the sumptuous room without another word.

Daniel understood now why Jacob Milborne had been so unsuccessful in Albany. The man craved self-importance. It made him rigid and incapable of empathy. After all, Ingoldsby and his men had come a long way to defend the colony. He had been sent on the king's authority, and yet, neither Milborne nor Leisler had made a move to welcome him when the first notification came of the arrival of the *Beaver* at Sandy Hook. Instead, he received a warm welcome from the likes of Stephanus van Cortlandt, who now shared meals with the major in place of Leisler.

But then again, it was true that neither did Ingoldsby, brash, stubborn, and resolutely set in his ways, strike Daniel as much of a negotiator. He was visibly so sure of his position of authority, which he apparently disliked being challenged, that he had seemed to lose sight of his mission's objective: to gain admission into the fort under Sloughter, who could be arriving in just a matter of days. Couldn't he simply accept the invitation to stay at an agreeable residence and bide his time in comfort? But his ego had evidently been nursed by Cortlandt and Philipse, who had only retreated to the prow of the ship after withdrawing from the captain's cabin, eager, no doubt, to learn about the outcome of the brief meeting with the usurper's man.

Moreover, how could Ingoldsby, who did not know New York any more than an English country squire, be so invasive, like a stranger who burst into your house and sat at your table uninvited? As they descended the rope ladder of the gunwale, Daniel wished to God for a day when New York would be governed by men who belonged to it, who were an integral part of its fabric, rather than an emissary sent from some gloomy, far-flung island.

Daniel's worst fears were realised the following day, January 30th, when Ingoldsby outright officially refused Leisler's authority as governor of New York. He did not acknowledge the letter of July 1689, thus undermining the very foundation of Leisler's rule. He refused any accommodation other than what he considered his rightful place at the fort. And he went so far as to summon the New York militia to his aid in ousting the usurper, insisting that if Leisler continued to refuse entry to the fort for the king's soldiers, then he would be no friend of the Crown of England.

To de-escalate the increasingly tense situation, Leisler lost no time in issuing a proclamation that summoned the militia of the province to his aid and instructed officers in King's County, where the *Beaver* was anchored, to obey no orders other than his own. He protested in the name of Their Majesties that without showing any order from the king or Governor Sloughter, Major Ingoldsby demanded the fort and then issued a call to arms. Leisler forbade any hostilities and declared Ingoldsby would be responsible if there were to be any bloodshed.

'Decidedly, let's hope Governor Sloughter arrives soon,' said Madame de Fontenay at the dining room table, after Daniel had relayed news of Leisler's response to Ingoldsby's threat. 'My husband would have said that these men have foolishly entrenched themselves into a stalemate.'

Daniel had returned home earlier than usual as the bleak winter's day began to turn purple. Seeing May's carriage parked in front of the house, Ducamp had followed him in to find his wife and children sharing the company of the ladies of the house. May had just returned from the Huguenot dame school in town where her daughter was schooled and, as per her habit, had stopped by the Darlingtons to impart the latest gossip. The little girl, Lily-Anne, who Ducamp had come to consider as his own daughter, sat in the vacant armchair by the fireside, proudly holding baby Francine. The two families had naturally bonded thanks to the difficult times that lay behind them and remained close friends in the uncertain times that lay ahead.

'Aye,' said Didier, who sat back from the table, having brought out his pipe, 'and I reckon they ought to be wary of the rabble-rousing counsellors!'

'I wouldn't be surprised to see Judith Bayard rubbing her hands together at the prospect of revenge,' said Marianne.

'Such a vengeful sow she is,' said May, not mincing her words after taking a puff from her husband's pipe. 'You must admit, though, Leisler's doing himself no favours being so ferociously against them.'

'He won't give up the fort or the seal until the new governor stands before him,' said Daniel. 'Claims it could be a trap otherwise, which, I admit, is nonsense.'

'But he really has no other choice,' said May. 'And I wouldn't be surprised if the grandees were deliberately using this major to force Leisler into a position of opposition.'

'Then why doesn't he simply let Ingoldsby in?' Marianne asked.

'That would be as good as confessing that he came to rule illegally,' said Madame de Fontenay. 'It would make him a usurper and a rebel by his own admission.'

'But he saved the city of New York,' said Marianne. 'Built up defences, and created an army...'

'A disastrous army,' said May.

'Granted,' said Daniel. 'Although the French have stood back, for the moment at least, it is true that he has no choice but to keep the fort till Sloughter arrives.'

'I worry that you two doing his bidding will do you no favours, Daniel,' said Marianne, expressing her deep concern.

'We don't have much choice. Anyway, I would rather pledge my allegiance to Leisler than to Ingoldsby.'

'Aye, same here,' said Ducamp.

'Let us hope things do not escalate,' said Madame de Fontenay. 'I only hope that even foolhardy men can see reason.'

But the next day, the exchange turned bitter. Ingoldsby accused Leisler's men on Long Island of firing shots at his soldiers, who had been given permission to set foot ashore in search of fresh provisions.

Leisler did not contest the incident but, so as not to pour fuel on the smouldering embers, asked for more details so that any culprit could be brought to justice. Ingoldsby declined and, again, rejected Leisler's offer of accommodation in town.

During the ensuing days, Daniel and Ducamp bore witness to the would-be council members rallying around the major and leveraging their supporters into forces, including those from Queen's County who had tried to rebel against Leisler's rule the previous summer.

A second ship from England, the Canterbury, arrived with additional men a few days later, bolstering Ingoldsby's confidence with the greater numbers. Daniel and Ducamp figured that the major now outnumbered Leisler's faction by five hundred men to two hundred. Yet, every day, new recruits arrived at the fort in response to Leisler's summons, some craftily ferried by Daniel to help balance the scales while on his way back from delivering Leisler's messages to the *Beaver*. 'My God,' he muttered one day as another small group of men from King's County boarded the ketch from a Long Island cove—where Daniel and Ducamp had stopped to pick up timber—'I can't believe it's come to this, a race against time.'

'Or is it a race to war?' Ducamp retorted.

The following day saw the Darlingtons and Ducamps attend the church wedding of Jacob Milborne and Leisler's twenty-one-year-old daughter.

As Daniel and Didier trotted home on horseback down Broad Street—having left the ladies to travel by May's carriage—Didier said, 'Lucky the ground's turning to mud. If the Canadians got wind that we were on the brink of civil war, they'd soon be down on us like a landslide. The mud will protect us, for the time being, at least.'

But at that moment, it was not so much the French soldiers on Daniel's mind as the English ones. After the ceremony, he had found himself in an intimate circle with Leisler at its centre. The governor had insisted they still try to bring Ingoldsby and his men into New York, where they could keep an eye on them, rather than letting them create havoc between King's County and Queen's.

'And we all know what that means,' said Marianne in her slight accent, when, back at home, Daniel related the conversation to her. 'The soldiers will be billeted, won't they?'

'I suppose so, at least those who cannot be garrisoned in the town buildings.'

'Then thank goodness we are outside the city wall. I don't want any soldiers stamping through my home.'

Daniel was not so sure they would be let off so lightly just because they were on the other side of the wall, especially given the number of soldiers to accommodate. He simply returned a nod while thinking to himself he would cross that bridge when they came to it. But his tacit response only prompted Marianne to say, 'Daniel, did you hear me? I am not having soldiers traipsing through this house!'

Three days later, on February 6th, under the pulsion of the incoming council and despite his constant refusal, Major Ingoldsby accepted the usage of New York City Hall and the adjacent buildings. It became clear to Daniel that the new council grandees were shrewdly utilising the major, who readily digested whatever information they fed him, and who was so easily riled into action against the 'usurper'. If the move gave Leisler the opportunity to keep watch on Ingoldsby, it also gave the anti-Leislerian council a foothold in New York and enabled them to covet the fort from close by.

Nicolas Bayard was on the list of council appointees, and the new future council soon presented a plea for his release. Leisler refused. Bayard would only fan the flame of discontent and rouse the differing factions even more. So, Leisler took the position to try to stave off any firebrands, to bide time to hand over New York to the incoming governor without bloodshed. For this to happen, he had to calm things down and treat the king's men well. It was during this episode that the Darlington household was shaken to its foundations. Leisler, in an effort to smooth over relations, issued a proclamation to prompt every home in the city and province to:

> *receive and entertain and bear all due respect and affection unto the said major and all under his command, not offering the least offence by word or deed, but as in duty bound to embrace, assist, help, and do all good offices imaginable, as being sent hither for Their Majesties' and our enemies, as they will answer the contrary at their utmost perils.*

Daniel had managed to place a word with the town constable in charge of billeting soldiers north of the town. He had found him at the public buildings adjacent to the town hall as soldiers in boatloads began streaming off frigates *Beaver* and *Canterbury*, now anchored off New York harbour.

'I have a full house already, Constable, two children with me and my wife, my two servants, and then there's my wife's elderly grandmother, who has taken our only spare room.'

'Can't she sleep in your room?' said the town constable, a short-legged man with a thick neck. 'That's what most do.'

'My youngest child is teething; it would be too difficult for her,' said Daniel, desperate to counter the constable's reasonable suggestion. Darlington knew he would have to give something in return. He went on, 'I can, however, make the barn loft comfortable.'

'And where they gonna eat?'

'I can allow for evening meals to be taken inside the house, Constable.' Marianne would just have to get used to strangers at their table. This was hardly the terrible days of the dragonnades.

After some deliberation, the constable said, 'That'll be two then, seeing as you've space in your barn. I'll give you two regulars, but no officers. And they don't come with officers' manners neither, I warn you.'

The barn was annexed to the house. Daniel and Ben had placed good sacking and bedding in the hayloft, where the men could put their heads down in rudimentary comfort after a hot meal.

Later that afternoon, through his glass now positioned at his study window, Daniel spied three soldiers in uniform ambling toward the house from the rutted city gate road. The one wearing a feathered tricorn, adorned with silver lace and a regimental cockade, peeled away from the other two and headed toward Ducamp's property further down, leaving two bedraggled privates to continue to the house that was surrounded by a trench and annexed by a barn.

Daniel often wondered afterwards what would have availed, had he vacated his study or the attic to make room for an officer.

When at last the soldiers stood at the front door in their greatcoats and muddy boots before Daniel—each with a sword at his side and a musket over his shoulder—one of the men, mid-twenties, of average height, more than made up for the silence of the large, lumbering, fresh-faced private who wore his hat cocked to one side. 'Gunner Gething. First name's William, like the king,' said the talkative one, doffing his simple tricorn to reveal a swab of straw-coloured hair. 'And this is James, like the old king, ha-ha!' he added, punctuating his speech with a rascally laugh. 'A bit shy for a bombardier, ain't ya, Jim?' he continued, knocking Jim's hat from his head, which Jim cheerfully caught. 'Never been kissed, see, if you know what I mean.'

Daniel got the feeling that Gunner William Gething would take some work and immediately took an aversion to the straw-topped Englishman who conducted himself without restraint, clearly deeming himself to be in conquered territory. Nevertheless, once they had removed their coats to reveal their red tunics, Darlington showed the soldiers into the dining room, where they found Marianne and her grandmother seated at the table. 'In you come, gentlemen,' said Madame de Fontenay. Daniel could not help noticing how thick her accent was.

'Yes, yes, in you come,' seconded Marianne, trying to be affable. 'Do not be shy, gentlemen.'

The soldiers gave the ladies a curt nod, then sat at the table laid with bread, cheese, ham, and some leek and ham soup. 'Nice place, here,' said William once he had settled in, which was as soon as he had taken a bite of his bread. 'Bit out of the way, mind you. Must be awkward getting back of a night, especially in this bloody rotten weather, eh?' Madame de Fontenay fidgeted in her seat, which made her mounted hair wobble.

'Gentlemen,' said Daniel, remaining congenial, 'I'd be grateful if you watched your language in the presence of the ladies of the house.'

'Oh, beg your pardon, gov'nor, been too long at sea. Speak proper English, does she then, your missus? I heard she was French.'

Marianne gave a thin-lipped smile. How did this soldier detect any accent? It was utterly vexing, and the frankness of it quite disarming. It made it difficult for her to utter another word. 'She is indeed,' said Daniel. Then, to make it clear whose side she was on, he added, 'Having escaped persecution in her own country.' Darlington regretted the justification the moment it left his mouth and could feel his wife's searching eyes upon him. William was not slow on the uptake.

'Fled from her own kind, did she? Seems even the French can't stand the French! Ha-ha. Just as well we're English born and bred, isn't it?' said William with exaggerated articulation. Did he realise he was being injurious? wondered Daniel but decided to give him the benefit of the doubt and put it down to ignorance.

After the meal, having prepared two lamps, one of which he handed to William, Daniel showed the soldiers to the barn. 'This where you're bunging us then, is it?' said Willliam, once inside, raising his lamp to view the ladder leading to the hayloft. 'Pity, I was quite looking forward to a proper rope bed after eight weeks at sea, weren't you, Jim boy?'

'You won't be cold up there,' said Darlington, keeping his focus and trying not to sound condescending. He refrained from telling them he had slept in plenty of barns worse than this one on his travels as a young man, and each time, he had been grateful for a dry space. Thankfully, he then heard a familiar voice that resonated from the barn door.

'Many a man would fight for a barn like this one to sleep in. You got the lucky draw, lads!' Didier Ducamp had stopped by to see how Daniel was getting on, the lieutenant billeted in his house having told him that the chatty soldier might be a handful.

'Who's he when he's at home?' said William, who did not seem keen to play along with Ducamp's spiel. 'Another Frenchie by the sounds of it! Cor, blimey, place is crawling with 'em!' he continued as he followed James up the ladder. Ducamp let it go; he and Daniel needed these lads to keep the lid on their flippancies and to behave themselves. There was no point in arousing resentment.

But from the day the soldiers were billeted in their barn, a subtle but persistent strain permeated the Darlington home. The first signs were innocuous enough—a misplaced comment about the family's allegiance, another remark about Marianne's French roots—but each word left a bitter aftertaste.

'Daniel, these men are a lot of work,' said Marianne a few days later, as Daniel joined her and her grandmother by the fire. 'I have tried to appeal to their better natures, but to no avail.'

'I would not give them the upper hand, my dear,' said Madame de Fontenay. 'Your grandfather used to say: you can never become friendly with the rank and file, for they become overfamiliar, and before you know it, they start answering you back.'

'They already do that, Grandma.'

'We have no choice,' said Daniel. 'Every household must take a man in. I cannot be seen as an exception.'

'No, but you did not need to take in two of them,' returned Marianne.

'I had to negotiate a barn stay rather than a room in the house. It was one of the conditions. It's the chatty one who's the problem; the man doesn't seem to know the boundaries of common decency.'

'The other one just smirks,' said Marianne, 'which goads him on. He might have been more manageable on his own.'

'Unfortunately, there's not much we can do about it now. Besides, we know what we've got. We don't know what we might get if we change.'

'Never mind, Daniel,' said Madame de Fontenay, holding up a knotted oak walking stick. 'I will watch over things in your absence, I have my special cane here, just in case!'

'Oh, but let's not forget these lads are our allies, though, ma'am.'

Madame de Fontenay gave Daniel the solemn promise that she would only use it if their lives were in danger. Daniel believed that she would.

The next four weeks saw the gunner and the bombardier up every morning at cockcrow and back in town, partaking in their various drills and duties with their cannon crew.

Except for the soldiers' insufferable day off, the Darlingtons were free of them the whole day through. And while they were at their posts, Daniel and Didier carried on their 'timber trips', now and then picking up volunteers for the fort. Darlington was reluctant to change the status quo and unnecessarily rock the boat. Until, that is, late one afternoon when Martha fetched Marianne into the dining room, where soldier William, uncommonly early for dinner, was casually rifling through a chest of family keepsakes—a collection of letters, hand-drawn portraits, and other personal memorabilia that told the story of her family. It was all she had recovered of her noble ancestry and had been going through them with her grandmother before the children needed feeding. 'How dare you!' cried Marianne. 'You have no right! Out of here!' Her sharp rebuke was met with a dismissive chuckle and a drawling glance at her breast, where her milk had soaked through her linen shift and had left a damp patch on her bodice.

'I hope we can trust you, Madame,' said private William, slowly getting to his feet, 'what with France and England always at each other's throats. You wouldn't be harbouring any sympathies for the enemy, now, would you?'

'That is my family! Get out of here!' Marianne cried out as her grandmother came charging into the room, brandishing her cane.

'You get out, young man!' she said forcefully in heavily accented English. 'You will be called when your food is ready!'

This was the first spark in what would become a steadily growing fire of resentment.

Night brought little respite. The clattering of drunken footsteps and raucous laughter often disrupted the once-peaceful evenings. On one such night, Daniel confronted them, his voice a controlled calm that thinly veiled his growing frustration, fuelled by Marianne's account of the recent violation of her small chest. 'This is a home, not a tavern!' he reminded them sternly, but his words seemed to fall on deaf ears as they tittered past him into the barn. What could he do about it? He could hardly complain to Ingoldsby.

During the day, May, ever vigilant, heard this all unfold from Marianne and her grandmother with a growing sense of unease. Her visits to check on Marianne became more frequent, her eyes often trailing the soldiers' movements with a wary sharpness during their day off, while Daniel and Ducamp were busy bringing in 'timber'.

The tension reached a boiling point one afternoon. Marianne, in an effort to create a warmer, more inviting environment amidst the starkness of military life, had carefully placed a cherished vase on the table. However, the more aggressive soldier, emboldened by his companion's laughter and Daniel's absence, overstepped during the meal. While reaching for a second helping of bread, he carelessly elbowed Marianne's vase, a family heirloom, knocking it off the table. The vase, filled with the first blooms of spring—a delicate arrangement of daffodils, crocuses, and snowdrops—shattered on the floor, its fragments and the flowers scattering across the room. His nonchalant apology, laced with a smirk, was the final straw. 'Oh dear, I do apologize,' said gunner William, his tone oozing with insincerity. 'But you do put on airs, ma'am, don't you? It must be the French in you, ma'am, always trying to seem more refined than everyone else.' Marianne's face turned pale with anger. 'That is enough,' she said firmly. 'From now on, you will be given your meals in the barn!'

Meanwhile, back in New York town, with the passing weeks, Daniel bore witness to the mounting antagonism. Both parties waited for Governor Sloughter, who still did not come.

Ingoldsby, giving in to the urge to take the fort, had been building up a strong presence, placing his men at strategic points. Daniel did not need Ducamp's military expertise to realise the major's intention. Such was the feeling of near siege that those in Queen's County who had once stood up against Leisler's rule met their counterparts of King's County, to agree on avoiding conflict and mutually preventing a bloodbath. Both Daniel and Ducamp gave a sigh of relief.

Daniel conveyed Leisler's summons to the major to disband. Ingoldsby refused, and the people of New York went about their business, knowing that a mere spark could ignite the tinder of civil war.

The two factions began antagonising and harassing each other, with Ingoldsby's men undermining Leisler's authority to the point of haranguing the fort men during their guard duties. A skirmish arose, and a handful of Ingoldsby's soldiers were arrested and held in the fort prison. But Leisler's struggle was not against these men. On the contrary, he wanted it to be known that he had housed the king's soldiers as best he could. Under Ingoldsby's protests, Leisler released them the same afternoon.

Again, seeing the major's soldiers stepping up their drills and patrols throughout the town, Leisler issued another summons to Ingoldsby to disband his forces to avoid an imminent confrontation. Learning of Ducamp's military past, he ordered him to hold the block house by force, if necessary, while Ingoldsby's *Beaver* positioned its guns on the battery. If only Leisler could hold the peace until the governor's arrival, Daniel thought. But it was clear that the newly intended council wanted him out. And where was Governor Sloughter's ship? What if it had been lost at sea? Could this state of extreme tension be sustained much longer before the first shots were fired?

Those first fatal shots came on March 17th, as Ingoldsby's men stood on parade in a show of defiance that clearly rejected Leisler's call to disband. It was in this context that a shocking scene at the Darlingtons' was about to play out. A scene that was to initiate a sequence of events that would end in a tragedy.

CHAPTER 24

March 17, 1691

NEW YORK

News of the fatal shooting at the fort spread around town faster than an exploding cannonball.

'Poor lads come all this way just to be killed by their own side! No casualties on the fort boys' side, though,' said Madame de Brey, the Huguenot teacher, an exacting, straitlaced woman who always seemed to be flushed to the cheeks whenever May Ducamp stopped to pick up her daughter. Her house was also an excellent source of information and gossip.

May boldly commented how quickly actions could become disproportionate to the situation when men put their foolish pride on the line. 'If only they could be dressed in women's clothing for a day, they would soon learn to eat humble pie and get over it.' The gaggle of women come to pick up their daughters nodded their heads reflectively, unsure whether to be shocked or amused. But everyone knew that May possessed the complaisance of money, so they laughed in a falsely shocked way as May went on, 'Men should run the world, but women should govern it, I say, ladies.'

Leaving the ladies to discuss the governance of their own houses, May then dived into her carriage behind her daughter, who was eager to recite a new song she had learnt in French.

As she listened patiently to her daughter finishing her song, May decided she had better pull up at Marianne's and tell her about the news of the shots. Those boy soldiers would no doubt amplify it out of all proportion, especially that private William, who would likely use it to exacerbate any division and swell his own sense of righteousness. She congratulated her daughter on her sweet performance. She always wanted her daughter to learn the enemy's language; it made you smarter for a start. Then, with her head half out of the window in the late afternoon spring sunshine, she hollered, 'Winden. Stop at Mrs Darlington's, would you?'

'Anywhere you say, long as it's out of this mad, godforsaken town, ma'am.'

'Yes, avoid the fort area at all costs.'

'I just don't get it. It's such a glorious, God-blessed day. Why can't folk just live in harmony? As if there ain't enough trouble wid dem French.'

'They lack your wisdom, Winden.'

'Ain't surprised my daughter and son-in-law is moving to Boston. I told 'em, they gonna be free as a bird. They'll be doing their grandparents proud; they can just up and get out of here. My old mom and pop weren't blessed wid freedom to just walk away like dat.'

'Oh. Will you be going with them?'

'All tings said and done, Mrs May, I'd be a burden to them. So, long as I can sit here warming this old seat and stroking my old Jeffrey, you can count me bein' wid ya.'

'Oh, so you don't mind becoming a burden to *me*, then,' said May. Winden let out a squeaky, joyful laugh. May could almost hear him slapping his thigh. She knew how he loved an outrageous jest. 'That's settled, then. We'll find some excuse to visit Boston once your daughter's settled in. Don't you worry, Winden.'

'Yes, ma'am.'

'Now, let's crack on, Winden, before this glorious day turns to night.'

'Yes, ma'am,' Winden laughed.

Winden gave the horse a gentle stroke with his stick. 'Giddy up, Jeffrey!' he called softly. No sooner was this said than the horse obeyed and broke into a smart trot along the cobbled street that ran along the wall of New York.

The north gate guards seemed more agitated than usual. Ordinarily, at this time of day, they would be standing, smoking, cussing, and whinging like old hens until the lady in the French wagon rolled into view. Then they would become bold, erect, and servile.

They all knew Mrs Ducamp, the auburn lady from the red house married to the French lieutenant. Shouldn't mess with the lieutenant's wife. They knew that if you did, you would get your pride knocked out of you, and she knew how to do it all in a mere sardonic glance and a quip.

Marianne, who was not quite the cook Martha was, prepared a hamper of ham, cheese, bread, black pudding, and wine for the resident soldiers, along with two pewter beakers.

Martha, having been taken ill, was lying in her bed with a fever. Ben was visiting family over at what the white folks called Negroes Causeway, a place where the black population owned

343

land. But to Ben, it was just the Causeway. So, it was up to Marianne to do the honours today.

Madame de Fontenay, still irresolutely set in her aristocratic ways, wondered how on earth her granddaughter would manage. But manage she did, and so, the old lady followed her granddaughter with a sprightly step, leaning on her oaken stick, to the barn. This had been Martha's chore since the episode of the vase.

On their way, Marianne thought back to that day at the dining table. In truth, it had been soldier William's attitude that had shocked her more than losing the vase that had belonged to Daniel's Dutch maternal grandparents. She could have nevertheless kicked herself for placing it where soldiers' elbows were within knocking range. It had been over a week, and she had been carrying the regret in her heart that she might have overreacted. Today would be like a peace offering. Even so, it was fair to say that mealtimes had become less strained, now that their visitors' dinner was dealt with and out of the way first. That constant antagonism was becoming a distant memory, already made less gross by the distance of time. But was the same true for the soldiers? She was about to find out.

Crossing the earthen threshold into the barn made her shiver in her clogs and realise what a damp den she had condemned the men to. She clomped with purpose past the haystack which was meant for the men's change of bedding. Suddenly, a blurred red shadow pounced in the corner of her eye and made her heart leap.

'Booga-booga!'

It was a slightly dishevelled soldier William who had jumped out from behind a wooden post. As her eyes grew used to the dim barn interior, Marianne also made out the large frame of James outlined in a pool of early evening sunlight streaming in through an upper window, whose shutter had been opened to let in some heat. He began guffawing like a braying donkey.

'Oh, it's the duchess!' exclaimed William, teasingly. 'Where's the slave girl?'

'Firstly, Martha is not a slave,' said Marianne, regaining her poise. 'Secondly, she is sick. And why would you be jumping out at her like that?'

'Ha-ha, firstly, all blacks are slaves here, far as I can see. Secondly, to tickle her fancy,' said William, now leaning on the post, chewing a straw. 'Don't it yours, Duchess?'

Outraged, Madame de Fontenay stepped vigorously to her granddaughter's side. 'Enough of that talk, young man! We come here with your supper.'

'Oh Lord, it's one-foot-in-the-grave Gran!' William was becoming flippant. A slurred flippancy that the old lady knew to be associated with alcohol, confirmed when she smelt it wafting nauseatingly from the soldier's person, even though there were five yards between them.

'No wonder Martha is ill,' said Marianne. In a flash, she recalled Martha's worried look when it came to taking the hamper out to the barn. Marianne suddenly wondered if the poor girl had undergone any indiscretion. Having to expose herself to indecent words and wandering hands alone would have put the nauseating swell of fear in her belly. It would have made anyone sick.

'Martha is as sweet as sweetmeat.' William grabbed the bottle of wine from the hamper Marianne was holding. 'Can you better her? I wonder,' he said, flirtatiously biting off the cork and taking a swig from the bottle.

'Put down the basket,' said Madame de Fontenay to her granddaughter in French. 'Let us go.'

Marianne had sensed the growing menace too. 'Here,' she said to soldier William, putting down the hamper, and began to retreat.

'Wait up, what's the rush, Madame Pompidoo? Eh? Your old man ain't due back till nightfall, is he? Not till he's dropped off his last load of passengers, eh? Nice of her to drop by, ain't it, Jim boy?'

'Yeah,' said soldier James, grinning widely, 'I'm starvin'!'

'And so am I in a way. Get the door, Jim boy, it's turning nippy in here.'

James went to close the door, which was ten yards in front of him.

Holding out her knotted stick as an extension of her reach, Madame de Fontenay charged briskly to intercept him. 'No, you don't, young man!'

'Hold on, hold on. Didn't anyone tell ya?' hollered William, becoming pedantic. 'You ain't in no position to be threatening the king's men. See, there's gonna be some scores to settle soon, you know. Some traitors to string up. Such as certain boatmen fetching rebels into the fort. Especially now there's been murders!'

'I don't know what you're talking about,' said Marianne, edging back to the haystack, where she had seen the pitchfork.

'That's all right, the magistrates will, won't they? Just as soon as we flush the rascals out come morning! Unless you've got somink nice to offer than smelly cheese and last week's pork. Somink fresh and perky, see what I mean, Duchess?'

'You stay back, William Gething. Get back!' Marianne reached for the pitchfork.

Madame de Fontenay rallied to her side. 'You stand aside!' she hurled sharply at the top of her voice. 'You, you...' She swung back her knotted stick. But at the pivot point, soldier James, coming up behind her, caught hold of it. The old lady twisted round her torso and clung to it as if it were her family jewels. Towering above her, James lifted the old lady off her feet, shook the cane from her grasp, and then brushed her aside with his free hand into the hay, where she landed with a bump against the post and lay limp and inert.

'Grandma!' cried Marianne, holding the pitchfork firmly with her two hands as if to charge.

'Sorry,' said James. 'I didn't mean to hurt the old girl, honest...'

'She's better off dead, what with what's coming. Besides, she was on the short list anyway. Now you, take the duchess from behind.'

'But this ain't right, is it, Will?'

'Never mind, Jim boy, the whole place'll be up in flames soon anyway. And you're in it up to the neck now, ain't ya! So just do as I say. Take the duchess before she does herself an injury!'

'You stay back!' growled Marianne, backing to where her grandmother lay. 'Touch me, and you will pay!'

'Well, the way I see it, barns burn,' said William teasingly, 'especially ones where silly women drop a flame into a bone-dry haystack! So just lay down the fork nicely, or you'll get injured.'

'You filthy scoundrel!' cried Marianne, lunging with the pitchfork. 'Get back!'

'Whoa, good boy!' said Winden as he pulled gently on the reins to slow Jeffrey to a walking pace.

There was a nasty patch of mud in front of the Darlingtons' now that the ground had thawed. Daniel had promised he would fetch in some clay bricks and pound them into it to make the ground firmer under foot, hoof, and wheel. But what with the timber runs, he hadn't gotten around to it. So, it had remained a quagmire, well-nigh impassable on wheels. So much so that the previous week, May's carriage had got stuck and had needed the help of an extra horse to yank it free.

As the carriage slowed, May thought she could hear a throaty cry up ahead. It definitely was not the sound of a baby. Could it have been a crow? But it came from the direction of the barn. She cupped her ear as they ambled up to the quagmire. There now came a distinct scream. Pushing aside the heavy canvas that covered the window opening, she said sharply, 'Winden, stop here! I want you to stay with Lily-Anne.

'Yes, ma'am.'

Turning to her daughter, she said, 'Darling, you stay with Winden. Don't let him follow me, you hear?'

'Yes, Mother, I hear you,' said the girl as her mother planted a kiss on her forehead. 'Was that Aunt Marianne?'

'You heard it too then.'

'Yes.' The girl gave an emphatic nod as her mother lost not another second. Raising her skirts, May pushed open the door and jumped down from the carriage, leaving the door open for Winden to haul himself inside.

She ran the remaining twenty yards to the barn, mud splaying up her dress as she hurried through the edge of the quagmire.

As she approached, she slowed to better hear the voices of the soldiers and Marianne, who was audibly in trouble. Keeping her head, May crept to the door that had remained ajar and peeked inside. Through the doorway, she could clearly see old Madame de Fontenay lying motionless on the hay.

May crept through the door opening, any noise covered by the voice of soldier William as he tried to manipulate James to join him in his criminal scheme. Moving stealthily to a thick

348

supporting post, she felt into the deep pockets she had attached around her shift, which were accessible through slits in her skirts and coat. The hard touch of smooth metal gave her instant reassurance. This would not be the first time she had to deal with unruly men. Before she had met Didier Ducamp, she had been escaping from her life as a courtesan and spy.

May clasped the handle of the small Acquafresca pistol adroitly lodged in her right-hand pocket and stood behind the post, peering at the scene being playing out before her, while assessing how best she could deal with it.

She quickly ascertained that soldier William was drunk as a lord and therefore unpredictable. Marianne was holding a pitchfork. Brave girl, May thought to herself. But she knew that Marianne would never stab a man. William just had to step up and wrench the fork from her.

'Take her, Jim,' commanded gunner William. 'I'll take her from the front.'

'No, Will. It's not right...'

'You're in it now, so just do it. Think later!'

Leaving no time for James to act, May stepped out from behind the post, her gun poised. In a low voice seething with pent-up anger, she said, 'Don't you move, James. You just stay put, or I'll blow your half-witted brains out!'

But James's gaze was now transfixed at the straw bedding. 'Look!' he exclaimed dumbly as Madame de Fontenay was coming to her senses.

'See, the old lady's not dead, James, and I saw it was an accident,' she lied. 'Now, you stand down if you know what's good for you!' May then switched her unforgiving glare to soldier William. Having fully cocked the hammer, she said, 'This is little Betsy. If you wanna kiss, you just keep coming, big boy!'

'Oh yeah, you've got one shot,' said William, playing dumb. 'Er, but there are two of us!'

May suddenly marched forward, opening the frizzen to expose the primed pan. There came a loud crack as she pressed the trigger ten yards from soldier William. Marianne let out a short scream, but the lead ball only hit and smashed the bottle of wine the soldier was holding.

'Bitch! I hadn't finished! Get her, Jim! She just blew her only chance!'

'Stay where you are, James,' said Madame de Fontenay, her hair still full of straw. The old lady had managed to grab her stick from where James had dropped it on the floor and was now holding it ready for a swipe. 'Or this will be my dying act!'

James hesitated.

'Get her, Jim,' coaxed William. 'She bloody shot at a king's soldier, man!'

Before James could process the thought, May pulled her left hand from her pocket. 'But Betsy's got a twin sister.' She brought out an identical small ornate pistol and cocked the hammer. 'Meet Beth!' she growled as she strode forward, opening the frizzen as before, closing the remaining distance between them, this time with the gun barrel aimed at William's head. The rapid movement brought soldier William crumbling to his knees in horror.

'All right, lady. Stop. Stop. Don't shoot. Only playing, weren't we, eh?'

Marianne stood with the pitchfork now aimed at James, who looked on, utterly confounded.

'NOW LIE DOWN, YOU WORM!' May roared.

'No, wait!' shouted Marianne, who sensed May would not hesitate to pull the trigger if soldier William got it into his drunken skull not to do as he was told.

It had been a tough afternoon. Daniel had ferried more armed volunteers from the Long Island coast directly to New York battery to save them from having to walk past Ingoldsby's soldiers into the fort. It was the only way to avoid unnecessary antagonism in these days of high tension. As for Ducamp, he had been ordered to supervise defences at the block house during the day watch.

Come the end of the day, the two men met according to their new custom at the stables, Daniel having moored his ketch for the night by the battery. After saddling their mounts, they rode under a foreboding sky up Broad Street, now fraught with traffic, where people were scurrying about their business after a day of high emotions. Ducamp continued filling Daniel in on the tragic event of the day which saw shots fired from both sides down at the fort.

'You heard right. I don't know who fired first, though,' said Ducamp, steering his horse around a handcart, 'but whatever happened, there was a volley. Two of Ingoldsby's men went down while on parade.'

'Killed?'

'I heard so.'

'Damn.'

'Leisler was furious. Ordered a cease-fire. Ingoldsby did likewise.'

'Why? It gave him a pretext to invade, surely.'

'At the cost of a bloodbath, though,' said Ducamp. 'And although he had a pretext, if he tried an assault on the fort, it would not have been in self-defence, would it? But don't you worry, he'll be considering his options. God knows what he's got cooking in that stubborn skull of his for the morning.'

'Let's just hope the night brings wise counsel.'

'Well, there ain't been much of that of late.'

351

'True,' said Daniel, who saluted the guards as they passed through the north gate. 'Will our men stand and fight?'

'I think they will. Especially when you consider we've got a melting pot of people over on our side. And Ingoldsby's been antagonising the Dutch, the Germans, and every other nationality except his own, and stoking up divisions between Protestants and remaining Catholics.'

'He doesn't know New York,' said Daniel.

'Aye, maybe someone ought to tell him. This might be under the English crown, but it ain't England, is it?' Ducamp then rose in his saddle at the fork that continued straight to his house. Turning his gaze towards the Darlingtons' along the right fork, squinting, he said, 'That May's carriage?'

As Ducamp said this, a shot rent the air and made the crows by the church graveyard outside the gate flap and squawk. Daniel and Ducamp gave each other just one glance, then kicked their steeds into a gallop.

A few minutes earlier, Lily-Anne was sitting on the edge of the carriage seat, having taken her mother's place, leaving Winden to climb in opposite her.

With the canvas drawn back despite the chill, she peered through the window opening, her eyes transfixed on the barn door. The seven-year-old's brow furrowed, and Winden recognised the feisty look of her mother. 'Winden,' she said, 'we can't just sit here. We should be at hand to help if there's a problem.'

'Your mother said to stay here, Miss Lily-Anne,' returned the old man, who was nevertheless thinking the same. Surely Madam May would have exited and given them a sign that all was well by now. What if she was in trouble and unable to call for help? He went on, 'But I can't say you're wrong, and it sure seems mighty quiet in there.' As he said this, he was assailed by terrible thoughts. A hand clasped over her mouth. A knife held to her throat. Unbearable thoughts to even imagine. So, Winden pushed open the carriage door. Stepping down, he said, 'You stay here while I just go and...'

'But Mother told us to stay together,' interrupted the girl with irresistible resolve.

That might be taking the girl to the lion's den, he thought to himself. But there again, at least she would be under his protection. Taking his gnarled root wood stick with the knotted head from under the driver's seat, in a grave tone, he said, 'All right, Miss Lily-Anne. But you just make sure you stay behind me all times. You hear? And not a word.'

The girl gave a double nod, sinking her kerchiefed and hooded head into her woollen shoulder cape while exaggeratedly clamping her mouth shut to show her lips were sealed.

Moments later, the pair were creeping toward the barn door through which May had disappeared. As Winden approached with the girl on his heels, there came a single shot and a terrible scream. He swiftly turned and picked the girl up and placed her flat against the outer timber wall. After signalling to her to stay put and keep silent, he rushed to the barn entrance, where he thrust open the door. The moment he did so, there came the thundering sound of galloping hooves from the track behind. He turned in time to see two men jump from their mud-splashed steeds.

'Mummy's inside!' yelled Lily-Anne.

'Keep by the wall, poppet. Winden, attach the horses!' commanded Ducamp, racing into the barn, where he found his wife holding a gun to soldier William's temple. Slowing to a halt, he could sense his wife's seething rage.

After rapidly assessing the situation, which was clear to him had developed from a standoff, in a breathy but controlled voice, he said, 'May! May, *cherie*. Don't. Shoot him, and we have a civil war on our hands.' He knew for a fact that she was capable of pulling that trigger. It was how they had first met. She had not only pulled the same gun on him, but she had also planted a knife in his side, although she had conciliatingly stitched him up again afterwards. During their brief and uncommon courtship, she had told him things in the name of self-preservation about her past life that even he, a former soldier and privateer, was shocked to hear.

Darlington was close behind. He seized the pitchfork from his wife's hands and tossed it to Winden, who had just entered, to guard James—just in case. Then he said, 'May, listen, whatever he has done, it's not worth the bloodshed his death would cause.'

'May, *ma cherie*,' pursued Ducamp, 'we have come a long way together. Remember our promise.'

Didier's calming voice at last brought her back to her senses, and she recalled that voyage to New York when they had each vowed to change their ways, to face the world, its trials, and tribulations together as God-fearing folk to the best of their ability. Her fury had sometimes gotten the better of her in the name of self-preservation. But although this man was prepared to rape and kill the very women who had come to feed him, she knew full well she could not put a bullet in every drunken, sex-starved soldier. There were too many of them for a start, and she would only end up dancing at the end of a rope. Besides that, she had made a promise to her two children, her husband, and to God. What if there really was an afterlife?

But as May lowered her pistol, soldier William, who would not be humiliated by a mere woman, pulled out his dagger from the sheath at his belt and lunged for Marianne, who had moved closer and was now standing three yards from Daniel on his right. May quickly took aim and fired unflinchingly to save her

354

friend. But the pistol gave a harmless click; the high level of humidity in the barn had dampened the powder.

Ducamp had seen the attack coming. It was ironically in a similar fashion that he had gotten cut by May barely two years earlier, before they fell in love. He sprung after the drunken soldier, grabbed him by the collar, and swung him round as Daniel pulled Marianne from the assailant's grasp.

'No, you don't!' bellowed Ducamp, who had expertly tripped up the soldier to force him to the ground and had snatched his knife. With one knee on the small of the culprit's back, Ducamp now held the knife to the soldier's throat. 'You are a lucky boy. I wouldn't have thought twice about putting you out of your misery not so long ago,' said Ducamp, who had decided to side with morality. It felt right.

'You know if I die, you die,' slurred gunner William between gnarled teeth, his lips kissing grit. 'But you're all gonna coppit anyway. You lot can't kill the king's men and get away with it. It's our bloody colony, not yours. You are just bloody tenants here!'

A hesitant voice came from a forgotten part of the barn. 'He doesn't mean it,' said James apologetically. 'It's the drink, turns him mad.'

'Stand where you are, boy,' said Winden, thrusting the pitchfork toward soldier James's face, while behind him, Lily-Anne ran to her mother. Daniel nodded to Ducamp, who returned a stern nod. 'He's spent,' he said.

'We will let you go,' said Daniel, passing his sharpened eyes from William to James. 'But tell your captain you ain't welcome here anymore!'

'Yes, sir,' said James indolently.

'Just make sure he gets back to your barracks!'

'I will. Promise, sir. Thank you, sir.'

Ducamp released his grip on William's throat. Getting up, he pulled the soldier to his feet by the scruff of his collar. 'Today's your lucky day, boy. Now get outta here, and don't let me see you again!'

'Ha, let's see if you're braver than your countrymen,' sneered William drunkenly. 'We've all heard tales of French courage... or the lack of.' James pulled his reluctant mate away as Winden stabbed the air with the pitchfork to herd the pair through the door.

With the sun balancing on the church steeple, Didier and Daniel remained to watch the pair of king's cannoneers stagger arm in arm back up the trail to the city gate in the last light of day, while the ladies and little Lily-Anne accompanied Madame de Fontenay into the house.

CHAPTER 25

March 18, 1691

NEW YORK

The morning sun cast a gentle light through the Darlington lattice kitchen window, making the utensils and copper pans hooked on the far wall glint. But it did little to dispel the shadows of fear that still clung to Martha as she stood by the stone sink.

Marianne was sitting at the table on the bench, burping her baby, along with her grandmother, who ordinarily deemed the kitchen, with its multitude of unfathomable utensils, to be the domain of servants. But this morning was an exception, testified by their faces that were still etched with the concerns of the previous night. It had been long, filled with bated breaths at every creak and crack of the timber-framed house.

Daniel and Ducamp entered, their arrival interrupting the reassuring words of Marianne. 'There'll be no soldiers coming today, Martha,' seconded Daniel gently, awkwardly trying to offer the maid a semblance of comfort.

'No soldiers, Mister Daniel,' she repeated, her voice a whisper, as if saying the words louder might make them less true.

'Aye, girl, they won't be bothering us here again,' affirmed Ducamp, who had come to fetch Daniel for their duties at the fort.

For a moment, Martha simply stared, the words slowly sinking in. Then, as the reality of the assurances took hold, tears began to well in her eyes. They spilled over, tracing silent paths down her cheeks. She wept not just from relief, but from the release of a tension she hadn't fully acknowledged until now.

The men exchanged a look, now understanding the depth of fear and anxiety Martha had been harbouring. 'You're safe here now, Martha,' said Ducamp, trying to reassure her though he knew it might not be enough. 'That's all that matters.'

But it wasn't all that mattered to Martha. She shook her head, wiping her tears with the back of her hand. 'It's too shameful,' she murmured, her voice barely audible. The unsaid words hung heavily in the room, a testament to the trauma she was unable to voice.

Daniel's expression hardened. If only he had known, perhaps he wouldn't have let the soldiers off so lightly. He exchanged another glance with Ducamp, seeing a similar resolve in his friend's eyes.

May, having removed her outer garment by the front door, now stepped sprightly into the kitchen, her concern nonetheless palpable. 'Martha, how are you bearing up?' she asked, her eyes searching Martha's face for the truth her words might not reveal.

Martha now offered a weary but genuine smile. 'Better, now that I know they won't be back.' Her voice was soft but carried a new undercurrent of resilience.

Ducamp nodded in understanding. 'We made sure of that,' he said, a protective firmness in his tone.

Martha looked up at them, her tear-streaked face a mirror of her inner turmoil. 'I just want to forget,' she whispered. 'I want to forget it all.' May walked over to the maid, placing a comforting hand on her shoulder. 'Whatever you've been through... no one should have to endure that,' she said gently.

Marianne, her voice firm but empathetic, added, 'Martha, you don't have to speak of it now, not unless you're ready.' Having once been physically attacked herself, Marianne knew how important it was to let the girl process her emotions in her own good time. 'Just know, we're all here for you.'

Madame de Fontenay, her usual stoicism softened by the circumstances, added, 'Indeed, dear. This house is your sanctuary, as much as it is ours.'

Daniel felt a surge of responsibility. 'We'll do everything we can to keep our houses safe,' he affirmed, glancing at Ducamp, who gave a grunt and nodded in agreement.

Martha, bolstered by the support, found her resolve. 'I just want to put it behind me,' she said firmly. 'And think about the days ahead.'

As the group in the Darlingtons' kitchen shared a moment of quiet solidarity, the back door swung open, and old Ben, the black servant from the French island of Guadeloupe, stepped in, his arms laden with baskets of provisions. His usual easygoing demeanour was replaced by a look of apprehension.

''Scuse me, ma'am, but everyone needs hear this,' he said in a French Creole accent, setting down the baskets on the table. Everyone turned their attention to him, sensing the urgency in his voice.

'What is it, Ben?' said Marianne, switching the baby to her other shoulder.

'Just come from the market,' he continued, catching his breath. 'Dey says all de roads leading to de fort been blocked off.

Folk can't even get near da marketplace. There's talk of cannons and soldiers everywhere.'

Daniel exchanged a quick, worried glance with Ducamp. 'Blocked off?' he asked, his mind racing with the implications. Was this the prelude to an assault?

'Yes, sir,' Ben answered. 'An' that ain't de whole story, yuh know. The market is in a real commotion. I managed to get what I could,' he motioned towards the baskets, 'but it's total chaos in town, truly.'

May stepped forward. 'This is getting out of hand,' she said, looking at Ducamp, concern furrowing her brow. 'What does this mean for everyone here? And for the town?'

Ducamp's expression was grim. 'It means Ingoldsby is tightening his grip.'

Marianne, cradling her sleeping baby, added, 'It is like we are under siege from our own people.'

There was a moment of silence as the gravity of Ben's news sank in. The conflict had moved beyond the confines of political struggle; it was now touching the lives of every New Yorker, master and servant, old and young, male and female, disrupting the rhythms of everyday life.

In a sweeping glance that embraced the whole kitchen, with a look of determination, Daniel said, 'We need to stay informed and do what we can to help those around us. This isn't just about the fort anymore.'

Daniel turned to Ducamp. 'We can still get into the fort,' he said in a low, determined voice. 'The shoreline outside the palisade along the north river is less guarded, if at all. If we move carefully, we can circle around to the battery.'

Ducamp nodded, his mind already mapping out the muddy route. 'Agreed. It's risky, but it's our best shot. The main entrances will be heavily fortified now; we're sure to be singled out. But they might not expect anyone to enter the fort from the shore.'

May interjected with a worried frown. 'Isn't that dangerous? And the river can be treacherous.'

'It is a risk,' Ducamp replied, 'but it is one we have to take. Staying outside the fort walls won't help anyone. We need to be where we can make a difference.'

Marianne, looking between the two men, added, 'Just be careful, both of you.'

Daniel gave her a reassuring nod. 'We will be. It's important to keep supporting those inside the fort. They're holding out for the governor's arrival, but until then, they need all the help they can get.'

Ben chimed in, 'Beggin' yer pardon, but if you're set on going, you gotta leave soon. At this hour, the tide will be in your favour. You'll be able to walk clear of de river sludge.'

'True,' Daniel said.

With a new sense of urgency, Daniel made for the front door, where he put on his thigh boots and greatcoat. He and Ducamp headed out and up the track without their mounts.

Those left in the kitchen shared a moment of silent solidarity. Each of them, in their own way, was increasingly affected by the unfolding events, and now they came together in the shared hope for a peaceful resolution and God's strength to endure the challenges ahead.

The previous evening, after the barn event, there was an awkward moment in the Ducamp household, where a lieutenant was billeted.

Didier had decided to come clean. After all, he hadn't harmed any of the soldiers; rather, he had kept them from committing

361

a heinous crime. It had come as no surprise to the lieutenant, who nonetheless voiced a warning. 'I do not doubt that another killing could have led to further bloodshed,' he cautioned, 'but despite this current state of affairs and misunderstandings, we are, after all, on the same side, are we not?'

'We are indeed, sir,' Ducamp replied.

'Things will hopefully return to order once the governor gets here,' said the lieutenant. 'After all, these men will need to fight together one day.'

But the governor's ship was still nowhere in sight, and Major Ingoldsby did not share the lieutenant's philosophical standpoint. Ingoldsby wanted the fort, and Leisler had become his personal adversary. Especially since the new intended counsel was impatient to get in, impatient for personal revenge, their urgency doing nothing to quash Ingoldsby's own frustrations.

Moreover, Nicholas Bayard, who had been selected to become one of the counsellors under the new governor, still languished in jail in that fort. Every day that went by exasperated the intended counsellors even more, exacerbating their desire to take the fort by force, especially given that armed men were still pouring in to defend it. How Ingoldsby could stand and watch as Leisler grew in strength was becoming beyond belief for the soon-to-be counsellors.

One of these, Matthew Clarkson, continued to petition for military support from the Connecticut governor. All he wanted was a nod to validate an incursion. But in his reply, Governor Treat invariably advised both parties to tolerate and redress any grievances rather than resort to irreversible force, the consequences of which could lead to civil war. There would be no winners if such were the case, except the irascible French, who would be left with an easy picking ground.

Jacob Leisler was no less furiously entrenched in his determination to hand over the fort to a sworn-in governor with a bona fide commission from the king. So, that morning of March 18th, in an effort to reverse the current threat to the fort, he sent word again for Ingoldsby to disband his troops and call off what had clearly become a siege of Fort William. Leisler, considering himself to be lawfully above everyone else, could not bring himself to bow before a pigheaded major. Moreover, he well knew that anything less would undercut his own conviction in the legality of his role. It would consequently undermine his defence, leaving him open to a severe condemnation. But little did he imagine the blow of fate that would later befall him.

Ingoldsby had no reason to post sentinels along the town's riverside palisade. So, it did not take long for Daniel and Ducamp to make their way along the Hudson riverbank, past the slow-moving windmill sails at the side of the fortress, to the battery that looked over New York Bay.

The stillness of the morning was punctuated by the sombre knell of the bell of the fort church, its wistful toll already coordinating shifts and rotations among the defenders inside the fort. Daniel quickened his stride, his eyes fixed on his vessel, anchored where he had left it the previous evening, its familiar masts and timbers glistening in the morning sun.

Ducamp, keeping pace, scanned the area, his soldier's instincts attuned to the cannon teams meticulously preparing, so it seemed, for an imminent attack from the sea. He noted how the reinforcing rings around the barrel of one of the cannons were being inspected. These rings helped contain the immense forces exerted when the cannon was fired. Each of the cannoneers of the battery was also inspecting his cannon barrel for cracks or fissures, the touchhole through which the ignition spark was introduced to ignite the main gunpowder charge, and the vent field where the fuse was placed. All part of the usual inspection protocol, thought Ducamp. He was no cannon captain himself, but he did know that a misfire at a critical moment during a battle could give the adversary the edge and lead to a catastrophe.

'She hasn't drifted, and looks like she's untouched,' Daniel remarked, his hand capping his felt hat, which in turn directed Ducamp's gaze toward the ketch, swaying gently in the dazzling sunshine.

'Aye, but we can't let our guard down,' said Ducamp, his eyes now running along the distant masts of the *Beaver* that towered above the houses overlooking the harbour. 'Ingoldsby's men will be watching, even if we don't see them. We need to be ready for whatever comes next.'

'True, probably just a matter of time before all this comes to a head,' murmured Daniel, his voice almost lost in the sound of shouted orders from the cannon crew captain. 'But we'll be ready. We have to be,' he said, the determination clear in his voice.

Both men saluted the cannon captain, then pressed on toward the guarded rear gate. Looking eastward, Daniel could clearly see the blockades across the market square that prevented anyone from entering the fortress from the town. If he looked out from the front gate, he knew he would see a similar blockade in Broad Way. 'I can hardly believe it's come to this,' he sighed, shaking his head in despair. 'Anyway, I suppose we'd better report for duty.'

Upon entering the fort, Daniel could feel a new energy within the fort quadrant that at this time harboured close to three hundred men preparing for another day of high tension. Sentinels armed with muskets were densely posted along the earthen battlements, and cannon crews were stationed at the four bastions that projected outward from the curtain wall to allow defensive fire in several directions. And men were being drilled on the dusty courtyard.

Looking up toward the town-facing bastions above him, Ducamp could perceive the butt ends of cannons that were chillingly angled to counter an offensive from the town.

They crossed the quadrant. Then Daniel knocked and pushed the door into the governor's office where, amid his close circle of advisors, Leisler was poring over a map of the town and a chart of New York Bay. Planting an index finger on the map that was spread out on the central table, he said, 'They have moved their battery to here.' He then turned around to acknowledge the newcomers. 'Ah, well timed, gentlemen. Ducamp, I want you to keep watch from the blockhouse on these,' he said, stabbing a point on the map with his finger as the two men stepped up to the table.

'From what I can see,' said Ducamp, 'they are cunningly just out of range of our fire, sir.'

'Yes, but their cannons can still hit our provision ships if they so desire.'

'With all due respect, sir, if they so desire, they can destroy the fort if we don't show them we mean to fight back.'

'Which is unfortunately what we did yesterday with the return fire that cost lives,' said Leisler, raising his voice. He was referring to the exchange of fire that left two of Ingoldsby's men dead. His gaze swept around the table as he went on. 'Let us remember, gentlemen, these men have come in support of our colony against the French. They are on our side. We only fire as a last resort. I do not want a bloodbath. Neither do we want to destroy our own town with return cannon fire. Is that clear?'

'Yes, sir,' said Ducamp in military fashion, while everyone else present nodded their heads gravely at the reminder that the soldiers directing their guns at the fort were actually here to protect them against a French offensive.

'I therefore must remind you to hold your men's fire.'

'Yes, sir.'

In a more reasonable voice, Leisler continued, 'Now, according to our estimations, Governor Sloughter's ship should arrive at any moment. We just need to hold the fort till then.'

'But what if it is lost at sea as some suspect?' said Jacob Milborne thoughtfully. He was standing to Leisler's right.

'Then there will be a bloodbath,' said Ducamp, struck by the solemn depth of his own voice.

'It must not come to pass,' said Leisler resolutely. 'Ingoldsby cannot risk such a catastrophe.'

'The added difficulty, as I see it,' Milborne returned, 'is that he is goaded on by the new council.'

'The intended council,' corrected Leisler. He pursued, 'Then let us pray he will have the good sense not to risk killing two of them with one of his cannonballs.'

'You mean Bayard and Nicholls,' said Daniel.

'Yes.'

'Very astute of you, sir,' said Milborne.

'And, Darlington,' said Leisler, ignoring Milborne's remark, 'I suggest you take it wider than usual as you head out this morning. They fired at Mazel's ship heading out earlier and missed. But you never know. And by the way, we are running out of corn for the windmills.'

'Noted. I'll remember to bring some back.'

'Their strategy is to try to starve us,' said Milborne. 'They have already blocked the roads.'

'Not such a bad sign,' returned Leisler. 'It means they will give us time. As long as we can keep the sea access open, we can hold out.'

'And provided Sloughter is safe and well,' said Ducamp, toward whom Leisler now turned.

Ignoring Didier's remark, Leisler said, 'Now, Ducamp, where was I? I want you to take command of the outer block-house. Send word back of any suspicious movement.'

'Yes, sir. My watch begins after our first run out.'

'Exceptionally today, I would rather you take position immediately. We're going to need all hands on deck, so to speak. I dare not imagine what is going through the minds of the grandees over there. But I have a feeling they won't be advocating for mutual peace.'

'But, sir...'

'It's all right,' interrupted Daniel. 'I will have Davey. He knows the ketch well enough now.'

Ducamp gave a reluctant nod. He was dubious about letting the ketch out without him. It would be lacking one of the crew, one of the three D's that had proven so successful of late: Daniel, Didier, and Davey. And even though he trusted the Dutchman, he wasn't a soldier; he did not have a soldier's reflex.

'Take Stevens with you too, then,' said Ducamp. 'He's got a sharp eye.'

An hour later, Daniel's hand was brushing the side of the vessel as he boarded.

It was a familiar and comforting touch that connected him with the many journeys he had undertaken on her. The creak of her timbers underfoot and the fresh breeze on his face were reminders of the countless times he had navigated these waters, smuggling supporters and supplies into the fort under the cover of fetching in timber. Those men, many of whom had wives and children who depended on them, had unflinchingly taken up the gauntlet in the name of justice and their love of freedom.

The ketch soon slipped away from the roadstead, gliding silently through the water, propelled by a light breeze in her jib sail. Daniel, at the helm, and Stevens, in the rigging—the latter an alert and agile young sailor one head shorter than Davey—kept a keen eye on the shore, watching for any signs of movement. Onwards they sailed, the silhouette of the windmill and the fort of New York soon looming in the distance, as Stevens and Davey now deftly deployed the mizzen sail.

Daniel took a moment to enjoy the calm of the bay, a stark contrast to the chaos brewing in the city. It was nevertheless the place he always loved coming home to from his voyages in the Caribbean. But unbeknownst to them all, among the shadows of the township, cannoneer William, fuelled by a desire for revenge, watched their departure with a malicious gaze.

Meanwhile, from the blockhouse situated outside the fort, Ducamp watched the ketch unfurling her main sail and setting out across the calm bay that shimmered in the midmorning sun. A splendid morning it was too, one that ordinarily put the spring back in his step.

But Ducamp, like many that morning, felt a growing pang of apprehension as he waited for the rest of the day to unfold. What would this world be like by the end of it? Would Ingoldsby, having received news of a disaster at sea involving the incoming governor, decide to go for the push? Would all the wives and children waiting for their husbands and fathers see them this evening? It was hardly conceivable that it had come to this. His French background made him question the moral legitimacy of the English army, capable of perhaps massacring its own.

That said, did the French not persecute, condemn to the galleys, and hang their own civilians just because they worshipped the same God differently? And had he not been part of it? Yes, but he had since turned a new chapter. He had relinquished his affiliation to France when he deserted the army all those years ago to join a privateer ship. Neither did he feel English, though. If anything, he felt American—as American as German-born Leisler but without the English affiliation—an American devoted to the freedom for every man to speak his mind and to choose his faith. All of a sudden, his thoughts were rudely interrupted by a thunderous boom.

'There!' roared one of the men in the blockhouse, peering through the square window that looked over the bay.

Ducamp swiftly joined him in time to see the water surge up with the impact of the cannon shot that narrowly missed an incoming sloop. Ingoldsby must have dwelt on Leisler's order to disband, he thought to himself, and this was his reply. But as long as the ships stayed out of range, there would be little chance of them getting hit. There came another deafening blast, and as if to prove him wrong, the shot struck the aft of the ship, sending splinters spraying into the air. Listing slightly with a damaged rudder, the ship managed to hold her course and soon was out of range as a third shot fell short.

Through his glass, Ducamp now focussed on the battery of cannons established in a wide street that ran from the marketplace on the coast side. He perceived the unmistakable large and bulky body shape of James. He then caught sight of the blond-haired William, who, judging by the congratulatory pats on the back from his comrades, Ducamp inferred to be the gunner responsible for aiming the cannon. Raising his hand, he said, 'Hold fire, lads!'

'Not bloody likely, sir,' said one wilful young man at the loophole next to Ducamp. 'The bloody bastards!'

'Leisler's orders,' said Ducamp sternly to the whole crew.

'But, sir, they just hit Mazel's ship!' The young man, having placed the barrel of his musket on the ledge of the loophole, now took aim. But Ducamp was quick to grasp the barrel, pulling it upwards as the soldier pulled the trigger. The shot went off skyward.

'I said hold fire!' he bellowed in the soldier's face. But the shot, despite it being fired in the air, prompted others to follow suit, and a quick volley was sent toward the battery of guns that turned out to be out of range anyway. 'HOLD. YOUR. FIRE!' roared Ducamp, whose order resonated over the musket shots, and silence returned.

Sporadic nervous fire from both town side and fort side punctuated the next few hours.

Meanwhile, one of the enemy gun carriages was heaved forward, an action that extended the cannon's reach over the bay. Ducamp quickly ascertained that it was that of gunner William. Initially, he failed to fathom the purpose of the manoeuvre as it now put them within range of being picked off by his men if they made fire again. But a moment later, everything became clear as he saw the massive bulk of the *Beaver*, Ingoldsby's warship, manoeuvring into the harbour with a straight line of fire up the south end of Broad Way to the exterior blockhouse that Ducamp was given to command.

A short while after Ducamp's observation, Leisler received an official reply to his order for Ingoldsby to disband his troops. It made no mention of disbanding; instead, it was a counter notification to surrender the blockhouse, or it would be destroyed with everyone inside it.

Leisler knew full well that the *Beaver*'s cannons would blow it to smithereens. Had he been outsmarted by Ingoldsby? But would he really execute his threat? Ordering fire from a land cannon was one thing, but firing on the king's subjects from the king's warship was another. The future governor, let alone the king, would not be impressed to learn of an English ship firing on crown colonists. What would it mean for Boston, for Connecticut, for Massachusetts? Would he really do it? Probably. It was a single building that had opened fire on his men. He would claim he fired in self-defence.

Leisler had summoned Ducamp who, having listened to Leisler's instructions, now reacted to the news. 'If we vacate the blockhouse, we lose the power to counter their gun that has edged further toward the bay. He wouldn't fire on the people he has been ordered to support, would he?'

'That is my final word, Lieutenant. Thank you for your bravery, but to remain would mean certain death. Tell your men to vacate the blockhouse immediately. Our ships will just have to sail wider.'

In truth, Ducamp saw no other solution either. Ingoldsby was a wily warrior. His manoeuvre left the fort ships open to cannon attack, thus preventing any provisions and men from supplying the fortress. But this also suggested that Ingoldsby was contemplating a long wait, didn't it?

Ten minutes later, as Ducamp looked through the blockhouse window on the coast side, he could swear he could see none other than William looking defiantly straight at him, his blond head of lank hair gleaming under the sun. 'An excellent target, now close enough to blow it off,' Ducamp thought to himself. As if in reply, William made an obscene gesture; then he drew

371

his thumb across his throat in a sign of death, following which he pointed puckishly across the bay. Ducamp, his glass pressed to his eye, skimmed the calm waters, only to spy Daniel's ketch coming in wider than before to avoid the enemy battery, but not wide enough to compensate for the new advance of William's cannon.

'My God!' he said incredulously to himself. 'He cannot. Surely, he wouldn't.' But Ducamp stood watching impuissant, while William continued fine-tuning the elevation and direction of the loaded cannon to set it on the trajectory of the incoming ketch. He had already experimented with Mazel's ship, which told Ducamp that cannoneer William was good at his job. He had thus already acquired his landscape markers in the guise of protruding coastal rocks as reference points to aid in aiming his cannon. Ducamp deduced then that there was regrettably a fair chance that William's shot would hit.

Ducamp had been ordered explicitly not to shoot first. But he couldn't just stand there and watch a cannon being primed with his friend in mind. Would William really go so far as to kill the man who had given him food and shelter, who had a wife and children to provide for? Without wasting another moment, Didier tumbled down the blockhouse steps and raced around the fort wall to the half-moon battery in the hope of sending out a warning. But the ketch was too far out. He swung his glass around to spy the enemy battery to his left, where he could clearly see bombardier James now waiting at the ready with his linstock—a kind of long staff with a forked end that held the slow match, the slow-burning cord with which he would ignite the cannon fuse.

William and the rest of the cannon crew were visibly eager, waiting for the ketch to advance into the anticipated strike area. Ducamp wished now he had incapacitated the scoundrel when he had the chance. Had he missed a Providential warning?

Maybe he should have remained at the blockhouse despite the threat. At least he would have been able to shoot the dogs. Desperately, he waved his arms to attract the attention of the incoming ketch. It needed to veer to port.

Looking through his glass from the vantage point of a balcony that looked over the bay, Major Ingoldsby, exasperated at yet another incoming ship conveying men and provisions to the fort, bellowed his order to his second in command. 'Sink that ship!' The officer then passed the order down the hierarchic line until it reached cannoneer William Gething.

Gunner Gething clasped his hands at the prospect of obliterating the incoming ketch. 'This will teach the bourgeois bitch to be high and mighty with an Englishman,' he thought to himself. William was the best gunner of the battery, which was how he had managed to get a billet rather than have to stay at the garrison. But he did not think back then that he would end up sleeping and eating in a dank and miserable barn. Worse, since last night, he and James had even been kicked out of that and sent to kip in the crowded garrison with filthy, snoring, smelly soldiers. In a rare spark of ingenuity, James had come up with an excuse to cover the fact that the pair of them had been evicted from their accommodation: 'The French lady of the house didn't like the way we eat,' he had lied. The garrison commander let it go, and nothing more was said, especially as William's impressive aim and talent for gauging the wind were legendary among those who knew anything about firing a cannon, and today was the day of all days for the artist to show off those talents in style. In truth, William had been stalking this ketch in particular whose destruction would smooth over the lump of indignation inflicted upon him at the Darlingtons'.

He had meticulously set the elevation and the distance, and had compensated for the wind that had dropped to but a gentle southwesterly breeze, which meant it blew roughly in the same direction as his sea-facing 12-pounder cannon. Perfect conditions for a successful shot, he thought to himself, and at a push, he had time to get three in before the ketch could slip away behind the coastline to the half-moon battery, located on the far side of the fort.

All was set, nothing left to chance or Providence. He had been carefully studying Darlington's comings and goings a long time before the barn incident. In fact, ever since he and James got barred from eating in the house by the haughty French tart. His recent observations unequivocally proved Darlington was smuggling armed men into the fort to counter Major Ingoldsby's intention to secure it for the king.

'You ready, Jim boy?' William called out as he watched the ketch slowly sail toward the engagement area. William's plan was not to sink the vessel immediately; instead, he planned to first deploy a cannister shot to clear the deck. The gunner knew full well that this type of shot was most effective at short ranges, but though it might sweep wide, it would still incapacitate. The cannister contained smaller projectiles, such as musket balls and other small metal pieces, packed into the stiff container. The objective was to scatter the projectiles over a wide area to maximize damage against the crew and the rigging. An 18-pounder rather than a 12-pounder would have been ideal; however, William had a trick or two up his sleeve that would enable him to keep the shot tight for as long as possible over the two-hundred-yard stretch to the strike area.

He had chosen a more tightly packed cannister, one whose packing he had personally adjusted himself to reduce any gaps. He had also carefully measured the charge to ensure that the cannister would not burst too early, keeping the shot pattern tighter as it hurled toward the target. 'Then she'll be like a lame duck on a mill pond,' William had gloated to James. All they would have to do then was fire a solid shot aimed below the waterline, and down she would plummet as good as a cormorant. If he angled the first shot right, there might be nothing left for the French tart to mourn apart from perhaps the head and a few limbs, if they were lucky enough to find them.

Gunner Gething raised his right arm above his head. As he did so, he gave a discreet wave of the left hand to Ducamp at the fort battery, but the Frenchman was too busy to respond.

Still holding his glass, he was frantically waving his arms to try to warn the ketch out on the bay.

William couldn't help a Machiavellian leer at the thought of how he had outsmarted Ducamp, who couldn't even fire a shot, just as Ingoldsby had outmanoeuvred the false governor who dared not fire on the king's men. 'This is the English army, mate!' the cannoneer muttered under his breath. 'Can't mess with the English army and get away with it!' He turned to James, brought down his right hand and, giving full voice to the two syllables, he yelled out, 'FI-RE!'

James touched the fuse with the slow match smouldering on the end of his linstock. William stepped back and plugged his ears with his fingers in anticipation of the beefy blast. He then stood wide-eyed, braced for the thrill of watching the dark, powerful cloud of shimmering projectiles hurtling through the air and into the ketch, and slicing everything in its path to shreds.

He waited another few seconds. Then, unplugging his ears, he turned to the bombardier. 'Put the fire to the bloody hole, man!' he bawled.

'I did, Will,' said James defensively. 'Powder must be damp or somink.'

William's eyes narrowed into horizontal slits as he recalled now how James had shown no enthusiasm when he had told him of his plans of revenge. 'Revenge in all legality, my son!' he had crowed. James had tried to reason that Darlington had given them decent food, that he had a family to provide for, and that, after all, they were on the same side. 'You've bloody sabotaged it!' the gunner hurled.

'No, Will. Must be a misfire,' said James on the back foot. Then as an afterthought, he added, 'Unless it's a hangfire.'

'Get out of my face!' roared William as he pushed the bombardier with such fury that he knocked the big, soft fella off his feet and sent him rolling down the slight elevation of ground, upon which they had hauled the gun carriage. Willliam was sure it wasn't a hangfire, which was when there was delayed ignition; it would have gone off by now anyway. But if it was, he knew he did not want to be standing in front of the muzzle. William took charge, ire coursing through his veins. He knew his crew could work quickly. They could reload in forty-five seconds. He could still get another two cracks at the target. He would just need to adjust the barrel slightly once it was loaded, and this time, he would take care of setting the fuse himself.

'Misfire! Reload! Reload!' he bellowed as the crew had already scrambled to their positions. Timing was everything. 'Remove the shot!' Done. 'Swab the barrel!' Done.

Meanwhile, recovering from the fall, James looked back at the rapid operation in train, an operation the crew had performed hundreds of times together. William was driving them on. 'Move it, she's slipping away!' he yelled as he took the dowser from the hands of the swabber. 'Enough! Load the charge!' Done. 'Load the wadding!' Done. 'Load the cannister!' Home.

But something was amiss, thought James to himself. He could feel it in his bones before it informed his mind. Then it hit him like a cannonball. 'Will!' he yelled, getting to his feet, 'remove the charge! Remove the first charge!' The first charge should have already been removed. Otherwise, in case of a misfire, there was a good chance it would be damp and inert.

William suddenly realised his error too. The inert charge would only create a barrier and prevent the fresh charge from igniting. But there was an even more important reason as well. Double the charge would exert too much force on the barrel. There was a chance it would explode. 'Damn it!' roared William. In his mad frustration, he snatched up the worm—which featured a double spiral attached to a long shaft, used to pull out unwanted material from the cannon barrel—and thrust it inside the barrel to reach for the cannister while the captain's calls continued fast and furious: 'Fire at the ship! Fire at the ship!

But as William hit the cannister with the tip of the worm, he heard a faint but alarming sound that filled him instantly with dread. It was the fizz of powder. He let go of the worm and stepped away from the muzzle. 'Hangfire!' he screamed out. But his alarm was cut short by an almighty, earth-quaking blast. Then it all became a terrible mess as gunner William and the other five members of the red-uniformed cannon crew were blown upward with the rise of the ground. The cannon had exploded in a flare of red and orange. Moments later, it was raining bits of red and black.

Down by the half-moon battery, Didier Ducamp caught the great flare of the blast, then heard the boom as it rolled like thunder slowly across the bay. The freak explosion momentarily convinced him of the Holy Spirit's undeniable presence, as he realised that gunner William's cannon had burst.

After the detonation that sent hundreds of gulls into flight, there befell an eerie silence as each man within and outside the fort endeavoured to comprehend what had happened. Ducamp instinctively crossed himself as per his Catholic upbringing but thanked the Protestant God that Darlington would make it back in one piece, and that Didier would not be duty bound, after all, to provide for his friend's family.

The shock wave had hurled James several yards further from the epicentre of the explosion. Moments later, dazed and sprawled amid a pile of mess and dust, he rolled over, pressing the ground with his left hand to pick himself up slowly to his stumbling feet, his ears still ringing.

He turned in a full circle to make sure his bearings were right and stopped, his eyes levelled at the space where the cannon had been. 'Will?' he called out as the sharp, acrid odour with undertones of metallic and burnt organic scents filled his nose. He coughed, squinted, and rubbed his bloodshot left eye with his left hand as the foul-smelling smoke and dust began to settle where the obliterated barrel and carriage had gouged the ground. It at last dawned on him that the crew and Will were gone, blown to smithereens.

Meanwhile, the shock and horror of the explosion began to hit home to the other battery artillerymen nearby, some covered in the grim fallout, who now approached to view the scene of desolation. Then all eyes fell on James. 'Weren't my fault,' he said dumbly.

'James, your arm, man!' said a squat soldier from Newcastle upon Tyne, ignoring James's comment.

'What?' said James, instinctively raising his right arm on which all eyes seemed to be fixed. But to his surprise, the space where his arm should have appeared was empty, and his limb felt weightless. Becoming panicked, he peered down his arm and rather comically felt the air at its extremity only to eventually realise that his forearm was missing. It must have been severed by a piece of falling shrapnel.

'Well, man,' said the Geordie, 'it might have been worse. I mean, you can still fire a cannon, can ya not?' But James there and then decided he no longer wanted to fire cannons. He just wanted to go home.

The detonation brought Major Ingoldsby from his viewpoint and charging out from his HQ. The tragedy would have a moral impact on his men, he thought to himself once he had found out what had happened. From experience, he knew that how he managed the situation would either bring him love or resentment. So, he ordered a cease-fire and an inquiry, although it slipped his mind to find out about the names of the victims.

A short while later, there came a knock on his HQ door, and instead of handing him a report on the cannon explosion, the messenger said, 'Sir, I am to inform you that Colonel Sloughter's ship has been sighted. Wind permitting, she should be in New York by tomorrow, sir.'

CHAPTER 26

March 19, 1691

NEW YORK

News of the arrival of the long-awaited governor had already rippled through the town to the fort by the time, the following day, Ingoldsby had dispatched Colonel Dudley with an urgent plea to H.M.S. *Archangel*.

Anchored in the Narrows, the man-of-war's advance into the bay of New York continued to be hampered by adverse winds. So, once Dudley had conveyed the critical need for the governor's presence onshore, Colonel Sloughter, standing tall in full regalia, sank one last draught of Madeira wine to fortify himself for the final passage to port. He had already survived one near disaster on the rocks of Barbados, where the *Archangel* had lost thirty-seven feet of her false keel—one reason for his delay—and he was loathe to court danger so soon again at his age. Yet, recognizing the urgency, he consented to an undignified row to shore, instead of waiting for the wind to turn.

Indeed, the people of New York, weary from the extended standoff between Leisler's defenders and Ingoldsby's forces, had been waiting all night and all morning in the hope that the new governor's arrival would herald the end of the conflict.

On that Thursday afternoon of March 19th, a cold north wind sent ominous clouds coursing over the half-moon battery, where Darlington and Ducamp were wrestling with furling the mainsail they had left out to dry that morning.

Looking out across the bay, Daniel caught sight of the silhouetted pinnace braving the choppy waters as it advanced toward the harbour, the oarsmen heaving into the wind, with two officials sitting bent forward holding their hats. So, they had got their man, Daniel thought to himself, realising the significance in the unceremonious arrival that underscored the weight of Sloughter's first mission: to weave together without prejudice the frayed thread of a divided city.

As the pinnace cut fiercely through the waves toward the heart of New York, it became clear to Daniel that Sloughter's landing would not simply herald a new chapter, but set the stage for a final, decisive confrontation that would determine the very fate of its people and governance for years to come. Would the old order be restored? Could Leisler find a place in this new arrangement? If that were so, how would he work with his rivals? Or would he and his council face retribution? Daniel knew the stakes were especially high for a foreign-born New Yorker like Leisler, who did not count among the town's grandees. And Sloughter, even though he was from far across the ocean, was after all one of them. Would these birds of a feather flock together against this popinjay?

If only Leisler could have acted on the news of the governor's arrival before his adversaries could get their grips on him, thought Darlington. Sloughter would arrive amidst the intended council's scorn of the elected governor and Ingoldsby's relish to see his demise.

Meanwhile, Ducamp finished fastening his side of the sail to the spar and joined Daniel's gaze over the turbulent bay. 'It'll take a strong leader to stand up to a pack of vengeful hounds.'

'I was just thinking the same thing,' returned Daniel.

'They won't be making any compliments about the restored defences or the new battery, for sure.'

'Nor the war efforts Leisler has personally financed to preserve us from the French.'

'True.'

'They'll portray him to Sloughter not as a New Yorker empowered by the people to safeguard their lives and livelihood, but as a usurper bent on taking the power from the crown.'

'Aye, my fear too,' said Ducamp with resignation in his voice. 'But at least we thwarted a civil war.'

'It came dangerously close, though.'

'Thank William for the cease-fire, eh?'

'Ha, still can't believe the scoundrel tried to sink me. But let us not speak too soon. Leisler will not accept anything less than a formal handover in due form.'

'That'll please Ingoldsby, for sure!'

A little later, they heard the bell of the Town Hall as it echoed through the subdued streets of New York, beckoning the townsfolk to gather to bear witness to an event that would mark a significant change.

Darlington left Ducamp at the battery to finish furling the last sail and rendezvoused at the fort. Ten minutes later, he was standing in Leisler's office, listening to a message being read out. 'The colonel has taken the oath as Governor Sloughter before the people of New York,' the messenger announced breathlessly. Daniel sensed both relief and apprehension amid the haze of pipe smoke. Leisler, who had stood firm in the face of adversity, seemed momentarily unmoored by the news. Sloughter's actions set a course that could not easily be undone, one that Leisler had long anticipated, yet its reality was stark. Daniel felt a deepening concern. The political landscape of New York was transforming as he breathed, and the implications for Leisler and his supporters were troubling.

The messenger continued, 'And the intended councillors have been sworn in, all except two.'

'Bayard and Nicholls, I presume,' Milborne interjected, his voice betraying a hint of concern.

'That is so,' the messenger confirmed.

'Well, they remain confined, though well attended to. Their freedom is the only thing they lack,' Milborne mused aloud. The room fell silent, each man lost in thought over the implications of this new development.

Daniel knew full well that the absence of Bayard and Nicholls from the council's swearing-in was a pointed act, one that did not bode well for the future. Their freedom, or lack thereof, was a chess piece in a game that was rapidly advancing towards an end.

Leisler's reaction was measured, his voice steady despite the undercurrents of tension. He lowered his pipe. 'We have acted in the interest of our city and its people, against all odds,' he stated, his gaze settling fleetingly on each of the members of his council before resting momentarily upon Daniel. He went on, 'Our actions have been in defence of our homes, our families, and our rights. This we have done with clear consciences and steadfast hearts.'

After a pause for collective thought, Milborne, ever the pragmatist, added, 'And now we must navigate these new waters with the same resolve and wisdom that have brought us this far. The arrival of Governor Sloughter and the establishment of his council mark a turning point, but our principles remain our guiding star. We still hold the power, and we have the support of the people.'

The atmosphere was heavy with the weight of the situation, each man balancing in his mind the complexities of loyalty, duty, and perhaps the inevitable return to the old order, with the grandees back in their seats of power. Daniel felt a resolve within him, a determination to stand by Leisler, come what may. The path ahead would be paved with uncertainty, but the bonds forged in the crucible of their shared struggle were unbreakable. He decided they would face the future together, united in their commitment to their community and their ideals of freedom of thought and choice of worship.

While the discussion continued in Leisler's office, under a flag of truce, Major Ingoldsby, escorted by his company of foot, presented himself at the fort gate. Instructions were given for him to be blindfolded before being conducted to Leisler's office a short distance into the courtyard. It seemed like an undiplomatic detail but one that the master of the guard, who took his job seriously, had established prior to Sloughter's arrival, as a security measure aimed at preventing any messenger from gathering intelligence on fortifications, troop deployments, or other strategic details.

Leisler, standing behind his desk, his close circle fanned out on either flank, gave the nod to remove the blindfold. Major Ingoldsby was not impressed. 'Sir, is this how your trainband treats an officer of His Majesty?' said the major forcefully. 'Never mind, I come from Governor Sloughter. His Excellency demands entry into the fort. What say you?'

'Come,' said Leisler amicably, in an effort to defuse the situation. 'How do I know this is not a ploy?'

Ingoldsby was in no mood for banter. 'Do you dare doubt the presence of His Excellency?' he thundered.

'I do not doubt it,' returned Leisler, becoming as pedantic as a Puritan priest, 'as I simply have no proof of his presence one way or the other, sir.'

'For the love of God, man, his ship is anchored in the narrows!'

'I cannot see it from here, sir. How could I possibly know?' Ingoldsby made some grunts of exasperation, but before he could formulate his thoughts into words, Jacob Leisler said, 'To bear witness to the said presence of the said governor, sir, allow me to send Mr Joost Stoll here with you.' Leisler gestured toward a stout, balding man approaching middle age who bounced twice upon his toes. 'He is the only man here who has encountered Colonel Sloughter and can thus vouch for his said presence. Mr Stoll will also personally deliver this letter to the said colonel.' Leisler handed the letter to Stoll, who gave a curt bow and accepted it. He had recently come back from London, where in 1689, he was sent by Leisler to deliver several documents intended to justify Leisler's control of New York and his military preparations.

'Then you refuse entry to your governor.'

'I do not refuse entry, sir. I simply demand to verify his identity according to the established protocol. Surely you agree it would be highly imprudent of me to instruct otherwise.'

'So be it. Whatever words you wrap it in, it is a refusal, nonetheless. I shall conduct your man to the governor with your persistent refusal, sir. I go.'

'Soldier, blindfold the major and escort him to the gate,' Leisler commanded.

'Confound you, man!' blasted Ingoldsby as the blindfold was immediately passed over his head and attached behind it.

The major turned and stomped off in a straight line until his arm was gently pulled and he was told to turn right. Stoll followed him to the gate, where they joined Ingoldsby's awaiting foot company. The thick wooden gate was bolted and barred, and the men marched through the dark puddles across the bare market field toward the Town Hall, situated at a cannon's shot from the fort by the harbour.

Meanwhile, back in Leisler's office, the hubbub of conversation was abruptly hushed by Milborne's commanding tenor voice as he sought to refocus the discussion. 'Gentlemen, gentlemen, thank you. In conclusion, then, they are simply obliged to negotiate the terms of our cession. It is unthinkable to surrender as though we were foes. To do so would be to consider us enemies of the king.'

'Nay, nay,' resounded from the floor of counsellors, some beating the table with their fingers.

'We have always stood to defend our Protestant king against the tyranny of the papists who would banish all freedom of religion,' said Counsellor Delanoy.

Making a calming movement with his hand, Milborne went on, 'Gentlemen, I say we stand firm. We are after all in a position of authority here, we have what they want, and so, gentlemen, we have the upper hand. Indeed, why could we not govern this colony ourselves until we reach an agreement with the king of England himself?'

'I agree,' said Leisler, finally emerging from his contemplation. He stood for an instant, his arms folded on his chest, observing the surprise of his own response. He knew that some of them entertained the unlikelihood of being able to push their hopes of self-governance even further. Then, unfolding his arms and pressing his fingers on his desk, he said, 'We need to speak to the governor in question. However, let us not diverge from our objective of handing over the running of this colony. This is not yet the time for it to seek independence; we still need the hand of a faraway king to defend us from other faraway kings. Now, I have sent the governor my message. Once he has read it, I have no doubt he will see sense and agree to sit around this table in a civilised manner to discuss the future of our beloved New York.'

As calls of approval bubbled over, Daniel began to realise that the topic of their own personal safety had not been broached, so consumed were they with defending their colonial position. What would happen if Sloughter declared them as being outside the law? 'And what about our futures, gentlemen?' said Daniel sharply. 'We do not know how we stand in the eyes of this governor. I for one distrust Ingoldsby, and trust even less the new counsellors. I believe only one thing that has become evident throughout this siege: it is that the grandees are out to seek revenge!'

'Good point, Daniel,' said Leisler as he picked up his pipe from the table and tilted the clay bowl to the flame of a fresh candle. Pulling his wooden chair beneath him, he sat back and said, 'Indeed, we must include our personal well-being and freedom from sanctions in the terms of the capitulation. Milborne, and you, Delanoy, I suggest you first study the terms with the governor while I hold the fort. My presence here will ensure that the governor treats you with the respect you, as counsellors of this city, deserve. I am sure Sloughter will see sense when he reads my note, that we have been deprived of welcoming him as befitting an incoming governor of New York because of Ingoldsby's tight guard. Provided, of course, that Stoll recognises him as being the man whom Ingoldsby claims him to be.'

There came another round of 'hear, hear' as the candle was passed round from one counsellor to the next. Discussion continued until the master of the guard entered, announcing that Ingoldsby and Ensign Stoll were returning from the Town Hall. Daniel pictured them being escorted by Ingoldsby's foot company across the market field in the encroaching darkness. 'Back from the Sloughter house,' jested Counsellor Delanoy, providing a moment of light relief in the otherwise tense atmosphere of the hazy, lamp-lit room.

A short while later, Stoll confirmed the identity. 'It is indeed the Colonel Sloughter I met in London, sir,' he said, bouncing on his toes while bowing his head almost apologetically, as Major Ingoldsby entered and wrenched off the blindfold himself.

Understanding the brief confirmation that had just been made, Ingoldsby, without banter or pleasantries, shot straight to the point. 'Now,' he said, clearing his throat. 'You are to give entrance to the fort, sir. Every man will lay down his arms and then leave the fort unmolested and go directly to his own home, except you, sir, and those you call your counsellors, who are to come with me and appear before your governor.'

'Major Ingoldsby,' said Leisler sternly, rising abruptly to his feet from behind his desk. 'I bid you to show respect!'

The major continued imperturbably, 'You are also to release Nicholas Bayard and William Nicholls, who are sworn-in members of His Excellency's council.'

'Not before we reach the terms of our capitulation.'

'For that, you are to come with me, sir.'

'Not I. We shall follow protocol. Milborne and Delanoy shall indeed go with you. They will discuss the terms upon which Governor Sloughter would take over this fort, should we capitulate.'

'*Should* you capitulate? Do you realise the gravity of that word, sir?'

'I speak not lightly, Major. Remember, we have here three hundred men in this fort. Neither I nor my counsellors have any intention to risk their lives, but there must be a proper transfer in full respect of the administrative protocol of this colony. Without it, there can be no order. Need I remind you, sir, without order, there can be no peace!'

Daniel long since suspected it would come to this: a battle of egos where each man sought to impose his own sense of importance on the other. But he hoped that, in the fire of the exchange, Ingoldsby did not read Leisler's threat as he had. For in it, Leisler clearly revealed he had no intention to risk any lives. There again, such subtlety would surely not have escaped a battle-hardened soldier like Ingoldsby, would it?

'I go, and let you think about the consequence of your words, sir.'

Leisler gave the master of the guard the nod. Ingoldsby was blindfolded, which now seemed as futile to Daniel as Leisler's threat. Then Milborne and Delanoy went with the major, their demeanour heavy with the gravity of their mission.

The damp and cold ink-black night brought little reassurance, only the glimmer of Ingoldsby's red-and-gold braided frock coat that emerged a third time from the market field. This time, he came bearing news that would strike a blow like a cannonball in the belly of a frigate.

Again, standing face to face, Ingoldsby fired first. 'I am to inform you that His Excellency has deemed it necessary to take your representatives into custody, sir.'

'What? Outrageous!' Leisler roared. 'Under what charge?'

'For one, the charge of unlawfully taking over the fort.'

Leisler's face seemed to turn to dull stone as he stared into the middle distance, illuminated by the tallow light from the wall sconces. These gave off a greasy scent as the candles within them burned. Standing in the shadows nearby, Daniel couldn't help but notice that Leisler's usual commanding presence, marked by his fingers arching on the table, now resembled more an effort to steady himself.

'Did you give my note to the governor, Stoll?' Leisler asked sharply, his gaze shifting slightly to the right as he broke eye contact with Ingoldsby.

'I did indeed,' Stoll replied.

Unmoved, Ingoldsby pressed on, 'You are to accompany me to meet your governor, sir.'

'You mean, so that he can arrest me too!'

'That decision rests with His Excellency. I am but the executioner of his orders, sir.'

'Ha, I will not go, and certainly not at this ungodly hour. I shall remain within these walls until His Excellency sees fit to engage with me and my council in proper and due form. Does he not realise that we command three hundred men within these fortifications, to say nothing of those beyond the town ready to bear arms in our defence?'

Ingoldsby's eyes narrowed, and his reply was sharp: 'We command over five hundred trained soldiers.' Then, moderating his tone, he added, 'So, you refuse for a third time, sir?'

'Indeed, I do, until the terms for an honourable cession are met. Furthermore, as you well know, capitulation after nightfall goes against all proper protocol.'

'It will make no difference,' returned Ingoldsby levelly. 'But, so be it recorded. Dare I say you are doing yourself no favours. You have until daylight to vacate the fort, or we will take it by force.' Ingoldsby turned smartly, leaving Leisler no time to give the nod to the guard master to apply the blindfold.

The major stepped to the door and made his way out into the fort courtyard, where he gave one sweeping look to his left. He recognised the demeanour of weary men huddled around open fires. He gave a gruff sigh as he turned sharply to his right. 'It would not take much to blow that gate in,' he thought to himself as he continued to the gate, where he joined his waiting company.

The room fell into a solemn silence as Leisler, still reeling from the shock, abruptly jerked back his head as if in disbelief, then slowly sat down. He would have to inform the men of the fort of the governor's position. For Darlington, too, the situation left no room for doubt: Sloughter had unequivocally chosen sides. Daniel wondered what he would hear if he were a fly on the wall in the great room of the Town Hall. He imagined the vociferous protests of the newly appointed council, their voices baying with disgust over Bayard and Nicholls' continued confinement in the fort jail, and echoing their call to arms. Then, the call of midnight would prompt Sloughter to adjourn the council meeting until the morning.

Darlington and Ducamp spent another night at the fort. As the sky began to pale over the harbour, it became apparent that a significant number of men had stolen out under cover of darkness.

The surprise was only partial for Daniel. He had suspected the previous night that, although most of the men had vowed to resist, they must have sensed Leisler's reluctance to defend the fort against the new governor. Once word had spread through the fort that the first leavers had passed through the city gates unhindered, many with families must have found it too tempting to resist going home.

The bleak light of dawn unveiled another surprise. Ingoldsby's cannons, previously aimed seaward, were now turned menacingly toward the fort. His forces had swelled to five hundred men, many strategically positioned just beyond musket range. This was no longer a siege posture: it was a formation poised to storm the fort at the risk of dreadful loss of life, all sanctioned by the governor himself. Daniel could hardly believe that the governor would rather destroy the fort than resort to other means.

After a restless night spent mulling over the possible outcomes and the consequences for the many families he had vowed to protect two and a half years earlier, Leisler summoned his counsellors and advisors to his office. 'Gentlemen,' he said from behind his desk to the ragged and weary-eyed men standing before him, 'it is my conviction that one must act fearlessly upon what one believes to be right. And so, I stand here before you and pray dear God that the Governor will see sense and accept my capitulation in proper and due form.' The counsellors solemnly intoned a chorus of 'amens' and unanimously grunted and hummed their consent, as did Daniel. How could anyone question the wisdom of seeking to negotiate their surrender to the sworn-in governor to prevent loss of life? he wondered to himself, provided it could be done in a way that preserved honour. Leisler pressed on, 'Here, I have written down again the essence of my letter to the governor for you all to recall.' Leisler picked up a scroll from his desk, the text of which he had composed from memory the previous night. He cleared his throat and read:

'Your Excellency,

'I understand that my adversaries are trying to trip me up, aiming to undermine my dedication to our revered king and queen. They wish to erase my loyal service, and that of my council's, up to this point. However, I trust that I have been careful not to make such a mistake, as I have always been committed and faithful to them. I kindly ask that you instruct the major to release me from the royal fort, handing over only the royal weapons and supplies. He should treat me in a manner befitting someone who will provide Your Excellency with a thorough report of all my actions and conduct, and my council's. With utmost respect,

'I am Your Excellency's most devoted servant.

'Jacob Leisler.'

There came another round of reflective hums and grunts. Leisler went on, 'Should he, for the love of God, agree to avoid bloodshed, then the men shall vacate the fort in an orderly fashion, lay down their arms as requested, and the council members and I shall surrender ourselves. Do you hear me, gentlemen?'

Heavy with gravitas, the council collectively voiced their acceptance, except for Counsellor Gerardus. Looking drawn and concerned, he coughed before asking, 'What would become of us?'

Leisler looked blankly at the round and portly Gerardus for an instant before responding. 'Good point, Doctor. I gather we would present ourselves before the governor. I can only presume he wishes to hear our voices and our allegiance to the crown, which, I trust, is undisputed among us. Am I right, gentlemen?'

A chorus of 'Hear, hear!' filled the room.

There was barely time to discuss further changes to the text intended to save lives and honour before the master of the guard stepped into the room with an announcement. Ingoldsby was again leading the charge, splashing through puddles in a straight line across the sodden market field.

Five minutes later, he was entering the governor's room without a blindfold, his boots caked in mud. Standing to attention, he said, 'To preserve peace throughout this province, His Excellency, with approbation from the council, has agreed to meet you for the transfer of this fort before the gate. Both His Excellency and the council will be present to officially carry out the transfer in *proper and due form*, sir, as you so term it.'

Leisler, standing calm and proud, said, 'I solemnly accept the transfer on those terms, Major, and shall be honoured to transfer the fort to the sworn-in governor appointed by our Gracious Majesties, King William and Queen Mary.'

There came a perceptible sigh of relief in the stuffy room as the full effect of Ingoldsby's words hit home. Daniel pulled open the windows that made the stale, smoke-filled air shift in one block, then slowly snake away into the fort quadrant. He knew that all these men sought was a dignified transfer to reaffirm their legal standing after two and a half years of devoted service. Daniel reflected on their leadership of New York and its province, carried out to the best of their ability despite the lack of guidance or support from the crown, too preoccupied as it was with its revolution in England and its war in Ireland. They had kept out the Jacobite papists who threatened the very liberty of conscience of the colony, one of the pillars of its foundation so cherished by New York's diverse population. Furthermore, they had reinforced the dilapidated wall and built sturdy defences, safeguarding the colony against the bellicose French and their Indian allies.

'I trust also that Milborne and Delanoy will be released from their shackles,' added Leisler.

'The governor and the council have deemed that shall be the case. In return, Counsellors Bayard and Nicholls are to be freed from their incarceration and brought out as you hand over the fort.'

'That shall be the case.'

'Then you are formally requested to file out of the fort on the stroke of nine by the Town Hall bell. Your men will vacate the fort first, line up on the parade ground in front, then lay down their arms, and make their way to their homes. You, sir, and your council shall present yourselves before His Excellency at the fort gate.'

'So be it, Major.'

Leisler gestured to the guard master to forget the blindfold as Ingoldsby turned on his heel and then marched out of the opened door, which brought in a draft and caused the windows to bang shut.

The major's demeanour was radically different, thought Daniel as the room became abuzz with celebratory utterances. But with just half an hour to the fateful hour, Leisler raised his voice to refocus operations. 'Gentlemen, the siege is ended, and our job is almost done.' There came a chorus of subdued cheers and nods of contemplation. 'Let us vacate these premises as befitting a lieutenant governor of New York and his council. And then let us return home to our loved ones. I, for one, have a new daughter who must wonder what her father looks like.'

The counsellors chortled at the jest and gave a hearty cheer. Leisler then gave instructions to assemble the men and prepare for their retreat. He would give them their instructions before they marched out.

A few minutes later, as the counsellors dispersed to prepare for the transfer, Leisler called Daniel aside. 'Darlington,' he said in a conversational tone of voice. 'You will make your way homeward with the men.'

'I will proudly stand with you, sir.'

'No, who knows what to expect from those grandees. They are all alike.'

'I will stand by you, come what may.'

'No, Daniel, I have used your loyalty enough. You have proved yourself worthy and done your parents proud. You have stood by freedom of worship, so cherished by your father and my dear friend. There will be another battle another day. But for now, I want you to go home to your family.'

'But Jacob, I...'

'You are not part of the council, Daniel,' said Leisler, his voice adopting a sterner tone. 'You will go home. That is an order.'

On the stroke of nine, Daniel watched the two hundred or so remaining men file out of the fort onto the parade ground in front of it.

Under the patchy March sky, Ingoldsby's officers were ready to usher them into place, bawling instructions for them to form into rows. 'Follow the man in front!' one officer yelled. 'You, start a row behind!' another commanded. To Daniel, it all seemed meticulously planned.

He watched through the gate as the men positioned them-selves on either side of the parade ground, forming a central aisle that led to Broad Way. This was the path where the two governors would meet. He and Ducamp had placed themselves among the last to leave the fort before Leisler began the formal march to welcome the new governor. Yet, after exchanging a final nod with Leisler, Daniel could not help a creeping sensation of vulnerability the moment he crossed the fort threshold. His eyes met a perimeter of Ingoldsby's red-uniformed soldiers, muskets in hand, surrounding the dishevelled ranks of fort men lining up in rows. Turning to Ducamp, Daniel said in a low voice, 'So, this is the point of no return.'

'Aye, easier prey there never was,' returned Ducamp under his breath. As they advanced, it dawned on Daniel with a heavy realisation that they were now already at the mercy of the new government. 'Thinking about it,' Ducamp uttered, 'it's not reassuring at all, is it?'

New Yorkers in their thousands had turned out for the transfer of power and were kept back from the parade ground. None were more vociferous than the anti-Leislerians, who now found themselves at liberty to hurl their insults at the fort men in all impunity. Daniel was acutely aware that among them were merchants he knew, frustrated by two and a half years of restrictions and taxes imposed to finance the war with New France. But how else were they to finance the major works required to fortify the colony? Daniel now realised that the protective perimeter of soldiers was also meant to keep the peace between the anti-Leislerians and the more numerous, yet more subdued, supporters of Leisler.

Daniel's gaze followed the central aisle, interspersed with soldiers, to a group of hecklers on the far-right corner. He recognised Mrs Bayard, caped in black under a felt hat, standing amidst her circle that included Mrs Cortland and their maids. Opposite them, in the far-left corner of the aisle, he then noticed Mrs Leisler and her daughter, young Mrs Milborne, solemnly surveying the grounds where some of the men had already prematurely laid down their arms. Daniel wondered if they, too, felt the vulnerability of their position under the new regime.

As if on cue, Major Ingoldsby now bellowed the order for all of Leisler's men to lay down their arms, which was relayed by the officers on the grounds. Leisler then emerged from the fort, regally attired and periwigged for the occasion—a red sash, pistol at his waist, and sword at his hip—waving to his supporters on one side, ignoring his detractors on the other.

He was followed by the council members, who received more jeers than cheers. Their mixed reception was quickly overshadowed by the loud applause and acclamations that greeted Bayard and Nicholls, who, escorted by guards, appeared rugged but well-nourished, and both with full beards. Daniel looked to his left, caught Judith Bayard's enthusiastic wave to her husband, and then noticed her jaw tighten as she cast a sharp glance towards Mrs Leisler.

The governor's cortege then came into view, with Colonel Sloughter at the forefront, his red face contrasting with his blond periwig. He was surrounded by guards in a tight box formation, followed by Milborne, Delanoy, and the governor's newly sworn-in counsellors. He advanced at a solemn pace, yet with nonchalant patience, like a man accustomed to such parades, until at last both governors halted, leaving two yards between them.

Daniel was standing ten yards away, his height affording him a clear view of Sloughter's high-arched, arrogant nose and his imperious eye—hallmarks of the aristocratic loftiness that Daniel so deeply loathed.

'Your Excellency,' said Leisler affably with a deep bow. 'We meet at last.'

'Do you have the seal?' said Sloughter levelly, with a stiff jerk of the neck that the most optimistic might have interpreted as a show of respect.

'Here, Your Excellency,' said Jacob Leisler, handing over the old broken seal of New York that he had used in place of the most recent one, which Stephanus van Cortlandt had taken to Albany two years earlier in an attempt to limit Leisler's authority. 'I trust you will find New York in a better condition than I found it, Your Excellency.'

'I am unaware of *how* you found it, Mr Lesser,' the governor replied, accepting the seal before absentmindedly passing it to Counsellor Dudley.

Before Leisler could respond, Major Ingoldsby stepped in. He had fetched Bayard and Nicholls from the cortege. 'It's Leisler,' the major corrected, 'Leisler. It's German.'

'Oh, is it? Well then, Mr Leisler...'

Ingoldsby then turned to the two disgruntled-looking men at his side and continued, 'May I present Counsellors Bayard and Nicholls.'

'Your Excellency,' Bayard began, extending his hand for the governor to shake. 'I must present my sincere gratitude for releasing me from the dreadful prison cell where I have been held for over a year,' he said, his voice tinged with injured pride. 'But alas, this is not the time for pleasantries, Your Excellency.' Turning towards Jacob Leisler with a disdainful sneer, Bayard continued, 'This man before us is the very scoundrel, the usurper, the tyrant who has so grievously misused the office entrusted by Their Majesties. I would boldly suggest, Your Excellency, that he be confined to jail forthwith.'

'Is that so?' the governor replied, eyeing Leisler as though he were assessing the character of the alleged tyrant. 'Well, such measures are now beyond consideration; the council has already granted an acquittal.'

'The council's decision requires my vote, Your Excellency,' insisted Bayard. 'As well as that of my fellow counsellor here, Mr William Nicholls, former attorney general. Without our vote, I therefore propose that the ruling be declared void.'

'Oh,' said the governor, searching for his advisors. 'Is this so, Mr Brooke?'

'Indeed, I believe it is, Your Excellency,' said Chidley Brooke, having stepped closer as the governor caught his eye. 'The ruling cannot stand without the vote of all the members of the council.'

'Two of whom were unjustly held captive in prison,' insisted Bayard, 'by this band of lascars, led by these two scoundrels, Leisler and Milborne, Your Excellency. I say they can and should be held in prison.'

Sloughter appeared to find himself at a slight loss. He turned to Ingoldsby. 'Is that so, Major?'

'As you are aware, Your Excellency, this man indeed unlawfully held the fort. He and his rabble prevented the king's men from entering, and his forces killed four of the king's soldiers. As the ringleader of these transgressions, I would advise that he and his accomplices be detained, Your Excellency, until a formal trial can be convened.'

'Ah, in that case, Mr Lesser...'

'It's Leisler, Your Excellency, Jacob Leisler. As I expressed in my letter to you, I find myself unjustly accused by these men. I implore you to consider my account of the events before making any rash decisions.'

Raising an eyebrow, Sloughter said, 'I am not in the habit of making rash decisions, sir. But fear not, you shall indeed have your say.'

'Thank you, Your Excellency.'

'However, until then, you are to be held in the king's jail.'

While Leisler, taken aback, was momentarily at a loss for words, Ingoldsby wasted no time. 'Guards!' he roared, signalling towards Leisler's counsellors with a twirl of his finger. 'Seize them and escort them to the fort prison.' Stepping up to Leisler, he then commanded, 'Lieutenant Collins, relieve this man of his sash, sword, and pistol!' Collins, aided by two burly guards, swiftly complied, stripping Leisler of his accoutrements. At that moment, a lady dressed in black marched up. She curtsied once to the governor, turned to Leisler, and spat in his face. It was Judith Bayard, who then tore off Leisler's periwig and brandished it to the anti-Leislerians, which provoked an uproar of laughter.

From ten yards away, Daniel watched in disbelief. 'No! No, this is all wrong!' he protested to Ducamp. Then, louder in desperation, he shouted, 'You are making a terrible mistake, Governor Sloughter. This man is a brave and honest hero!' But the plea went unheeded as Leisler was manhandled, his legs clapped in irons, and his person frog-marched back the way he had come. Pushing through the jeering crowd that had forced its way between the soldiers, Daniel caught Leisler's eye. The older man gave a stern shake of the head. 'Go back. It will be all right! Go home!' he shouted. Then, locking eyes with Ducamp, who had kept up behind in the chaos, Leisler gave an emphatic shake of the head.

Ducamp immediately understood. He caught Daniel by the arm. 'Daniel, leave it!' he yelled sternly. 'Daniel, you don't want to go back in there!'

But Daniel continued to fight his way through the surging crowd. 'Didier, this is horribly unjust—'

'There's nothing we can do now with five hundred muskets aimed our way.'

As this unfolded, Ingoldsby's voice rose above the clamour. 'Men, leave your arms here, and you are free to go. Stay, and you will face arrest!'

'Daniel. Let's go now!' urged Ducamp, as the fort men surged toward the harbour, with others making for the city gate at the top of Broad Way. 'We must leave now. Your family needs you. Come on!'

As Leisler was swept through the fort gates, with the horde of counsellors claiming their innocence and decrying the injustice, he gave Daniel a final nod, urging him to leave. Daniel then shot a glance back at Bayard, who was smugly receiving accolades from Sloughter's council members; his wife's eyes gleamed with triumph as they fixed on Mrs Leisler. Yet, amidst the turmoil, Mrs Leisler stood concerned but dignified. Her daughter hastily drew her away while the crowd, divided in their loyalties, either disputed or cheered the arrests. They were kept in check only by the intervening soldiers.

'They've got their revenge,' said Daniel darkly, upon seeing how Sloughter's counsellors were now revelling in their ascendancy.

'We have been deceived!' was the final outcry Daniel heard from Leisler's council, as Ducamp hastened him away from the scene of betrayal.

Daniel was still catching up on lost sleep when, in the midst of reliving the tragic transfer ceremony, the rumbling of approaching carriage wheels brought him from his slumber, and he opened his eyes.

He could tell by the chill in the air and the fading light through the shutter pulled ajar that it was later in the day than he hoped. Marianne must have let him oversleep, he thought to himself. Uncharacteristically, he felt for his old pistol, which he had cleaned and greased as soon as he had arrived home. He had left his new one along with his musket on the parade ground, where he had laid them down that tragic morning. Once everything had blown over, he figured he would go recover them from the Town Hall or wherever it was they were stored. But would it blow over? He still could hardly believe this rule of impartial law, brought here to New York by this new governor from the old country.

Then he looked around the shaded room in search of his clothes that Marianne had folded on the chair by her dressing table. It occurred to him how much he valued her thoughtful gestures, her manners, and her practical sense of organisation. Just two and a half years after crossing paths with the young, ferociously independent woman, he now admired her sense of motherhood. She brought a whole new meaning to his life. How could he ever live without her? As these thoughts entered his mind, little did he know the twists that fate had in store, twists that were about to cast long shadows over the life they had built together as Mr and Mrs Darlington of New York.

Three minutes later, he was waiting on the threshold with Marianne, babe on her hip, to greet May and Didier Ducamp as they jumped down from the carriage parked in front of the barn. Little Samuel was being tended to by Claudine. 'I suggest we all meet in the kitchen,' said May in her no-non-sense manner, which didn't sound much like a suggestion at all. 'I have some important news fresh from town.'

'I'll get Martha to put the water on,' said Marianne, mim-icking the sense of urgency. Madame de Fontenay joined the 'kitchen party' as she called it.

Moments later, in the kitchen where Martha had put on the water for some tea, May said, 'They are going to try Leisler and his council for high treason and murder.'

'What? You can't be serious,' exclaimed Daniel, standing by the window, too agitated to be seated.

'Aye,' said Ducamp, seated next to his wife, 'that was my reaction when May told me.' He had also been catching up with sleep before his wife had stopped at their house down the road and told him of the news.

'Then we came straight here,' continued May.

'How did you find out?' asked Marianne.

'Got it from the horse's mouth!' said May. 'I spoke with Judith Bayard, who wants everyone to know about her triumph. She says Bayard wants everyone in Leisler's close circle to dance at the end of a rope.'

'Good God!' exclaimed Daniel. 'Is there no end to the spite of those people?'

'I think not, and worst of all, he has the governor's ear,' said Didier.

May continued, 'Daniel, you were close to him.'

'I wasn't a counsellor, though. Otherwise, I'd be in prison right now.'

'And they'd have thrown away the key,' said May. 'Judith told me they've put Leisler in the same prison as her husband, with the addition of clamping him in irons.'

'How is that possible?' asked Daniel.

'Very possible and in all legality,' said May. 'Anyway, it doesn't matter that you weren't a counsellor. Burghers and advisors in town have already been rounded up. I suspect you haven't been yet because you are outside the wall. But it's just a matter of time before they come knocking on your door, Daniel.'

'Once inside,' added Ducamp, 'they won't be letting you out any time soon.'

'Daniel, then we must leave,' declared Marianne.

'Our trenches won't serve any purpose then,' said Madame de Fontenay. 'Not even against the English!'

'Grandmother!'

'They did help morale, though. We shall just have to leave without testing them.'

'But I did nothing untoward,' continued Daniel. 'I'll stand my ground.'

'In their eyes, you did,' said May. 'You ferried men to the fort. You enabled Leisler to strengthen his position. They will go as far as to blame you for the deaths.'

'I killed no one.'

'Aye, man, but let's face it,' said Ducamp, 'without the ketch runs, some would never have fired a shot, and even that cannon might never have blown up.'

'Daniel, May is right,' said Marianne.

'I cannot betray my friends.'

'You heard Leisler, Daniel,' urged Ducamp. 'He told you to clear out. For the sake of your family, you must leave.'

After a pause, as Martha placed the tea paraphernalia on the table and more remonstrance ensued, Daniel finally said, 'Where would we go?'

'We'll go north,' said Marianne, 'stop at Little Rock. We'll change our name. No one will be the wiser until we know where we stand. At least, until after the trial.'

'We have a plot, but nothing's built on it,' said Daniel.

'There is an inn there, at least. We can decide what to do when we get there. Thankfully, it'll soon be spring.'

'Yes, and in spring, the French will be coming!'

'Pity,' said Madame de Fontenay wistfully, 'I would have liked to try our trenches.' Her remark sparked a moment of nervous laughter, making the acceptance of the dramatic turn of events perhaps more palatable.

May brought the conversation back round to the urgent matter at hand. 'You'd better prepare some belongings; you must leave in the morning. Soldiers will likely be rounding up

405

more of Leisler's people at dawn. You must depart an hour before daybreak at the latest, before the darkness begins to pale.'

'The night is without moon, and there will be cloud cover. I don't know the East River as well as the north. There's a risk of hitting rocks at Hell Gate,' said Daniel, coming round to the idea of escape.

'Take my carriage instead of your own,' said May swiftly.

Marianne nodded resolutely, quickly grasping the switch.

Daniel said, 'They are bound to follow us.'

'Not if I create a diversion,' remarked Ducamp. 'I'll take the ketch out to get some lumber. And the market vendors from the country will soon cover your tracks. If they do come knocking, they will only find Ben, who will tell them you've gone to visit friends. He won't know how you travelled there.'

'And what about you, my friend?'

'They won't be after me,' said Ducamp. 'I was only following orders. Besides, I have my guardian angel right by my side.' He clasped May's hand and held it up.

May said, 'Believe me, it can be useful to stay on even terms with your foes.'

Ducamp pursued, 'The post road is safe enough. Besides, the human vermin of this world don't get up till late; you'll be all right. And by the time Ingoldsby's men catch up with me fetching in timber, you'll be long gone.'

'The truth is,' said May, 'you have no choice. Marianne, you will take my pistols.'

The younger woman nodded brazenly. 'Just show me how to load them, and I'll do the rest!'

'That's the spirit!' said Madame de Fontenay. 'And if anyone comes near, they'll feel my cane!'

CHAPTER 27

Fall, 1699

EIGHT YEARS LATER

As the early morning mist clung to the bustling docks of New York, the Delpech family disembarked with trepidation and hope.

Paul, weakened from the voyage and alarmingly feverish, leaned heavily on Jacob as he limped down the gangway from the merchant ship, the *Nassau*. It came as a saving grace to Jacob when he found that the entry conditions into the city were less procedural than in Boston. 'I suggest you first find a refuge for your family,' said the busy customs official on the quayside. 'You can return afterward to put your goods into storage.'

As Jacob led the way to a nearby inn, followed by a barrow boy hauling their personal belongings, the uncertainty of their future in this burgeoning city weighed heavily upon him. Yet deep down, he sensed that this was a necessary rite of passage that should mark the beginning of a new and hopeful chapter in the saga of the Delpech family.

As for Jeanne, the place felt both alien and promising. She was sensitive to the different languages spoken among the clamour of conversations she heard along the way. At one point, she instinctively turned her head, almost certain she had heard French spoken in an accent of southern France. It was all very different from Boston, where English was the predominant language. And mercifully, there would be no more sea voyages, she considered with relief, as she glanced back to see Paul hopping along the cobbles on his crutch.

Jeanne woke early the next morning, content to be in a bed that did not sway, albeit in a musty inn. The youngest children were still asleep beside her bed, and Paul was lying on the paillasse on the floor. With a frown of concern, she reached over and touched his brow and realised his fever had grown worse than before. 'Burning,' she said to herself, while Isabelle and Pierre began to stir. As soon as Jacob returned, she planned to fetch a draught from a pharmacy to bring down his temperature, she thought as she got up to prepare a cold press for his forehead.

Jacob had risen early, excited to embark on his errands. After kissing his wife on the cheek and his children on the forehead as they slept, he first set off for the State House to inquire about that plot in New Rochelle. They might have records of deeds, given New Rochelle's jurisdiction under New York province. Then he would make his way up Broad Way and through the land gate in the remote hope of finding the Darlingtons at home, although he was under the impression they must have moved—why else would there have been no reply from them all these years?

As the city awoke to the hustle of early risers and the distant calls of the harbour, Jacob found himself tracing familiar streets that had become paved and cleaner in the decade of his absence. He vividly remembered trudging through the muddy, pig-filled streets back in the old days. Now, the air was charged with the energy of change as the vibrant evolution of the city unfolded before him in the form of an array of new buildings. Many of the wooden shacks down by the harbour had disappeared, replaced by more solid warehouses built of brick. Having secured his goods in storage the previous afternoon, Jacob was now free to focus on the two actions that would determine his future: securing the plot of land and finding the Darlingtons.

A short while later, Jacob was standing in the large room of the Stadt House by the harbour. 'Now, let's see. Delpech, you say?' said the clerk, who had returned with a large ledger.

'That's right,' said Jacob eagerly, yet almost dreading the reply. He had recognised the clerk from his first arrival in New York a decade ago; the man now had less hair and had adopted a stoop. Jacob wondered how different he himself would appear to the Darlingtons. But thankfully, he still possessed his maternal grandmother's full head of hair, though he didn't recall it being tinged with ash grey at the temples back then.

'Hmmm. Well, I can safely say there is no Delpech registered on the deeds for New Rochelle.'

Jacob unfolded a worn, yellow piece of paper. 'But what about this letter of reservation?'

The clerk peered at the note Jacob presented. 'It is dated from ten years ago, sir,' he replied evenly. 'A lot can change here in one year, let alone ten. Indeed, by the time this year is over, we shall all be moving into the new City Hall, no less.'

Jacob's heart sank with the clerk's words, but then a new thought sparked hope. He pressed on, 'Would there be a Mr Darlington in the register?'

The clerk readjusted his lunette on his nose as he looked down at the vast page. 'D...D...Darlington... No, sir. There is no such name either.'

'I am sorry to hear that, truly, I am,' said Jacob. 'But pray, would you perchance happen to know of a Daniel Darlington here in New York? He has a house opposite the church grave-yard outside the wall.'

'You mean Wall *Street*. That's where the new City Hall is being built. I'm afraid you'll find New York has changed quite a bit in ten years, sir,' said the clerk, peering over his lunette. 'I apologise, but I cannot remember the names of every living soul in New York.'

'Of course,' said Jacob, feeling slightly ridiculous. 'So, in short, my reservation isn't worth the paper it's written on.'

'I would suggest you make enquiries at New Rochelle it-self, if you had dealings, as you say you did, with its founding burghers.'

In the early autumn sunshine, Jacob was glad for the familiar sight of the fort as he turned onto Broad Way, now an avenue lined with tall brick and timber houses, some featuring bricks of different hues laid in checkered patterns.

But the wall, where was the wall? he wondered as he came upon the new church where once stood the land gate and the graveyard. Peering down Wall Street to his right where the wall once stood, he could clearly see what, going by the clerk, must be the new City Hall in an advanced state of construction. 'Clever,' he thought to himself, 'I wager they used the stone foundations from the wall blockhouses to build it.'

He walked on from the new church to find the view distinctly changed. It was pretty, refined, and tamed, and it was dressed in the ruddy hues and golden browns of autumn. For Broad Way now led into the distance in a tree-lined country avenue, with pleasantly laid-out gardens and streets branching off it in an orderly fashion. He walked a bit further amid a carpet of fallen leaves, then took a right onto a hard-earth track. His heart rose when a little further down the lane, his gaze met the charming two-storey house where he had stayed during that winter of '89. Spacious houses with pretty gardens had mushroomed around it, and the view once so beautiful to the forest edge was now replaced by quaint two-storey brick and timber houses.

As he approached, he noted the Darlington house had seen better days. One of the shutters had lost a hinge, and the garden, where once a goat was attached to a picket, was overgrown. He pushed open the sticking gate into the path that led to the front door, where he recalled Marianne once had stood pregnant and radiant, greeting him with a caring smile. 'Lord, where have those years gone?' he said, hanging his head in contemplation. What had become of those dear friends he once knew? Would he ever see them again in this world? Or would they remain forever young in his memory as he had left them, a decade ago on that cold spring New York morning? Jacob felt a soft swell of nostalgia in his heart. 'Silly old stick,' he told himself, wiping a moist eye. He sometimes wished he was not so sensitive. Yet there were no regrets to be had; after all, his departure had meant he had been able to reunite with his wife and see his children grow.

'Good day, sir.'

Jacob gave a start as, turning his head, his eyes were met by a tall black man standing at the entrance of the barn at the side of the house. He was holding a hefty scythe in his broad hand and wearing a look of affable curiosity.

'Oh, sorry. Yes, yes, I was about to knock.'

'No one there no more, sir,' said the man with a look of concern.

'Oh. You see, I used to know the people who once lived here, by the name of Darlington. Daniel and Marianne Darlington. They were friends of mine. Do you know them, by any chance?'

'Oh, no, sir, not me. The house is due for demolition, that's all I know.'

'Do you work here?'

'Yes, sir. Just using this old barn to sharpen me tools to trim the grass. But you just wait here, my boy will fetch me boss. He might know your friend. And if he don't, I'll wager a tobacco twist his lady do. She knows everyone.'

The man turned to a boy whom Jacob had not noticed. The lad ran off, while Jacob stood evaluating the place as if he were considering a purchase, provided it wasn't too late. As he warmed to the idea, he realised it would not only resolve their immediate housing problem but also prove to be a sound investment. The old house wouldn't require much work to restore; he recalled it had been solidly built. This would allow them to be settled in their own home before the onset of winter.

It wasn't long before Jacob heard galloping hooves that interrupted his blossoming thoughts of a purchase. Looking up, he saw a stern-faced, broad-shouldered man riding a majestic bay stallion, its coat gleaming in the sunlight like polished mahogany. As it drew closer, Jacob stood up from his seated position on a tree trunk, the very one he liked to sit on in those early days of spring of '89.

The man dismounted. 'Morning, sir,' he said in a deep voice, tipping his wide-brimmed hat. 'Can I help?'

'Good day, sir. Yes, I was enquiring about the house. I used to know the owner.'

'Ah, Mr Fontney,' said the man. 'He ain't been seen around here for a long time.' Jacob realised that the house must have changed ownership. But then his train of thought was disrupted as the approaching man gave him the shock of his life. The shock was reciprocated as the man halted in his tracks a few yards from the garden gate. Both men stood for a moment, staring at each other in disbelief.

'Monsieur Ducamp?' said Jacob, breaking the spell in English. 'Well, bless my soul, can it be?'

The reply came in French. '*Monsieur Delpech, ma parole!* What brings you?' Then, checking himself: 'Forgive me, monsieur, my wife often tells me I lack manners,' said Didier, extending his hand as he stepped more vigorously forward. The two men grasped each other's hand over the garden gate.

Jacob was filled with a mix of emotions. This was the man, the very lieutenant who had marched his men into his house in Montauban in the name of the French king during the dragonnades of 1685. And yet, the same man later saved his life on a privateer ship more than once. Despite the past, their smiles held a genuine warmth, a testament to the unlikely friendship forged in the most unexpected circumstances. Moreover, Jacob had found an unlikely friend in this town that seemed so foreign to him now.

'I live in the house down the road with my wife and children,' said Didier, after the initial exchange of surprise. 'So, what in the world brings you here, Monsieur Delpech?'

'I have come to settle in New York with my family,' said Jacob, continuing in French. 'I was hoping to find the Darlingtons. Did you know them?'

'I did indeed, sir, some years ago now. They left only a year after we arrived.'

'Do you know where they went?'

'Sorry, I can't say. They just took off one day after the troubles here. Now the house belongs to Steven Fontney. Never set foot

413

in it, mind. And now he's selling it. The price of a plot here has risen sharply, you see. But where are you staying?'

'At the inn near the harbour.'

'It is hardly a suitable abode for a family, I would venture to say, Monsieur Delpech.'

'No, indeed, especially as my son is rather poorly.'

'Then seeing as you once knew this house, you must stay here until your affairs are in order.'

'Oh, really? I can tender rent, naturally,' said Jacob. Pleasantly surprised, he turned with a sweeping glance that encompassed the house. 'And, actually, if the present owner is open to selling...'

'No need,' insisted Ducamp. 'I have the key. We keep an eye on the place for him, you see.'

'Oh, but...'

'It's furnished, just needs a good clean and airing. I can send our maid with the birch broom and linen cloths to see to the dust and grime. She can bring along a good stock of lye soap for the linens and floors. And we'll have bunches of lavender and rosemary spread about to sweeten the air.'

'Well, I don't know what to say,' Jacob said, clearly overwhelmed by the show of kindness.

'Then let us speak no more of it,' Ducamp said genially. 'I am simply delighted we meet again. To tell the truth, monsieur, if it weren't for you, I swear I would be facing damnation. I owe you my life. But I'll explain that later.' Didier opened the garden gate, and gesturing for Jacob to step through it, he said, 'Come, Monsieur Delpech, I want you to meet my family. You look as though you could do with some refreshment.'

That afternoon, Jacob presented the house to Jeanne. Inside, it was dusty, cold, and damp. Mould had developed in room corners, spread across doors, and grown on exposed surfaces. Yellowing linen sheets, once covering furniture, had been tugged off and now lay gnawed by vermin.

But while Jeanne held her kerchief over her nose in disgust, Jacob, lost in his imagination, saw the Darlington house as he had remembered it. 'This was my room where I stayed through that winter,' he said enthusiastically, as he opened the shutter of the upstairs attic room. 'Longview's gone, pity... but thankfully, they've left the rope bed.'

Nevertheless, Jeanne, forcing herself to see beyond the grime and the ravages of time, said, 'Then this is where we'll start, so Paul can have a room to convalesce.'

The next day, all the shutters of the Darlington house were pushed out, like a ship at full sail, catching the autumn breeze.

For the Ducamps, who came to greet their new neighbours before May took her youngest girl to dame school, it was a heartening sight to see the old house come alive again with family life. Their eldest daughter, Lily-Anne, came along too, and their youngest, Francine, quickly found two new playmates: Pierre, a boy of her own age, nine, and his elder sister, Isabelle.

The joy of finding an abode was overshadowed by Paul's persistent illness, and by Jeanne's polite but distant verbal exchanges with the Ducamps, who had insisted on helping with preparations. Didier volunteered to assist Jacob with mending shutters and fixing sticking doors, a welcome offer given that Paul was laid up with a temperature. However, Jeanne did not share Jacob's enthusiasm for the place as a home, nor could she envision herself living there permanently. Neither could she bring herself to warm to Monsieur Ducamp, the very lieutenant who had ushered his dragoons into their house in Montauban in that terrible August of 1685. Jacob had taken pains to prepare

415

her for the encounter, but the shock of seeing Ducamp again made her silently livid, despite his visible attempts to be pleasant to her.

How could she chase away those horrid memories of soldiers traipsing through her house, even though Jacob reminded her that Ducamp had been the more sympathetic of the two dragoon lieutenants? It was the bullish second lieutenant who had thrown her out of her home, despite her being on the verge of giving birth to Isabelle. No, she would never be wholly happy in this house. Besides, she was a country girl at heart. Oh, how she missed the pastures and tilled fields of the Chateau of Verlhac, memories that seemed to grow more vivid with each passing day. Moreover, with Jacob having spoken so much about the plot of farmland in New Rochelle, she had never imagined herself surrounded by a sprawling city, in a house that would soon be engulfed by it. And wasn't it supposed to be torn down after the winter, anyway?

Later that morning, Jeanne was in the larder, pouring the pickled foods that had been left for many a year in crocks and pots into a bucket she had placed on the table. They consisted of an assortment of fruit, vegetables, tongue, and fish, pickled in wine vinegar blended with spices and herbs, all unmistakably French. She recalled how her neighbours in Ireland would question her on the quality of her winter foods and the colour of her vinegar, which was much lighter than that of the locals. To Jeanne, it was a sign that this house had been well maintained and cared for through the years, indicating that the owners had means and high standards. Through these little details, she realised that goodness and love had resided here.

May had been helping clean the kitchen, and moments after she had left, Didier now entered to repair one of the shutters. In truth, having sensed Madame Delpech's discomfort, he had been eyeing the opportunity to speak to her alone.

As he passed by the larder, he stopped in his tracks. 'Oh, I can carry that out to the compost for you, Madame Delpech,' he offered.

'No need, Monsieur Ducamp,' said Jeanne, as she emptied another ceramic crock of cabbage into the wooden bucket. 'Thank you, anyway,' she added, without looking up.

After a shallow exchange about the clement weather, Didier lingered. Then, true to his character, he dived in: 'Madame, I've been wanting to tell you how regretful I am about what happened to you and your family in France.' As Jeanne picked up another crock and poured its contents of cornichons into the wooden bucket, Didier pressed on. 'I tried my best to ease your suffering... I eventually deserted the French army because of it. But I know that nothing can replace the life you lost.'

Jeanne glanced up, and with calm eloquence, she said, 'I appreciate your concern, Monsieur Ducamp, but we have come to learn to live through hard times, and indeed, God has often tested us. Yet I find solace in knowing that He has never forsaken us, always carrying us through man's wrongful deeds one way or another.' Having vented her rancour and reaffirmed her steadfast faith, she poured another crock of spoiled pickles into the bucket that was becoming full.

'Amen, madame,' said Ducamp earnestly. 'I want you to know I truly admire you and your husband for standing firm in your convictions and beliefs. I see things more clearly now, whereas before, I thought the only solution for you was to abjure. It is fitting you have come to these clement shores; we need folk of your moral fibre to help shape this place into a land of freedom of worship and liberty to speak freely. Thanks to those ready to defend their convictions like you do, I have hope that we can build this spirit of freedom into the foundations of this place—a place that folk of all walks of life can call home.'

417

The bucket was full. She couldn't pour in any more putrefied pickles or risk it being spilt as it was carried through the house to the compost heap. This time, Jeanne looked at Ducamp levelly in the eye. 'That is well, monsieur. However, from what I have seen, it appears that this newfound spirit of freedom doesn't show itself to everyone. What about the black slaves? Shouldn't they benefit from it?'

'Some say that God made them subordinates to those who know better.'

'Come now, Monsieur Ducamp, that's preposterous, and you know it.'

'I do, Madame, which is why there are no slaves in my household.' Ducamp almost gave a sigh of relief, as he had been considering getting one or two, despite May being against it. Jeanne's very clear reasoning lightened his lantern.

'And the native peoples? Have they found God with us, or have we brought them the devil?'

'The choice is theirs, Madame. We have taken and settled on their lands. It would be a further wrong to impose upon their beliefs, wouldn't it?'

'True, but, as my father used to say, why must one man's joy be the cause of another man's sorrow?'

'I am just a simple man trying to do what's right, trying to amend the wrongs of a lifetime. I cannot mend the whole world.'

She read sincerity in Ducamp's expression as she recalled Jacob's stories of how he had suffered, including the loss of his first wife and child. Jeanne now saw before her a man earnestly seeking to make amends. Who was she to stand in the way of his redemption? In a softer tone of voice, she said, 'I daresay, Monsieur Ducamp, neither of us has time left to mend the entire world. That task will fall upon our children. But in the meantime, let us endeavour to make it a better place, shall we?'

418

'To that, I wholeheartedly agree, Madame Delpech,' said Ducamp, with a crackle of emotion in his voice. 'Now, please allow me to take that bucket and bring in some water. My wife has gone to fetch the girls, and then she will be back with a hamper.'

'Thank you, Monsieur Ducamp,' said Jeanne, conceding. 'Yes, she said so. It is very thoughtful of her.'

Work paused for a meal of cold cuts, bread, cheese, and watered-down wine, laid out on the table over which May had thrown a tablecloth.

It was a solemn moment when Jacob began grace, choosing words that resonated with the themes of new friendships and beginnings. Before concluding, Ducamp added, 'And praise to the Lord for granting forgiveness on earth as in heaven.' Jeanne recognized that holding onto grudges would only impoverish their lives. If this was to be a fresh start, then it was essential to wipe the slate clean. Moved by Ducamp's words, she bowed her head more deeply. Then she added, 'Let us pray for Paul, that his fever may abate and that he sees a new way ahead.'

To break the ice and perhaps prevail upon Jacob's wife, Ducamp began with one of the nicer anecdotes from his past with her husband, about a Bible. He recounted how Jacob had given the Bible to him when they parted ways. Jacob was headed for Nassau to join a ship bound for New York, and from there, make his way to his wife in England. Meanwhile, Ducamp continued on his way in the infamous privateer ship he was serving on, Bible in hand. Sometime later, having met a fine young lady by the name of May Stuart, that Bible saved them from a terrible injustice. 'We were stopped by English soldiers in Charlestown,' said Ducamp, with a glance to May who discreetly egged him on with her eyes. He went on, 'Lily-Anne must have been just five at the time and could have been deprived of her mother and new stepfather. But when I pulled out my Huguenot Bible, printed in French instead of Latin, one look at it was enough to reassure the captain that if anything, we would be fleeing the French rather than conspiring against the English.'

'Bravo, sir,' said Jacob with enthusiasm.

Didier added, 'Then we set sail for New York, where we married in the Huguenot church and set up home.'

'Wonderful,' continued Jacob heartily. 'I am so glad that the Word, or should I say, the words of our Lord, came to your aid in such a mysterious way.' As for Jeanne, the story made her wonder what Monsieur Ducamp had been doing on the privateer ship, yet she conceded to smile nonetheless.

Jeanne took kindly to Ducamp's flaming-haired wife. May, the exuberant woman of means who had been born into poverty, normally would have stood in stark contrast to Jeanne, a high-minded noble lady who had fallen on hard times in later life. Yet both women found they had one thing in common: they had both clawed their way out of adversity.

Having sensed Jeanne's initial discomfort toward Didier, May patiently waited for an opportunity to gain Jeanne's trust. When dealing with prey, folk, and feelings, she had learnt that there was always a favourable moment for those who bided their time. Armed with patience, charm, exuberance, and an acute ability to read others, May had learnt to understand the most subtle of signals, and her gregarious nature had helped her to understand body language. She was, after all, in her previous life, a past master in the art of extracting intelligence, a skill that now served her well in navigating new relationships.

Throughout the morning, she had made herself agreeable to Jeanne and willingly let her lead. Not because of the age difference of a decade between them or any notion of hierarchy, but rather because Madame Delpech radiated a calming presence. May observed her poised demeanour, refined manners, and the grace of her upbringing with a sense of serenity and admiration. Madame Delpech embodied the quintessence of a distinguished French lady: a woman of fine tradition and heritage, level-headed and sure of herself. In short, May had at last met the fine lady she herself had once aspired to become. But now older and more mature, May—a former spy and courtesan—found contentment in being Mrs Ducamp, in a place where money trumped class. She now proudly asserted herself as being still a diamond in the rough.

Jeanne was grateful for Mrs Ducamp's help in preparing the house; May had also provided extra linen and their midday meal. It made Jeanne smile when Mrs Ducamp amusingly remarked she was 'struck over like a nine-pin' to see how much more the noble lady, born with a particle in her name, knew about cleaning linen than she did.

During those first moments of breaking bread together, the conversation seemed to mysteriously steer away from the present and previous owners of the house—a topic that Jeanne knew Jacob was burning to broach. After the happy conclusion of Monsieur Ducamp's story that had helped to relax the atmosphere, she now raised a question. 'Why has this house been abandoned for so long?' Surprisingly, the Ducamps had little to offer beyond the fact that it was slated for demolition.

'In that case,' Jacob began eagerly, 'I shall stop and make enquiries about these plans for demolition on my way to the storage sheds to fetch our blankets. For we might consider purchasing it ourselves, given its ideal location for a trader. I would go as far as to say that it is better placed than in Darlington's day, as it is no longer outside the city wall.' Marking a pause, Jacob noted the lack of reaction at the mention of Darlington. He went on, 'So, I will visit the State House this afternoon.'

'You might have to wait, I'm afraid, Monsieur Delpech,' May interposed. 'The State House is transferring to the new Town Hall, and they say it could take up to a week to transfer and classify the records. Your efforts might be in vain.'

'I was there only yesterday.'

'Yes, I heard that you might find some of the older records still there, but the recent ones will most certainly be moved to the new Town Hall in Wall Street.'

'Ah, I see...'

'In the meantime,' said Didier, 'I'll send word out to the present owner with your query.'

'Thank you, yes, I would be most obliged, Monsieur Ducamp. And if there is anything to pay for the use of this house, as I said yesterday, we can naturally discuss a rental agreement.' Didier gestured with his hand that there was no need.

Jeanne, sensing a rush in Jacob's plans, suggested calmly, 'Shouldn't we wait, Jacob, until we see what other opportunities there might be?'

'I'm merely keeping our options open, my dear. Things tend to move more quickly here in New York, you see. We don't want to miss out.'

'That is true, but, if I may say...' said May, picking up on Jeanne's reserve, 'there are as many opportunities as there are transactions, assuming you have the means. We came here at a time when the landscape outside the wall was still very wild. You could see the edge of the forest on the hill and hear the call of the wolves at night. Now it's gone—although it's by far safer nowadays. I recall once when the former owner built a trench around this house in case of French invasion, would you believe! Anyway, the only reason we stay here now is for Lily-Anne and Francine. They attend the school of Madame de Brey. I shall introduce you to her at church on Sunday, Madame Delpech.

She is a Huguenot too. But frankly, as you have no ties, you will find other possibilities if you look.'

'Quite,' concurred Jeanne, grateful for the support. 'There will be other opportunities, Jacob. You might be attached to this house because you stayed here. But there is possibly a valid reason for its demolition. It is infested with vermin, for one.'

'Oh, we can always get a cat and a terrier,' chuckled Jacob half-jokingly.

Persisting gently, Jeanne added, 'But the very foundations of the house could be at risk, Jacob. It's been vacant for eight years!'

'Ah, that is a good point,' Jacob acknowledged, suddenly remembering his promise about not making decisions without a proper family discussion. The fact was, he had only raised the possibility of a purchase yesterday. She hadn't warmed to the idea any more than she had to the idea of having Lieutenant Ducamp as a neighbour. Jacob then questioned tactfully, 'Even so, we could always build a new house on the plot, couldn't we?'

'I suggest we keep an open mind,' said Jeanne.

'Agreed,' said Jacob. Turning to Didier, he said, 'It is nonetheless worth asking the current proprietor about his position.' Didier bowed his head, trying to appear helpful and modest before Madame Delpech.

But Jeanne's thoughts had already shifted to their son. The room upstairs would soon be ready, but how would they fetch him from the inn? He would refuse to travel by handcart, and he wouldn't be able to mount a horse in his condition. She said, 'Anyway, Jacob, how are we going to bring Paul from the inn?'

Before Jacob could respond, May chimed in. 'Oh, I thought you had three children, with one still in France.'

'No, Mrs Ducamp, we have three children here, not including Elizabeth, our eldest, who is the one who remained in France. Our eldest son, Paul, is still at the inn, recovering from a broken leg and a fever.'

'How old is he?' May enquired.

'Twenty-one,' replied Jeanne.

Jacob harrumphed. 'I gave him another tincture this morning, but it seems futile. I am even contemplating leeching.' Jacob went on to explain that Paul had lost all appetite. 'Given that his leg seems to be setting as well as can be, I presume there must be something else that is untreatable with medicinal herbs alone.' Jacob was referring to the humours. Although he did not say so, he believed Paul had fallen to a case of black bile, the disease that deprived a man of all hope, all strength to fight, and all desire. It could also deprive a man of the will to live.

'Let me see him,' offered May. 'I have dealt with fevers before. I am immune to smallpox, you see, so I have often been called in when there have been outbreaks.'

'Oh no, it's not smallpox, Mrs Ducamp,' asserted Jacob. 'I believe it runs deeper; it is more of a disheartenment.'

'A case of melancholy. I have treated many such cases in my day, Mr Delpech,' said May confidently. 'I suspect there is some impediment in his mind.' Jacob glanced fleetingly to Jeanne, who kept Paul's whim about going to sea to herself. May continued, 'But first, we must bring down this fever. And leeching doesn't help, any more than bloodletting. The natives here don't do it at all.'

'I must confess, that has been my observation too,' acknowledged Jacob, nodding his head pensively.

Young Lily-Anne was sitting at the end of the table, tending to the three children. She had already learnt about Paul's nasty fall from Pierre while they were playing a game of nine pins in the freshly scythed garden. Lily-Anne wondered what Paul looked like, and imagined from his parents and siblings that he would be blue-eyed and quite tall, with dark hair and an olive complexion. She was becoming weary of being consigned to the care of the younger ones. So, when she overheard the adults discussing Paul's fever, she boldly interjected, 'There's an indigenous remedy for fevers. I know a healer who used it to treat Louise Granger.'

'You mean Ama, the Lenape healer, Lily dear?'

'Yes, she showed me how to make the draught with black cohosh.'

'Black cohosh?' repeated Jacob sceptically.

May clarified, 'It's a root foraged in autumn.' Then she proposed that Jacob use her carriage to fetch his blankets and for Paul's retrieval, while she walked Francine back to school. Lily-Anne eagerly volunteered to source some black cohosh.

'I can get some fresh from Ama if she's in town. If not, I'll try at the apothecary.'

'Let me give you some money,' said Jacob.

'She only accepts barter. But she will accept some needles if you have any. And I can use them at the apothecary too if I can't find her.'

'I have plenty of those,' said Jeanne promptly. 'I will fetch some this instant.'

Later that afternoon, an hour before sunset, Jeanne stood beside Paul's bed, having opened the curtain and the canvas-covered window to let out the musty air that May claimed was too warm. Earlier, Jacob had borrowed May's carriage to fetch the lad from the inn.

'Paul,' she said, gently shaking him from his slumber. 'Here are our neighbours come to see you, Mrs Ducamp and her daughter.' Paul cracked open an eye, then became more alert upon seeing the two strangers at the foot of his bed. The first thing his eyes lighted upon was a blaze of red, silky hair—two shocks of it in abundance. Of equal height, mother and daugh-

425

ter were similar in every way except for their age difference. Paul pushed on his elbows as Jeanne propped up his bolster pillow. 'Oh, pleased to meet you,' he said. 'I apologise you find me in such an unflattering condition.'

'We shall bring you something to ease your fever,' said May, affably but with no nonsense. She had long since learned that her presence alone—her demeanour and physical appearance—sufficed to make her both accepted and sought after, breaking down barriers with ease, even now as she aged.

Echoing her mother's manner, Lily-Anne said: 'It is to be taken three times a day, with some soup, bread, and cheese.'

'Thank you,' said Paul, feeling obliged, although he was eager for the awkward encounter to end.

'There is much to do downstairs. We need you on your feet, young man,' May cheered, her request delivered with a smile yet carrying a sense of finality.

Lily-Anne was taken aback. Instead of the tall, handsome young man that her imagination had conjured, she found a frail figure glistening with sweat, his complexion sallow. His hair was lank, his nose was sharp and more pronounced against his drawn features, and purple bags underlined his eyes, which seemed too large for his gaunt face.

Jeanne said, 'We shall begin by frequently airing the room.' Paul looked at his mother, recalling how he had insisted on keeping the canvas-covered window firmly shut and the fire lit to fend off the autumn chill. Now he pursed his lips.

May observed his muted reluctance and added, 'The chill you feel comes from within, not from the outside air. A healthy young man wouldn't find it cold. It's your illness that is deceiving you, making you feel cold so it can thrive cosily inside you.'

'My thoughts exactly,' said Jeanne, who now realised she should have stuck to her position. With her mind crowded with preparations around the house, she was grateful for Mrs Ducamp's discerning eye, which was quick to identify what was amiss.

Lily-Anne nodded firmly in agreement with the ladies' reasoning, her large blue eyes conveying the need for the patient to get a grip on himself. Paul let the moment pass; he could always close the window once they were gone. 'It is important to get a hold of the fever, unless you would rather succumb to it,' said Lily-Anne, surprising herself by the force of her own words. She could not bear the thought of this newcomer languishing out of sheer obstinacy, and potentially needlessly dying. It would be foolish, and she had little patience for foolish people.

After their departure, Paul sank wearily beneath the covers.

An hour later, there was a flurry of activity in the main room as May and Jeanne found themselves chasing a mouse that had scurried under a chest of drawers.

Having displaced the piece of furniture, they discovered yet another entryway for the unwelcome guests. They promptly stuffed the mouse hole up with rags as a temporary measure, resolving to have Didier seal it with plaster the following morning. Meanwhile, Lily-Anne had been busy brewing a decoction from the dried black cohosh roots she obtained from the apothecary. Amid the commotion, she now slipped away with Sarah, her mother's maid, to the room upstairs where the feverish young man lay.

'My apologies for being rather blunt earlier, or sharp, depending on how you took it,' said Lily-Anne after she entered the bedroom.

'Sharp-ish,' said Paul in a crackly voice as he feebly heaved himself up upon his elbows.

'Good. Because dumb people would say blunt,' she said encouragingly, effectively putting him on a pedestal. She had learnt from her mother how to be clever and flattering without seeming so. It was a well-honed skill her mother used to 'unwrinkle', as her mother would put it, even the grouchiest of characters; she even managed to smooth out old Mrs Bayard. Lily-Anne continued, 'It was meant to make you aware of your condition and spur you on to fight it.' Paul remained quiet as he watched Lily-Anne take the earthen beaker of the warm concoction from the tray the maid was holding. 'You will need to take this brew several times a day, assuming, of course, you are willing,' said Lily-Anne, instinctively knowing that her patient needed to feel he was in control. She moved a step closer with the beaker despite the nauseating smell wafting from his person. Obligingly, he accepted it, while the maid went to close the shutters. 'Goodness,' Lily-Anne said, waving her hand in front of her nose, 'you'll be needing a restorative bath filled with lavender all to yourself.' Her playful remark surprised herself when it popped out of her mouth, but at least it put some colour back into his cheeks.

'No doubt. Once I am repaired,' he replied, slightly mortified.

'You must be on the mend already,' she said satisfied, 'otherwise you wouldn't have left the window open, and you would have died in your own bad air, wouldn't you?'

'Would I?' said Paul, unamused. 'Then I would not be bothered about windows, draughts, and restorative baths, would I?' he snapped.

She fired back teasingly, 'No, because you would be six feet under in a box to keep in the smell!' Then, deciding to let him stew, she said, 'I will be back in a while,' as she left the room.

Sipping his draught, Paul pondered the outrageous and pretty young girl. Her voice was overly confident for her age; he was not used to such offhand remarks. Was he expected to listen to such impertinence after sharing the rigging with veteran sailors of the world? 'Thank you for the draught,' he said to the maid as she too departed after stoking the fire and taking his empty beaker. 'Please tell Miss Lily-Anne she needn't return.'

But return, she did, with the maid. And with a clean nightgown that smelt of lavender.

The following morning, sitting up in bed in the fresh nightgown, he muttered to her, 'I had a better night. I owe you my thanks.' He had felt contrite in the face of the unwavering care the girl showed. No one forced her to care, but she clearly did. He saw it in her determined brow when she asked how he was feeling while Sarah stood three paces behind her. The maid's presence ensured that May's spirited daughter was properly accompanied in what were the girl's first steps into a young man's quarters.

'That's a good start,' she returned, passing him the decoction. 'It means you are conscious of gratitude.' Sensing he was beginning to open up, she added, 'And I hope you have said your prayers. They will help. They always do. Have you?'

'No,' he admitted, after a sip of the snakeroot brew.

'Then you should. It teaches humility, for one...'

'I prayed for my leg to heal,' he said sullenly. 'But did it?'

'Oh, but I believe it has,' she countered.

'I will be left with a permanent limp.'

'It did get better, though, didn't it?' she said brightly. 'Now I suggest you pray for a change of attitude. Be thankful you didn't land on your head for a start! What if it had robbed you of your senses? It sometimes happens when a man gets a whack on the head, you know—because it always seems to happen to men, rarely women. Then they forget where they are, and sometimes it lasts, as if part of them had died.'

Feeling his lips tremble into a smile, he let slip an indulgent chuckle.

'Am I wrong?' she probed gently, coaxing him further. 'Shouldn't you be thankful your father managed to save your leg?'

Caught by her engaging manner, and unable to contain his despair any longer, he muttered, 'I am. But it's not much use for climbing.'

'What do you want to go climbing for?'

'Rigging, for one. Without being able to climb rigging, my hopes of making my fortune through trade at sea are dashed.'

Softly, she said, 'Is that what troubles you?'

'I had a dream to sail the high seas,' he confessed, like an offering.

'There are plenty of winding roads you can meander down around here,' she said encouragingly, 'and the land is as vast as an ocean.'

'You can't possibly understand without feeling the call of the sea,' he said dismissively.

'Perhaps not, but if I were to lose the full use of a leg, I would develop another aspect of my person.' Paul noticed the determined furrow between her eyebrows as she said this.

He asked teasingly, 'And what if you were to lose your hair and your beauty?'

'I'd wear a hat!' she retorted, sidestepping his mention of beauty, though nonetheless pleased by it. 'Besides, my hair will go grey when I get old. And then I will seek the wisdom of elders like Ama. She's the wise Lenape woman who told me how to brew that decoction.'

'You seem wise beyond your years, already. How old are you?'

'I'm nearing sixteen.'

'Hah, I thought as much,' chaffed Paul, hiding his disappointment with banter. 'You seem to know so much, but what real experiences do you have?'

'Plenty, and I've read plenty in books about the travels of Marco Polo, the odyssey of Ulysses, the journey of Christian in *Pilgrim's Progress*, and the exploits of Captain Morgan.'

'Do you think those books can lead to fortune?' he said solemnly.

'No, but the knowledge they contain can. Knowledge is power, and power, rightly wielded, can make you a fortune. Otherwise, you are just a pirate, a thief, a mindless thug. That's what my father says, and he was once a privateer himself!'

'That may be,' Paul conceded reluctantly.

'Here lies opportunity for those who seize it. This is a whole New World in the making, and one you can help shape if you have the heart to do so, and the knowledge.'

'What exactly do you mean?'

'By reading and studying, you can acquire knowledge that others lack, giving you the upper hand. Considering your handicap, it might be your best path to acquire the fortune you seek—unless, of course, you prefer the life of a modest farmer, which is fine too, but you might not become rich.'

'Crops make money,' he argued defiantly, then glugged down the rest of his decoction.

'True, but selling them is where the money lies,' Lily-Anne retorted.

'Hah, must you always have the last word?'

'Not if it's already been said.'

Paul, half smiling, conceded. 'Then I shall ponder over your counsel, doctor.'

'Good. I hope to see you in better form.' Before he could reply, Lily-Anne swiped the beaker from his hand, turned, and left the room with Sarah in tow.

In the short period of Paul's convalescence, their exchanges deepened. Paul, nonetheless, remained indulgent and slightly aloof, and sometimes overbearing to this intelligent and spirited girl who, pretty though she was, was not yet a grown woman in his eyes. However, expressing his inner deceptions opened him up to more meaningful dialogue. Perhaps she was right. Perhaps he would need to study. He could learn the rules of commerce and the laws of the land.

On the third day, he rose with a renewed sense of purpose for his future. Dressed in clean clothes, he hobbled downstairs to find the house looking spruced up with flowers before the window. Everyone was delighted to see a resemblance of their son and brother.

On that same third day, the new Town Hall was officially inaugurated. In the afternoon, despite Ducamp's warnings of impending demolition and Jeanne's reservations about staying at the house beyond the winter, Jacob went to enquire about the Darlington house. He trusted in Jeanne's knack of making the best of a situation. She was naturally averse to change, but once committed, she always adapted admirably. He fondly remembered how, with a few select pieces of furniture and touches reminiscent of southern France, she had made his rooms in London feel like their townhouse in Montauban.

He found the same civil servant as before, clad in the same attire, bearing the same expression and stoop. It struck Jacob how some people remained unaltered by time or circumstance. This clerk had reluctantly come to this statelier building, and yet he had instantly made it his own domain.

'Mr Fontney has agreed, in principle, to the demolition of the said property to make way for new development,' the clerk revealed, adding that the house was no longer for sale. Jacob pressed for a chance to speak with the owner, but the clerk was unable to provide an address for Mr Fontney.

The following day, Paul was sitting on the floor, his left leg bound with new ligatures and supported by new splints, filling in more vermin holes in the kitchen, when there came an unexpected knock at the front door.

He felt a rush to the head and asked Isabelle to answer it. 'Don't you think it's Lily-Anne coming to see you?' she said teasingly. It turned out to be Lily-Anne's stepfather, who stood at the door accompanied by a stranger, a tall gentleman, well attired in riding gear, with a mysterious smile that she instantly distrusted. Why would anyone smile for nothing? Then Mr Ducamp introduced him as the owner, causing Isabelle to cover her mouth in shock and dash upstairs to tell her father, who was tightening rope beds with her mother.

'Father, come quick, it's Mr Fontney, the owner!'

'Good heavens!' exclaimed Jacob, getting up from his knees. 'Perhaps he would like to sell after all.'

Jeanne glanced back at him with a look of alarm. 'Or perhaps he is wondering what we are doing occupying his house without his permission and without paying any rent!'

'Mr Ducamp assured me all was in order.'

'But are you sure we can trust Mr Ducamp, Jacob?' Jeanne asked in a hushed tone.

'Come, my dear,' said Jacob gently. 'I once trusted him with my life, and I would do it again.'

Nevertheless, with concern marking his brow, Jacob made his way down the staircase, with Jeanne following behind. But his face quickly smoothed over when he saw the tall figure of the gentleman standing near the window, in discussion with Paul and Didier Ducamp.

'Papa, this is Mr Fontney,' said Paul, turning to his father. Like his sister, Paul had assumed the gentleman's identity based on Monsieur Ducamp's introduction of him as 'the owner'.

'No, it isn't,' said Jacob, as he advanced into the room, smiling broadly. 'Why, it is Daniel Darlington! My dear fellow!'

'Jacob Delpech,' returned Darlington, as the two men warmly shook hands. 'You cannot begin to imagine how pleased one little lady is going to be when she hears confirmation of your arrival here in New York with your dear wife and children.'

Jacob introduced Jeanne and their children to Daniel. Jeanne glanced sharply at Ducamp as if to ask why he had not informed them earlier. But Jacob, bubbling with questions, pressed on, 'So, where, or rather, who is Mr Fontney?'

'One and the same,' intervened Ducamp as they all took a seat around the dining table. He turned to Jeanne to address her reproving glance earlier. 'I couldn't let on, I'm afraid, Mrs Delpech. You see, I was sworn to secrecy, and so shall you be.'

Darlington explained, 'I took a new name after the troubles that could have cost me my life and fortune.'

'I thought I recognised the name somehow,' said Jacob, placing beer beakers on the table.

'Marianne's idea. She took her grandmother's name and made it sound more English. But as Jacob Leisler's good name has been officially restored now, I could revert back, I suppose. But allow me to linger on that episode another time perhaps. I see the house has been put to good use.' Sensing Jeanne's concern, Darlington added, 'I am so glad it will have served one last purpose before the papers for its demolition are signed. There are plans to build a new French church here.'

'Oh, really,' said Jacob with a hint of disappointment. 'So, it is final then.'

'I am afraid so, but do not despair, my dear friend. I have here something that belongs to you.' Daniel reached into his frock coat pocket and pulled out some neatly folded papers. 'These are the deeds of your plot in New Rochelle. I simply need to sign them over to you in exchange for the initial asking price.' Jacob could hardly believe his ears, whereas Jeanne looked momentarily lost, awaiting confirmation of what she thought Darlington had just said. As Jacob listened, open-mouthed, fumbling for words that would not come, Daniel continued, 'I purchased the plots, yours and mine, for a rather good price in the name of Fontney, so that you would not miss out should you decide to return. The burghers agreed, but I'm afraid I was unable to inform you directly in writing as, in the aftermath of the troubles, I suspected the post of being under surveillance. I must confess, I was rather preoccupied with keeping a low profile at the time. However, I did write to you eventually, but by then to no avail. Your church wrote back, stating they had lost your address and knew not where you had settled.'

'We went to Ireland,' said Jacob, regaining his composure.

Daniel gave a meditative nod and then continued. 'I did go to London with Leisler's son to support him in the defence of his late father. But I promised Marianne I would not reveal my true name until everything was signed and settled—she had been traumatised by Jacob Leisler's downfall. Once there, I enquired at the French church, but they explained there had been a fire incident, which is why they had lost your address, and that was that. So, when Didier sent me word of your arrival, I sent a man immediately to instruct Didier to hand over the key to this house, which, I am thankful to say, he had already done anyway. I believe you know each other from previous experience.'

Leaning on his walking stick, Paul, gobsmacked, but less so than Jacob, said, 'Does that mean then, Mr Darlington, that we have the plot my father has been making us dream about all these years, after all?'

'It does indeed, young man.'

'I think we are in need of some refreshment,' said Jacob, who finished pouring the contents of the jug of beer into the beakers. He then sat down at the dining table, where he had sat on many occasions with the New Rochelle delegation and Jacob Leisler, and where he had helped to structure an irrigation system and divide the land accordingly. Jeanne pressed his arm as he discreetly brushed away some moisture welling in his eye.

'You will find it has changed, hasn't it, Didier?' said Daniel, turning away to Ducamp.

With a measured nod, Ducamp said, 'It certainly has that.'

'I am finding this place does not seem to stop changing,' said Jacob.

'Indeed, my good friend, that is why this house will make way for new development, to lay the proper foundations for a new French church.'

'I am sorry to hear that, truly. But you bring such better news.'

'I do heartily concur with my husband, Mr Darlington,' said Jeanne. 'Life in the countryside has always been more to my liking.' Glancing more softly toward Ducamp, she added, 'Even though we have been made to feel most welcome here, thanks to our charming neighbours.'

'Then allow me to suggest that we all make the journey to New Rochelle before the week is over. Your possessions will be safe here in the meantime. And the village boasts a fine inn, it being on the post road.'

'Yes,' said Jacob, 'I well remember.'

'But I insist you lodge at my house,' added Daniel.

After much jubilation, it was decided to take a cart to New Rochelle on the following Saturday, the day after next, which would leave Daniel time to fulfil his business obligations. Daniel insisted on staying at an inn in town, but Jeanne and Jacob insisted they all dine together the following evening with the Ducamps to celebrate their merry reunion.

The following evening, gathered around a lavishly set table dressed with beef, pork, carp, oysters, and fine wine, the conversation turned to what Daniel preferred to term the 'Leisler Stand'—in contrast to those who deemed it a rebellion. 'Then what happened?' Paul asked eagerly, wanting to know the fate of the man in question. By then, the children had gone to bed, and after some deliberation, Daniel agreed to recount the tragic end of Jacob Leisler.

CHAPTER 28

Fall, 1699

NEW YORK

Isabelle quietly got up, pulled up her woollen stockings, and slipped on her nightgown over her shift, leaving little Pierre sound asleep in their parents' bed.

She tiptoed to the top of the stairs, careful not to make the floorboards creak. Perched on the third step from the top, she then peeked into the downstairs room toward the front window, whose shutters had been pulled shut. In the warm glow of the dining table lamps, Mr Darlington appeared gravely serious as he sat opposite her parents, who had their backs to her. To his left, May Ducamp sat next to her husband. Lily-Anne was sitting at one end of the table, between Darlington and her father, while Paul attentively listened to Mr Darlington's every word from the opposite end. The Ducamp's youngest was curled up with a blanket placed over her in an armchair by the glowing hearth. Isabelle wriggled to find a comfortable position, then trained her ear to the sombre voice of Daniel Darlington.

He was saying, 'While holding New York for William and Mary, never did Leisler think he would one day risk a condemnation of treason at the hands of their appointees. But when he handed over the fort, he was immediately tied up and put into irons, as was his son-in-law, Jacob Milborne. They were detained in the fort prison, as were other members of Leisler's council and close circle. Then our worthy friend was indicted for treason and murder.'

'I can still hardly believe it,' said Jacob, seated directly opposite, as he served Daniel some more wine.

'Neither could he,' said Darlington. 'But it must have dawned on him quickly that there would be little chance of a fair trial, for he refused to enter a plea and instead petitioned to be tried in England, where he hoped he could plead his innocence to an impartial jury directly under the king. By pleading in New York, he would have effectively empowered the jury to make them judges of fact. Moreover, he rightly asked for his power as governor to be determined first.

'But alas, that was not to be. Instead, the ensuing mockery of a trial was cruel and arbitrary, with the judge from the anti-Leislerian faction and the jury mostly composed of its prominent members, including none other than Major Ingoldsby.'

'The same who had laid siege to the fort before the governor's arrival?'

'The very same,' said Daniel, turning toward Paul further down the table. Darlington pressed on, 'Ingoldsby, Bayard, Nicholls, van Cortlandt, and other members of the elite were all in consort to bring Leisler down and to influence the new governor, who, I should add, was residing with the Bayards in their townhouse, no less.'

'It is hardly conceivable,' said Jacob. 'Mercifully, you were able to narrowly evade capture yourself.'

Daniel gestured to May and Didier sitting to his left. 'Thanks to my good friends here, I was indeed able to flee to New Rochelle with my family. But as soon as things calmed down, I returned under my assumed name, wearing a gentleman's periwig and a wide-brimmed hat, complete with a full beard and moustache, and a promise to Marianne to keep a low profile. I was eager to find out about the proceedings, and how I could help without breaking my promise to my dear wife.'

'But what exactly was Leisler accused of?' said Paul, leaning forward on the table, his wooden bowl pushed aside.

'Illegal usurpation of authority, thereby constituting high treason. He was even accused of being the root cause of the massacre at Schenectady by the French and their Indian allies, which, of course, was absurd. For if our Indian allies had watched the trial as they had agreed to, there would have been ample warning to counter the surprise attack. But that's another story.'

Jacob asked, 'Was there no protest from the people of New York who petitioned him to lead them in the first place?'

'There was indeed a great deal of division and uproar. Even Domine Daillé, the Huguenot priest of the fort temple, who chastised Leisler many a time throughout his governance, was adamantly against what was clearly becoming a travesty of justice. Daillé collected near two thousand signatures for his petition to remove Leisler and Milborne to England to be judged more fairly by Their Majesties. But as soon as the authorities got wind, he was arrested.'

'What became of that petition?' asked Paul.

'Well, fearing for the lives of her family and the subscribers, when the good priest was arrested, his wife burnt it. She is not to be blamed, for if the other priests had stepped in to offer their support, it might have been a very different story. But they did not.'

'And the protesters?'

'To quell any further dissent, a bill, crafted at the behest of Bayard, quashed any unrest from potential protesters, who would henceforth be deemed as rebels. And let us not forget that Ingoldsby had brought an army with him! Never was there such fear, suspicion, and political division as during Leisler's trial.'

'That's true,' said Ducamp as Darlington swirled his wine in his glass meditatively. 'The anti-Leislers became all the more confident in their accusations, now that they understood which way the council's weathercock was turning.'

'Anyway, the long and short of it was that the accused were found guilty of treason, punishable by death. Leisler's counsellors were detained in confinement until their charges were reversed by order of Queen Mary the following year. But as for Leisler and Milborne, five members of Sloughter's council that included Bayard, Nicholls, van Cortlandt, Philipse, and Minivielle, voted for their execution. Yet there was still a chance of saving them while word was expected from England and while Sloughter hesitated to sign the death sentence.

'However, Bayard and Nicholls soon throttled that last hope. I suspect they prevailed upon the governor, pretexting that if he were to let them live much longer, it would open the floodgates to all kinds of dissent among the populace. Which was utter balderdash.'

'Truly,' said Ducamp, 'they were bent on making an example of our governor.'

'Yes,' said Daniel, 'and despite the fact that Leisler had been holding the governorship for King William in whom he had blind faith, and to uphold our Protestant values of freedom of worship.'

'To say nothing of preparing our defences against the French from the north,' added May, 'who threatened to attack New York just as they had destroyed Schenectady.'

'Those were fearsome times when you think about it,' said Ducamp.

'Indeed, they were,' said Daniel with a fleeting thought for his dear Aunt Millie, whose husband, their son, his wife and children, perished in the tragedy. With a mournful chuckle, he added, 'There are still remnants of the trenches around this house that my wife made in the futile hope of halting any potential assailants.'

'But why did the governor not simply wait for advice from the king?' questioned Paul, who knew nothing of Daniel's loss.

Coming back to himself, Daniel said, 'He deemed that if they cut away what he and the council saw as the root of dissidence, peace and calm would be restored.'

'Some say the governor succumbed to their promise of wealth,' added Ducamp.

'True, I heard it said as well,' said Daniel. 'And it doesn't surprise me either, as he was not a wealthy man; quite the contrary.'

'I remember his wife certainly yielded,' said May, 'influenced as she was by Judith Bayard.'

'Whatever the reason, after Sloughter signed the execution order, it fell upon Domine Selyns to visit Leisler and Milborne in prison. Had he supported Domine Daillé's petition, he might have played a crucial role in saving their lives. Instead, on the fourteenth day of May, a Thursday, I recall, the priest informed them of the grim decision as they were about to eat their dinner together. He told them there was good news and bad news. He then gave them the good news that their comrades were to be spared, held in confinement until the pleasure of the king was known. Then, he delivered the bad news.'

'Which was?' prompted Paul as Daniel took a sip of wine to moisten his tongue.

'They were to die the following Saturday, to be hung, gutted, quartered, and beheaded.'

'That's barbaric! I can't imagine them having much of an appetite after hearing that,' said Paul solemnly.

'How awful!' added Jeanne. 'So unfair! Surely Leisler should have spoken up to defend himself?'

'Leisler and Milborne indeed sent notes, and their family and supporters beseeched Sloughter to defer the execution, at least until the king's pleasure was known, but to no avail. His mind was made up, based on the advice of Leisler's decriers. Without granting a single meeting with his predecessor, Sloughter condemned the two men to the gallows at the scratch of a signature.'

'They say Sloughter signed under duress, and was drunk,' said May.

'That wouldn't surprise me,' said Daniel. 'But if so, why did he not retract his authorisation when he became sober the following day? There really can be no excuse in my mind. He was as guilty as the rest of them. I wouldn't be surprised if his death a few months later was due to a deep sense of guilt.'

'God will have judged him,' said Jeanne.

'And just to rub in the salt,' Daniel continued, 'preparations were made for the gallows to be set up on Leisler's own confiscated grounds that once belonged to the contested Lockermans estate. Surely the cherry on the cake of revenge for the Bayards, who had been at the centre of a long-standing family feud over the estate, which the Leislers inherited through Leisler's wife while the Bayards claimed it should have gone to them.'

'Yet another reason for this man Bayard to fear his Maker on the day of judgement,' said Jacob.

'So, Leisler was executed the next day then?' asked Paul, quite taken aback but keen to know more.

'Yes, the following morning.'

'I recall it well,' said Ducamp. 'The place was swarming despite the bad weather and the early hour of the day.'

'It was May 16th,' continued Daniel gravely, 'in the year of our Lord 1691. The day was as grey and wet as the crowd was forlorn and dismayed. The condemned men, who once led New York, were jeered in the drizzle by hecklers planted along the way from the fort prison to the gallows that stood by the State House. I was standing at one corner of the grim platform, and I will never forget when Leisler's voice resonated, clear as a bell over the silenced crowd, whether they were supporters or not. He declared before God that what he had done was for King William and Queen Mary, for the defence of the Protestant religion, and for the good of the colony. He begged forgiveness for his enemies in the name of peace, and then committed his soul to God.'

'Incredible,' said Paul, 'right up to his last breath, he championed unity among the people.'

'God's blood!' chimed in May. 'I'd have gone out fighting tooth and nail, and fie on those who would have gotten in my way!'

'Milborne then followed,' Daniel pursued. 'I distinctly recall the sheriff asking him if he would bless the king and queen, to which Milborne replied, "It is for the king and queen I die, and for the Protestant religion!" Then they covered his eyes. "I am ready," he said, and then, as it had done for Leisler, the trap opened beneath him. They were hanged until close to death, then beheaded.'

'How awful,' said Jeanne, holding her napkin to her mouth.

'Unlawful and so unfair,' said Paul bitterly.

'A worthy governor indeed,' said Jacob.

'A brave and honest man who gave his life to save New York. He governed our city in the name of the people, when its so-called elites were still wondering whether they should stay loyal to the Catholic James II, or embrace our hard-earned freedom of worship and the Protestant values proclaimed by King

William. Once the turncoats had evaluated the situation, they conspired against the man who had stepped up and replaced them to save New York. Thus ended the life of Jacob Leisler, the first governor of New York to be elected by its people. Let us remember him.'

'Amen,' said Jacob. Then after a reflective silence, he asked, 'What is the situation nowadays, Daniel? Did his death quell passions and stem any further division?'

'Quite the contrary, I'd say. I for one more than ever advocate judicial reform and New York's self-governance, even though Leisler was against the latter. And I'm not alone, especially since Bellomont, the current governor, recently upheld Their Majesties' decision to restore Leisler's honour and return his estate to his family, following Jacob Leisler the younger's successful defence of his father in London. Parliament reversed the attainder against Leisler and Milborne in 1695, clearing their names. It was found that charges against him were void as the indictment against Leisler began on the 17th of March, whereas Sloughter did not arrive in New York until the 19th. This meant there had been no treason because Ingoldsby had been entrusted with no powers in government, and Leisler had offered no resistance to Colonel Sloughter thereafter. In fact, it was found that Ingoldsby should have obeyed Leisler, who was legally the commander-in-chief of the province. It was Ingoldsby who could have been condemned for high treason for laying siege to the fort, not Leisler for holding it.'

'So, Leisler was right all along,' said Paul with gritted satisfaction.

'He certainly was. Yet, despite the crown's late intervention, I still often wonder why a king from a distant land should dictate our fate here in New York. In response to this, Leisler once said: *For the time present, we need the hand of a faraway king to defend us from other faraway kings*. But I believe that time will come to an end. As our numbers grow, I hope we'll achieve the freedom to establish our own judiciary system, ensuring an opposition party to call to account the government in place, and to institute a guarantee of a fair trial for anyone condemned by that power, regardless of their political viewpoint, caste, or class.'

'Hear, hear,' said Paul, enthusiastically tapping the table with his fingers.

Darlington went on, 'And one day, I hope and pray we shall be victorious in forming our own state system for the people of these lands, who will have the right to choose their assembly—not for folk who have never set foot in it.'

'Well said, sir,' said Paul. As he spoke, the young man found himself captivated by the prospect of a new avenue for his studies, while at the same time, he felt eyes upon him from the opposite end of the table.

Isabelle, sitting in the shadows at the top of the stairs, caught sight of Paul exchanging glances with Lily-Anne, whose fiery beauty seemed to radiate even more in the soft glow of the tallow lamplight. For a fleeting moment, she held his gaze, her large blue eyes sparkling intensely. Isabelle conjectured that Lily-Anne too could see the transformation in Paul. He was no longer the bedridden patient of a few days past, but an engaging young man, full of spirit.

CHAPTER 29

Fall, 1699

NEW ROCHELLE

The next morning, Jacob carefully drove a flatbed cart, equipped with an added passenger bench, out of the barn. He brought the two strong horses to a halt before the house, where Jeanne, the children, May, Didier, and Daniel were waiting on the path, bathed in the hues of dawn.

The Ducamps, amid the twittering of sparrows in a nearby tree, were wishing Jeanne a safe journey. 'Rather you than me,' said May lightheartedly, stamping her feet against the early morning chill. 'I could never stray too far from city life and its gossip. But I look forward to seeing you all next week.'

'Thank you for making our arrival so much less strenuous,' said Jeanne, her cheeks flushed with cold. 'You have truly made a world of difference.' Her words were sincere, yet her eyes betrayed a tint of anxiety, as the two ladies from very different worlds fell into each other's arms in a dignified embrace.

Meanwhile, from his perch in the cart driver's seat, Jacob hailed cheerily, 'Here we are, all packed and ready to roll.'

Patting the cart that had rolled up beside him, Ducamp said, 'I had Lenny grease the axels and tighten the spokes, and I only had the rims refitted last week, so I trust you will have no problem getting there.'

'We are indebted to you, Monsieur Ducamp,' said Jacob. He had spent the previous afternoon with Jeanne and the children loading the cart with blankets, linen, and crates of extra clothing. Earlier, at the break of day, Daniel, who had stayed the night in his old study, had helped load the cart with provisions for the journey, which included urns of wine and water, and a hamper of food.

He now mounted his snorting steed. 'Weather permitting, we aim to be there by late afternoon,' he said, once in the saddle, while pushing his hat down more firmly on his head.

'If not, there be plenty of inns along the way,' said Ducamp, giving a leg up into the cart to Isabelle and Pierre, who were warmly wrapped up for the season, while Jeanne took her place on the rear bench that she had covered with a folded woollen blanket for rudimentary comfort. Isabelle, who had scrambled to the front, saw Paul look expectantly left and right before solemnly placing his walking stick in the cart and hoisting himself, stiff legged, beside their father at the front. Amid waves and calls of thanks and well-being, Ducamp closed the barn doors. Then, he and May, arm in arm, watched the cart trundle off into the crisp autumn morning, toward the post road that ran along the misty East River.

They had barely travelled fifty yards when Isabelle saw a shock of auburn hair shimmering like a dancing flame in the early morning sun. She tapped Paul on the shoulder. As he looked around, his eyes lit upon Lily-Anne running across the adjacent meadow that he assumed must have backed onto her house. She was wearing clogs and had thrown a shawl over her shift. He concluded that she had not long gotten up. 'Come back soon!' she called out, slowing to a walking pace, and waving now that she had attracted their attention.

'See you next week, probably,' Paul hollered, a smile spreading across his lips as the children and their parents waved back. The cart continued up the lane between fields of winter barley and ripe corn ready for picking, toward the dawn of their new lives.

Jacob found that the road was no longer the trail in the wilderness he had known back when New Rochelle was nothing more than a cluster of settlers' shacks.

He found it straighter, more level, and surfaced in places with gravel where once there was nothing but soft mud. As they passed early birds carting their wares to New York market, he found himself reflecting that a fine autumn day was perhaps the perfect time to travel, the ground being softer than during the summer bake and the winter freeze. Past the Bronx, they halted briefly at Kingsbridge to pay the toll over the creek and to water the horses in the babbling brook there. By late morning, the road had taken them past pretty hamlets, each mile carrying them further from their old life and closer to their new.

They stopped at midday under the shade of an old elm tree for a moment of respite and a shared meal of cold cuts, chestnuts, and cider. While tightening the cartwheel spokes by tapping the wedges with a mallet, Jacob reflected on how Ducamp had become gentrified despite his former ruggedness, perhaps becoming the man he was always meant to be. It made Jacob all the gladder he had given away his Bible to Ducamp when they had gone their separate ways. How wonderful it was to reap the fruits of a charitable act rather than the misery that can only result from a misdemeanour. Somehow, he thought to himself, that charitable act had led to them all riding in this cart to their new home today.

Daniel Darlington, responding to Jeanne's seemingly trivial comment about fitting in, said encouragingly, 'You have done so in Ireland; I have no doubt you will have no problem doing so again.' However, Jeanne had not known that many people in Ireland, given that they lived in the tamed countryside, only meeting their Huguenot friends once a week at church. She kept it to herself.

After their meal, keeping his leg straight, Paul took over the reins. Jeanne rode up front beside him to let Jacob spread himself out in the body of the cart on a blanket to ease his aching bones. He dozed with the warm autumn sun gentle on his face, but his rest was shallow, shadowed by a weighty concern. He had led his family halfway across the world to be on this road. They were all riding on the hope that it was taking them to a place they could definitively call home, be free, and flourish.

Their progress was marked by the steady clop of hooves and the creak of the cart amid the tall trees and the fall of their leaves, and the last bumble of bees humming in the gentle air. Jeanne looked over her shoulder to see the children at play, cross-legged on either side of their father, his belly serving as a card table, and their laughter a balm to both their parents' concerns. Jeanne and Jacob exchanged glances, finding solace in shared strength.

Three hours past high noon, Daniel, who usually rode ahead to ensure the passage was clear of storm debris, landslides, and rockfalls, fell back alongside the cart. By then, Jacob had taken up the reins again with his wife beside him, while Paul rested his leg in the back. The washboard road had mercifully become flatter and had recently been resurfaced with gravel in anticipation of the winter weather, especially as the post road was the major link between New York and Boston during those harsher winter months.

'Remember this hill?' said Daniel.

Jacob looked around him, unable to place the scene with precision in his memory. 'Last time I came this way,' he said, 'there was a covering of snow.'

'True,' said Daniel, as the horses clopped over the crest of the hill. 'It leads down to the village.'

'What village is that?'

'Home,' said Daniel.

'My goodness, you mean we're almost there already?'

Daniel made a sweeping gesture with his hand and said, 'Mesdames, messieurs, I give you New Rochelle!'

The view before them descended into an area of gently sloping fields on the backdrop of the East River, glistening in the late autumn sunshine. Before the shore, where once stood a huddle of shacks, Jacob now viewed a picturesque village with homes made of stone and outbuildings made of timber. The land around it was cultivated. Fields of barley, wheat, and sweet corn lay before him, swaying in the afternoon sun like a beautiful blond sea.

'See over there?' said Daniel, pointing to the far south-facing side of the valley where there stood a large house. 'That is where I live.'

'My word,' said Jacob, who had reined the cart to a standstill, and now cast his eyes over the distant stone building.

Jeanne compared the sight of the neatly laid-out valley, drenched in the late afternoon sunlight, to a Garden of Eden. 'It's beautiful, Daniel,' she said, 'truly.' This was Jacob's dream. She had been so worried it would not meet his expectations. But by the look on his face as his gaze now swept across the laboured fields, she worried no more.

451

Daniel proceeded to give a tour of his property, using his finger to point out the various features. 'You see the farmhands in the fields over there?' he began.

Jacob followed Daniel's gesture. 'Yes,' he replied, shielding his eyes from the sun, 'near that great elm tree next to the country lane.'

'Exactly,' Daniel continued. 'That's part of my land, near two hundred acres in all.'

'Impressive,' said Jacob. 'Did you ever try tobacco?'

'Too mild here,' returned Daniel. 'But what I want to show you is beyond that elm. You see the stretch of land that goes all the way down to the stream and across to the edge of the forest?'

Jacob confirmed. 'Yes, I see it.'

'Well, my friend, that is your land.'

Jacob raked his hair with his hand and, inadvertently knocking off his hat in the process, turned to his wife and children. 'You see, my dears, it is true!' he cheered. 'Right there before our very eyes—our new home!'

'Put your hat on, Jacob, before you get heatstroke,' replied Jeanne, laughing delightedly with their children. 'And before we all get carried away,' she continued lightheartedly, 'let us not forget there is much to do before we turn those fields into arable farmland.'

'And where are we going to live then?' asked Pierre.

'We're going to build a tepee, of course,' said Isabelle dramatically.

'Wow! Really?' exclaimed Pierre innocently.

'It's called a wigwam in these parts,' Paul corrected, straight-faced.

'We're going to live in a wigwam then,' said Isabelle pertly. 'And Paul is going to make one for Lily-Anne.'

'What are you talking about, Isabelle?' Paul retorted.

As the children's banter about tepees and wigwams continued, Daniel, overhearing their conversation, leaned over in his saddle with a gentle smile. 'Actually,' he interjected softly, capturing their attention, 'the native peoples around here live in structures quite different from tepees or wigwams. They are called longhouses, built from the trees, and designed for the climate and community life here.' He gestured towards the surrounding landscape, rich with forests that had been home to indigenous tribes for generations. 'These lands hold many stories and ways of living that we're all still learning about.'

To prevent further escalation of the banter, Jeanne said levelly, 'For the time being, children, we are fortunate to be spending the winter at Mr Darlington's in New York until we have built our own house.'

'Well, actually,' said Daniel affably, 'you needn't go back to New York if you'd rather winter here.' Then, moving on, he added, 'But first, to cross over to the other side, we must pass through the village.'

It was an unintentionally sharp reminder to Jeanne that they would still need to fit into a tightly knit community. Would they be accepted? Their roots lay in Montauban, in southern France, far from the western French city of La Rochelle, from which these settlers originated. Confronted with the notion of being outsiders once more, it seemed now to Jeanne that they were facing the dauting task of adapting to a different culture, another country, all over again.

'I wonder if I'll recognise anyone,' remarked Jacob, too modest to ask if anyone would remember him.

Jeanne smiled into her husband's eyes and said assertively, 'No matter, Jacob, we have our plot. At least we no longer need to search.'

The cart rattled on down the slope, plunging between fragrant orchards laden with apples and pears. As they neared the village set amid orderly fields of corn, pumpkins, and root crops, Jacob perceived villagers gathering near a quaint church. Curious, he called ahead to Daniel, who was riding a few lengths in front. 'Is there a harvest festival in the village today?'

Daniel half turned in his saddle with a knowing smile. 'You'll soon see,' he replied enigmatically.

Ten minutes later, the cart was finally rolling into the village, where villagers returning from the fields amicably bowed or doffed their hats.

They soon reached the little church where, by now, a veritable crowd had congregated and was cheering the newcomers. A burly man wearing a blacksmith's leather apron took one of the horses by the bridle and eased the cart to a halt in the shade of a maple tree, its leaves a canopy of vibrant yellow, deep orange, and reds. It began to dawn on Jeanne that this was no harvest festival after all: it was a reception in their honour. She smiled broadly and without restraint as she heard cheers of welcome in her native tongue.

Meanwhile, Jacob recognised none other than Messieurs Bonnefoy and Le Conte, who ambled up to the cart with welcoming smiles. They were impeccably dressed for the occasion in woollen coats worn over waistcoats, knee breeches, and linen shirts that allowed a modest frill at the collar and cuffs. 'Monsieur Jacob Delpech, at last you return!' declared the portlier of these two founding burghers of New Rochelle.

'Good heavens,' said Jacob, 'why, it's Monsieur Bonnefoy!'

'There's a bit more of me since we last met, as you can see,' Bonnefoy quipped, clapping his hands on his prodigious belly. 'But you look in fine fettle, my word.' The two men firmly shook hands.

Then came the turn of Monsieur Le Conte, a tall figure attired in dark browns for the season. 'Welcome back to New

Rochelle,' he said. 'We are mighty glad to have you back, Monsieur Delpech, after all this time, especially with your family.'

At that moment, Jacob, already quite overwhelmed as more hands were thrust toward him—the same hands he had shaken on his departure ten years earlier—caught sight of a young lady making her way assertively through the crowd. He recognised the burgeoning smile of Marianne. 'My oh my,' he cheered, now quite beside himself.

'My dear Uncle Jacob!' Marianne exclaimed joyfully, hastening toward him.

'My dear niece!' Jacob called out, opening his arms for Marianne's tender embrace.

'It is so good to see you,' she said, as four young children gathered around her, the two youngest peering shyly from behind her skirts. The crowd then respectfully parted to make way for a dignified old lady leaning on a cane with one hand and holding her maid's arm with the other.

'Madame de Fontenay, bless my soul!' exclaimed Jacob warmly. 'I can hardly believe my eyes.' Marianne's grandmother, though more reliant on her maid's arm than before, had lost nothing of her indomitable spirit, commanding respect while prodding onlookers out of the way with her stick as she approached.

She grasped Jacob's outstretched hand and pulled it toward her with commanding affection. 'Did you think I would depart from this world without seeing you settle here with your family first?' she said in playful reproach. 'Well, you can imagine how overjoyed I am to see you, Monsieur Delpech, here with your lovely family! At last, I shall be able to rest in peace, knowing that you've made it home.'

After Jacob had proudly introduced his wife and children, Jeanne quickly entered into excited conversation with the ladies. Together, they were all escorted to the church for a welcoming ceremony, with the promise of a hearty feast at the inn to follow. As the words expressed in Jeanne's native French washed over her like a wave of well-being, she instinctively felt that this place, with its warm embrace and shared language, was as close to home as they could ever hope for.

CHAPTER 30

Winter, 1699

NEW ROCHELLE

Jeanne was glad to be within her own walls by the time the first snows came.

'It might not be the Château of Verlhac, Jacob, but we didn't have much choice,' she remarked, when they first moved into the one-storey wooden dwelling, erected just a stone's throw away from the Darlingtons' house. She was reacting to Jacob's fleeting bout of disenchantment. 'But at least it is our own roof over our heads. This Sunday at church, we shall thank God and all who assisted in getting it built in time for the winter.' They had been lodging with the Darlingtons and Madame de Fontenay. It had gone well; Madame de Fontenay was an inspiration, and Marianne was a delight. But the time had come to regain the intimacy of family life.

'It's just that it is considerably more confined than I had anticipated,' said Jacob, his anxiety melting away as he warmed his hands by the crackling fire and snowflakes pattered lightly on the oil-paper windows. He continued in a brighter tone of voice, 'But you are right, my dear Jeanne, as always you are. We must look beyond the present; we shall build outward and upward once we have traversed this freezing cold winter.'

All in all, Jacob agreed it had turned out to be a wise decision to build the house in stages. With ample help from the villagers, it had taken little time to clear the land, lay the stone foundation, and build the rudimentary wooden structure, especially since the timber in abundance was already hewn and seasoned. The settlement had wisely erected a sawmill and had designated a place for wood storage for such new builds.

This first stage of the house comprised a kitchen with a cooking fireplace, a hall that doubled as a common room by day and a bedchamber for the boys by night, and a separate bedroom where Jacob, Jeanne, and Isabelle slept in simple rope beds. This setup was sufficient for the family to spend the winter within the New Rochelle community, rather than in New York. They found the community spirit of these devout people was a constant that ran deep, and villagers turned out whenever the construction had required extra hands, such as when placing the beams.

Isabelle and Pierre quickly made new friends at the village church, where the children were schooled. Marianne introduced Jeanne to the women's gatherings, where she shared her knowledge of spinning and weaving that surprised everyone, and Jacob was often solicited by the burghers for his advice on the new watermill and irrigation management. Paul, meanwhile, had developed an interest in law, and devoured Jacob's old books on the subject by lamplight.

It was a momentous day for everyone when the joiner and his apprentice delivered the table, two benches, and a pair of spindle-back chairs, which they placed before the stone hearth.

'That's so much better,' Jeanne declared. 'Now, it truly feels like our family home.'

Jacob said, 'The first thing I shall do on it is write a short note to my suppliers.'

'And I shall write another long letter to our dear Elizabeth,' added Jeanne with a distant look in her eyes. She thought of her eldest daughter who, when still a girl, had chosen to remain in France with her aunt at the cost of her forced conversion to the Catholic faith. Yet there was some solace in knowing that Elizabeth had married into a family of former Huguenots who, despite outward appearances, quietly kept their Huguenot beliefs.

Whenever inclement weather prevented Jacob and Paul from working on outdoor improvements, Paul would study while Jacob drew up plans for the evolution of the modest dwelling into *a palace fit for a princess*, as he liked to call it. There would be a stable for the new horse and cart, outhouses, and a barn too. They might even have a cow or three, and a pig. Pierre, ever enthusiastic, added, 'And a goat, like at Uncle Daniel's, to keep the grass trim.'

However, for the time being, the family's focus was to come through winter with a clear plan for business ventures, farming, and future extensions to their dwelling. Jeanne especially looked forward to the arrival of warmer weather, which would allow a journey to New York to purchase the glass for the windows to replace the makeshift oiled paper. It would make a world of difference to let the sunlight into their little house. Furthermore, she sensed that a trip back to New York would give Paul, in particular, something to look forward to.

She noticed that his limp had become less pronounced these days, despite the cold outside. Yet there were times when she caught a faraway look in his eyes, and she wondered what he was thinking. There were young ladies in the village who, she had noted, had shown an interest in him, but Paul's regard seemed always to be elsewhere. 'Perhaps the spring will bring a change of heart,' she mused.

CHAPTER 31

Spring, 1700

NEW YORK

'We must pay a visit to the Ducamps tomorrow,' said Jacob to Paul over a tankard of cider with some bread, ham, pickles, and boiled eggs.

'No place better to catch up with the latest news, I'd say,' Paul remarked indifferently and without irony after knocking back another throatful of the delicious, thirst-slaking beverage.

They had spent the better part of the day sharing the reins along the muddy post road, now lined here and there with budding trees and the first blooms of spring. Once through the east gate of the city, they had trundled down to the busy harbour, then parked and chained the cart in their lock-up after loading their sacks of grain and the farm tools into it. After locking the door with the heavy padlock and chain, Paul had led their sturdy horse to the nearby stable to be watered, fed, and brushed down, while Jacob went to order refreshments and a bed at the inn. After a reassuring pat on the horse's flank and murmuring quiet words of gratitude for the day's haul, Paul had then left it to rest and joined his father at the inn that was humming with conversation and gossip.

'First rule of thumb in trade and politics, my boy—maintain your best connections,' continued Jacob with a passing thought for the meandering maze of life. For it was safe to say, the former dragoon lieutenant, his former oppressor, had become a good friend and had found himself a surprising and vibrant lady with character, to say the least. Jacob had suspected May of being a woman of the world the moment he had laid eyes on her, and a woman of means too, the type of lady he would never have encountered in his old life.

'Yes, Father,' said Paul, recollecting the day he saw Mrs Ducamp and her daughter at the foot of his bed: that determined brow, those becoming eyes, and the confident, mature voice that emerged from Lily-Anne's cupid's-bow lips, defying her age.

'But first, I want to send my letter to my suppliers so that we can have something to sell before the year's harvest.'

'Why don't we buy and sell something other than wine from France, Father?'

'Because, my dear boy, I know about wines of France better than the tobaccos from Virginia, and it's better to deal in something you know about, and preferably like. Although, I must say, I do enjoy a pipe of Virginian tobacco.' Jacob popped a chunk of pickle into his mouth with an indulgent chuckle.

'But knowledge can be acquired,' insisted Paul, inadvertently catching the eye of a middle-aged, one-armed gentleman with a scar across his bristly jaw, sitting at the next table by the window. The gentleman gave a polite nod, which Paul returned. He was being attended by the barmaid, who had brought him a clay cup of rum, a jug of milk, and a small bowl of sugar and spices, which

Paul found quite likable somehow. Paul pressed on, 'I mean, you yourself had to learn about wines at some point.'

'That is true,' said Jacob, 'but I enjoyed it long before I traded in it.'

'You still had to learn how to import it from Amsterdam to Ireland, though.'

'And if I had known then what a headache it would be, I would have stuck to planting. But I did learn, and now I can safely say, it will be easier this time round despite the extra distance between us and our suppliers, because it's something I know about.'

'Well, look at Mr Darlington,' said Paul, pausing before asserting his favourite counterargument, having already discussed the matter of trade along the road from New Rochelle. 'He went to the Caribbean with nothing but his grandfather's sword and a pouch of coins, and came back a wealthy man.' Paul was referring to the many evenings after dinner spent captivated by Daniel's Caribbean tales at the Darlingtons' (otherwise known as the Fontneys' house) in New Rochelle. This was before the construction of the Delpech abode was advanced enough for them to move in.

'That is true,' said Jacob good-heartedly while lighting his pipe. 'And as you heard him say, he came close to losing his life on more than one occasion in the process. Thankfully so, mind you, otherwise he might never have stopped to repair his ship at Cow Island, and we would probably not be sitting here discussing trade today.' Such was the surprise of life, thought Jacob as he said this, fleetingly contemplating the life he had led so far while taking another drag on his pipe. And yet it seemed that some things were of God's will, and only after the event, he thought to himself, did one see their correlation to the tapestry of one's existence. And now, here he was in another world, discussing the intricacies of trade with his grown-up son. Everything was yet to be built or cultivated: the house, the business, the land. Yet at that instant, having eaten and drunk to fulfilment, he was a man content. What more could he ask for?

Sensing his father's relaxed mood, Paul pressed on, 'That's exactly what I mean, Father—fortune favours the brave.'

'But don't forget that Darlington knew the Caribbean like the back of his hand before he made his fortune,' said Jacob.

'So could we,' thought Paul, but he kept the thought to himself, seeing that his father was still unwilling to yield.

Jacob, as during their ride into New York, resolutely stuck to his guns with his tried and tested business formula, which he deemed watertight. The only added inconvenience he saw was the extra distance his barrels would need to travel from France to their destination in New York. The goods would take longer to arrive, and there were consequently increased risks of loss at sea. But he was confident that, by not putting all his eggs in one basket, he would make a sustainable profit, especially here where wine was for expensive tastes. Above all, to underpin his strategy, Jacob had built up a good standing with his suppliers over the years, who would wait for payment until after the first harvest.

Paul said, 'I just thought there was more profit to be made with goods from the West Indies. We could sell it here or ship part of it to Europe, simple! And then purchase more wine and tools, if you insist, with part of the proceeds.'

Sitting forward in his chair, Jacob said, 'The thing is, Paul, we may no longer be at war, but by consequence of privateers losing their letters of marque, the Caribbean Sea will be a hunting ground for pirates, believe me.'

'The risk is equivalent to sailing across the ocean, surely.'

'That is why we shall split the orders between two ships,' said Jacob. 'I learnt the hard way back in Dublin when an order was lost with a ship from Amsterdam. It would have sunk us too if I hadn't split the main order between two shipments.'

'But surely you can do the same from the West Indies to reduce the risks of loss likewise.'

'Also, there is relatively little competition for wine here.'

'That's perhaps because people might not care for it due to its high price,' countered Paul resolutely. 'But I do know that rum is in high demand. They put it in everything.' The young man glanced toward the window table, where the seafarer was ostentatiously mixing milk and spices into his rum.

'Well, my boy,' said Jacob, with a sweeping glance around at the few clusters of merchants and sailors at the tables despite the slack hour of the day. 'We simply need to maintain a steady flow, and we can have a good life here. We don't need pots of gold,' he concluded with a smile of finality.

But Paul was not enthused by a good life. He wanted more, and in his heart of hearts, he was becoming a little disappointed with this New World that supposedly held so much promise—promise that now seemed just beyond his grasp. As they rose to leave, the one-armed sailor, seated by the window behind Jacob, gave a cordial nod goodbye, which Paul returned.

A few moments later, they were pushing the door into the busy lane. The air was blithe with spring sunshine and filled with the calls of dockers and the rattle of handcarts amid the deep grunts of cormorants and the ever-present screech of gulls.

Jacob led the way, with the sun casting long shadows between the Dutch-styled buildings that lined the cobbled thoroughfares. Their destination: Milyer's glassworks on Beaver Street, a well-known venue to any settler seeking to build. On their approach, the rhythmic sounds of artisans shaping the molten glass guided them to the workshop's entrance. The air was tainted with the smell of woodsmoke from the furnace, and the

465

heat of creation that brought about the translucent sheets that would illuminate their home.

Jacob had sent a note a week earlier with the order for the glass to be made and cut to size, according to the given dimensions to make lattice windows set with lead cames. He negotiated the payment partly in coin and the rest in surplus seed from his lock-up, given that he had decided to begin planting only over the most sun-filled parcels of his land this first year. For the rest, he needed to see how the land lay through the seasons and consequently whether he could grow orchards that, once mature, would not need replanting each year as would annual crops. So, the grain would sustain them for the immediate future; then the orchards would enhance their earnings in a couple of years when the trees began to yield in abundance. Moreover, there was no point overworking: it was enough to sustain a family. For now, the project was the house. The glass windows would make Jeanne feel so much better, now that the more clement days of spring were upon them. Jacob had ordered extra panes for the future extensions of the house. It would save having to use oiled paper as well as a trip to New York.

'We can have them packaged and ready by the morning for you,' said Mr Milyer, a stocky man with large, burly forearms that showed the scars of his trade. The clinking and blowing noises continued in the workshop amid the glow of the furnace under the great bellows. 'How are you travelling? By boat, I presume.'

'Actually, we have brought our cart. Didn't want to risk losing our seed, you see,' said Jacob, anticipating the question of why they had not taken a sloop. He had heard about the treacherous strait known as Hell Gate, with its dangerous currents, shallow waters, and submerged rocks that made it one of the most hazardous passages along the American East Coast. He did not say he was loathe to take the waterway, though.

Milyer was nevertheless concerned they would be risking breakage if they transported it all the way to New Rochelle over the bumpy post road. He strongly suggested it would be safer by sloop. 'The sloop lads are well-versed in the waters of the straits. Once your order's loaded, it won't go nowhere, and it won't get shaken about like in a rattling cart. Honestly, you're better off sending your glass panes by the river, Mr Delpech.' Finding no argument against Milyer's sound reasoning and given that he would need to pick up a new set of seals he had yet to order anyway, Jacob agreed to return by boat, possibly the following week.

Next, father and son headed to the candlemaker's to procure some rushlights and a selection of candles for the home, the church, and the community at large. There were never too many, what with it still being the season of long nights and with Easter not far away. Jeanne had asked for a selection of beeswax candles specifically for the main room and the bedchamber. They burned more brightly with the sweet-smelling fragrance of honey, as opposed to the tallow ones that smoked, gave off a dim light, and smelt beefy.

It was early evening by the time they had finished these errands, and as they were in the vicinity of the harbour area, Paul, in spite of his limp, steadfastly insisted on carrying the straw-padded crate of candles back to the lock-up where they had parked the cart under lock and key. Jacob, meanwhile, would deliver a letter from the pastor of New Rochelle to the pastor of Saint Trinity's. Father and son agreed to meet later at the inn.

It was suppertime at the inn when Paul entered, paused for a moment, and glanced around the lamplit room for his father.

The place was a babble of voices with clusters of patrons—merchants and seafarers mostly—spooning down bowls of broth and eating sausages, and oysters by the dozen, raw on the half shell or roasted. But Jacob was not there yet.

A generously proportioned maid, her tray laden with tankards of beer and cider as well as cups of kill devil, flashed Paul a becoming smile as she crossed his path. She urged him to take a stool at the counter. Having once fallen in bad company in such a place in Boston, Paul knew better this time not to indulge in spirits. So, while waiting for his father, he ordered a tankard of cider instead.

As he took his first sip, he heard the dull, cadenced thud of wood on wood that reminded him of the walking stick he had long since discarded. Flicking his eyes to his right, he saw a one-armed man with a limp settling atop the stool next to him. 'All right, John?' greeted the bald tavernkeeper with a respectful nod to the newcomer. Without waiting for a response, he placed a spoon, a bowl of broth, and a mug of ale in front of him. Paul deduced by this exchange that the gentleman must be a respected regular of the establishment, perhaps a captain, judging by the fine cut of his clothes.

'You not eating, young man?' asked the patron, whom Paul, turning to face him, recognised as the gentlemen sipping rum and milk at the window earlier in the day.

'I'm waiting for my father,' said Paul, returning the one-armed patron's affable smile.

His genial manner allowed for easy conversation, and as Paul sipped his cider, the pair soon bonded over the recollection of that drink of milk and rum.

'We're settling in New Rochelle,' said Paul in reply to the gentleman's question about his origins. 'Originally from France, though, before we moved to Ireland.'

'Ah, I pegged you as Huguenots,' said the patron, pausing from eating his broth.

Surprised, Paul said, 'How did you know that?'

'Heard you speaking in French with your father earlier. But where's my manners?' Setting down his spoon, he extended his strong right hand, that of a seasoned mariner, which Paul took in a brief but firm handshake. 'John Barbeck, occasional merchant, former shipmaster, and agent to any ship's captain willing to listen to a piece of good sense,' he said.

'Pleased to meet you, sir. I'm Paul Delpech, merchant's son and failed sailor,' said Paul with a light chuckle. Upon being asked, Paul shared how he fell from the rigging of the ship that brought him to the New World and broke his leg, preventing him from ever climbing again.

'Hah, lad, there's more to seafaring than climbing the shrouds. Plenty of opportunity to learn the ropes without scaling them. In all me twenty years at sea, I never climbed them more than twice,' John said with a knowing grin.

Paul, intrigued, asked, 'But then, how could you become a shipmaster, sir?'

'Oh, I ain't always been such. I began as a modest cook's mate,' John explained openly, 'aboard a merchantman bound for the Caribbean. I learned the ropes, seizing one opportunity after the next, and here I am, twenty years later, having lost a limb in a foolish turn of events. Could've carried on, I s'pose, but decided to let the sun set on me seafaring days. Now I sit before you, content to be a ship's agent.'

'What does a ship's agent do?' asked Paul.

'I handle provisioning, docking arrangements, repairs, and maintenance, so the lads aboard can enjoy their time ashore. And I also dabble in recruitment,' he added, lowering his voice to a confidential level, 'speaking of which, there's a merchantman southbound at port that you might like to know about. Needs a carpenter's mate, in case you feel inclined to inquire.'

'No, thank you, sir,' replied Paul, more sternly than he intended. Softening his tone, he added, 'I must accompany my father back to the village.'

'Take no offence,' said John reassuringly. 'The only reason I ask is that you don't strike me as a village lad somehow. You see, sometimes, when opportunity knocks, you've got to seize it, because it might not come knocking again for a good while.'

'To be honest, I wasn't expecting such an offer on my first trip back to New York this year.'

'Well, let me know if you want me to put in a word. The *Bonaventura* leaves on the morning tide. Just ask for me at the quayside. John Barbeck.'

'Thank you, sir, but really, it's not for me.'

A few minutes later, the former shipmaster left a coin on the counter, then cordially took his leave as Paul's father entered the inn.

'Who was that?' said Jacob, sitting down on the vacant stool.

'A shipmaster turned ship's agent.'

'Did you get his name?'

'Barbeck. John Barbeck.'

'Good,' said Jacob heartily. Then, adding with a wink, 'You never know when we might want to purchase some rum from the Caribbean.' Then he called for two bowls of broth, some sausages, and two dozen raw oysters on the half shell.

Paul rose quietly the following morning before high tide. Leaving his father snoring peacefully in his sleep, he crept downstairs and let himself out into the freshness of the early morning, and then ambled down to the gull-screeching quayside.

It was alive with activity, with two streams of dockers hauling sacks on their backs before each of the three vessels due out that morning. Among them, he saw the *Bonaventura*, a magnificent Dutch-built fluyt, her tall masts crawling with mariners preparing her sails to be unfurled to catch the wind. Paul fondly recollected that the combination of square sails on the main and foremasts were for propulsion, and the smaller triangular topsails on the mizzenmast served for manoeuvrability. Her figurehead, an ornately carved and painted wooden sculpture, depicted a patron saint that was supposed to protect the ship and all souls aboard on their onward journey. *She must be well over a hundred feet long*, he thought to himself, as he cast his eyes over the decks, where sailors were securing the last of the cargo and ensuring that the cannons were ready for defence against pirates. It looked like she was equipped with several cannons positioned along the gunwales to defend against these villains of the sea.

He sensed the anticipation for the voyage ahead, and imagined the ship's carpenter, surgeon, and cook checking their supplies and instruments of their trade, while the captain would be poring over maps and charts, planning the route.

As he watched the dockers hauling the last of the sacks of grain from a horse-drawn cart to the gangplank, a pleasant voice spoke to him from behind. 'There she is. Are you ready to join her?'

Paul turned to greet John Barbeck, who smiled disarmingly. 'She is quite a beauty, isn't she?' said Paul, still quite awestruck.

'Aye, verily, she is that,' said John, running his eyes over the *Bonaventura* as he stood beside the young man.

'What is she carrying?'

'Wares of all sorts, tools, textiles, plenty of grain... And she could still do with an extra pair of hands to help keep her shipshape and seaworthy.'

'Thank you, but, unfortunately, I know nothing about woodworking.'

'Hah, lad, they say necessity is the father of invention. You will learn quick.'

'No, I really must return to New Rochelle with my father. There is so much to do there.'

'There will always be so much to do.'

'True, but I must go.'

'Well then, if that is your final word, that's fine,' said John reassuringly. 'And you are wise to take it in the sober light of day. For it is a decision that you will look back upon for the rest of your life, one way or the other,' he said, gazing appreciatively along the ship's graceful flank. Turning back to Paul, he added, 'She weighs anchor within the hour. Join her if you will.'

'I... I really must be going,' said Paul, pulling himself away. Then he walked at a brisk pace the way he came, without turning back.

A little later that morning, Jacob and Paul were walking along Dock Street under an overcast sky where fingers of sunshine edged between gilt-tinged clouds. 'Something on your mind, Paul?' said Jacob to his son, who had been quieter than usual since their breakfast of porridge washed down with a mug of cider.

'Hardly,' said Paul evenly. 'I was just wondering about the glass.'

'It should be easy to return next week by boat to fetch it back to New Rochelle. I mentioned it to the pastor yesterday; he said there'll be far more sailings back and forth, what with the warmer weather.'

Indeed, Paul could smell and see spring about them in the burgeoning city trees and gardens they had passed along as New Yorkers went about their business. 'Good,' said Paul as his gaze turned seaward to the *Bonaventura* sailing out into the bay, her figurehead cutting gracefully through the enamel-like water. 'I shall look forward to sailing again.'

They sliced their way through the busy marketplace crowd, where they ignored vendors calling out their wares, and then strode out into the elbow of Broad Way that straightened into an extended avenue. Half an hour later, they were passing by the old Darlington house, where they had lodged upon their arrival in New York. It was also the place of Paul's convalescence and where he first set eyes on that young girl full of spirit, bordering on impropriety. Now the half-demolished house seemed to reflect the ruins of his abandoned dream.

They continued until they came to the Ducamps' place, which comprised a main residence and Didier's office. Jacob had since learnt more about Ducamp's occupation. Didier had purchased Darlington's ketch after Daniel's flight from New York. Didier then had little by little, with his wife's financial backing, built up a lumber business, which now boasted an extra couple of ketches to deal with the shipments brought in from along the Hudson and East rivers, and Long Island. Jacob's visit was not only a social call then, but also a business visit in that he wanted to pick Didier's brain about clearing some land of trees, when to fell them, and how much their sale was likely to bring. Then there was the question of the grain mill he intended to place near a stream. He hoped Didier could point him to a mill builder who could design one.

Ducamp gave them as warm a greeting as his taciturn nature could muster; then he accompanied them to his fine house across the lumber yard, grown too small for his needs.

Moreover, he explained, most of the land he previously rented for wood storage had been sold, as the land north of Wall Street was becoming increasingly residential. 'We have a wood storage place down by the shore now,' he told Jacob as they crossed the yard, while his wife's carriage was pulling up outside the house. May had just seen her youngest to the Huguenot dame school and greeted the two visitors in her usual exuberant and friendly manner, which contrasted with Didier's more confidential demeanour. It seemed the pair were a perfect match of opposites, thought Jacob. He guessed that May was behind the networking side of the business.

The equally fiery bonnet of her eldest daughter soon appeared from the dim carriage. It seemed to Paul that over the winter, she had changed shape. Her hips were wider, although still slender, and her bust had deepened. He made an effort to refrain from overtly looking her up and down, but his surprise was no less impressed on his face, which made Lily-Anne smile knowingly, in turn making Paul feel slightly awkward. After all, this was the young lady who had nursed him back to life, had listened to his deepest disappointments, and had cared for him enough to show him a clear way forward from the fog of despair in which he had found himself. His eyes seemed to thank her as they exchanged a meaningful glance and shared a nod of greeting.

Jacob insisted they would not stop long—they still needed to pay a visit to the seal cutter's to order a new set of seals—but they would gladly stay for tea and *ontbijtkoek*, a delicious spicy cake sweetened with molasses.

Questions infused with good humour and genuine concern were exchanged around the dining table in the panelled common room, which May had tastefully decorated in the French style. Yes, Jeanne and the children were in good health and enjoyed village life in New Rochelle. Indeed, it had been very cold, but no lack of timber meant they were able to keep warm in their new abode. Jacob was tacitly impressed by what he had seen—the outside office building, the house and gardens, and now the room—all of which were clear indications of how a man of Ducamp's modest station could aspire to rise in society here.

The conversation soon shifted to business. 'Here it is,' said Jacob, bringing out a slip of folded paper upon which he had carefully drawn his main seal. Around its perimeter, he had inscribed *Delpech & Son* along with *New York* at the centre, the whole adorned with an elaborate design of two barrels and a grapevine, which everyone found admirable, although possibly a little intricate. 'We shall be back in a week or two to pick up the seals,' said Jacob, who explained they would keep their lock-up in New York in the same way they had kept their business address in Dublin, even though they had resided in the country.

When Jacob put the question about the construction of watermills, May said she could point him to a clever carpenter who would fulfil his needs for his small mill, while Didier went into detail regarding tree felling and associated costs. As May rose to fetch an address, Lily-Anne, taking advantage of the interruption, asked if she could show Paul the new horse she had received for her birthday. Giving Paul no choice, she beckoned him to follow her to the stable that annexed the house.

'There,' she said, a few minutes later, once they were at the stable doors, 'I wanted to save you from a drawn-out conversation between old folks.' Paul looked quite shocked at her remark, but then she laughed out loud. 'Only joking,' she said as she unbarred the door, which Paul pulled open to the sound of a nickering horse and the scent of fresh manure. 'I just wanted to see your face. But Daddy can go on for hours about how to fell a poor tree, which quite makes me cringe. The only time the Indians fell a tree is for making their canoes. Ama says every time you cut one down, it's like destroying a medicine store. Anyway, how is New Rochelle?'

'Well, where to begin? It is a village,' said Paul drily as he followed her into the dim stable, where she lovingly greeted her horse with her forehead pressed between its ears. Paul went on, 'A nice one, though, with good people.'

'But it's a village all the same,' said Lily-Anne, detecting a note of frustration. 'But it will grow. And according to your father, your business will be partly here in New York anyway.'

'True,' said Paul, holding out his hand for the horse to sniff.

'Meet Ahanu,' said Lily-Anne, pleased to see the horse's friendly greeting. 'It means *joyful*.'

Paul, sensing the animal was proud but good-natured, gave him an affectionate pat on the neck. 'Handsome fella,' he said, rubbing the horse's shoulder, which brought him physically closer to Lily-Anne.

'I see you no longer need a stick,' she said from the opposite side of Ahanu's muzzle.

'I threw it on the fire,' said Paul, smiling.

'And I hope you are equally cured of thoughts of going to sea.'

How could she possibly suspect he still entertained such thoughts? he wondered. 'Actually, I have been studying my father's law books. I hope perhaps to learn about court proceedings.'

'Have you told your father your plans?' Clearly, she too had noticed *and son* on the sketch of the seal.

'Not yet. I shall do so when the time is right.' Lily-Anne said nothing. Paul continued, 'I do believe I could be good at it. But I will need to find out if I can join a firm to learn the ropes, for there is no school here where I can study.'

'I'm glad you will be learning the ropes on land rather than at sea. I feel quite proud of you, for some reason.'

'I cannot say the sea is entirely out of my system, though,' said Paul truthfully, realising he was in danger of becoming self-centred. But she had a way of pulling the words out of him. So, he pressed on, 'But I did manage to refuse an offer only this morning. A good one, on a merchant ship called the *Bonaventura*.'

'I thought they wouldn't take you if you can't climb.'

'I wouldn't need to for some jobs, apparently. But there is nothing more to say on the matter as that ship sailed this morning.' Paul jerked his head away as the horse snorted and swung its muzzle toward him. 'Whoa, boy, good boy,' he said gently.

'I'm glad you've found your anchor in books.' She had chosen her words well, thought Paul. It was indeed as though he had anchored himself to books to keep him from wandering. Yet what would he do once those books had run out? He hoped that further learning and an occupation would keep him anchored, but for that to happen, he would need to further his knowledge. The question was, where? Where would he continue his schooling? How would he enter a firm at his age? Lily-Anne continued, 'I saw a book on law the other day. It belonged to a deceased juror, so I thought of you.'

'Thank you!' said Paul, bashfully deflecting the kindness of her thought with a lighthearted jerk of the head, while she kissed her horse on the nose.

'Ha-ha, not because it belonged to a dead juror,' she guffawed. The horse gave a snort as if he got the jest too, which made them both laugh. 'So, tell me more about New Rochelle.'

He told her they had begun preparing the ground—at least, a few plots of it, the most exposed to the sun—and hoped to start planting barley and peas when they got home. But their chat was abruptly interrupted by a call from the scullery door. 'Lily-Anne!' her mother hollered. 'Come and show Mr Delpech your medicinal tinctures for a bad back.'

He wanted to talk more, to listen more, to get back to the depths of their previous exchanges. But the call stopped him in his tracks as Lily-Anne yelled out, 'Coming, Mother!'

Jacob held the reins loosely as the cart, filled with sacks of seed, tools, and baskets of provisions, rolled tranquilly along the East River Road, with the bedazzling rising sun on his right.

Paul, sitting on his left, his gaze locked on the dewy verge, was lost in his thoughts. All said and done, he mused to himself, he was not really suited to become a carpenter's mate anyway. He had no inclination for carpentry as some lads had, and besides, wasn't he too old to be ordered about like a lackey? He concluded that either John Barbeck had underestimated his age, or he was desperate to fill the position. As they rattled along, he marvelled at how, within the short space of their visit to New York, the surrounding pearling vegetation had made stunning progress. Clusters of bright yellow, white, and purple blooms showed here and there.

Jacob noticed it too. Lowering his pipe, he turned to Paul and said, 'Time to plant, by the looks of it.'

'Yes,' said Paul, coming back to himself. 'Hopefully, we can get it in before we return for the glass and seals.' The haunting caw-caw of crows in the mist caused him to glance back over his left shoulder toward the sprawling town, now without a wall and open to the misty hinterland of Manhattan. He focussed his sight on the gleaming sheen of a cantering horse as it disturbed the birds dipping into the soft earth of a field. Then he recognised the blazing head of the young lady riding sidesaddle, her fallen hat fluttering against her back. Paul's heart rose in his chest as he elbowed his father, who looked back and then pulled the cart to a standstill at a clearing beside the river, leaving ample breadth for an oncoming market cart to easily pass by.

At last, Lily-Anne halted her horse abreast of the cart, beside Paul. Catching her breath, she said, 'I missed you at the inn. They said you'd already taken to the road. So, I'm glad I didn't have to venture far.' She was as fresh as the spring morning, racy and splendid as she sat on her horse in her best riding clothes, her thick green skirts falling to the top of her boots. Her large, captivating blue eyes, the whiteness of her complexion, and her heavy locks of auburn hair that tumbled upon her slender shoulders made Paul's heart beat faster as he greeted her. From a leather saddlebag, she brought out a ceramic pot wrapped in cloth. 'Mr Delpech,' she said to Jacob spiritedly, passing the pot to Paul, 'this is what you'll need for your back. It's an ointment. You just need to rub it in, and it will relieve stiffness, although it won't make it go away, I'm afraid.' Jacob took the gift with thanks, while Lily-Anne reached into her pouch and brought out a thick book which she handed to Paul. 'This is the book I told you about. I happened to stumble upon it again when I picked up my sister yesterday afternoon from her school.'

'*The Third Part of the Institutes of the Laws of England* by Edward Coke,' Paul read out as he took the hefty book from her slender hands. 'Thank you very much,' he said, unflinchingly grateful as he placed the book on his knees and turned the first page in awe. 'This will be an essential addition to my collection. Thank you, Lily-Anne. I will repay you for it on my return.'

'No need,' she returned forthrightly. 'Anyway, can't stand here on parade, and you've a long road ahead of you. Have a safe journey back!' Pushing Ahanu onward, she then swung him round. 'Come back soon!' she hollered and then cantered off as quickly as she had arrived, amid the orange haze of sunlight.

'A thoughtful young lady, indeed,' said Jacob, glancing at Paul out of the corner of his eye.

'Father, she is just a friend. Besides, she is still a child.'

'Women become wiser and fuller quicker than us men, my boy,' said Jacob, giving a shake of the reins. 'Hyah!' With that, the cart trundled forward, as Paul glanced back at the fiery shock of hair flowing over the dewy fields on the outskirts of town.

CHAPTER 32

Spring, 1700

Two days before the sloop was slated to sail from New Rochelle to New York, Jacob put his back out while taking a turn at manoeuvring the heavy wooden plough behind the draft horse. Paul had warned him to leave the ploughing and harrowing to the younger farmhands, who were used to manoeuvring on a slope. But Jacob had wanted to show them that he was not just a settler with means.

If truth be told, however, he wasn't excessively put out at being too incapacitated to make the voyage; he had never enjoyed travelling by waterway anyway, and he had not been looking forward to navigating the infamous waters of Hell Gate, albeit in a shallow-draft vessel. At table the day before the due departure, Jacob gave Paul instructions which he had written down on paper, even though Jeanne would have preferred to put back the trip to the following week, when Jacob would have recovered.

'Worry not, Mother, I shall take it all in my stride,' said Paul in an attempt to gain the upper hand. Then to press home his statement, he added, 'Just as I did when I travelled from Montauban to Geneva when I was just a boy.'

'You had a guide, Paul,' said Jeanne, quick to remind him—perhaps too quick and too defensive, for she still often saw the young boy he once was, and sometimes spoke to him as such, which Paul was finding increasingly exasperating. Would this ascendance stick to him like horse glue for the rest of his life?

'Mother, I am twenty-one,' he sighed. 'I can look after myself very well.'

She gave him the sharp stare from when he was a boy. 'Paul, my dear, I haven't gone through deprivation, separation, and hardship to see my children put themselves into harm's reach.'

'With respect, Mother, aren't you forgetting that I too went through equal hardship? It was hard, but I too made it through, even though I didn't entirely understand why we were fleeing. I had no choice anyway. Neither did I have any choice in leaving behind Ireland and my hopes of becoming a soldier.' At last, it was out. Paul had been finding it increasingly challenging to keep his frustrations bubbling under his hat. He just wanted to make a point. Not wanting to be hurtful, he added more gently, 'But now I do have a choice, Mother. I am going to New York. I will fetch the glass for the house and the seals for Papa.'

'And in that case, do tell Lily-Anne for me that her ointment has helped,' interrupted Jacob, trying to calm things down while gently stamping his agreement to let his son go.

Jeanne pursed her lips at Jacob's clever reminder of the girl. He had told her about the parting gifts, but she had accredited the gesture with nothing beyond innocent thoughtfulness. Yet wasn't she still rather young? Nevertheless, Jeanne had the abrupt realisation that there would be another Mrs Delpech one day. 'In that case, my dear son,' she said with the gallant smile of one defeated, 'if you see Mrs Ducamp, give her my fond regards.' Jacob gave her one of his furtive glances of approval and gratitude. She had no choice but to concede.

Yet, call it instinct or motherly concern, she experienced a visceral inkling that this trip would change the course of her son's life forever. Nevertheless, *ce qui sera, sera*, she tried to tell herself, as Jacob continued to explain the details of Paul's mission to him. Firstly, he was to check the seals before acceptance. Secondly, he had to fetch the glass and oversee its safe loading aboard the return ship in accordance with Jacob's meticulous packaging instructions.

As she watched father and son speak man to man, it dawned on her again that Paul must have been traumatised, indeed all her children must have been, by the consequences of her life choices that they had not chosen, only endured. Had she done them wrong? But then, she told herself that the hardest thing was not being able to become the parent you dearly wanted to be. There were times when many exterior forces obliged you to make choices that you would never have even entertained in an ideal world, which this certainly was not. However, there was no point in adding another layer of self-pity. There was no point in letting prior hardships stand in the way of self-improvement. All she could do now was give encouragement to her fledgling son to fly with his own wings. But that was not an easy thing to do when all she desired was his well-being.

The men at last finished going over the ins and outs of packaging the glass panes with hay in crates, using wooden dividers and securing the crates aboard the sloop. With a furrow of concern on her brow, Jeanne said, 'Promise you will keep your two feet on the deck at all times.'

'I promise, Mother,' said Paul indulgently, content with her implicit blessing to let him go. 'I couldn't do otherwise anyway, even if I tried. I would be as artful as... as an elephant on ice!' The witticism made Isabelle laugh out loud. She then explained to Pierre that the elephant would slip, slide, and crash through the ice and sink to the bottom. Pierre didn't find it funny at all and suggested that a hippopotamus would be more appropriate because it could walk underwater, whereas an elephant would drown. That made everyone laugh, except young Pierre, who had been learning about the exotic animals in the Ark.

The following morning, Paul experienced a sense of liberation the moment he embarked as a passenger aboard the sloop, even though he knew full well it would be short-lived. For he would soon have to return to his place as a villager and planter.

The day-long voyage southward down the tidal East River—much of which he spent reading the book Lily-Anne had given him—through the perilous Hell Gate, and on toward New York harbour passed relatively smoothly. He admired the crew's savvy navigational skills, even though none of them would probably venture any further than the port of New York, he thought.

But while sailing down a wide and easy stretch of the river, when he put the question of going further afield to one of the seasoned sailors, he was quite surprised at the reply. 'Ah, I been a deal further than New York, matey. Aye, done me time on a Caribbean merchantman up and down the coast, seeing the sights 'n' all.' He then went on to give a colourful account of his many travels, including his encounters with whales, giant turtles, and obliging mermaids—the latter of which Paul took with a pinch of salt—and the bountiful lands of the Caribbean islands where birds of bright hues sang their beautiful songs.

On the morning after his arrival in New York, he oversaw the lading of the glass as per his father's meticulous instructions.

After a busy morning, he sat down to a bowl of gruel and a mug of cider by the harbour-side window at the inn. At a nearby table, a knot of mariners was gabbling on about the fabled lands of the Caribbean and the various ways a savvy matelot could make a heap of coin, legally or otherwise. While tending a discreet ear and spooning down his porridge, Paul felt a shadow loom over him, which made him look up, unsure whether to frown or smile.

It was John Barbeck who, after congenial pleasantries, slammed down his tankard of beer and pulled a stool under his butt. 'I'll be brief,' he said, leaning closer to Paul. 'There's a position on a four-hundred-ton East Indiaman, a beauty. I believe it will be more to your liking. She was moored at the anchorage when last you came, so you probably didn't see her. Right now, her hold's brimming with merchandise, and she's nearly all shipshape for a long voyage to La Martinique.' The very name evoked an air of the exotic to Paul's ears, but his mouth was about to formulate a refusal when John, raising his only hand, pressed on with an affable smile, 'Hear me out, young fella. La Martinique is a French-speaking island in the Caribbean, and the purser's in need of a mate who knows French.'

'French is my mother tongue,' said Paul matter-of-factly, unable to resist the lure of disclosing his linguistic talent.

'Aye, that's why I'm glad to see you,' said John, reaching over and clasping Paul's shoulder in a comradely manner. 'She's slated to sail on the morrow.'

'I am sorry, sir, I cannot go,' said Paul, shaking his head. 'I have my responsibilities to my family in New Rochelle.'

'Ah, you didn't tell me you were wed,' said John Barbek, looking like his hopes had just been dashed.

'I'm not. My responsibilities are to my parents and siblings.'

'Your father, is he unwell?'

'No, he's just strained his back. That's why I'm here alone.'

'Well then, young man, the decision is all yours to make. But if you don't go this time, there's a strong likelihood that you never will,' said John, as he sat upright on his stool with a sigh of resignation.

Paul kept his thoughts to himself, while the matelots at the nearby table continued their lively banter about exotic places and pretty girls, and sugar and spice, all rolled into the same destination: La Martinique. They did not look like the rough types he had been accosted by in Boston; these sailors spoke in a confusion of French and English, one of them with an Irish lilt. John Barbeck leaned in once more. 'You can't deny it's a rare opportunity that in my opinion suits you down to the ground. Now, if you're willing to seize it, point your toes to the *Providence* at the quayside tomorrow morning, an hour before high tide at the latest, or I'll be obliged to find a replacement.'

Paul remembered it was on the mid-morning rising tide too that the sloop back to New Rochelle was due to set sail, to take advantage of the deeper waters once at Hell Gate. After a final nod, John Barbeck ambled away to another table, leaving Paul with much to ponder while finishing his breakfast.

Time was on his side: he only had to pay a visit to the seal cutter's, and all his errands in New York were done, he thought to himself as he turned into a backstreet that led to the cobbled quayside.

For now, his gaze was drawn across the harbour to the *Providence*, the impressive East Indiaman. From the mouth of the alleyway, with his felt hat pulled firmly over his head in case Barbeck was lurking, he stood for a while in admiration of her three masts, rigged with an intricate web of lines and sails that exuded power. He imagined himself up there, free as a bird, deploying the mainsails and feeling the sudden acceleration as she harnessed the mighty force of the wind. Even from this distance, with his view intermittently screened by passing dockers and boy carters, he could discern the row of cannon ports lining her vast, streamlined hull that gleamed in the garish afternoon sun. Here was a vessel seriously armed to defend her cargo and crew against the ever-present threat of pirates. The sight of such a maritime leviathan, superbly poised amid the flurry of lighters, was a vivid reminder of the perils at sea. But for a young man of twenty-one, she embodied the epitome of excitement and adventure. And she needed a purser's mate who spoke French fluently.

From beneath the wide brim of his hat, he spied the matelots from the inn ambling toward the ship, laughing and chaffing each other as they went, with taps on shoulders in the palpable excitement of another voyage. It made Paul feel a pang of solitude and one of nostalgia for the comrades he had left behind in the emerald hills of Ireland.

He dared not approach any further or even linger an instant longer. Instead, he resolutely turned his feet back up the alleyway. He had not forgotten that he had promised to pay Lily-Anne a visit when back in town, and besides, he wanted to find out where she had found the law book so he could perhaps procure the other volumes. The thought of the spirited girl brought a secret smile to his lips, which he tried to disguise from passers-by with a hand to his mouth and a harrumph in his throat. He told himself he would honour his promise after his trip to the seal cutter's.

Paul lengthened his stride along the dock and turned right up Broad Street, arriving at the busy junction with Wall Street—a thriving commercial, legal, and administrative centre, graced with a new City Hall at the head of the Broad Street junction.

From City Hall, he weaved his way through the hurrying crowd along Wall Street before turning left onto a sedate cobbled lane. A short way down, he recognised the weathered façade of the modest establishment he had visited with his father two weeks earlier. The seal cutter's shop was nestled between two more recently erected, taller buildings, with a faded sign above the door depicting a finely engraved seal and intricate scrollwork.

Pushing open the heavy wooden door, he stepped into a realm where time seemed to stand still. The air was thick with the sweet smell of beeswax, the sharp tang of metal filings, and the rich scent of wood shavings. Sunlight softly seeped through the paned windows, casting long shadows over the workbenches arrayed with unfinished stamps, materials, and tools of the trade: chisels, mallets, and engraving tools, along with bars of red wax and sheets of brass. From behind the bench on Paul's left, an apprentice wearing a hessian apron looked up without a word, then fell back to his creation.

Paul glanced around the workshop, a sanctuary of precision and craftsmanship, shelves lined with an assortment of seals and stamps of varying sizes awaiting their final touches. On his right, the master seal cutter, a sinewy silhouette of concentration, was hunched over his workbench, engraving minute details into a piece of metal, and seemingly oblivious to the world beyond his magnifying glass. 'Good afternoon, gentlemen,' said Paul, who patiently waited a few moments until the man finally looked up, as if lifting his head out of a reverie.

'Yes?' he said, seemingly surprised to see the young man standing before the counter.

'I have come to collect my father's stamps and seal,' said Paul affably, holding out the numbered sketch that Jacob had given him. 'The name's Delpech.' The man slowly rose from his stool and, with deliberate movements, approached the counter. He took the paper and brought it to within arm's length of his long face, etched with lines of thought, and tipped with an impeccably trimmed, grey-tinged goatee.

He reached under the counter and brought out a small, dovetailed wooden box. 'Mr Delpech, Jacob,' he said, peering probingly over the sketch at the young man standing before him.

'Yes, sir, that is my father,' Paul said patiently. 'I was with him when he placed the order. My name is Paul Delpech.'

'I see,' said the man, his tone marked by scepticism. 'I usually hand over seals to the person who placed the order, unless I am acquainted with the person collecting them, of course.'

'I understand your concern, sir,' replied Paul, as it was becoming clear to him that his father, with his large personality, had effectively left him completely overshadowed the last time they stopped at the shop together. Paul persisted, 'But I am Paul Delpech, his son. Unfortunately, my father is bedridden in New Rochelle with a strained back.'

'I see,' said the seal cutter, visibly tumbling over in his mind if he had seen this young man before.

Paul was not without understanding the necessity for the man's caution. Obviously, he could not simply hand over something as precious as a seal to anyone who showed up. But Paul did have the sketch. He insisted, 'I have the number, sir, and I can assure you, I was with my father when he placed the order.'

'So you said,' said the seal cutter, looking dubiously back at the young man.

But just then, Paul was saved from an awkward moment by a ray of light as the door was pushed open. 'Good afternoon, gentlemen,' chimed a rich feminine voice. 'Isaac, I swear you haven't moved since I came here last!' The apprentice, a younger version of the master, looked up, his long face lit up with a bright smile. The master seal cutter peered at the young lady too with newfound buoyancy, as Paul turned to see the uplifting, brightly coloured person of Lily-Anne.

'Paul Delpech!' she exclaimed. 'What are you doing here?'

'Lily-Anne, I might say the same thing. I've come to pick up my father's seals.'

'Then we are two of a kind!' she quipped.

The master seal cutter looked back at Paul and then, with a nod, handed him the seals in their box. Paul inspected them while Lily-Anne made small talk with young Isaac, her presence immediately brightening the subdued ambiance. She was clad in a cerulean dress with a fitted bodice and a full skirt made of wool that flowed down to her ankles. The dress was modestly adorned with delicate white lace at the cuffs and collar, providing a pleasing contrast that highlighted her vibrant copper-coloured hair. Her attire was completed with a pair of calf-length and sturdy low-heeled leather boots peeking out from under her skirts, practical for walking through the cobbled streets of New York.

'I was going to pay you a visit,' a beaming Paul said to her a few minutes later, having taken up his box.

'I should think so too,' said Lily-Anne playfully, 'or you would be a gentleman who doesn't keep his word, which is not a gentleman at all.'

Paul, feeling slightly awkward about displaying his con- nection with the young lady, chuckled lightly and said, 'I will wait for you outside.'

Moments later, he was eyeing her through the small, glass panes, which offered a slightly distorted view of her as she conducted her business with evident charm, father and son hanging on her every word.

Stepping out of the workshop into the dimming lane, the sun having begun its descent and its warmth being replaced by the late afternoon chill, she said, 'Sorted. Now, where are you going?'

'My word,' said Paul, 'I was honestly going to pay you a visit.'

'Good, then I shall accompany you,' she said playfully. 'You wouldn't have found me at home earlier anyway. I have just come back from Ama's; she is teaching me about the white pine resin, which is what your father's ointment is made of. It's a salve for sores and muscle pains, you know. Anyway, I promised Father I would stop at Mr Pike's and pick up these.' She indicated the box in her basket, which Paul noticed was lovingly wrapped in brown paper and secured with twine. 'My father wanted to have some new ones when he saw your father's,' she added; then she reached for her shawl inside her basket. It was a fine piece of thick fabric in a soft shade of ivory that complemented her vibrant dress.

Without a word, placing his box under one arm, he stepped closer, taking the woollen shawl from her hands with a gentle touch. 'Allow me,' he said softly, draping it around her shoulders with careful attention. At one moment, their hands brushed. Paul felt a subtle yet undeniable attraction pass between them, like two loadstones compelling one to the other. Lily-Anne's large blue eyes met his, holding a spark of something unspoken. His simple act of adjusting the shawl to ensure it sat comfortably on her slender shoulders became a lingering moment, filling him with a yearning for her warmth in the cool spring air.

'Thank you, Paul,' she said, her voice carrying a hint of something new, as they walked side by side.

'It is a happy coincidence that you stopped by,' said Paul, as they turned into Wall Street, with the setting sun beginning to sink behind the gambrel roof of the recently built Trinity Church. 'Otherwise, the old man might not have handed me my box of seals.' He briefly filled her in about the seal setter's reticence.

'He was just being cautious,' she said, looking up, her eyes targeting his. 'But once you have his trust, he can be as gentle as a spring lamb.'

'I could see that,' said Paul. 'You had them eating out of the palm of your hand.'

'Oh, I've known Isaac since we were at Madame de Brey's school together. Malleable as copperplate, really.'

'They certainly cheered up on seeing your pretty copper top, if I may say!' quipped Paul. However, not wanting to risk becoming overly personal, he regretted the pun on her beauty the moment it came out. But Lily-Anne took it in her stride and gave a merry laugh.

'Hah, I wish I could manage it as easily,' she joked. 'I have to keep it attached, or it flies all over the place. Look. See?' She clasped and drew back a loose tendril of silky hair behind her ear. Paul complimented her on her resourceful hairstyle. She had pulled it back from her face in a simple yet elegant manner, its thick locks twisted into a low chignon at the nape of her neck.

'It gives you poise,' he said.

'Anyway, you haven't come to talk about my hair. When did you arrive?'

'Late yesterday. I spent all morning packing and loading the glass panes.'

'I'm sure your mother will be delighted to have some sunlight in the house. Where's your father, by the way?'

'Strained his back.'

'Maybe I put a spell on him, hah!' she said spiritedly, knowing that a Puritan mind could well accuse her of witchery. But this was not Boston, and Paul was not a Puritan; thankfully, he was a Huguenot, and he was not shocked at the jest.

'Actually, he asked me to thank you for the ointment,' he said matter-of-factly, 'It has helped ease the pain.'

'Or perhaps he is simply glad for your mother's soft touch as she rubs it in.'

'I dare not think,' said Paul, shuddering at the unimaginable thought, which made her laugh. 'In any case, he is not a keen sailor at the best of times.'

'Unlike his son,' said Lily-Anne, quick to recall Paul's past dilemma. 'Are you cured of the sea now?'

Paul was never bored in her company. She was daring, surprising, sometimes shocking, but always on cue, with her unswerving wit that invariably hit home.

'Actually, I have been offered another job only this morning. A purser's mate.'

'Will you take it?'

'You know I cannot.'

'No, you must not even think about it. I seem to remember you saying you desired another way forward.'

'Yes. There again, this purser's mate wouldn't need to climb the shrouds. He would only be required to be organised and down to earth, have a head for figures, and speak French.'

'Oh, I'm sure that all would suit you very well, except for the down-to-earth part,' she said with a note of irony.

'Indeed, it does.'

'But you would risk losing your grip on your law studies if you took it.'

'Worry not, I told him I couldn't go.' Paul looked up as an ox-drawn cart rattled past them. They had already turned onto the wide thoroughfare of Broad Way and were passing the new church, not far from where she lived beyond the graveyard. He continued, 'And speaking of the law, I must ask where you found that law book which, try as I might, I've found quite the puzzle to understand. But there's another one of the series that interests me. It is to do with commercial law.'

'The four came in one batch, so I must have them.'

'Oh?'

'I thought I'd give them to you one at a time,' chuckled Lily-Anne. 'I didn't want to overload your cart!'

'True, they are hefty books. But pray, let me pay you for them.'

'No need, they hardly cost the paper they were printed on.'

'Really?' said Paul, surprised. These books, rare in New York, were like a grimoire to a law student.

'Well, if they don't anchor you here, I don't know what will!'

'The only problem is I need to anchor my learning too, otherwise everything seems so foggy. But there aren't any such places of learning in New York, are there?'

'You can always learn in the halls of justice, and perhaps secure guidance under the tutelage of a learned jurist. Isn't that what your father used to be in France?'

'Yes, but here it's English law. I would need to come to New York often. Not that I'd mind; I harbour no desire to tether myself to a life as a villager and planter. I must admit I got itchy feet when he said I could join that ship. I just had to point my toes, and I would have been aboard.'

'I think you need to keep your focus. You have a life here,' she said with almost intimate conviction. 'Your father's business will surely flourish, and you will grow with it.'

'That's the problem. I don't think I want to. I initially wanted to go into the army, but then we left Ireland. Then I broke my leg on the ship, and I do believe my mother found solace in my doing so, for it meant she would keep her grip on me.'

'That's not fair. You can't blame her!'

'Don't get me wrong, I have great love and respect for my parents. Yet there is a strong desire within me to be the master of my own fate. I mean, that seal cutter didn't even acknowledge my presence the last time I went there with my father. I can't think how I will ever escape the shadow of my parents.'

'Paul, the way I see it,' said Lily-Anne, slowing her pace as they approached the graveyard, where daffodils were growing in clusters, 'perhaps you need to redefine your station and your path forward with your parents. Why could you not open an office here in New York? It would make perfect sense.'

'That is true.'

'Then you could indulge in trade from the Caribbean. And at the same time work toward your law studies.'

'If I didn't know better, I would say you are trying to put me off going to sea.' He laughed lightly. 'Have you been speaking to my mother?'

'No, not at all,' chimed Lily-Anne; then, becoming grave, she said, 'I just like to know that you will be here in New York, where I can come and pester you every day.'

They had naturally come to a pause under a flowering crab apple tree; the scent of its mellow white blossom seemingly compelled them to linger. 'Then I should look forward to it,' he said, falling deeper into the pools of her eyes. He smiled briefly and said hesitantly, 'I am glad to see you when I come here.' Then, spontaneously, he added, 'But I am twenty-one, Lily-Anne.'

'And I am sixteen,' she returned, quick to the word draw. 'One day, I too will be twenty-one, Paul. Then twenty-seven, then thirty... But whatever our ages, our difference will still be smaller than that of both our parents.'

'I must go, I will visit tomorrow,' he said, feeling confused by her emotional plea.

'I had better go too,' she said, presenting her cheek in the French fashion. But as he approached, a movement in the hedgerow made her turn slightly, and their lips brushed, and then they kissed on the mouth, the tingle of burgeoning love swelling both their hearts.

He fleetingly glanced around to make sure no one was looking. Thankfully, the shade of the tree veiled their kiss to a certain degree. It would put her in a terrible predicament if they were caught, although she didn't seem to care. 'I do have feelings for you,' he said, his eyes searching hers.

'I too have feelings, and I dearly want you to stay here in New York. I want to see you often.'

But Paul turned away. She caught his hand in time and said softly, 'I will see you tomorrow at the quayside with another book.' Letting go, she added, 'I ought to go now.'

He was left speechless by the power of the sudden burst of passion as he watched her walk hastily to her house until she had entered the flowering garden. Then he turned and briskly walked away from the strange emotion tinged with guilt.

That night, under the low wooden beams of the inn's shared bedchamber, the snoring of fellow travellers kept Paul from sleep. As he lay on his straw-filled mattress, his thoughts kept reverting to those intense moments with Lily-Anne.

He felt guilty, and yet he had done nothing to invite her kiss. He had returned that kiss when perhaps he ought to have restrained himself, and yet she was so enchanting. But she was only sixteen. How could he justify such a liaison to his parents, let alone to hers? And truth be told, despite the ease with which he, perhaps too easily, shared his intimate frustrations with her, he scarcely knew her. Only that her parents were prosperous, that her stepfather—none other than one of the lieutenants who had occupied their house in Montauban during the drag-onnades—had served with his own father aboard a privateer ship. And that her mother had been successful, during the war-ring years between England and France, in various ventures in Cuba and other places in the Caribbean. There, that place again, Paul mused, that Caribbean. Further evidence that fortunes could indeed be made there. The melodious sound of its name alone evoked images of wondrous lands and exotic products far beyond his imagination: sugar, spice, coffee, indigo, cocoa, rum.

But now, what of Lily-Anne? She was spirited, confident, astute, and beguilingly beautiful. She was clever with herbs and inquisitive about the native Indians, who knew about these lands and the remedies nature had to offer here. He was glad Didier Ducamp was not her real father, for if his parents had forgiven him for entering their house in France, Paul still found it challenging. So, in actual fact, perhaps he did know her rather well after all. What more could an honest man desire in a wife? And what did she see in him?

His neighbour momentarily broke his introspection with a crackling fart. As Paul turned restlessly over, it occurred to him that he had hardly arrived in this New World of fabled oppor-tunity and yet, here he was, assessing the qualities of a wife, which was all the more stifling in this sonorous, foul-smelling darkness. What would he say to her in the morning? Certainly, he would be happy to see her, but would they touch hands? Would they kiss? He certainly would want to. At last, sleep came as he lay with a forearm over his exposed ear.

However, no sooner had he nodded off than a gentle nudge from a boot, together with a whispering voice, brought him back. It said, 'She's leaving in an hour for La Martinique.' Upon the whisper of that magical name, Paul turned over brusquely. He opened wide his eyes to see John Barbeck holding a dimmed lantern in the snorting darkness of the room. 'If you are going,' he rasped, 'you'd better gather your kit and make haste to the quayside. Cap'n wants to catch the dawn wind out on the rising tide. Come with me now, or I'll have to take someone else to meet the purser.'

'But I have glass panes to deliver to New Rochelle.'

'Are they aboard?'

'Loaded them yesterday.'

'Then they will be delivered anyway with or without you, come what may. I'll give you some paper later so you can write down your instructions on it. I'll see that it's handed to the captain of the New Rochelle sloop.'

'I don't know,' said Paul, now sitting up, rubbing his stubbly chin, while desperately trying to weigh up his quandaries that tied him to shore: his promise to himself to pursue law, his duty to his parents, and now the situation with Lily-Anne. *Should I stay or should I go?* he asked himself, as he ran his hand through his hair.

'You won't get another chance as good as this one, lad,' said John, on cue. 'If you refuse again, I wager my right arm, you will never have the courage to leave here, mark my words! I've seen it happen before, and I've seen plenty mourn the chance of a lifetime. And I shall simply bid you good day next time I see you.'

Lying in her bed that night, Lily-Anne reviewed the encounter in her mind, fondly recalling her deep desire to take Paul by the hand when he admitted he had feelings for her.

She knew from her strong-willed mother that here in New York, it was often the woman who held the reins. This was especially the case of the Dutch women who traditionally held the purse strings, women like the detestable Judith Bayard, who was clearly the driving force behind her perfidious husband. As Lily-Anne lay awake, she recalled the power of secretly riding her horse astride for the first time, and wondered if she could also steer the potential of this principled and romantic young man and harness his burning desire to succeed. She felt sure she could turn him into someone who counted, if only he would let her. She was dreaming they were kissing when she suddenly awoke, gripped by a terrible presentiment. Although he had admitted he had feelings for her, had she not underestimated the lure of a rival?

In the half light of early morning, careful not to wake her young sister, she rose and quickly slipped her dress and shawl over her shift. She soon found herself scurrying down Broad Way, which was vacant and bathed at this hour in the orange hues of the cloudless new day, before making her way toward the harbour.

To her horror, the ship Paul had spoken of was no longer at quay. Catching her breath in the brisk dawn wind, she swung round only to see the Indiaman slipping with majestic poise into the rising bay, her sails taut and glimmering in the sunrise. 'No, Paul. Please don't be on that ship,' she said anxiously as she hurried onward to the inn, the wind coursing through her copper locks.

'Is Mr Delpech still here?' she asked the good-natured innkeeper, a barrel-shaped man with a balding crown and a bushy beard. He was hobbling back to the counter after tending to the cauldron hanging over the newly made fire in the tiled hearth. The air was filled with the savoury aroma of simmering broth, underlaid by the pervasive scents of wood smoke, cold tobacco, spirits, and ale.

'Ah, me old knees givin' me gip,' he said while processing her question. 'Who d'ya say again, miss?'

'Paul Delpech,' Lily-Anne said more pressingly, 'a young gentleman from La Rochelle. He is taking the sloop back this morning.'

'Oh aye, I know who you mean. And you are?'

'Miss Ducamp, Lily-Anne Ducamp.'

'Thought you was,' he said, glancing at her hair, which conformed to the description that Paul had given of her. Did she detect a note of pity in his voice? While fumbling for something beneath the counter, he continued more softly, 'He left just before dawn, with Mr Barbeck. Seemed in quite a hurry, they were. Mentioned something about an Indiaman, not a sloop, my dear.' The innkeeper's words hit her like a cold wave, confirming her worst fear. Her rival was a ship named *Providence*. 'Here, he left you this.' The innkeeper passed her a sealed letter with her name on it, along with a locked seal box. Showing a brave face despite her heavy heart, she thanked him, took the box and letter, and headed back the way she had come.

Pausing at the quayside, she cracked open the letter and read:

My Dear Lily-Anne,

It is with haste that I write these lines, for the ship on which I am about to sail is ready to depart. Please forgive me, but I feel I must make headway before life passes me by. I entrust you with these seals, which I have instructed my father to collect the next time he is in town. I have sent my parents a letter so they will know of my parting. I sincerely hope and pray they will find strength in their hearts to forgive my precipitated departure, but the call of the sea was too strong, and this opportunity too rare to pass up.

Please keep the books for me for my return. I might yet find an anchor in their pages, for I realise now that I lost mine when I was a boy after leaving my hometown, during the dragonnades that your stepfather knows about too well.

I pray you remain in good health, my dear Lily-Anne, and as pretty as when I last saw you.
Yours, most affectionately,
Paul Delpech

Leaning on a mooring post to steady herself, Lily-Anne cast her eyes out to the bay, where the *Providence* was becoming engulfed by the sea mist. 'Don't you go climbing that bloody rigging,' she found herself saying as the calming dawn wind brushed against her face.

Epilogue

EASTER, 1700, NEW ROCHELLE

After the solemnity of the Easter service, Jeanne, Jacob, Pierre, and Isabelle mingled with their fellow villagers as they made their way from the little stone church to the sunlit meadow, where the ambiance was bright and *bon enfant*.

Paul would be reaching Carolina by now, perhaps even Florida, Jacob thought to himself as he walked along with Daniel Darlington, nodding graciously and offering the peace of Christ here and there. After leaving their wives to settle on a seat and the children to scamper off with their friends, the two men made a beeline for the tapped barrels, one of small beer, the other of cider. The barrels sat on wooden racks among the trestle tables that fussing ladies were arraying with more savoury homemade dishes. Laid out in a line, these tables were regally garnished with an assortment of cold meats, goat cheese, savoury crusty tourtes still warm from the baker's oven, plump bass pulled from the river, oysters collected down by Echoe Bay, succulent smoked eel, pickled cucumbers and beets, nuts, dried fruits, delicious honey-coated *pain perdu* and *pains d'épices*, crispy corn bread, and hard-boiled eggs now that the chickens were laying again.

With the help of Darlington, the pastor, and the ironmonger, Jacob had carted the barrels from his lock-up down by the harbour, having previously purchased them on his last trip to New York. He had insisted on providing the small beer and cider to mark this special celebration of the resurrection of Jesus, and his family's first Easter in their new home. As Daniel engaged in pleasantries, Jacob took a step back to briefly reflect how their modest homestead and his business would still grow, albeit more slowly, despite Paul having taken to sea. But somehow, he felt that there was no great rush now they had covered their minimum requirements, as he looked ahead with a feeling of serenity he had not experienced in a long time. In fact, he had not felt this way since his days at Château Verlhac many years ago, where, upon his ban to practice his profession as a Huguenot juror, he had taken over the fields around Jeanne's family estate and had become a successful planter and merchant. Little could he imagine then that he would be standing here today on the other side of the world in a village built by Huguenots.

'Fine day,' said Daniel, rejoining Jacob, who had let his eyes travel over the Huguenot community that had tamed this former wilderness and turned it into a village similar to many in France. 'They did a good job with the scythe,' continued Daniel. 'It was knee deep only yesterday.' He was referring to the meadow that had been closely cropped the previous afternoon to reduce the risk of encounters with snakes and bees, the latter attracted by the flowering clover. Jacob remarked on the clusters of bright blooms of spring flowers here and there that the men with scythes had been careful to cut around and leave to flourish.

But then his brow furrowed at the sight of Mr Fournier who, Jacob now recalled, had lent his black slaves to do the job. Jacob knew from Darlington that Fournier had brought them with him from the south when he moved to New Rochelle the previous year. There he was with his young wife, accompanied by one of the slave girls dressed up for the occasion, nodding and shaking hands as he advanced across the meadow from the church. It brought back a stabbing memory of the vicious plantation owner in Leogane, a certain irascible Verbizier whose name he would rather forget. Jacob suspected Fournier, an outspoken and stocky man in his forties, of desiring to make a point by parading the pretty girl for all to see. He had audaciously presented the farmers and aldermen with an economical argument for the purchase of slaves, which Jacob had vehemently opposed. The Darlingtons and the majority of those present had stood by Jacob when he offered his testament of what slavery meant to any individual, no matter the colour of a person's skin. 'It is inhuman, it is unchristian!' he had hammered after relating his own experience in slavery on the island of Saint Domingue, where he had borne witness to black men cruelly worked to death on the sugarcane crushers. Though he could not stop the current trend of purchasing slaves in New York, it must at least be stemmed in this settlement, he had vowed to himself. But that struggle would have to be for another day. Today, as he watched children in their Sunday best playing tag and darting between the adults, their laughter rising above the soft murmur of conversations and the occasional clink of cider cups, he told himself to keep his thoughts to himself.

His brow smoothed over like a passing cloud as his eyes found Pierre and Isabelle with young Samuel Darlington, running across the green expanse to Jeanne and Marianne. The ladies had taken a seat on a bench under a blossoming dogwood tree.

'You may,' said Jeanne to Isabelle's petition for them to join the children's tug of war. Isabelle then rushed off with her brother and Samuel, who had received the same reply from his mother.

At last, the ladies could relax in the dappled shade and chat for a spell. They had been up with the lark and had spent the morning with the village wives, making the final preparations for the feast. Marianne remarked that the roast lamb was cooking nicely on the spit, its aroma blending deliciously with the sweet fragrance of the dogwood blossom dripping above them. 'Truly, I am famished and quite fatigued,' she added, with a hand instinctively placed upon her belly, 'but, I hasten to add, it is a good sort of fatigue.'

'Me too,' said Jeanne, with a smile that comforted, 'it is so pleasant just to sit for a moment in the sunshine, isn't it? I would never have thought it possible, though, this time last year. I am very glad to be here.'

'Ah, we are so glad to have you here,' said Marianne. 'You have become such a pillar of our little community, if I may say so. Everyone loves your weaving class, and Uncle is so active among the elders, helping to set plantation fence heights to preserve the peace and everything, he seems to be everywhere.' Marianne had not ceased calling Jacob thus, to the extent that the villagers thought they really were related. Jeanne took it in her stride, sensing that the pseudo affiliation filled a need in the younger woman, who was bereft of all but one member of her ancestral family.

'Perhaps, one invests oneself where one feels most welcome,' returned Jeanne. 'And how is your grandmother?'

'She is "hanging on", her words, not mine,' said Marianne with a light laugh. 'She says she wants to feel the summer sun on her face before she goes anywhere, including to the celestial kingdom. She says she doesn't want to be knocking on heaven's door in the freezing cold!'

Jeanne gave an indulgent laugh at the old lady's wit. Madame de Fontenay had caught a chill and had taken Jeanne's advice to stay indoors until it passed. 'I have no doubt she will be with us for some time yet, God willing. I told her I would pop in and see her later.'

'Oh, she'll be counting on it. She says she will not find another French marquise in this neck of the woods, even if she lived to a hundred and seven.' Touching the back of Jeanne's hand and speaking in a more sedate tone, Marianne said, 'But tell me, Jeanne, how are you bearing up since Paul's departure?'

It was still an open wound, but Jeanne was coming to terms with the fact that her son had entered manhood under full sail, and there was nothing she could do to hold back the sands of time as Paul charted his own course. 'He will be sorely missed, that is for sure,' she said with a ghost of a smile. 'Jacob has lowered our expectations in terms of trade and farming, now that Paul is not here. He was hoping to set up a counter for Paul to manage in New York, deeming it would suit a young man better than life in the village. Didier and May would have been at hand in case of any trouble. I suggested to Jacob to tell Paul before he took the boat to New York, but he wanted to see how he would fare. Jacob regrets it now, of course. But for me, the hardest part is not having been able to become the parent I hoped to be.'

'I do believe that is a universal concern, dear Jeanne,' remarked Marianne consolingly. 'Indeed, I sometimes think I am not doing everything I can, and I haven't had such a tough time of it as you have.'

With maternal reassurance, Jeanne said, 'You are doing fine, my sweet Marianne, I can assure you. But you must take care not to overdo it now that you are nearing your term.'

'The sooner, the better,' said Marianne. 'I'm praying for an early June baby. My back is killing me already.'

'My poor dear,' said Jeanne, 'let us hope you'll be spared the hot weather. I remember I had to carry Isabelle all through the hottest months of summer back in '85 in Montauban. Insufferable.' The mere mention of her hometown never failed to induce a glint of reminiscence in her eyes for the place she had loved, where she had left her eldest daughter and the grave of her darling Lulu.

Marianne said, 'And on top of that, the soldiers came and ate you out of house and home, and then threw you out into the street as you were about to go into labour.'

'It changed everything forever.'

'And I was so shocked to find out that Didier Ducamp had played a part in it.'

'Oh, Didier was not the worst. On the contrary, he tried to protect us. But then, he had to depart, and a cruel lieutenant took over. I am at peace with Didier now; he has been redeemed in my eyes. It was Didier who taught Jacob how to defend himself while they served on a privateer ship together. And we need friends in New York. So, I am all the gladder he fell upon a strong woman to support him.'

'True, May is a formidable woman, indeed.'

'But we prevailed through heartache and sorrow, and now I appreciate days like this all the more. My only qualm is that my decisions must have hurt my children. I did not realise it at the time. I just thought of our commitment to God and to freedom. I do see now, however, that my escape from France left Paul without an anchor, which is why I suppose he has gone seeking one at sea.'

'I pray he will return in fine fettle,' said Marianne, pressing Jeanne on the arm supportively. 'Perhaps with a wife on his arm; you never know! Look what happened to Daniel, and here I am!' She laughed. 'We married in Charles Town on the way up. After encountering such rough seas along the coast of Florida, I did not want either of us to die without being wed. But I do sympathise with you, dear Jeanne. Although, I must say, I sometimes can't wait for the day when Samuel must leave the family nest. I suppose wisdom tells us we must do what we can to enable our fledglings to fly with their own wings.'

'You are quite right, my dear, and then we pray every day for their well-being. But I am reminded of Paul by the window-panes that bring light into our home. Thankfully, he had packed them well; only a couple of panes were broken when they arrived from New York. Luckily, Jacob had thought to order extras.'

The ladies lifted their eyes from their deep conversation to see Jacob and Daniel as they appeared before them, handing an earthenware beaker of cider to each of them. 'Tell me what you think of it,' said Jacob, 'I thought it could allow us to wait until my order arrives from France.'

'Thank you, my uncle,' said Marianne.

'We were speaking about the windowpanes and the lovely light they bring into the house,' said Jeanne.

'Ah, yes,' said Jacob, catching onto Jeanne's implied meaning. 'I was saying to Daniel that Paul must be nearing the climes of Florida by now.'

'I avow,' said Daniel, 'he is not without reminding me of my own youth. I alas did the same to my dear mother and father. But I did return with my own ship. My father was so proud, but my mother was furious because she knew it meant I would be going away again.'

'Jeanne blames herself for Paul's losing his bearings, as she sees it,' said Jacob informatively.

'Oh, I shouldn't, honestly, Jeanne. I was born and bred in that house where you first stayed in New York, and yet I too felt an inclination to make my own headway. I suspect that for some people, it is in the air here. After all, this is supposed to be a land of opportunity, is it not?'

'It is that, although not for all of us, alas,' interrupted Jacob, looping his head toward Fournier, who was moseying with his crowd toward the food table on the other side of the green.

Chiming in to steer the conversation away from the looming shadow of the slave trade, Jeanne said, 'Nevertheless, in a way, I suppose I am proud of Paul, really. For after all, it must have been a bold and difficult choice for any young man. And his departure is nonetheless a testament to the values of freedom we so cherish. I suppose we all have a calling, don't we? Some answer it, some don't. All things said and done, I am nonetheless content that he answered his call of freedom as we did ours.'

'Hear, hear!' said Daniel, raising his beaker. 'To God and freedom!' As he said this, everyone raised their beakers to Daniel's spontaneous toast while a child crashed into his legs.

'Papa,' said Delphine, his eldest daughter, 'the Easter hunt is about to begin. Come!'

The two ladies were each offered a steady hand and happily rose from the half-shaded bench. 'That'll be Madame Delrose who is organising that one,' remarked Jeanne. 'I am conducting the egg rolling with Mrs Portier and Mrs Legrand.'

Jeanne advanced with Jacob and their friends into the merry gathering, where the sack-race heats had begun in the gentle embrace of that first spring of the new century—the first spring of many for the Delpech family.

The End

Acknowledgements

This has been a long and eventful journey in writing this series of novels, involving many years of delving into archives, contemporary journals, and other writings, which I have thoroughly enjoyed. I would like to thank all the historians over the years who have compiled research, allowing authors like myself to gain quicker access to crucial information. My heartfelt thanks also go to my family and friends for their unwavering support and encouragement throughout this process. Special thanks to my editors and my advance reader team, who helped weed out any typos and inconsistencies. The Leisler Institute has been invaluable in this journey, particularly David William Voorhees, who unreservedly shared his great wealth of knowledge and with whom I had the honour to correspond while writing this novel. Finally, to the readers who have followed this series, your support and enthusiasm have been a source of great motivation.

Enjoy this book? You can make a big difference.

Thanks so much for listening to *Call of Freedom*, I hope you enjoyed it.

Honest reviews of my books help bring them to the attention of other readers. If you've enjoyed reading this book I would be very grateful if you could spend just a few minutes leaving a review on my website at www.paulcrmonk.com and on the platform you used to purchase it.

Thank you so much,

Paul

MAY STUART

A standalone novel set in the thrilling world of the Huguenot Chronicles series.

Port-de-Paix, 1691. May Stuart is ready to start a new life with her young daughter. No longer content with her role as an English spy and courtesan, she gains passage on a merchant vessel under a false identity. But her journey to collect her beloved child is thrown off course when ruthless corsairs raid the ship.

Former French Lieutenant Didier Ducamp fears he's lost his moral compass. After the deaths of his wife and daughter, he sank to carrying out terrible deeds as a pirate. But when he spares a beautiful hostage from his bloody-minded fellow sailors, he never expected his noble act would become the catalyst for a rich new future.

May Stuart is a standalone novel set in the world of the thrilling Huguenot Chronicles trilogy. If you enjoy unlikely romance, period-authentic details, and rip-roaring tales of redemption, then you'll love this tale on the high seas.

What readers are saying:

"A most enjoyable, uplifting read."

"Great story of a woman with other ideas of her future."

"Entertaining and so well written that the characters come alive with realism."

Available now at paulcrmonk.com and other retail platforms!

GET BEFORE THE STORM 1685

Building a relationship with my readers is one of the best things about writing. I occasionally send newsletters with details on new releases, special offers and other bits of news relating to my historical fiction series. You can get a free copy of my prequel novella **BEFORE THE STORM 1685** by signing up at BookHip.com/FSZRFG

About the author

Paul C.R. Monk is the author of *The Huguenot Chronicles* historical fiction series and more. You can connect with Paul on Facebook at www.facebook.com/paulcrmonkauthor and, should the mood take you, you can send him an email at paul@paulcrmonk.com

Also by Paul C.R. Monk

In The Huguenot Chronicles series:
Merchants of Virtue
Voyage of Malice
Land of Hope
Call of Freedom

Also in the Huguenot series:
Before The Storm 1685 (prequel)
May Stuart

Other works:
Love in a Forbidden City
Strange Metamorphosis
Subterranean Peril

Printed in Great Britain
by Amazon